NEOLITHICA

DAN SOULE

READER BONUSES

Should you love this novel, **at the end you will find a link to a bonus behind the scenes ebook**, exclusive to NEOLITHICA readers. It includes an alternative ending and an in-depth interview with the author, Dan Soule, about the writing of this epic novel.

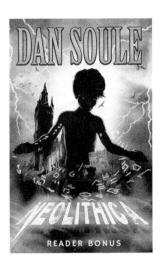

More books:
Join Dan Soule's *Rotten Row Reader's Club*
And get FREE books at www.dansoule.com

For Jenny...

with whom I walk through this life, as we make our own song.

PROLOGUE

Tk"lo, *Bear Paw,* sat cross-legged staring into the fire, embers dancing into the endless night sky. He was warm enough under fur blankets, one of beaver, the other of wolf, and looked up at the other blanket he sat beneath: a sky of countless stars, so many that they were like the froth of river rapids. His people believed they had been born from the tumult of those churning heavenly waters, and to the waters they would return, once the spirit of this body was done with the world. Tk'lo, an old man, the oldest of his tribe, was not sure he still believed this, though he sang the old stories, even the ones his children, and their children, could never remember because they could no longer walk the songlines.

He waited now on the edge of the known, where the land remained as it always had. The trees at the perimeter of the snow-covered clearing marked the ever-encroaching boundary that ate into their world. As the fire crackled, sending up another spray of dancing sparks, a growl came from the treeline.

Tk'lo did not reach for the stone knife at his hip, or for the stone axe lying beside him, which he had learnt to copy from the one he'd traded with the milk drinkers many years ago. It was the same type of axe those foreign people had used to cut down all the trees and take the memories in their songlines, the ones only Tk'lo could remember.

The tribe was once a great melody of life, moving through the land singing together. Now they were barely more than a few families left with a handful of songs. Each year more of them walked beyond the treeline and into the land of no memories to eat grass and drink milk. Tk'lo let out a hollow laugh at the idea of drinking milk. He had tried it several times, but he would always end up behind a bush farting like a giant urus bull.

Another growl came from the treeline.

"Ha! You try drinking milk, Ulv'nor," he joked. If the spirit of the great wolf was there, it made no reply. He pulled the beaver blanket around his shoulders a little tighter.

He looked skyward one last time and shuddered. Why, Tk'lo could not be sure. Perhaps it was the glint of reflected light in the eyes shining from the darkness of the treeline. There was something in the great black river that the other tribespeople could not see. Even after he and his brothers brought news of it back, carrying a dark song on their lips, they were loath to sing, they still were not believed.

And now, the last of his people had moved into colder lands to try to learn the songs of others like them, those moving with the migrating animals and the changing of the seasons. The dark song and its warning would die with him. Tk'lo looked into its eyes staring from the darkness behind the stars; the stars shone with the light of another world beyond this one, glinting off the thing's obsidian scales. Its tail curled around their world. Its serpent's tongue licked the air, tasting the avarice of a place of no true songs.

The crow croaked as it flew over Tk'lo's head. It opened its wings, turning on the air, coming to rest by the fire as a pack of wolves padded from the treeline. Their heads hung low. The sound of their growls rumbled with the power of a gathering wave. The crow screeched again and the old man kicked out with his arthritic foot. He only succeeded in making the crow hop back and make a noise that sounded like a laugh.

"You can wait for your meal," Tk'lo told the crow, knowing the crow was here for him. They always knew when death was coming.

Tk'lo's father had once said to him he 'wished to sit by the fire tonight with Ulv'nor', that it was time to sing with him. Better that an old man feed the wolves and crows than slow down his tribe and take food from the young ones. They all needed their strength in these meagre times, and learning new songs would not be easy.

As the growls grew louder, Tk'lo began to sing the song of the great wolf.

From the night of the land with no songs came the boy with eyes black as the scales of the thing from behind the stars. Tk'lo remembered the boy and felt the bile rise, burning his old throat. Now, he reached for his blade. He wished it was a blade of black stone.

Naked in the snow, and with wolves at his flanks and a crow at his feet, the boy smiled without kindness through fire-cast shadows, which made the small markings on his skin come alive. The boy looked beyond the old man in the direction his tribe had fled.

Tk'lo, finding a strength that had long since left his frail body, rose from his fur blankets. They fell to the ground like heavy snowflakes. He had stayed here to die and knew that what he did was nothing more than a futile gesture of a dying old man, but still he gave one last cry of battle.

The crow let out a laughing caw, and the boy grinned with fire dancing in his black eyes.

PART I

1

MARY LOVED the sound of the pigeons talking together. They said only good things, and to her looked very like the people she saw in Glasgow. Some were beautiful and clean, with plump chests and nice feathers. Others, Mary thought, looked more like her: dirty, old, maybe with a toe or an eye missing. All of them, however, had a rainbow around their necks. The thought made her happy, stood in the middle of Sauchiehall Street, a hundred birds flocking around her, and a dozen more perched on her arms, shoulders, and the woolly hat on her head. She fed them bread while the people of the city rushed around her, parting like the waters of a river around a rock.

Mary did so like to catch up on all the pigeons' news, cooing to them softly as they pecked bread from her hands and from the crumbs she'd scattered around her feet.

Then, as if she had said something wrong, they all took flight with a fricative trill of wings. Mary felt a little sad her friends had gone. She was about to pick up all of her things, packed neatly into a large, square polyethylene shopping bag, when the reason for her friends leaving cocked its black head at her and croaked.

"Stupid Mary," the crow said, hopping closer.

Mary hated crows. Nasty things they were. Never a nice word to say about anyone. Not like pigeons or most dogs. More like cats but less sarcastic. Mary ignored it and picked up her heavy bag.

"Don't be stupid, Stupid Mary," the crow laughed, but it wasn't a nice laugh. It reminded her of the laugh the cruel porter used to make back when Mary was younger and lived in Lennoxcastle. The porter was called Eddie. She'd never met a nice Eddie and guessed it was the name given to nasty people. In fact, Mary would guess every crow in the whole world was called Eddie, even the girl crows.

"Go 'way, crow," she told it with a pouting scowl.

"Where you going to go, Stupid Mary? You haven't got a home. You haven't even got a brain." The crow thought this was very fun and hopped in Mary's way so she couldn't get away.

"Don't want to talk to you," Mary said, trying to shuffle to the side, but the crow hopped laterally to block her way.

"Stupid Mary, quite contrary. Just trying to help."

"You've helped no one, horrid crow." Mary made a break for it, using her bag to knock the crow away and join the stream of people. The crow wouldn't follow her there. Instead, it fluttered into the air, shouting after her.

"Run away, Stupid Mary. It won't matter."

Then, stretching out the black cloak of his wings, the crow was gone.

2

IT WASN'T A GOOD DAY. No, actually, it was a great day, even in the Scottish rain, which had begun to feel like a familiar friend to Stephen. *Driech* was the word the guys on the site used, and Stephen liked it. In his mouth, the word had the quality of the day: grey and with a touch of morose acceptance. It shouldn't be something to like, but he did. More and more he had felt affinity for this rugged place. Its landscape and its people had rougher edges than the soft, lilting Nottinghamshire countryside he had grown up in south of the border.

Stephen's whole family were settling in nicely. The girls had started at the new school in Kirkintilloch at the beginning of the school year in August. A bit of a change for them from the English timetable. He wondered at how adaptable his girls were, even hearing a few Scottish notes in their accents already. Janet, his wife, had found a job in a good Glasgow accountancy firm. And for Stephen there was plenty of work on the horizon. The risk of the move seemed to have paid off. The cost of living was amazing compared to the southeast of England and London in particular, where they had moved from. They had initially expected to buy in one of the upmarket suburbs around Glasgow, Bearsden, or Milngavie. Instead, they had fallen in love with a house and then the small village in which it sat, Milton of Campsie, lying at the foot of the Campsie Fells. When they drove toward the place, the fells had risen dramatically behind the village.

The house was large and a little quirky, like their decision to move from everything they knew in England. And the fact that the property was a quarter the price of similar properties around London didn't hurt either. Even better, the local high school was a high-performing comprehensive, and so they didn't even have to pay for schooling.

They were having the best of all worlds. They'd quickly stopped telling themselves they could go home to England at any time, back to the long commute, back to all the frantic pace of life and the high cost of living. They were putting down roots, making friends, feeling at home. Stephen thought all these things as he turned off the motorway, a coffee in one hand and the promotional brochure and the plan of works sitting on the passenger seat next to him in the Range Rover.

'Bringing us closer to nature' read the brochure's title. It didn't much appeal to Stephen. The advertising copy was a little contrived, but that wasn't his department. He was a civil engineer and the project manager, and this wasn't a big job anyway. Another six months to go, nine months maximum.

A local environmental group had taken exception to the project. There had been a minor bit of local press coverage and a small piece on the national Scottish news. Hardly anything, really. The environmentalists were a regular fixture at the site entrance and were really quite friendly. Stephen knew several of them by name. There was Meredith, the lady with the grey, curly hair, always in a stripy jumper. Susie, a young, pretty girl in her early twenties, who would have been quite a stunner, Stephen thought, if it wasn't for those thick dreadlocks she sported. Still, it takes all sorts. And there was Jerry, a dumpy man on the wrong side of middle age who fancied himself as something of a firebrand, shop steward type. He'd mellowed when he saw Stephen's Derby County woolly hat one cold day. Apparently, Jerry's father had been from Derby and it was still his team. Well, apart from Glasgow Rangers, of course.

Meredith, Susie, Jerry, and a handful of others were there every morning with their flasks of tea and homemade placards. The group would have a go at a protest chant in the morning and usually another when the heavy vehicles on the site stopped for lunch. By the evening, though, their numbers had normally thinned out, and instead of chanting, both sides would wave each other off. The whole thing was rather convivial. Okay, they didn't see eye to eye on the need for the project, but Stephen could see where they were coming from. In a way, they both kind of wanted the same thing. It was only a small road, cutting into a little bit of the peat land. The protesters' main objection was the destruction of a historic natural habitat, peat being laid down over thousands of years. Stephen's company were building to help the National Trust and the Department for the Environment bring more people to the natural world to promote conservation. Their ultimate goals were the same. As such, even the protesters made Stephen feel good about his decision to move the whole family to Scotland.

Just one small thing played on his mind this morning. Last week, his eldest, Tilly, had come home with a dark cloud over her. Janet dug into it. Matilda was a forthright nine-year-old, confident in her opinions, which Stephen knew all too well could cause an argument at home from time to time. There is nothing quite as maddening as a nine-year-old who knows the answer to everything.

It seemed during a playground game one of Tilly's new friends had said for her to "stop being so English." Tilly didn't know exactly what that meant, but knew it wasn't a compliment. Stephen had had a similar experience two months back with one of the workmen on a different project. He was an older man with a lot of building experience and set in his ways. Stephen required the new health and safety paperwork filled out in the new format. The old-timer, Alistair, didn't see the importance of it or couldn't be bothered. Alistair strongly resisted completing the new paperwork. Holding his ground, Stephen made his case again, but Alistair still wouldn't listen. Stephen had no other choice but to put his foot down and insist. Alistair had walked away, and Stephen heard him mutter, "English twat." Alistair was well liked; Stephen got his own way, and so he let it go. Though he did ask for Alistair not to be selected for any of his further projects.

Stephen and Janet talked about the work incident and Tilly's playground problems at home, deciding in the end they weren't anything to be too concerned over. There were always a few bigots wherever you go. Weighing it all up, it was a small price to pay for the benefits of their new life. They were more relaxed, had more time with the kids in a great house set within breath-taking nature, and all with money in the bank.

As he passed the protesters to pull onto the site, Stephen slowed the car and gave them a *wee* wave. A couple of them waved back. Jerry good-naturedly brandished his placard, and the others cheered with small plastic thermos cups of tea in their hands.

The smooth surface of the road gave way to the compacted gravel of the work site. Stephen's four-by-four suspension lolled him up and down like a boat entering the choppy waters on the edge of a storm.

He could see the site ahead. Most of the team had already started work. Willie, though the guys pronounced that more like *woolly*, was in the earthmover about to cut into a swath of dark peat. The huge yellow claw gouged into the bank of ancient peatland, ripping a bucket of earth into the air. Clods of dark brown soil dripped from it like decaying flesh.

In his temperature-controlled cabin, Stephen felt a gust of stagnant cold air brush his skin. What the hell was that smell? It was like someone had opened a tomb. His flesh goose-bumped.

Nausea surged from the pit of his stomach, and his sphincter tightened in fear. At that same moment, the Range Rover cut out. Everything electrical went dead. The satellite navigation turned black. Dashboard gauges fell limp and lifeless. The digger, with its monstrous claw, along with all the other machinery on the site, also ground to a halt. In unison with their machinery, all the builders had stopped dead. It was as though they were all feeling the same thing Stephen was. What colour they had in their faces on this *driech* morning drained away, and the sky darkened with a rumble of thunder.

His Range Rover still moving, luckily not at speed, Stephen finally remembered to apply the brakes to the three tons of lumbering metal. The brake pedal wouldn't respond. He pumped it twice, feeling the panic of falling in a dream and missing the final hold before oblivion. With fumbling fingers, damp with sweat, he found the handbrake. It was enough to stop the Range Rover with a scratching skid.

The necrotic smell was still with him. Stephen caught the vomit in his mouth, scrabbling for the door handle. Flinging it open, he half fell out of his vehicle, giving in to the nausea. His breakfast of coffee and porridge spewed onto the ground between his feet, splashing his smart leather shoes. He tried to breathe.

Stephen's work boots were in the back of the Rover. He would normally put them on before walking onto the sodden site, but at that moment angry shouts came from his men. He looked up from between his knees to see Big Tam being pulled off Ronnie by the site foreman, Jackie.

Spitting bile into the dirt, Stephen rushed down to help. Mud enveloped his smart shoes and dirty water splashed up from bloated puddles, caking his trousers and soaking his feet through to the skin. Each step felt heavier and heavier with sucking mud, draining the energy from him. Part of him wanted to flee. It cried somewhere in the back of his mind like a terrified child, and for one moment Stephen thought his girls were here crying. But of course, that was a silly idea, and so he dismissed it and forced himself on.

It wouldn't be the first time an accident on a site had caused a fight, though it was odd amongst this group, who had only ever seemed good-natured to Stephen. Their work had been full of laughter, practical jokes, and banter about football, sex, politics, and even religion, with a Catholic-Protestant division Stephen didn't wholly understand. Another reason to hurry. There were more months of work ahead. Better to bury the hatchet now than let things fester.

Jackie had managed to calm things down by the time Stephen arrived a little out of breath.

"Right, you two. Enough," the foreman growled like only a Glaswegian could.

His usual ruddy complexion gone, Jackie was pale. The old foreman looked just like Stephen felt: worried and ill. Stephen saw it in the faces of every person stood on the site. They had aged ten years, and he was sure if he looked in the mirror he'd see the same thing.

Stephen approached, a palm facing each man as if holding back an invisible wall between the two fighting men. Jackie was doing the same but from a position directly between Big Tam and Ronnie, his back to the wall of peat. Jackie was Stephen's right- hand man. He liked him and hoped to work with him a lot more in the future. They exchanged a perplexed look, gilded with worry on both sides. In the other, neither saw someone who had any answers. There was silence. Things were calming down. The simmering pressure was still there, but the trouble must have passed, whatever it was.

Willie, having come out of his cab in the dead digging machine, exclaimed, "Dear God!"

Stephen knew Willie wasn't a religious man, though he loved his Celtic FC with a sports fan's fervour, and yet he said the words like someone facing the reality of their own mortality. They all turned slowly, the sense of dread growing in the pits of their stomachs.

Out of a fallen clod of peat, a disembodied hand protruded, glistening brown like wet leather in the rain.

"What the fuck is that?" Willie said, slipping and staggering over to them.

"It's a fucking hand," Jackie growled.

"I can see it's a fucking hand," Willie said, panic rising in his tone.

The hand was a dark, leathery brown, and no bigger than a child's Tilly's age. The claw of the digger must have cut cleanly through its arm.

As he stared at the dead hand, Stephen was consumed with the idea that he wanted to punch Jackie in the face. He wasn't sure where that thought came from. He only knew that it seemed like a great idea. Self-righteous prick, always shitting on Stephen's suggestions, thinking he was the boss.

A noise from behind startled him. He turned to see the protest group brandishing placards. One of them had a hammer.

"Aye, what tha' fuck are yous hippie cunts aboot?" Big Tam shouted. Although, in his Glaswegian growl, it sounded more like a challenge.

The kindling was ignited, setting the two groups at each other. They ran, meeting Stephen in the middle, who stood with his arms opened wide, shouting, "Come on then, you *bastards.*"

Stephen, who hadn't had a fight since he was eleven, threw the first punch, hitting the old woman, Meredith, with the curly, grey hair, so hard her head snapped back. She hit the ground with a massive slap, knocking all the wind out of her, her delicate nose now a crushed smear across her face. Stephen jumped on her, straddling her body, raining down blows on her unconscious face, just as the hammer carried by one of the protesters buried its head in Ronnie's skull. He stood, twitching for a moment as thick red rivulets ran like oil down his face.

Stephen's screams of rage only stopped when the two-by-four of a placard caught him clean on the side of the neck. He fell sideways off the old woman, consciousness briefly leaving him. He tried to push himself to his knees again, only to receive a second blow from the two-by-four, spinning his head and dislocating his jaw. He fell face-first into the mud. The blood pouring from him didn't matter. He would kill whichever bastard had done that to him. He would kill them all. Or he would have done, had the two-by-four not struck a third and final time. It came down with full strength on the vertebrae connecting Stephen's head to his body. A snap, and Stephen did a brief danse macabre in the mud.

His new life in Scotland was over.

3

NOT SINCE THE ACCIDENT, since she had lost him, lost almost everything, had they walked through the park to take Oran to school. It
had been a year. Autumn in Glasgow was always their favourite time
of the year. Mirin and Omar would walk either side of Oran, holding
his hands, swinging him between them – when he didn't want to
chase pigeons or stroke a passing dog, that is. It was a time of year
that reminded them of meeting at university when they were barely
adults and everything seemed possible.

Now, with Omar gone, the piles of golden leaves in Kelvingrove
Park looked dead. The portent of a long, dark winter to come.

The little boy ran ahead, wriggling to free himself from his
mother's grip so that he could kick great showers of gold and brown
into the air, clapping his hands with the sheer joy of it. This
brought a smile to Mirin's face. He was the only thing she had left,
the only thing she lived for, and the only thing during the long
nights in the last twelve months that had prevented her from
joining her beloved Omar. This was her most private thought,
something Mirin had never shared with anyone, not even her grief
counsellor.

They came out of the park on to Gibson Street, turning right to
walk past the short parade of coffee shops, bars, and restaurants, up

to Oran's school at the crossroads. Behind that, the university spread up and over Gilmore Hill.

Mirin swallowed the ball of anxiety in her throat. She could see the other parents dropping off children in cars or walking together in small groups. School had been going since August. Now, early October, Oran was starting back late. This would be his first day at school in more than a year, and Mirin's first day back to work as well. She had talked it over with her counsellor. Apparently, it marked a big step in her grief and was an indication of the real progress she'd made. Intellectually, Mirin understood that actions sometimes need to precede belief until the mind could catch up with the body. Mirin never had trouble understanding things intellectually. That was her job, a job that up until a year ago had been so important. But the physical part, the actual doing that her counsellor was keen on, well, she guessed she had to take in one clichéd step at a time.

The noise of children in the playground grew to a crashing wave. Mirin's heart leapt, feeling as though it might fall forever if she didn't catch it with another hard swallow. She squeezed Oran's hand.

Nearing the gate, Mirin could feel him wanting to pull away again and run to see his friends. The other parents were looking at her. She needed this. Oran needed this.

Mirin wanted to hug her son and tell him how much she loved him. She crouched at his level. His hair was snaked in tight curls. His brown eyes stared back at her. She would tell him that everything was going to be all right.

But Oran spoke first.

"Are we getting back to normal now, Mummy?"

"Yes, my little darling, we are."

"Will it ever be normal again without Daddy?"

Mirin held back the tears threatening to boil over.

"No, I don't suppose it will, darling."

"We'll just do the best we can then, Mummy." The little boy gave his mother a hug, throwing his thin arms around her neck.

"Yes, we will," Mirin said, marvelling at the child's resilience. "Now, you have a great first day at school." She closed her eyes, planting a kiss on his forehead. It felt warm and real. He let her go with one last squeeze and ran into the playground amongst the other children shouting back over his shoulder, "You have a great first day too, Mummy."

Mirin watched him for a moment, then that ball was in her throat again. She looked up the hill to the main campus of the university. She had got through the first hurdle. Now all she had to do was keep going, one hurdle at a time, until the day was done.

"Professor Hassan, how good to see you."

Mirin stiffened. It was Mrs Stewart, the deputy head.

"We all wanted to let you know how devastated we were when…"

Mirin couldn't do this right now.

"Thanks," she said. "Can't stop. It's my first day back. Thanks again. Sorry." Mirin had already started up the hill at pace, leaving the school behind her.

Mrs Stewart's quizzical look disappeared the second Toby McBride pushed over Sally Pinker.

"Tony McBride, come here at once."

Mirin didn't look back. Now all she had to do was get through a day in the archaeology department. With any luck, she could spend the next week just going through a year's worth of emails.

4

Constable Hardeep Bhaskar, or Dip to nearly everybody, was doing his usual beat, stopping in at various places. It was good to touch base with the community: shop owners, farmers. He'd pick up a coffee from the shop, which doubled as a post office, and maybe one of those Danish pastries they had too. He shouldn't but he usually did, resulting in the slight belly his mother always chided him about.

"You can let yourself go after you're married, Hardeep."

She meant well and it wasn't as if he *wasn't* in the market for a wife. The opportunity just never seemed to present itself out here in the countryside. Dip wasn't exactly lonely, but he had found himself softening to his mother's occasional hints about potential arrangements she and her cousins had been scheming about for years.

Whether it was a result of solitude or not, Dip liked this part of his job: getting everyone to know his face. He tried to give out a friendly persona so people felt they could talk to him. It was also one of the big pillars of community policing. Managing rural crime without the cooperation of locals would be nearly impossible.

The next stop was one of his favourites: the small road development at the nature reserve, where a little protest had camped out ever since the project started. It was very good-natured on both sides, which made a refreshing change from the vitriol he saw more and more on the news these days.

Coming down the road, Dip noticed that the protesters were no longer there. His initial thought was that they must have moved on, maybe to a new, bigger threat to the environment. There was a little piece of him that was sad at that idea. There wouldn't be a reason to come by regularly and see how everyone was getting on.

The indicator on his police car clicked rhythmically as he slowed down to make the turn into the site. Something seemed a little out of place. A couple of placard tops lay discarded on the ground. They had been torn off and the sticks left as careless litter. Flasks of tea were scattered around the once-campsite, plastic cups surrounding them. Usually they were placed neatly bottom-down. Surely the environmentalists would tidy up after themselves?

Of course, they wouldn't be the first group of hypocrites he'd ever met. However, they hadn't struck Dip that way. They'd seemed an honest and sincere bunch, not protesting for the sake of getting riled up, but with a genuine cause they were prepared to quietly advocate for. It was a pity, but once he tracked them down, he would have to write them up for the violation. He allowed a small sigh at the thought of the paperwork.

His suspicions were confirmed as soon as he turned off the main road. The project manager's Range Rover wasn't parked up in its usual spot. Instead, it sat abandoned in the middle gravel access road, its driver door left open. The large vehicles beyond were uncharacteristically still. By this time of morning, the digger was normally in full swing. The place normally resembled a veritable hive, trucks and diggers crawling around carrying their payloads of dirt and minerals. All lay silent.

Dip parked up behind the Range Rover and got out. The thought crossed his mind that he should call it in, but what would he say? What was he calling in? He didn't know anything yet. He'd have to go down and check. Gravel crunching under foot, Constable Bhaskar approached the Range Rover. Glancing inside, he saw nothing untoward. Then his eyes found the carnage ahead.

Reflexively, his hand went to his radio. Nothing happened. A hollow button-click. There wasn't even any static. He clicked it again, and still nothing. Eyes scanning left to right, he walked down towards the site, still trying his radio for dispatch. Dip could see bodies lying on the ground and slumped against vehicles, their limbs at funny angles, heads slumped, necks twisted, and blood. So much blood.

Click. Click. Click. Still no answer. Blood pounded in his ears. Dip slipped and stumbled through the mud until he reached the first body.

What might have been the old lady lay face up next to the body of Stephen, the project manager, who was face down in the mud. Dip felt bile rising and his stomach clenched; he brought a hand to his mouth, fearing the retch. The old woman's face was unrecognisable, nothing but red pulp. Only her curly grey locks identified her as Meredith.

Stephen's head was turned sideways, eyes staring blankly. His neck looked as though it had been broken, leaving an unnatural valley between the back of his shoulders and the base of his skull. His jaw was dislocated, twisted into hyper-extended palsy.

Dip couldn't hold it back any longer and vomited on the floor next to Meredith. The constable straightened up, wiping his mouth. He needed to take in the details of the scene but all he wanted to do was un-see the tableau of violence. He noted Ronnie's body: brains spilled out of his skull. The body of Big Tam between two dead protesters, Sam and Ollie, a pickaxe buried between the big man's shoulder blades. Willie lay slumped against the wall gouged into the peat, frozen, eyes staring wildly.

A small movement caught Dip's eye. It was the young girl, Susie. He ran to her, falling to his knees, mud drenching his uniform. She was breathing, though the breaths were shallow and rapid; one of her eyes was swollen shut. Her nose was broken, as were several of her fingers. In places, her clothes were torn, suggesting another kind of physical violence Dip didn't want to contemplate. He took Susie's mangled hand. She looked through him, as though he wasn't there. Taking one last ragged breath, her chest rose and then her body went limp. She exhaled in a long, slow, ghostly gasp, and she was gone.

His mind snapped back to the radio but it was still useless. *Click.*

Click. Click. He was beginning to hate that sound. It was the mocking sound of futility.

"Christ!" he said out loud. Dip tried to gather his thoughts and make sense of it all. Overwrought with emotion, he needed to draw on all his training and follow procedure to take control of the situation.

Bodies were everywhere. It was like a damn battlefield. The two sides had seemingly gone to war, killing each other with their bare hands or whatever tools they had available: two-by-fours, hammers, pickaxes, screwdrivers... But to what end? It didn't make any sense. It had been all so good-natured. What could have happened to make them want to kill their fellows? Dip searched and found no answers. He clicked the button of his radio once again to no avail. He called desperately into the silence for someone to answer, "Come in. Is anyone there, please?"

Somebody answered.

The shuffle of muddy boots came from behind the JCB digger. Dip turned and saw Jackie, the foreman, covered in blood, holding a crowbar. He had hate in his eyes and slashed across his face in a slicing grin. Jackie raised the crowbar over his head.

"Fucking Paki," Jackie growled through broken teeth and a mouth full of blood.

Dip hadn't been called that in a while, probably not since he was a probationary officer arresting drunks on a Friday night. The words gave the officer an emotional stab, picking at a lifetime of unseen scars: from the playground, on the bus with a group of mates, random insults walking down the street, even a joke he'd overheard in the changing rooms at work years ago, and which he'd never complained about. And that wasn't the half of it. Not really.

The crowbar had already begun its downward swing. He raised his forearm in a protective upward block, and the crowbar connected. The impact shattered his arm, but saved his life.

Dip rolled away, trying to put space between him and Jackie, who was already bearing down on him for the second swing. The sodden ground slipped under Dip's boots. He felt like a cartoon character, wheeling his legs on the spot and getting nowhere.

Scrambling past the metal bucket of the JCB, Dip's back came to rest against the caterpillar track. There was nowhere else to go except for maybe under the earth mover, but time had run out. Jackie came on slow and steady and had closed the distance, repeating his racist slur. He spat the words with victorious intensity, which belied every single interaction Dip had had with Jackie.

Dip fumbled one-handed with his utility belt. Jackie raised the iron bar above his head to finish off the constable. There was no time for the verbal de-escalation they had all been taught in the academy. It was now or never. Jackie took one final stride forward. Dip pulled free the canister from his belt and lifted it as high as he could, depressing the button on the pepper spray. The jet of burning liquid shot out of the canister into Jackie's face. The foreman cried out in pain, dropping the crowbar, which hit him on the back of the head.

Bringing his blood- and mud-caked hands to his face, Jackie staggered, thrashing side to side. Blinded, he slipped. With his hands engaged with trying to clear his eyes, Jackie didn't put his arms out for balance and so his entire body pitched in the air and fell back heavily to the ground. His skull landed on one of the upturned teeth of the earth mover's bucket. There was a wet crunch of shattering bone. Jackie's body convulsed as though in protest of his sudden death, legs and arms giving involuntary twitches.

Dip approached the body cautiously, holding his broken arm to his chest. Jackie stopped twitching, as dead as all the other bodies on the site. What Dip suspected was brain matter dripped glutinously out of the back of Jackie's skull and on to the muddy ground.

Dip began to shake. His arm was numb with shock and he found himself panting involuntarily, unable to pull in enough air. Every fibre of his being was telling him to run away, to get as far away from here as possible, but his training told him to take control of the situation, that people were relying on him. But the situation didn't need controlling any more. Everyone was dead. Fucking hell, they were all dead, and he had just killed a man.

He looked around, as if hoping to see an answer in the carnage.

That was when his eyes, which had seen too much for one day already, alighted on something that somehow appeared incongruous even in these horrific circumstances: a severed hand, a small and delicate and leathery brown hand.

Buried in the bank, at about the same level as Ronnie's chest, concealed deep within the peat, was the face of a young boy, his eyes closed as if he were asleep. Tangles of black curly hair were plastered to his beautiful face.

Constable Hardeep Bhaskar could not draw his gaze away from the face of a beautiful boy entombed in the wall of peat. He was perfectly preserved, but for a dark leathery brown to his skin. Lying peacefully on his side, he looked as though he was merely sleeping, his face miraculously untouched by the earth mover's claw.

As Dip stared at the sleeping visage, fear began to grow in his heart, rising like a wall of black water about to crash down over him like a wave.

5

MIRIN STOOD outside the Gregory Building, with the circular stone sculpture at its entrance resembling an enormous six-foot millstone. She was rooted to the spot, as if the great stone was around her neck, not standing inertly beside her. The Department of Archaeology lay inside. Undergraduates floated around her. If she stayed there, passed over by the current of life, maybe she would dissolve away.

One step at a time, she told herself. Mirin had spent twelve months avoiding this moment, but now it could not be avoided.

She entered, winding down familiar corridors, like maze-tunnels from a distant dream, until at last she came to the staff offices and research labs. Mirin swiped her staff card; the little LED light remained red. She tried again and yanked at the door, which remained steadfastly shut. For one second, the thought crossed her mind that this was all a big mistake, that she had imagined living this life that was not hers. That she was never a professor, a wife, a mother, a widow, a grieving parent, that she didn't really exist in this nightmare, that in fact she was dreaming, or had woken in someone else's life and the nightmare was not hers. But this idea was too good to be true. The truth could never be like a twist in a pulp psychological thriller. She had read about the psychedelic-like qualities of grief, the profound changes in brain chemistry, the loss of self, the Jungian ideas about passing through an underworld that led to either redemption or damnation, depending on how the subject responded. But no matter how much she read, it couldn't make up for the doing.

A cough came from behind Mirin.

It was Charles, curly hair thinning more on top since she last saw him at the funeral.

"Hello, Mirin." He fumbled with the card and keys hanging on a lanyard around his neck. "They put in a new entry system a few months ago. Part of the new data protection policy, apparently. I'm not exactly sure what data we have that would be worth stealing, mind you."

He held the door open for her.

"Thanks," she said.

Charles was one of the top guys in the world on sandstone erosion, based in the neighbouring Geology Department. He was also terrifyingly awkward, and as a result, didn't hang around to make chitchat, but vanished with a curt nod and stooped scurry. Today, Mirin was grateful for it.

The department was full of life: the bustle of students and staff, their eyes glued to phones or notice boards, chatting in small groups without a care in the world other than the extent of their student overdraft, the latest assignment due date, or the price of beer in Glasgow University's two student unions. There was something homely about it, even given how she felt.

She meandered unnoticed until she came to the PhD lab. She stopped at the window beside the door, looking in. Inside, her former PhD student, Portia, was sat at her desk laughing, throwing back her head, flicking her long red hair. Mirin could imagine the brightly coloured bangles on Portia's thin, pale wrists jangling as she looked up at the man perched on her desk. The sleeves on his pressed herringbone shirt were rolled up. Their legs were almost close enough to touch. Then Portia's green eyes flicked away from the man and found Mirin's staring in from the corridor. The smile on Portia's face faltered a little and then brightened again in recognition. The man turned at this. Seeing Mirin he straightened. Mirin felt like a voyeur caught in the act and a blush reached her cheeks. But the pair simply smiled. Portia was now waving at Mirin enthusiastically, and the man opened the door.

"Mirin, you're here!" David said.

"Hello, David. Hi, Portia."

"Shall we move to my office and have a chat?"

"Do you mind if I go to my office first and get my bearings?"

"Of course. I'll come to see you in an hour. How's that?"

Mirin nodded and made her escape.

There was a little picture on her desk. Three smiling faces, huddled together; little Oran between his two parents. It wasn't that the fact that it was a picture of Omar that caused her grief. Her house was still full of them; she couldn't imagine a time she would ever take them down. It was that she hadn't seen this one for a year.

She swallowed the ball of anxiety once more and clicked the email icon on her desktop. There were thousands of unread emails. All the recent stuff at the top was the usual barrage of unnecessary department circulars or messages from faculty committees Mirin used to sit on or chair. Then there was alumni news, requests to contribute to colleagues' birthdays or retirement presents, automated journal notifications, and conference call invites. But lower down they began: the sympathy messages. Mirin clicked on each one, high-lighting them all. She hesitated for a moment and pressed delete. They disappeared from the screen as a knock came at the door.

Professor David Hamill's head appeared around the door. Apart from their brief meeting on the way into work this morning, Mirin hadn't seen David for a year. Some of her colleagues had tried to call in to see her at home. She pretended to be out or put them off if they messaged her beforehand. David had sent an email as well at some point. Mirin never read it. It came with the avalanche of other sympathy notes, which from the first were already too much.

How much David had changed in the last year, but in the opposite direction from Mirin. While her life imploded and her career stagnated (not that she cared much about the latter) he had soared into the stratosphere. The university had made him a professor, as they had done her two years previously. However, importantly from the university's point of view, David had become something of a media darling. He fronted a new series for the BBC combining archaeology with genealogy, science with stories, called *Digging up the Past*. It was nominated for a BAFTA, and David got another gig on a prime-time comedy panel show rife with intellectual badinage. Barely a new professor, the university made David head of department when old Michael Pillsbury finally retired three months ago. Before Mirin had left, before Omar had died, Mirin might well have been in line for the same post. She wasn't jealous. Mirin's perspective had changed. The lens through which she viewed the world had been irrevocably altered.

"Is it okay to have a word?" he asked, coming straight in.

Mirin spun in her chair, expected him to take the small seat between the bookshelf and a filing cabinet on the other side of the narrow office. Instead, he sat himself down on the edge of her desk, like he had in the lab with Portia, sitting over Mirin and looking down at her. Mirin pushed her chair back slightly so as not to be looking up at him like a child. David shuffled forward a little in response.

Mirin knew this was coming. In her absence, she hadn't paid attention to office politics. But when she decided, or rather realised, she would have to go back to work if she was to do things like keep paying a mortgage or giving Oran a future, she'd known David would now be her line manager. He was head of department. It couldn't be anybody else, even though technically she was the more senior professor.

"Look," David began, "I wanted to let you know, we are all so pleased to have you back. And we know it has been a really hard year for you. I want you to know, there's no pressure. There's no need to hurry. Ease your way back into things. Phased return is still on the cards, if you want it. You don't have to be here five days a week doing the full grind that everyone else is doing."

"Thanks, David. That's good of you, but I'll be okay. I've got to get back into things at some point. Undergraduates won't teach themselves. And..."

"Oh, I asked Portia to cover your undergraduate lectures. She worked all summer preparing slides on Neolithic and early Iron Age religious practices. I may pitch in a little too but..."

"Portia?"

"Yes, she's quite the little talent. Of course, you know that already. Her PhD is coming along quite nicely. Preliminary results on Palaeolithic bog pollen make quite interesting reading. She is presenting at a conference in Helsinki in a couple of months. I'm keynoting, of course."

"Is that the International Conference on Archaeology and Biochemistry?"

"That's right. I know you normally present at that conference."

"Well, I organised the last two and edited the proceedings."

"Oh, that's right," he said genially.

"I didn't know you had expertise in biochemistry."

"Well, I'd hardly say expertise. Really, I think it was more to do with all the TV things. You know how it is." He waved his hand carelessly. "I really didn't feel able to say no!"

And yet, that's exactly what you should have said, thought Mirin. And then she caught herself. She was perhaps being unkind; the old Mirin talking. The one that stayed late to finish grant applications and research articles and caught up on all her reading at the weekend while Omar and Oran played.

"No, I suppose not," she agreed.

"Besides, it's a great opportunity to promote the department and the university. It will give Portia a nice bit of exposure too." David smiled at this, a winning TV smile. It was a smile Mirin had known since graduate school, a smile which had more layers than it seemed. Today of all days, Mirin really couldn't be bothered playing this game.

"That's all wonderful. I *would* like to take back the lead supervisor's role for Portia's PhD, however, being my area of speciality."

David's smile faltered a touch, but he recovered.

"Absolutely. That's something we can talk about. I'm sure there's enough of Portia to go around. I don't need to keep her all to myself."

He rose from the desk, fixing his tie with a habitual push and tug at the silken knot. As he left, he said once more, "I know things have changed. I know things have been hard for you..." He chewed his lip in an almost convincing impression of doubt. "... I feel bad..."

"David, it's fine. I'm happy for you."

"Really? I've often thought it could have been you up there on the television instead of me. You've got the looks and..."

"Honestly, David? I have no interest in making TV programmes. None whatsoever."

Again, that winning smile faltered slightly. Those teeth, lasered white, flashed back as if defeating the briefest moment of self-doubt.

"We'll talk again soon," he said, opening the door. "It's good to have you back."

6

THE PLASTER CAST was too big and clumsy, making Dip fumble with his keys, dropping them on the doorstep of his home. His arm and head hurt. His body was heavy with fatigue and an adrenaline crash. And his mind spun with the events of the day, trying to make sense of the violence. The paramedics told him he was in shock and he could still feel the effects of it. Now he was dog tired and filthy from the muck of the site and the things he had done. He wanted a shower, followed by sleep, to forget, if that was at all possible.

Home was a small cottage rented from a farmer in the Stirlingshire countryside, with whitewashed walls and a slate roof, which might have once been thatched. The door was freshly painted red. And the whole property sat in almost complete darkness, isolated between fields down a narrow lane. The darkness didn't help in finding the key on the mat.

Finally, Dip managed to locate it and then the keyhole. The freshly painted door stuck. Dip put the shoulder of his good arm to it and almost fell into his front room.

Jackie Chan immediately assaulted his master. The small pug dog came skidding out of the galley kitchen, little paws winning no traction on the tiled floor. A chorus of tiny yaps accompanied the little dog's enthusiastic welcome. He jumped up at his master, his paws managing to reach Dip's knee.

"Hey there, buddy," Dip said, pressing the plaster-cast fist into the palm of his other hand at chest height and making a little bow to Jackie Chan, a private ritual. Then Dip made a noise like "*whoar!*" in a high-pitched tone and put up his fists in a fighting stance. Jackie Chan immediately sat down on his haunches, stopped barking, and raised one leg and pawed the air a few times.

"Good boy." Dip ruffled the pug's head, who in return licked his master's hand while snuffling at the strange new scents he'd brought into their home.

It was not something he would usually do on a work night, but Dip poured himself a large measure of single malt. He wasn't expected at work tomorrow, though he would go anyway. If nothing else, today had produced a mountain of paperwork. Paperwork that wouldn't end for a long time due to so many unanswered questions. Not least how two groups of quite pleasant people had started brutally killing each other over something as innocuous as building a road into a nature reserve. He thought about this, swallowing the first mouthful of whisky, letting it work its warmth down his throat.

Dip sat down heavily in an armchair with a bottle of sixteen-year-old Lagavulin he had been given at Christmas. Dried mud flaked off him, but he felt too tired to care. He poured another large measure, noting his right hand trembling; he knocked back the whisky in another single gulp. The second one burnt unpleasantly. However, the alcohol had already begun to hit him, seeping into his muscles, relaxing him, dampening the speed of his thoughts.

On the third measure, Dip's face scrunched as the liquid burnt down his gullet and then warmed his belly. The savoury afternotes washed his palate, shortly followed by the almost antiseptic taste of peat. The taste brought his mind unwillingly back to the day, what he'd seen, what he'd done. He poured a fourth large measure and knocked it back. The sharp edges of his mind were numbing. Better.

Dip staggered to the kitchen and put some food out for Jackie Chan. On his way back to the chair he turned on the television. It was a mistake. Of course, the incident was on the news. He was even there, in the background, sitting in the back of an ambulance being tended to by paramedics. They didn't show any of the gore, just the emergency services busying about the site behind Lucy Walker. The fact that Lucy Walker was there, with her feline cheekbones and black hair tied back in a tight ponytail, said everything about how big a news story it was. She was normally anchoring, or interrogating some politician or celebrity, rarely in the field getting her designer shoes wet. Dip reached for the remote when the lights overhead flickered, and all the power went out in the cottage.

Jackie Chan growled and began to bark, the hackles bristling on his little back. With a sigh of inevitability, Dip checked the fuse box under the stairs. Half-drunk, his mobile phone seemingly out of battery as well, meaning he had no flashlight to hand, Dip found the fuses with some difficulty. He realised his phone probably got damaged in his pocket at the incident today. Feeling along the line of fuses, he found the culprit and flicked the main switch up. Lights came back on and electrical equipment gave bleeps of starting up. The wiring is getting old in this place, Dip thought, mentally noting to tell his landlord.

Jackie Chan gave another bark, shook the folds of his skin rattling his collar, and with a deferential lick of his own nose, looked up expectantly at his master for their next move.

"I think it's time to give up on today, buddy," Dip told the pug.

They climbed the thin stairs to the attic bedroom. The house felt cold and the wooden stairs squeaked underfoot. Every bone in Dip's body now seemed to be aching, along with a pounding head. Shapes oozed into one another in the dark until Dip turned on the light upstairs. The pain came in pulses that bloomed and retracted, never to the point of comfort. He took another mouthful of the water of life along with two of the strong painkillers from the hospital. Hopefully the combination would knock him out for the night. He turned on the shower in the en suite while he pulled off his clothes, leaving them discarded in a pile.

Jackie Chan paced in a circle at the foot of the bed, sat down, his glassy eyes fixed on his master in the adjoining bathroom. He whimpered. Dip stepped over the side of the bathtub, feeling every injury as he did so. The water was warm on his belly, matting the hair. He would be quick. Shower enough to clean off the dirt. Raising the plaster cast above the shower to rest on the tiled wall, Dip submerged his head. As he did, his consciousness waned like an undertow, first with an initial tug like a head rush before Dip was roughly peeled away from the shore of reality.

In a rush of foamy water, he was sucked back over the pebbles of time.

———

Dip found himself amidst a twilight expanse of bogland, shrouded in mist, a fine Scottish rain falling. It was so fine as to hardly be there at all and yet pervade everywhere. Bird calls were at once close and yet far off, distorted by mist that moved like a swirling serpent. He walked through the bog, sometimes losing his footing, sinking in to the knee. The path must be trodden carefully. Dip felt a great sense of unease in this place, and yet he strode with a confidence that was unfamiliar to him. *Hunting.*

When the water covered his feet, it felt as though it would suck him under and hold him beneath the surface forever. But there was nowhere else to go. How he got here wasn't a question on his mind. He was playing the role with the total commitment one gives to a dream.

He emerged from the mist. Someone knelt ahead of him. A woman, beautiful and young, her hair in braids, a simple cloth dress covering her body. She wore flowers in her hair. They could not be from here, he knew, because there were no flowers to be seen in this marshland.

A hiss left his lips. Clasped to her breast she held a stone knife: its blade of sharp, black obsidian; its hilt of antler. She whispered to herself, muttering over and over. The language was foreign to Dip, but whatever it was, she was repeating it in a chant or religious invocation. The mist enclosed them, unnaturally thick. The chant was insistent. Not a chant but a song, he realised. It filled him with pure rage, not uncontrolled, but distilled down to a sharpness as deadly as the black knife the young woman held.

The mist hemmed him in. Looking down to place a foot on the precarious ground, Dip caught his reflection. He was a boy of maybe nine or ten years of age. Slight. His skin was light brown, his hair a short mane of silken, black curls now dripping wet and clinging to his face. The blackness of his hair matched his eyes, which in the reflection appeared the glaucous colour of flint. Dip recognised his dream-face. He had seen it earlier that day encased within the peat of the nature reserve.

Dip wanted to leave now. He wanted to wake up. The unified consciousness of a moment ago began to split. The dreamer became aware of the dream. He had a terrible sense that something was about to happen. The power of the boy's rage was evidence of that. But what could a boy do against a woman with a knife? And why was he searching her out?

The thought of earlier that day, of looking in at the Range Rover and thinking he should call it in, that he should trust his gut, came back to him. The same feeling gripped him now, only amplified.

The boy, Dip, moved closer to the woman, the sound of the bog squelching with each step. Dip could see markings on his own naked body, black on brown, in regular patterns made with thin lines and dots. Tattoos. The boy smiled. His perfectly black teeth reflected in the dank pools around them, in the place of neither earth nor water. Those pools were a black of the same matted sheen as the obsidian knife the woman held in her hands.

The woman's song built in intensity, growing louder and ever more insistent, pulling Dip closer, allowing him to see something else. It wasn't something in the bogland surrounding them but some-thing within the woman. His mind could see her open heart and the soul beneath that. He knew which gods she worshipped. He knew her fears, her sins, and her most fundamental beliefs.

Catching it in his mind, like a snowflake on his palm, he fed one of those beliefs, adding to it, building its strength, magnifying it, distorting it. Her belief, this tasty little thing, was in the stories she'd been told as a little girl to make her behave. It was the fear that he, the boy, would come, as he had come to other places. It was the lie that they did not make him and that their gods would save them. It was a nightmare that had become a reality, walking out from the shadows of her imagination. It was an easy thought to feed, to cultivate and grow. And they, thought the boy, they do love to propagate in every sense of the word. They will do anything to propagate, believe anything, and he would help them get what they deserved. This was his gift to them. The gift of themselves.

Still chanting, the woman's shaking hands grasped around the handle of the obsidian knife, began to lift it from her chest, turning the point towards her belly. The young woman opened her eyes. They were two panicked emeralds illuminated with fear. The chant became strained with terror. But, with sheer force of will, she continued to sing.

Her arms straightened, preparing to stab the blade into her stomach. The song was now almost a scream reaching its apogee. She shook her head side to side, maintaining the song, tears streaming down her cheeks, mixing with the fine rain beading on her shivering alabaster skin. Muscles in her forearms corded, betraying the internal battle, a battle Dip knew she had lost. The purity of her conviction had been sullied. It was too easy. They did it to themselves.

Dip too fought contradictory impulses: he, the dreamer, wanted to run away, to wake up; the other, the boy, relished the forthcoming violence. Dip could hear the countless screams, from countless lands, echoing in the boy's memory.

The knife was about to fall. He would have her cut slowly and watch her own entrails spill out before her terrified gaze. The smile broadened on the boy's face. It would be over soon, and he would seek out the others. Then his concentration, his control over the woman, was broken.

The water exploded around him. Warriors sprang from its depths, spitting reeds from their mouths, spray showering their bodies. They grabbed hold of the boy's slender limbs, two men to each, pulling him to the ground. He screamed and cursed them, spitting and gnashing his teeth: "Izora zaitez, artaburu. Tortalori. Zahorra!"

A large man, with muscles as hard as granite, grabbed a handful of his hair, pulled back his head, and pushed it into the water. The boy writhed and struggled, the eight men holding him down barely able to keep him there. They screamed and shouted urgently. They would not be able to hold him for long. Bog water covered Dip's face. Its taste filled his mouth and nose, making him cough and splutter but not enough to smother the rage. He fought, bringing his head above the water.

The man with granite muscles held on, as if wrestling a gigantic beast. Opening his eyes, Dip could now see that the young woman was standing astride him, brandishing the black stone knife. The men screamed for her to do it, and in one fast, scything movement, her hand slashed through the air beneath Dip's chin. It cut as though it met no resistance. Dip thought she had missed, but then a gout of inkish-blood ejected from his throat, spraying the woman. The coldness of the blood shocked her, staggering her back.

Consciousness was leaving Dip now. He felt his great strength ebb and his limbs grow very weak. Eight men lifted him from the ground and carried him a short way. The blood formed a black mask across the boy's face. Blood dripped to the sodden ground from the gaping wound. The party now sang together.

Reaching a predetermined spot, the group came to a halt.

His vision blurring, Dip could see the water beneath him. They tied something around his waist. The cord bit into his numbing flesh and they threw him forward. A heavy stone pulled him into the depths. Brown liquid filled his lungs. Blood stained the water black. The faint light of the world faded.

With a clawing gasp, Dip lurched from his slumped position in the bath. He shivered beneath the hot water. Jackie Chan growled at the foot of the bed and then let out a bark from the next room.

The lights flickered again, keeping this reality in a world of shadow and outline, real but not yet substantial. The pain in Dip's arm had returned, along with the mother of all headaches. Whisky furred Dip's mouth, and its stale peat-tinge made his heart lurch. He slipped in the bath, nearly cracking his broken arm on the edge.

Jackie Chan continued to growl.

"What's the matter with you, buddy?" Dip said hoarsely, struggling out of the bath.

Jackie Chan barked.

"Hey, boy, it's me." This time Jackie Chan gave a plaintive whimper. One handed, Dip attempted to dry himself, teeth chattering with the spectral cold of his dream.

"That's it, Jackie. It's me. It's okay. I had a bad dream was all. Just a dream." Jackie Chan jumped clumsily from the bed and ran to the doorway of the bathroom, panting and licking his snout apologetically. Dip ruffled the fur on the back of Jackie Chan's neck, and breathed through the pain in his arm. "It was just a bad dream, boy. A bad day mixed with booze and painkillers."

7

A STRIP LIGHT illuminated the office a little too harshly, while outside autumn's night had already wrapped a dark blanket over the city. The department was all but empty. David looked up from the notes he was outlining on the computer. He rubbed his palms across his eyes, trying to grind away the brain fog gathered from the meeting. Above the desk, his own face stared back at him from a poster of his acclaimed television series. A gift from the production team. The picture had an elegant black frame. Season two had been commissioned already, and David was working on pre-production notes to send over later this week to his producers at the BBC.

He was trying to clear his mind of the faculty committee meeting, which had left him drained. It was one thing to be made a professor, and quite another to be made head of department. Nothing quite prepares one, David thought, for the full weight of university procedure and the excruciatingly long meetings. Academics love to talk. And they are polite to a fault. As a result, everyone got to speak. The problem was that some people, most of them, liked to say the same thing at least three times, and no one was rude enough to interrupt, just in case anyone got their feelings hurt. David didn't want to hurt anyone's feelings. Actually, that wasn't true. He would have loved to have told them to shut their mouths. Could they make a decision sometime this century? But David knew the game and had ambitions. So, he kept his mouth shut and smiled as encouragingly as possible. However, he wasn't sure he could face the next thirty years listening to everything in triplicate.

The university would undoubtedly give him time off for his next TV show though. The vice chancellor could hardly contain his enthusiasm when they last met at an event with members of the Scottish Parliament at the university's Hunterian Gallery. When he would get to do a little bit of research was harder to say. He could piggyback onto some of the graduate students' research papers, the lovely Portia not least. But that wasn't really his research. The Antonine Wall was what he did his PhD on, and he'd been expanding on it ever since. He had made something of an academic reputation in that area. Not much but enough, he told himself, to make professor even without the television show. Everyone loves the Romans.

Looking at his poster-self profile gazing pensively over the landscape of the British Isles, David mused that perhaps his talents lay in communicating the big ideas to more popular audiences. That was important work, wasn't it? The idea danced in his mind like something slightly forbidden. He liked that idea. He knew that some of his colleagues looked down on what he was doing. Jealousy, that's all it was.

As if the gods had been listening to him, the boxy telephone on his desk, at least ten years out of date with current technology but standard university issue, began to ring.

"Hello. Yes, it is... That's awful... Yes, you've been sent to the right place. That's exactly the type of thing that we do. In fact, we have one of the world's leading specialists in the area... Yes, I understand. I saw it on the news... Of course, I didn't realise that such a discovery was also made. And the coroner is pretty sure?... Yes, we will act with the utmost confidentiality... When? I think we should be able to put a team together and be with you by the day after tomorrow. The longer something like that is exposed, the higher the risk of degradation... Of course, and it's a crime scene as well... Yes, I'll see you Wednesday... Thank you, DCI Dalgleish."

David put down the phone and immediately Mirin became the object of his mind. Would she be up to it? He needed her. This was her specialism. There were only a handful of other people in Europe qualified to do this, and if the university didn't step up to the mark, then it was highly likely they would lose this opportunity. Paddy Drogheda was only a short flight away in Dublin. And Carl Jorgensen would be on a plane quicker than he could get drunk at a conference dinner if he heard about this. David lay money on Carl being on the phone by the end of the week to talk to him, to see if he could lend any resources, i.e. get a piece of the action. No, no, this was going to turn out to be a once in a lifetime opportunity...

He went over what the DCI told him. A bog body, the head at least and a hand, which was still an amazing find. Old Croghan Man was only a torso and arms, and Paddy Drogheda still dined out on the income more than thirty years later. David didn't know all the details of bog bodies but finding it with the head intact was a boon. Hundreds of bog bodies had been discovered all over Northern Europe, but only forty or so were intact. Mirin would know the exact details. Yes, this could be big, professionally speaking.

Professor David Hamill did not believe in luck or greater powers guiding his fate: he was a man of science, but a thrill of exhilaration tingled through his body when the telephone began to ring for a second time.

"Hello, Professor Hamill? It's Lucy Walker."

"Lucy," David said with polished enthusiasm. "Wonderful to hear from you. And don't start with all that professor nonsense. You know you can call me David."

"Well, David, my sources tell me there might be a little discovery at the recent tragic events up in Stirlingshire."

"I'm afraid I couldn't possibly comment, Lucy."

"Don't be coy. I know all about the potential archaeological discovery of a lifetime wrapped up in a gruesome set of murders. At a national beauty spot, no less. I was there earlier. I don't know about you, David, but I smell a story, maybe an award-winning documentary."

"Things are rarely as dramatic as they are made to appear."

"Well, you'd know all about that, Professor," Lucy Walker said lightly.

"David. Call me David."

"Yes, I will, except when I see you tomorrow on camera. Wouldn't want you to look unprepared. Then when we know what we've really got we can have a little chat. Work something out that might be in both of our interests."

"Wouldn't that be nice?"

"Yes, it would, wouldn't it, Professor?"

"Call me David." David heard Lucy laugh playfully, the way she did with guests sometimes, lulling them into a feeling of trust. "See you tomorrow... Professor." David leant back in his chair, marvelling. The academic life could be a slow molasses of procedure and habit, but it also contained the real prize of genuine discovery. Most researchers were content with the small incremental finds and new niche observations. That was science and that had been the story of David's research career so far. It was nothing exceptional. But every academic dreamed of the big discovery, the kind of thing that elevated them among their peers and put them into the stratosphere. Could this be it? he wondered.

David was married to his career like everyone else. This past year, however, had given him a taste for the exotic, and there was a small piece of him that felt that he was being unfaithful to his vocation. But the more he did it, the more fan mail he received. With every television and newspaper interview he did he felt a little less unfaithful. His bank account didn't mind either. He stretched out in his chair, wondering if perhaps something was about to bring these two sides of his life together explosively. Who could tell? That was what was so exciting about research: the possibility of failure or the discovery of a lifetime.

A knock came at his door, and David knew before it opened who it would be.

"Come in," he said, swivelling his chair to face the door, his face on the large poster looking wistful and wise behind him.

Slipping inside, Portia shut the door with her backside.

"It's time for supervision, Professor."

No, David didn't believe in luck or fate, but like any good scientist he knew one should keep an open mind when presented with new data. Portia, now, she had an open mind, David thought to himself as his graduate student clicked the lock of his office door.

8

PULLING UP TO THE SITE, uniformed police held back press and a few members of the public trying to film with their phones. A short way from the road, forensic tents stood obscuring the site, making it look like a travelling caravan of scientists had briefly taken a few days' holiday on the land.

The van bumped on the uneven ground. Portia gave a small grunt when she hit her head on the windowpane. Chin, a research assistant Mirin thought had promise despite being almost painfully quiet, held some of the equipment in place.

"Sorry," David called into the back, evidently relishing the outing.

He pulled the vehicle to a sudden halt, throwing the rest of the group forward with a jolt, and sprang out of the van.

"We'll take a preliminary look and then see what we need," Mirin said to the others.

Portia and Chin nodded, although Portia was looking at David. Mirin followed her gaze. He was talking to a small group, presenting himself to the camera and the pretty woman with angular cheekbones, styled and fixed hair, a Barbor jacket and blue wellington boots, replete with a trim of white silhouetted hares.

"It looks like we have an audience." Mirin tried to keep her tone neutral. "Try not to pay attention to them. We've a job to do. David will handle the rest."

They disembarked from the van, green wellies squelching in the mud.

"There she is..." David opened his arms to the team trudging through the quagmire left by rain. "Our expert."

The cameraman panned to Mirin. "What do you think you've found?" Lucy Walker offered a microphone out of shot.

"I don't know. We haven't seen it yet," Mirin said, keeping her team moving to the site.

Portia tried not to snort at Mirin's reply, attempting to muffle it behind her sleeve. Lucy's face darkened, her jaw tightening under her cheekbones. She dropped the microphone to her side with a roll of the eyes and a pointed look at David.

Two people, a man and a woman, peeled off from David's side. Mirin noted they looked about as pleased to be on camera as she was.

A smile pinged back onto David's face.

"On me in three, two, and..." he said, addressing the camera. "What we know so far is..."

The man and woman intercepted Mirin's group. "Good morning," said the woman, fishing in her pocket. "DCI Connie Shepard. This is DI Stuart Blair." They flashed their IDs, Connie falling in beside Mirin, Stuart next to Portia and Chin, a yard behind. "You'd be Professor Hassan?"

The detective offered her hand, already covered in a latex glove. Mirin met it with her own gloved hand. The handshake was brief but firm, Mirin noted. A hand used to being crushed and which had grown strong and prepared. Connie wore smart slacks and a shirt under a raincoat, warm and reaching down to her knees, the type of item probably stored in the boot of her car, with a change of clothes in another bag. Mirin got the picture of someone very practical and efficient, like her handshake.

"What can you tell us?" Mirin asked.

"Not much. The pathologist and our forensics team are sure it's nothing to do with the crime scene. It's much older."

"I heard it was a real horror shop," Portia offered from behind.

DCI Shepard nodded. "Ten dead," and gave no further details.

Mud squelching underfoot, the group approached with their breath frosting in the autumn air. Despite the sun having been up for several hours, it hid behind a marble of white clouds, mottled with seams of grey.

"You alright?" DI Blair asked Portia, whose already pale skin had drained to a porcelain white.

"Just want to get this right. It could be important," Portia said. It sounded like a lie to Mirin. Something was off with her PhD student, but Mirin couldn't pin-point why. Portia looked nervous, anxious even.

The police had cleared the scene thoroughly, removing all traces of blood, and the rain had done its part too. But the site, gouged out of the peatland, had the look of an open wound in the flesh of the earth.

Only feet away now, the site was so arresting that Mirin came up short. The rest of the group halted, except for DCI Shepard. The police officer turned, observing Mirin. The archaeologist could not tear her eyes away from the face of the young boy, his features perfectly preserved. Even from some twelve feet away, the boy's black hair was striking, framing what anyone would call a beautiful face. His eyes were shut, emphasising his unnaturally long lashes, and his head was on its side, as though he lay asleep peacefully under the blanket of the earth. He looked, Mirin thought with a leap of her heart, like her son, Oran. The boy was a little older perhaps but had the same dark hair and long eyelashes.

Mirin knew the gruesome fate which had befallen many of the bog bodies. Whether the rest of his body was still intact would only be revealed once they cleared the surrounding material.

Mirin and DCI Shepard turned quickly at the noise behind them.

Portia was bent double, throwing up between her legs, hands on her knees. It was at that moment David, Lucy Walker, and her cameraman decided to join them, the cameraman recording every-thing. Portia raised her head, realising she was being filmed. Chin and DI Blair were bending to help her.

"I'm okay." She waved them off. "It must have been something I ate." David looked at her with a frown.

Lucy and the cameraman flanked the group, goading them forward like sheepdogs.

"The face is remarkably well preserved. We'll start much wider in case there is any more to find," Mirin instructed her group.

"Is that normal? Will the whole body be preserved like that? How old do you think it is?" Lucy asked.

"Everything is unusual when it comes to bog bodies. We rarely get a complete body, but it's common for what we do find to appear frozen in time. Fingerprints are often still visible. We might find the contents of a last meal in the stomach, and even brain matter can remain in bodies thousands of years old."

"How is that possible?" Lucy sounded genuinely interested, and Mirin was about to answer.

"The bog..." David began. The camera panned to him. "... performs a process of natural mummification. Many people know about Egyptian mummies, or some of the Peruvian examples perhaps, where arid conditions, in addition to embalming techniques, contribute to halting the normal processes of decay. However, bogs have a unique chemical make-up, which, despite being a wet environment, preserves the soft tissues of the bodies so well that, as in the famous example of Tollund Man, it can appear the body could have died only days ago."

David carried on in the background as Portia and Chin returned with the necessary equipment. Then they set to their delicate task of exploring the find. David would occasionally appear with a trowel, when he wasn't talking to the camera. The detectives had backed off to give them room, checking their watches from time to time. Visibly white and now sweating, Portia soldiered on.

"Are you alright?" Mirin asked her out of earshot of Lucy and her microphone.

"I'll be okay." She cast a glance at David performing for the camera.

"You let me know if you need to stop," Mirin told her, carefully removing a clod of peat just above the face of the boy. "My God!"

Portia moved in to get a closer look as Mirin inspected the area. Talking into the camera, David stuttered mid-sentence, double-taking over his shoulder. The cameraman moved away from David, with Lucy following tightly behind, a hound moving in on a powerful scent.

"What have you found, Professor Hassan?" Lucy peered over Mirin's shoulder.

"We've more than a face," Mirin said. "It appears we have the whole head, and it's connected to his torso. This is significant. *Very* significant."

Mirin worked to reveal more and more of the dead boy's body.

The whole team, David included, were involved now, digging with careful urgency. They were engrossed and quiet but for an occasional gasp or exclamation.

The boy they were steadily revealing lay on his side lengthways. The lower half was still encased in the peat, but what they had exposed looked like a complete body, minus the severed hand.

Sweating and dirty, the team took a pause, exchanging glances.

"What?" Lucy said, who, to her credit, had been silently letting them work for the last few hours.

Mirin nodded to David in silent agreement. He had dropped the polished veneer. He was every bit the archaeologist in the field getting his hands dirty.

"It's significant," he said, looking up from the dirt to the camera. "We appear to have a complete, or near-complete, body. The levels of preservation are truly amazing, which means..." He trailed off.

"What? What does it mean?" Lucy asked.

"It means," Mirin when on, "that either we have one of the most significant finds of the decade, particularly at this depth, or –"

"Or what?" said Lucy, sensing a story either way this would break.

"Or, given the level of preservation, we are looking at a relatively recent burial. At the moment things don't add up."

"Like what?" Lucy moved closer.

"The discolouration of the skin implies that the body has been in the ground for some time. It could be anywhere back to the Iron Age, possibly even older. We'll only know more once we can test samples in the lab. However, the level of preservation is incredible. There seems to be very little disfiguration of the skull and face. The pressure of the bog and the softness of the tissues would have typically flattened the body to varying degrees."

Mirin was interrupted.

"Look at this." It was almost a whisper from Chin.

David peered closer at what Chin was pointing to with the end of his trowel. "Are those markings? Tattoos perhaps?"

They were all looking closely now, Lucy and the cameraman trying to film over their shoulders.

"They don't look European, if they are." Lightly Mirin touched a globule of peat to brush it away. Portia retched, falling back from the group and puking in hot, violent heaves.

Raised voices reached them from the main road. There weren't as many onlookers now, but the uniformed police still stood guard. They parted for a man who stumbled through, nearly losing his footing. One of his arms was in plaster from the elbow down. He was shouting something out of earshot.

"Bloody hell, he's come back," Mirin heard DI Blair mutter to DCI Shepard. "You want me to get rid of him?"

The man was running now, slipping on the churned-up ground, waving his arms and calling out. "Wait! Stop! Don't!"

DI Blair stepped forward, blocking the man, placing a hand on his chest to halt his advance.

"Please stop. Don't disturb him!" the man shouted over Blair's shoulder, moving from side to side, blocked at each step by the DI.

"What's he saying?" asked David.

"He was the copper who reported the incident and your find," DCI Shepard told them.

Lucy nudged her cameraman, but he had already turned his lens on the new character in play. The man sidestepped one way. DI Blair went to follow, but it was a fake, and the man slipped under his arm on the other side, breaking into a clumsy run toward the group.

DCI Shepard put her hands up now.

"That's enough, Constable Bhaskar."

Dip skidded to a halt in front of her, falling forward, barely catching himself with his good hand. His plaster cast pushed into the gluttonous mud. "Stop! Don't!" he pleaded, looking like he hadn't slept or shaved in at least a couple of days.

"That's enough!" came DCI Shepard's voice. He looked at her with plaintive eyes, then they shifted to the boy.

"God, no!" Dip shouted. "You've uncovered him. Put him back. Put him back. Put him back." Dip slipped again and his flailing plaster cast caught DI Blair across the cheek.

Blair grabbed Dip by his broken arm, forcing it behind his back, causing Dip to cry out in pain and momentarily stop his tirade as Blair dragged him back from the scene.

"DI Blair, ease up," Connie said, following the two struggling police officers. Blair apparently had his ire up and continued to haul Dip through the mud struggling.

"Please stop. You must put him back. We'll all die. Please."

Portia looked as though she was about to keel over and steadied herself on David, whose television smile had faltered. The sudden burst of chaos into the mystery of their find, at a recent murder scene, evoked a feeling Mirin was too familiar with, a loss of control.

"Enough, Stuart. God damn it, that's an order," Connie said.

Stuart released Dip, and kneeling in the mud he said, almost weeping, "God? He can't help us."

9

Douglas Wallace stared at himself in the mirror. He knew that he looked awful. The skin of his face was waxy and pale. He felt awful as well. The lack of sleep hadn't helped. The same dream kept waking him up, repeated over and over.

Ever since that crime scene at the nature reserve in Stirlingshire things had been different. He was more honest, for one. And mentally, he'd never felt better. The only way he could explain it to himself was that he'd had an epiphany.

Douglas had seen plenty of death during his years as a forensic scientist for the police. Never that many bodies at once, it was true, but that wasn't what was keeping him up at night. It was the hand he'd found, brown and leathery, looking like it didn't belong in that place, severed several inches above the wrist.

Douglas had thought and dreamed of that hand a lot since that day. He'd handled it with the usual forensics' precision, bagging and logging it. It had been recorded as part of the crime scene, although they quickly realised it wasn't relevant, particularly once the state pathologist confirmed the body was much older.

He'd dreamt of the boy's face too. Along with the hand, it had lingered in his thoughts, followed him into his dreams. How delicate they both were. How beautiful. In reality, he hadn't spent that long looking at either, but their details were stamped on his mind: the perfection of the little nail beds, the curl of his dark eyelashes, and even the fingerprints.

Trying to make himself look presentable, Douglas combed back his hair, even adding a little product like he might have done when he was younger, and Mary was still with him. He put on a clean shirt, fixed his tie, and ran through his plan for the evening.

It had been so long since they'd had a proper family dinner. The kids were grown up. Diane went first to Dundee University, and was now wasting her law degree working as an administrator that barely covered her debts. She'd shacked up with that Susan girl she'd met at work. Susan was coming tonight too. Mary was surprised when Douglas suggested it, given his previous opinion about their relationship.

Then there was Connor. He was still at university, living with his mother, and attending lectures at the smaller and far less prestigious Caledonian University. The Polytechnique, Douglas called it. The boy seemed hung-over or high most of the time, studying media of all things. Mary said they had to let them live their own lives, of course, even though Douglas was expected to pay for those lives. He had thought for a long while that maybe he had been too hard on them all. He loved that boy. God, how he loved him.

They used to go and watch Celtic games together. Those moments were almost perfect memories. Douglas would take Connor to play football on a Sunday for local boys' teams. There'd been a chance for Connor to seriously make it. Partick Thistle and Motherwell had been sniffing around him when he was twelve. He had trials when he was fourteen. One more shot and he might have made it, if he had applied himself. But Connor wasn't interested in anything, apart from girls. Much like his sister, Douglas thought with no little bitterness. Mary had told Douglas it was more his dream than Connor's. It really hurt Douglas' feelings when Connor had decided to go and live with his mother.

And Mary, his beloved Mary? They had been through so much together. He still thought about her all the time, thought of her as his wife: until death do us part. Douglas believed in that, he always had.

He couldn't imagine being with anyone else. Maybe he didn't show it, maybe that was at the root of all their problems, but Douglas was a romantic, an old-fashioned romantic. Traditional. He still went to church on Sundays and took communion, even though the rest of the family stopped not long after the children's confirmations. Douglas let it happen. It was his fault, giving in too easily to Mary.

Like that other thing that weighed heavily on him.

He'd turned forty-seven. Diane had just left for university. Connor was beginning to prepare for exams in secondary school when they had a little accident. Mary fell pregnant. Douglas had been so happy when she told him. Then he read her face. She'd already made up her mind. They were too old to have another baby in their late forties. Christ, they would have been forty-eight by the time it arrived. Douglas didn't like it, but Mary went through with the sin.

In many ways Mary was right. Her reasons were valid. However, in his heart, Douglas could never reconcile himself to doing that thing. He saw it as taking a life, or at least stopping one that had every right to exist. But he loved Mary. She always got her way, and he was weak. It was that which forced a wedge between them. They quickly began to drift apart. Mary said it was a long time coming, before the abortion even. That hurt. It cut deeply. But he could see clearly now. He could see how it had been all his fault, how he hadn't done the right things.

Tonight, he would make up for it all. He was bringing the whole family together. He was going to be the father and husband that he should have always been for them.

Everything was prepared. They'd soon be here. Only the finishing touches needed adding. The sight of him at a stove, Mary would have laughed, he thought, as he pulled on an apron, tying it behind his back. Since they parted, he'd learned to do a lot of things: cooking for himself was not the least of them. They were all going to have one great meal together.

A last supper.

Douglas seasoned the pots simmering on the stove with the white powder he had prepared earlier. Weighing out another measure, Douglas added it to the mayonnaise, casting an eye at the clock.

Putting an extra dash of Tabasco sauce and a couple of tablespoons of ketchup to the mix, he poured it over each small dish of prawns lying on a bed of lettuce.

One of the advantages of his job was his knowledge of things the average person didn't have any right to know. The LD50, or lethal dose, of most legal and illegal drugs, for example, and how to calculate for body weight. There was enough time to lay the table and get the glasses ready for drinks before Mary would arrive. She was always on time.

Douglas untied his apron, hung it on the back of the kitchen door, checked himself in the mirror one last time, palming down his hair, and went to the small utility room at the back of the kitchen.

Everything was going perfectly. Douglas finished checking there were enough heavy plastic sheets, cleaning equipment, large plastic buckets, the appropriate amount of hydrofluoric acid and a bone saw borrowed from work.

As if on cue, the doorbell rang.

He was ready to show his family the love they needed and deserved.

10

"WHAT DO you think of Constable Bhaskar's outburst yesterday?" Gone were Lucy Walker's designer boots and Barbour jacket. Today she had donned the white lab coat of science. Her makeup applied for a natural effect, hair tied back in a ponytail, not quite as tight as it would be for interviewing a politician. It was lower and looser.

David looked pensive for a moment, considering his words, either for dramatic effect, or merely an opportunity for the editor to cut the audio and video together as they wished. The edges of his mouth turned up a touch.

"You mean, are we dealing with something supernatural here?" Again, a pause, a slight tilt of the head sympathetically. "No, I'm afraid not. I think what we saw yesterday was the result of extreme stress from a traumatic event. I'm no psychologist, but I think that is far more likely than our remarkable specimen being the harbinger of our doom."

Mirin, Portia, and Chin were pulling the body out of a brushed steel, temperature-controlled storage unit set into the lab wall. The unit was dented in places, with scuff marks showing its age. Between them, they carefully loaded the body, wrapped in plastic on a large metal bed, onto a trolley. Lucy's cameraman, who today at last introduced himself as Robert (or Bob, he didn't mind which), filmed them with Lucy and David in the foreground, providing colour to the process.

"Could there be some religious significance to the boy's death?" asked Lucy.

"That's a very interesting question," David answered, while the others began to lift the body onto an examination table in the middle of the brightly lit lab in the basement of the Gregory Building. "It is a common feature of bog bodies to demonstrate different forms of peri-mortem injury."

"Perimortem?" Lucy queried.

David smiled confidently, white teeth glinting through. "At or just after the moment of death," he clarified. "The famous Scandinavian Tollund Man, for example, was hanged and found with the rope still tied around his neck, while the Graubelle Man had his throat cut; Lindow Man, a British example, strangled, hit on the head, and his throat cut; and then the Irish find of Old Croghan Man was perhaps the grisliest of all. Only his torso and arms were found. A big man by even today's standards, from his wingspan it is estimated he would have stood at an impressive six feet and six inches. He had been decapitated and the head was never recovered. His lower body, below the ribs, had also been cut clean through. We also know from the hazel withy, a kind of wooden rope, that he'd been restrained with it by piercing it through his biceps.

"But back to your point about the religious significance of these deaths: we cannot know for sure. Certainly, the killings in the cases I mentioned appear ritualistic, but that could also be associated with rites around death penalties. In the case of the Old Croghan Man, his body was located at the boundary of very ancient tribal lands in Ireland. Some archaeologists have speculated that he was a failed chieftain, and his death was a ritualistic offering to the gods, possibly associated with fertility rites and the promise of a better harvest in the future. In which case, the deaths could be both a punishment *and* a religious ritual, with a high-status offering to the gods. Our modern minds tend to see these things as entirely separate. But in the Iron Age, as really was the case for us up until the Enlightenment, religion touched every part of every person's life. Their beliefs shaped even the most mundane of practices."

Mirin and her small team had now carefully removed the peat from the top of the body. The boy lay as they'd found him, the lower half still encased. Sweat began to pearl on Portia's forehead despite how cool the lab was, and her complexion had turned pale. She wiped away the moisture with the cuff of her lab coat.

"Do you feel okay?" Mirin asked.

Portia nodded, swallowing hard. "Yes, I'm fine. Just a bug, nothing serious." She looked as though she hadn't slept, and her cheeks were drawn. Mirin noted the similarity with Constable Bhaskar.

"The level of preservation is astounding," Mirin said.

"Why bogs? Is there some special significance to them or were they just a form of convenient rubbish dump?"

Portia tutted. Lucy cast a glance but maintained a professional demeanour.

"That's a very good question indeed, Lucy," began David, his latex gloves still spotless. "It is generally thought that bogs, marshes, and fenland indeed held special significance for Iron Age societies and probably earlier societies too. They are inherently dangerous places. Neither land nor water. Local people would guard safely the knowledge of how to move through these semi-aquatic areas of their land. And because they were neither one thing nor the other, 'liminal' is the archaeologist's term, it is thought they represented to the ancient mind a kind of limbo between this world and the next. A place where spirits might percolate up and be able to exist more easily on our mortal plane. And similarly, a place where mortals of the physical world might wander into the eternity of the afterlife and remain trapped there."

"That is until archaeologists come along and dig them up," Lucy quipped, and both she and David laughed.

"My God, can you see this?" Portia whispered. She had removed the dirt around the boy's face and neck.

The whole team moved to hunch over the body, pulling an overhead light to illuminate proceedings. Lucy and Bob the cameraman jockeyed for position over their shoulders, trying to get a better look.

Mirin took a short, sharp intake of breath. "You're right."

"What is it? What have you found?" Lucy sounded breathless.

"His throat was cut. See here, the wound?" Mirin pointed, moving her gloved finger slowly up, following the line of the clean slash deep in the boy's throat. It was packed with dirt they would need to remove.

Despite the grisly injury, the boy's eyes were closed as if he was at peace. The ringlets of his black hair fell about his face and eyes.

"Is it a human sacrifice? Is this common? How barbaric these people must have been!" Lucy said.

David didn't have time to answer her because Chin made another discovery.

"I think I found the weapon." Chin carefully removed dirt at about the level of the boy's belly. They hadn't seen it before because they needed to dig down through the layers of the dirt to safely remove the whole body without further damage. Mirin moved in to help Chin. Even David got in on the action, repositioning the light overhead for them. It took all their mental effort to resist the urge to work more quickly. The more they revealed, the more excitement they felt.

"Is that what I think it is?" said Portia hesitantly.

"A knife," said Chin, barely audible.

"A what?" said Lucy.

"Not just a knife, by the looks of things," concurred David.

"What is it then? What have you found?"

Mirin had cleared the handle of bone, while Chin had uncovered the blade.

Mirin looked up to Lucy, smiling. "Unbelievable! It's an obsidian knife."

Realisation formed in Mirin's mind: all the implications, the potential significance of the find - *if* proved legitimate. Words were forming in her throat, ready to breathe the discovery into the world.

"I think that it is safe to say," began David, "that this might prove to be one of the most significant finds in the last century."

The statement made Mirin snap her mouth shut. Portia raised her eyebrows and looked between Mirin and Chin. Chin lowered his gaze back to the knife and continued to work. Bob had swung his camera to David, coming in close, filling the shot with David's head and shoulders, ready for the professor's punchline.

"We have a specimen with an unusual level of preservation. He looks practically perfect, but for the slit in his throat. And unusually for a bog body, which are themselves rare finds indeed, he is an even rarer thing: a child. Bog bodies are typically Iron Age or younger. But this is a stone tool, more typical of the Neolithic, perhaps better known as the Stone Age. No bog body has ever been found from that era, let alone of this quality, and so unusual. And I come back to the religious motif. Obsidian, the black basalt stone, possible to work into one of the sharpest-edged blades known to mankind, historically speaking, has long been associated with magic and even witchcraft. It is a material associated with black magic, and here, indeed, we seem to have found the smoking gun, or rather the blooded blade, of child sacrifice."

11

PORTIA STAYED to do extra work after the intrusion of the TV crew during the day. The lab was now quiet. The northern autumn had a bite to it, eating away the sun by late afternoon, so that inhabitants of the city hurried about the business of getting home under the orange gloam of the streetlights.

Portia looked down at the severed hand. She had kept it out of storage, carefully removing the earth that caked it. The more she removed, the more remarkable it appeared. It was exquisitely preserved. Acidity levels in the bog had performed a chemical alchemy, halting the process of putrefaction by bacteria, rendering flesh immortal. During her master's degree, Portia had been lucky enough to travel to Ireland to see the Old Croghan Man. Maybe it had been her fire-red hair that had secured her the placement. Maybe because she laughed at old Professor Drogheda's jokes. Maybe it was something else.

Portia had caught the old professor looking at her arse more than once, though he never did anything else. He would look away when she caught him staring, as though her behind was one of many scientific anomalies he might be looking at in the environment. David had been the same, though less of a gentleman, and younger and handsome.

Portia had charmed Paddy Drogheda so much he helped persuade the museum's curator to let Portia inspect the actual specimen instead of looking at it through the glass display case. That had set her dissertation apart from the others in her year at Oxford and led to the PhD opportunity with Professor Hassan and then David.

Whereas the Old Croghan Man had truly enormous hands, the hands of this new find were small and fine: the fingers willowy, the wrist thin and elegant. Other than the discolouration from being so long in the bog, it was perfect. Even the usual compression as a result of immersion had hardly affected it.

It would be nice for her colleagues to pay attention to her mind once in a while. That was the principal reason she'd chosen to come all the way north to study with Mirin Hassan. Professor Drogheda had seemed disappointed his offer of a studentship to study at Trinity College Dublin was declined.

Staying late, even feeling ill, it was all worth it. This was the opportunity of a lifetime. Being associated with this project could help make her career even before it had begun.

With a small plastic spatula, Portia scraped a globule of mud to reveal the bare skin closest to the point at which the limb had been severed. Even through the headache and nausea, which hadn't abated since their field trip, the rush of excitement at what she uncovered was exhilarating, like a drug flushing through her veins.

Each careful scrape of her spatula, and judicious use of deionised water to wash away the debris and smears, revealed more of the sculpture-like corpse. Portia's heart quickened again. The skin bore markings: tattoos perhaps? They looked like symbols, not just patterns. More than decoration. Reaching for her notepad, she hurriedly scribbled her initial impressions before returning to the hand. A final wash showed the markings wound in a regular pattern of lines down to the wrist and beyond where the hand had been severed. Portia picked up her pen again, wrote a single word on the paper with a question mark: 'Writing'?

This wasn't merely a pattern or a collection of symbolic images. They reminded her of words, similar to...? She couldn't put her finger on it. Ideograms: small pictures, she thought. Proto-writing scripts, what were they called? Although far from being an expert in philology, Portia could see some similarities with cuneiform, the Mesopotamian script, but enough differences to stymie that theory. She remembered reading somewhere about the development of writing from pictograms, and an old theory that writing grew out of earlier symbolic activities. The picture language of oral cultures, memory boards, and knotted systems of South America. A few scholars had even discussed the possibility that tattoos and scarification acted as mnemonics, a memory aid, in shamanic and storytelling practices of the ancient world. Even the word 'glamour' she knew had come from an older Scots mispronunciation of 'grammar'. The ability of the written word to capture, store, and carry meaning appeared magical to largely illiterate cultures. Or so the theory went.

Early writing was a difficult area to investigate because oral cultures naturally leave very little textual evidence behind. But it was well accepted from the studies of indigenous peoples from Australia, the Polynesia Islands, the First Nations of the Americas and others that stories, until and even after the initial appearance of writing, weren't just for entertainment. They were the repository for all of a society's knowledge. Telling them was quite literally a reliving and remaking of their knowledge. The storyteller that sang the song around the campfire or in the mead hall was a historian, priest, cultural touchstone, and fortune-teller in one. Portia's heart raced. Was their little boy a shaman, a storyteller, a singer of songs? *How poetic*, she thought.

Portia rubbed her eyes. This would definitely be worth changing her thesis for. Mirin was nice, a classic academic, measured and interested in the intellectual development of her students. She'd only been her PhD advisor for six months before her life fell apart, and she lost so much. She was back now, although there seemed to be a little bit of her that hadn't returned. Portia still wasn't clear whether Mirin was her lead supervisor anymore. Which, of course, meant David had power over her projects. He'd become an important man in the university, having raised the profile of the department. He was the toast of the city, if not the country, fronting on award-winning shows, invited to speak on everything from breakfast television to political debates. He could speak eloquently and tell a good story. And he was telegenic. God, was he telegenic. Portia thought of Lucy, smiling and touching his wrist during the day. It made her sick in the pit of her stomach, and jealous. Was he just an actor? Was he using her or was she using him? Was everyone just using everyone else? The cold cynicism of this thought twisted in her chest.

Another wave of nausea hit Portia, but it was much smaller than it had been before. She'd felt so embarrassed when she threw up in front of her colleagues at the dig site. David had patted her on the knee in the front of the van on the way back to the university when no one was looking. They hadn't been alone now for a few days. He'd been so busy and preoccupied with this find. They all had. Graduate school had become so competitive, as was the job market. You'd need a PhD to work in McDonald's soon enough. David was becoming the most prominent archaeologist in the whole country, if not beyond. His name and support could open doors, and she thought maybe there was more there. There wasn't anything wrong with that, was there? People working together got drawn to each other.

Lucy slunk into her mind again, flirtatiously flicking her hair through the day, showing her whitened teeth, playing with the hem of her tight skirt. She wasn't the only one who could play that game. *Bitch*, Portia thought.

She tried to keep her mind on the task at hand, the work, but her hand became unsteady due to fantasies of David with his hands all over Lucy, and Lucy's hands all over him, pulling at each other's clothes, feeling each other's bodies, grabbing, kissing, biting. Open mouths exploring. In her mind's eye, Portia could see David pushing Lucy against the wall of his office as she wrapped one of her long legs around his hips. Her nails clawed at his back while they both grunted like animals.

The image was burned so hotly in Portia's mind that before she knew what she was doing she was in the corridor and walking towards David's office, where she knew he was working late.

Portia left the hand on the workbench under the microscope. If she had taken one last look, she might have seen the letters begin to move across the mahogany- brown skin.

63

Portia knew the journalist was gone, but the vision of David making love to Lucy in his office filled her with rage. Half expecting to find her there, or hear the muffled grunts behind the door, Portia knocked. She'd been here before after hours.

David replied with the usual "Come in." He swivelled on his chair; Portia shut the door behind her. The room was dark but for the desk lamp. She stood, her chest rising and falling with quickened breath. Flame-red hair fell about her face like dangerous sparks from a fire about to burn out of control. She kicked the door shut behind her and locked it.

"I'm kind of busy tonight," David said.

Walking forward, Portia undid the buttons of her shirt and threw it along with her lab coat to the office floor. She unfastened her bra, her pink nipples already hard.

"Portia, I really don't think..."

She unbuttoned her jeans, slipping them down to her ankles slowly, along with her panties. She stepped out of her clothes to stand in front of him naked. She could tell he was already hard. Even though he was twice her age he was always hard like a teenager. His eyes fixed on the thin thatch of fiery hair between Portia's legs. Reaching down, she put a hand on his crotch and rubbed. He let out a gasp. "I shouldn't. I have..."

Portia covered his mouth with hers as she unzipped his fly, releasing him. Despite it all, she felt tense, self-conscious. Perhaps it was whatever had made her unwell the last couple of days, her clammy complexion, maybe the weight she'd lost even the last two days and the bags under her eyes. Or maybe it was David; maybe he was now interested in that bitch journalist. But he was still hard, and she was ready for him.

Portia climbed astride his hips, one hand behind his head, pulling him into a deeper kiss. They both moaned through their embrace, and she felt him give in. They sank into each other. Tonight, she would give him something other than a journalist to think about.

Back in the lab, strip lights flickered overhead. On the workbench the severed hand began to move. At first it was a twitch of the middle finger, and then the other digits began to move one by one, until it flexed and clenched into a fist. When the hand relaxed, it began to turn itself over, pulling its thumb towards its little finger. Like some ancient spider, it landed on its palm. The fingers splayed, flexing, and the palm of the thing, now its body, rose. It scuttled towards the edge of the table. The lights overhead stuttered once more.

It paused, one finger raised.

The lights failed.

In the black, where only imagination has sight, something went hunting.

12

IT SCURRIED, seeking the shadows, pausing and then moving at speed. Down black corridors, pushing doors ajar with preternatural strength, scuttling up onto desks, across sills and shelves, searching, drawn. It perceived without sight, feeling their emotions, fragile things that quiver in the night.

It found a hole behind a cabinet and squeezed its way through.

Finding brick beneath its fingertips, it crawled down the wall. The beam of a flashlight barely missed it. The security guard on duty, Johnny, thought he saw something out of the corner of his eye moving down the side of a wall. But when he looked there was nothing there. *Probably a drain spider,* he thought. Feeling cold, he pulled his coat around himself, a wave of nausea rippling up from his stomach, and he thought he might be getting sick.

"Bloody students are like a walking Petri dish," Johnny mumbled.

It crawled on, at the edge of things, pausing when the wrong vessels walked by talking and laughing. They did not quiver enough. They were not the right shape. They were not receptive to what *he* had to fill them with.

Bushes covered its progress up the edge of concrete steps, which led to a throng of noise. It skittered itself into the clammy heat of the

Queen Margaret students' union. This place was rich with open vessels.

Stopping in the shadows, feet moving past. They were not right, but then...

Yesss, you are one. Not a good one, but one nonetheless. You will not spread what needs to be propagated, but you will be filled, and devour yourself. So sad behind the smile. So lonely among friends. No, they won't miss you. Yesss, they would be better without you. You are a burden. It isn't worth the struggle. Those pills the doctor gave you, with the ones the boy in the toilet sold you, and the ten pounds in your pocket for a bottle of vodka from the off-licence. Put your phone down the toilet. Lock your door. Put a chair under the handle. Do it properly. Just leave. They won't know you've gone. Goodbye.

And on to the next. *So angry for those things they did to you when you were little. That's why you lift those weights and hit that bag. Yesss, he bumped into you on purpose. You shouldn't let him get away with that. You're a grown-up now, can't keep getting pushed around. He's laughing as he says sorry. You should give him something to be sorry about. When he goes to the toilet follow him. Hurt him. Break him until he weeps like you did as a child. Yesss.* And on to the next one.

It slipped between shadows and stumbling feet until... *Perfffect!*

"You know, I honestly think we should do away with the idea of gendered names." Kevin took a sip of his half pint of beer, looking up over the rim at Rachel, who sat on the other side of the table next to that huge oaf Gerald. What was he doing here anyway? This was the Queen Margaret Union. All the toff rugby players were supposed to hang out in the Glasgow Union at the bottom of University Avenue. But here he was with all his muscles and private school education, slumming it in the QMU, while the alternative music tried its best to drown out their conversation.

"Why would we do that?" Gerald leant forward, shouting over the sticky table between them.

Kevin rolled his eyes and took a deep breath. "So it'll be a level playing field," he explained.

Gerald looked bemused. Kevin thought he could actually see the cogs turning. He imagined they were probably gold and had a butler to oil them.

"Sorry. I don't get it. How have boys' and girls' names got anything to do with it?" Gerald asked.

Really, his whole class needed pitying, if it wasn't for the fact that they were probably the reason the whole world was in this mess. It was hard to pity people with money and opportunity. Actually, it wasn't hard, it was impossible. Gerald was a rich white male, brought up to believe he would inherit the earth. This kind of thing was like a fish trying to understand running.

"Look, *you...*" Kevin pointed his finger and spoke slowly and loudly, and not just because of the music, "...are a white male. It makes me so mad. The whole goddamn system is a self-perpetuating patriarchy, perpetrating its violence on women and people of colour."

This wasn't working. Rachel looked a little uncomfortable. But, damn, someone had to point out the emperor has no clothes.

Kevin had been sidling up to Rachel in tutorials all last semester. He'd tagged her into his tweets all the way through the summer, and she'd responded to more than a few of them. Kevin was sure she liked him before Gerald came along. But when they came back for the start of the third year, Gerald and his muscles were doing her honour's psychology course. At least they didn't look like they were an item. Not yet anyway.

Something brushed against Rachel's leg. She shivered and even in the brooding light show of the union the colour looked to have drained out of her face.

"Don't," she said when Kevin tried to put a hand on hers. She pulled away, and Kevin noticed her wipe the back of her hand down her jeans. He thought he felt her foot rub up his calf under the table.

"Sorry. You looked unwell," Kevin said.

"God, are you alright?" Gerald looked concerned as Rachel heaved and clasped her mouth.

"Of course she's alright, Gerry. She doesn't need a man to look after her." Kevin took another sip from his half pint of shandy.

"My name isn't Gerry, dickhead."

Rachel jumped up from the table, still covering her mouth with

68

her hand. A bottle of beer and a couple of empties took a tumble in the rush. She clutched her belly as she ran from the bar.

"Now look what you've done," Kevin said. "You're so toxically masculine."

"Whatever, Kev." Gerald went after her.

Kevin watched them go, gritting his teeth. He could just imagine what they were about to get up to. She could do so much better than him. The problem was that she didn't even know what she wanted. False consciousness. Gerald was merely the cultural manifestation of consumer capitalism, wrapped up in the muscles of economic security. She couldn't help it. It was what the culture had conditioned her to think ever since it forced her first dolly onto her. Rachel didn't really know what was good for her, none of them did. Kevin swallowed bile, a deep draught of it. He could feel it festering, growing like a dark seed into an obsidian flower.

VOMIT WAS ALREADY SPRAYING between her fingers by the time Rachel reached the bottom step of the student union. There was a brief reprise once her stomach was empty, and the cold autumn air hit her face.

"Are you all right, hen?" a bouncer called after her.

Rachel stumbled off down University Gardens, a parade of converted townhouses from the turn of the nineteenth century, now occupied by various departments of the humanities. Stopping briefly at the entrance to an alleyway, Rachel felt another stomach cramp and rushed into the privacy of the alley, letting the spasm have its way. Unable to stand, she fell to one knee, clutching at the damp stone of the building. Again, a hot torrent of liquid rushed out of her nose and mouth. A moment of suffocating panic gripped her, the thought that this would never stop, and she would die choking on her own vomit. But finally, the spasms stopped.

Taking a gasp of air, Rachel could only taste acid and spat thickly. Her heart raced; her breathing was heavy. When she tried to bring both under control, something scuttled behind her in the alleyway.

Peering out of the dark towards the faint orange glow from the street-lights Rachel listened. The union bar thumped bass into the night. Something quietly scuttled towards her through the shadows. Her heart quickened, and she strained to see what it was, thinking she should rise to her feet. But nothing emerged. A raucous laugh, somewhere in the distance, broke the illusion.

It was the alcohol, or something she ate, though Rachel had neither eaten nor drunk much that evening. She had been hoping that she and Gerald would get a kebab and head back to hers. Then maybe...

Three thin legs crept from the shadows. Startled, Rachel fell back, landing in the pool of her own vomit. Another leg and a form that reflected the sheen of night on its wet body.

Pushing backwards on hands and feet, Rachel slipped in the lumpy puddle beneath her. That seemed to provoke it. It began to run, its legs a spasmodic blur. Rachel caught herself, remembering to scream, taking a huge breath as the thing leapt.

The scream was stifled as the thing landed on her face. Rachel shook her head from side to side, trying to free herself from the cold, wet animal. It smelled of earth and decay. The more she tried to scream, the harder it gripped. Two of its legs pressed on her eyeballs, the others gripped her cheeks at either side of her jawbone. Rachel brought a hand to the thing to try and peel it off. It clenched harder. She felt her right eye pop first, like an enormous boil finally lanced. She screamed, even though her mouth was smothered with the taste of fetid skin. She fell to the concrete, pulling with two hands now, as her other eye popped out of its socket.

The thing moved downward, finding her screaming mouth. The legs, or perhaps they were fingers, gripped her tongue. It pulled itself deeper, forcing her jaw wide, until the jaw popped in dislocation, and the muffled screaming was replaced by the sounds of choking.

––––––

"DID YOU SEE A GIRL, lads? Brunette, about so big." Gerald indicated Rachel's height with his hand coming up to just below his chin. "She might be worse for wear." He'd checked the toilets first, including the ones up on the second floor, but couldn't find her anywhere. The two bouncers nodded at the pile of sick at the bottom of the stairs.

"Your girlfriend did that," one said and pointed Gerald off down the road.

Gerald jogged off and at first ran past the bottom of the alleyway. Maybe he heard something, maybe he saw something in the corner of his eye, or maybe it was the feeling he got. It was hard to pin down. The closest thing to it was a time when he was twelve and back home from boarding school for the summer. His little brother had been bugging him all week to play. He knew he just missed him and looked up to him. Coming home from boarding school was always a bit weird. It took a couple of weeks to settle back into things. They had gone boating, and little Charlie was showing off. Gerald wasn't really paying attention, and Charlie cut himself with a penknife trying to gut a fish in the hull of the boat. The knife had slashed lengthways up his wrist. There had been so much blood. In that moment he could have sworn Charlie was going to die. Of course, the little git was fine. They got back to shore, phoned Mum and Dad, tied the wrist off and kept the bleeding to a minimum until the ambulance came. It was a close call, but in that close call Gerald saw a whole different future, one with a dead little brother and angry parents and an end to everything that he really loved. That was the feeling that made him stop, the kind of feeling he'd hoped to never feel again.

Cautiously, Gerald jogged a few paces back to the opening of the alley. He could hear muffled noises, scuffling. He stepped into the dark, his mouth already dry from the old feeling of dread.

Rachel lay on her back, drowning in the muddy shadows settling around her like silt. Her legs kicked feebly. One hand was at her mouth, tugging ineffectually at something. Her other hand lolled, pulling at phantoms. Gerald stood for what felt like an age. Shock passed from his eyes to his brain. He was frozen, unable to make a decision. When finally he unfroze, his mind seemed to say several things at once. Run. Scream. Fight. Don't look. Forget. No.

Some other part of Gerald's body made the decision, the same part that rowed his brother to shore and thought to apply a tourniquet to his arm, while his own imagination ran wild in the background. He stepped forward, slipping on something wet, but managing to keep his footing. The sound he made disturbed whatever was attacking Rachel. He could see it, a dark lump over her mouth. It paused as if listening.

A prickle of cold revulsion tightened Gerald's skin. A rat. It must be a rat. A rat with five legs. A rat with no hair and skin that shone dully. It crawled out of Rachel's mouth. She went limp, head falling to the side, her dislocated jaw hanging slackly, something oozing from now empty eye sockets. Gerald did not want to see. He did not want to remember her like that.

The weight of his legs felt impossibly heavy, and his hands began to shake with fear but also rage.

The thing turned and walked stutteringly down Rachel's chest. Gerald lunged to grab it, but the thing jumped, meeting him halfway.

Gerald missed the thing, fingers closing on empty air. It hit him in the throat, wrapping around his windpipe. His hands wrestled with its cold and slippery body. There was no space to work his fingers underneath it. Pressure built in Gerald's head. His breaths were gargled, spit threading from his mouth. The desire to breathe became an all-consuming panic. Like the lens in a black and white movie as the credits were about to roll, the world around him narrowed to a pinprick. There was a sound of something crunching, and Gerald could only squeak. Like a rat. Then the pressure was relieved.

Gerald sank to his knees, one last effort to desperately pull air into his lungs, each breath causing pain, like razor blades down his throat. Why the thing had stopped Gerald didn't know, but he was thankful.

A noise. Someone coming down the alleyway! Gerald managed to turn his head to see the silhouette of a man. Only a strangled rasp came out when he tried to ask for help. He fell beside Rachel.

The figure walked towards him, in no hurry. Gerald tried again to ask for help. The shadowy figure appeared to look between the two bodies on the ground. Gerald held up a pleading hand. The figure held his fists clenched tight at his sides. A sense of relief blossomed in Gerald as the figure's face swam into clarity. There was hope.

Someone had come to help them. Rachel, God, Rachel, maybe she could be saved. The hope was a weak one, but it was hope. Kevin had found them.

The severed hand crouched, sensing. It waited for its meal to ripen. If it could, it would have purred.

"Help Rach..." A searing cough burnt his throat.

His fists clenching and unclenching, Kevin raised his foot. He was wearing a thick boot. There were urgent voices nearby, but they would not come in time. Kevin brought his foot down as hard as he could on Gerald's skull.

Under the cover of night, the hand returned to its owner, well fed and growing in strength.

13

READING by the light of the lamp, Mirin sat up in bed, going through the pictures they had taken that day of the bog body. She had a spreadsheet open on her laptop, planning out the order of the investigation. But the last few days had taken their toll, and exhaustion made her rub her eyes and close the laptop. She told herself this was normal. Going back to work and dealing with office politics was bound to feel like a chore, even without the added emotional rollercoaster of such a major career event as this find. But even so, Mirin still couldn't understand why she was so angry at David. Was it that deep down she was jealous of him, that she wanted the things he had? No, not any more. It was that the job, the archaeology, the science was a concrete thing to her. It was a careful process that dealt in facts and hedged interpretations based on evidence. It was something she could count on. It was something without emotion, and how she needed that. David would turn it into a circus with all his grandstanding. She knew it would be good for the department, for its profile, for research impact, for student numbers, for funding, and all the rest. But David's pronouncement about the significance of what they were dealing with still felt like a betrayal. This was the thought that slipped in and out of Mirin's mind as her eyes began to droop, papers still on her lap.

The bedroom door creaked open, the noise bringing Mirin out of the foothills of sleep. Oran put his head around the door and seeing that his mother was awake padded like a small elephant across the apartment's broad wooden floorboards. Mirin had already pulled back the bed sheets on what used to be Omar's side of the bed, and Oran jumped in.

"What's the matter, sweetheart? Bad dream again?"

Oran nodded and snuggled down, cuddling warmly, and Mirin rubbed his little back.

"Do you want to tell me about it?"

He had a look on his face that made him look older than his seven years. She thought the last year had made him grow up quickly.

"There was a hand."

"A hand?"

"It was running in the dark like a spider."

Mirin stroked his hair. "That sounds like a funny dream. Whose hand was it?"

"There was only a hand. I didn't like it. It ran after me, and I ran but it was going to get me, and..." He trailed off, squeezing his mother tightly, and Oran pointed with his finger to a few inches of his wrist.

Mirin felt a chill. "Did you see something on my computer today?"

The little boy shook his head again. "No, Mummy. Why?" The last word came out as a yawn and his eyes were already closing.

"It's nothing, my sweet. What was the hand doing?"

"Bad things."

"What kind of bad things?"

"I don't know. Just bad."

"It was only a dream. Everything is all right now."

Oran turned over, hunkering down under the covers.

"Sing to me, Mummy."

Mirin switched off the light and held her son. She put her arm on his shoulder and sang the song Omar used to sing. She had learnt the Arabic by heart, though knew few of the words.

"Sleep well; your sleep is flawless; the flowers of moonlight are a thousand colours; don't awaken from your fairy tale dreams; don't step into a world of despair; sleep well; Mother's eyes are wide awake; like every night there is a mother behind the walls; and there is no longer a string attached to your kite..." Mirin sang in a whisper, curled protectively around her son. Together, they floated away from reality.

IT WAS a beautiful day at the end of summer, and they only had a couple more days left holidaying in the Cairngorms. The rain had been falling heavily for the last few days, swelling the river, but Omar thought the level had begun to drop. Water moved fast, dark black over granite boulders. Mirin zipped up Oran's life jacket, while Omar sorted the paddles into the green fibreglass kayak.

"You don't think it's too rough?" Mirin zipped up the front of her own life jacket.

Omar looked out over the river. "Not this bit. We'll get off before the rapids downstream. It will be exciting, hey, buddy?" He ruffled his son's hair.

Mirin's heart always ached a little when she saw him smile at her son like that. He was such a good father. *Was*, she remembered. This was a dream. No, not again. No, I don't want to. But they were already getting in the boat, the force of the dream's story carrying her along, as it always did, as an unwilling participant.

They pushed off from the bank, the current catching the boat and nearly leaving Omar behind. Oran laughed with his father. They paddled, riding the currents as they had many times before. It was a passion Mirin and Omar had shared since university, exploring the wilds of Scotland. They wanted to share it with their son. He sat holding on in the middle of the boat, laughing and screaming with delight when the boat would land heavily after hitting a wave, or gyre in an eddy before straightening out.

Like a madwoman, Mirin laughed, paddling through her dream with knowing terror. They approached a bend in the river, one they had navigated many times before when it was just the two of them. A large boulder caused a trough in the flow, which would momentarily suck the boat down and then spit them out the other side. Paddling hard, they kept the boat straight and level. They hit the trough. The boat lurched back. Smiles marked their faces, their eyes thrilled as they flirted with danger. Mirin felt the burn in her shoulders as she dug the paddle into the water, Omar doing the same at the front of the boat. Then her paddle stuck between two rocks; the rough vibrations travelled up the shaft to her hands. She tugged to free it but as she did an eddy grabbed the boat, shaking it in a short, violent jerk. The paddle sprang from her grip. She made a desperate grab for it, her fingertips reaching its surface and finding no purchase. It fell into the water and was sucked from view. Mirin must have called out because Omar and Oran looked over their shoulders. Their smiles washed away as quickly as Mirin's paddle when they saw her face. Omar turned back to the front of the boat, furiously paddling the churning water. The boat seemed to edge up the trough through Omar's brute force. He slowed only for a moment and the kayak was sucked back, water washing over Mirin and soaking Oran, who for the first time screamed, not in delight but fear. The kind of scream that made Mirin want to rush to him, to gather him up and never let him go, no matter what. The trough sucked the stern of the boat under. Water flooded the hull. A wave crashed into the side. Oran screamed again, a soul-piercing squeal. The boat flipped.

Mirin woke with a start, as if coming up for air. The dream washed away. The black smother of churning water was replaced with the dark loneliness of night. Mirin wiped the tears from her eyes. She turned to hold her son. Oran murmured in his sleep and she kissed the black curls of his hair. Breathing him in filled her with relief that he was here like a lifebuoy she would never let go of.

14

PUSHING down the plunger of the coffee press, Dip watched the dark granules churn in the thick, glossy liquid. He already had heartburn and another cup was not what his body needed, but he still couldn't face sleep. The past few days he had only slept in fitful bursts when he could no longer keep his eyes open. Each time he would pull himself out of the dream to protect against what might be lurking there. Wakefulness wasn't a much better state of existence. It was simply the one he felt in more control of.

After adding three sugars to the coffee mug, Dip turned on the television with the hope it would take his mind off things. Jackie Chan jumped up on his lap, spilling hot coffee over Dip's thighs. He held the cup away with a familiar resignation, while the little dog performed his ritual: walking in two little circles before thunking his pot belly down with a harrumph.

Despite the bright morning, every light in the cottage was on, and Dip kept his heavy black patrol torch by his side. It wasn't merely for the purposes of illumination. Its weight was reassuring, weapon-like, although he knew it would likely be ineffectual against the spectre of which he was afraid. Being in this house was the last thing he wanted but it had been forced upon him now that he was the laughingstock of his station. His commanding officer had ordered him to take sick leave.

The broken arm was one thing, but on top of that his colleagues thought he was a raving madman. Compassionate leave, his commanding officer had labelled it. He'd talked about trauma for a while before making Dip an appointment with the clinical psychologist attached to the force. Dip accepted it all. He couldn't figure out what else to do. No one would believe him. Heck, a few days ago he wouldn't have believed it either. Now he was stuck in his cottage knowing something was coming. He felt it. He'd seen it and had not gone near the shower since, instead washing carefully in the sink, afraid of the water. His stubble was growing into a beard as dark as the bags under his eyes.

The morning news was on the television. As a boy brought up in the West End of Glasgow, Dip recognised the location in the news report. His family owned a restaurant near the university. He used to do everything from cleaning dishes to waiting tables and acting as sous chef to his mother. Students and faculty were regular patrons and so he knew the area intimately. Jackie Chan grumbled as Dip disturbed him to find the remote. It was lodged somewhere down the side of the seat. He found it and turned up the volume to see why his home turf was on the news.

"...truly shocked and saddened that something of this nature could have happened at this great university," commented the university's vice chancellor to the reporter, his name and position appearing in a graphic at the bottom of the screen. "We're providing whatever support we can to the family of the victims and helping the police in whatever way we can."

The reporter turned back to the camera. Over his shoulder, Dip knew the location on the curving road of old townhouses on University Gardens, which jarred with the 1970s concrete modernist architecture of the Queen Margaret Union. Police forensic officers busied themselves around the scene in white coveralls.

"This is John Shepherd reporting from Glasgow University, where last night two young people were brutally murdered by a fellow student. Staff and students are struggling to come to terms with this shocking event. The motivation for the attack is as yet unknown. The suspect remains in police custody for questioning."

The half-full coffee cup slipped from Dip's hand, smashing on the tiles. The location in the news report was a short walk across the road from the archaeology department where he knew they had taken the body from the bog. An acid sting of bile caught in Dip's throat, along with a sense of panic. Pulling the phone from his pocket, he searched and found what he needed in a few keystrokes.

He dialled the number. The university switchboard put him through to the right department. A secretary answered and he asked to speak to Professor David Hamill. The secretary asked who Dip was, ready to palm him off with some excuse that the celebrity professor was too busy. However, being a police officer had its uses and on hearing his credentials, she changed her tone.

"I'm afraid the professor isn't available at the moment. However, I could put you through to Professor Hassan, who is also working on the body."

That would have to do. She transferred Dip. The phone rang a few times before a woman picked up.

"Hello, Constable Bhaskar? How can I help you?" Mirin's voice sounded cautious, with a note of surprise, indicating to Dip that she remembered who he was. *That could be a good thing or a bad thing*, he thought.

"It's about the murders last night on campus. It was on the morning news," Dip began, trying to disguise the urgency in his voice.

"It's terrible. We are all quite shocked that fellow students could do that to each other. But I don't see what that has to do with..."

"No, you don't understand. Have you noticed anything about the boy from the bog? Anything unusual?"

"I'm sorry, Constable." Mirin's voice was kind, and Dip gritted his teeth in frustration. "You're right, I don't understand. Are you phoning as part of the investigation? I was under the impression they caught the perpetrator."

Dip knew he sounded ridiculous. But what else could he do? If he did nothing, more people were going to die. He knew that with terrible certainty. But he also knew that he couldn't prove it, not yet.

"Yes, no," he stuttered. He thought fast. "I'm sorry. I know I must have seemed a bit, well, crazy the other day at the site. I was in shock. I think I'm still a little confused. I saw the murders on the news, and it reminded me of the boy. And I wondered if you had any news about him. I'm on leave at the moment. It is purely a personal interest."

There was a brief silence at the other end of the phone.

"I see," Mirin said. "It's really too early to tell. All I can say is that he is presenting us with a mystery to solve."

"A mystery. Really? How so?" Dip tried to not sound desperate.

"I'm sorry, Constable. I really can't say any more at this stage."

Dip knew he wasn't going to get anywhere else without causing more trouble for himself, so he ended the call.

The young man in custody for the murders wasn't fully responsible for what he did. Dip knew that. Just as what happened between the builders and protesters at the peat bog was something far more dangerous than a good-natured protest turned ugly. Dip had seen it and felt it, the power of the boy. The feelings of impotence and desperation welled up in him.

With the TV talking to itself, Dip looked around the cottage, thinking. Jackie Chan wriggled in protest when Dip plucked him from his damp, coffee-stained lap and placed him on the floor. Jackie gave a yap in protest while Dip hurried around the cottage gathering what he needed, stuffing some clothes in an overnight bag and then snatching up car keys. Jackie Chan stood sentinel in the front room, his head tipped to one side as his master opened the door.

Someone had to do something before it was too late. Maybe it already was, or maybe he really was crazy. But Dip didn't believe that.

"Come on, boy," Dip called. Jackie Chan gave a small woof and ran out the door past his master.

15

Jackie Chan barked at the rain from the front seat of Dip's car. It was lashing down heavily, drowning out the noise of the struggling engine of the small car. The windscreen wipers rushed back and forth, ineffective against the torrent, giving Dip brief glimpses of the motorway on his approach to Glasgow. Spray kicked up from the vehicle in front as their brake lights came to life. Hitting his own brakes, the car aquaplaned for a moment, threatening to lose control before its wheels gripped again and the car slid to a halt. The windscreen wipers rushed frantically to and fro. Something up ahead had brought traffic to a standstill.

Mirin and Portia washed the boy's skin with the specially prepared deionized water. A camera, provided by Lucy Walker, was set up on a tripod, recording their work. Mirin took photographs as they exposed another piece of skin, unveiling more of the symbols Portia had found on the boy's hand.

It was quiet work, with the two of them knowing their jobs and having no need to talk. They each savoured the thrill of discovery in their own silent reverie. Chin was running some tests on a skin sample they had harvested for dating and compositional analysis. However, the results wouldn't be available for a few days at least.

Now washed clean, the intricate pattern of black marks on the boy's body and arms had become clear. Mirin intended to share the photographs with a friend in the Linguistics Department who was a specialist in comparative philology. News of the boy had already spread widely around the university, and any department with a potential interest had offered help.

Mirin checked her watch and began pulling off her latex gloves when David walked into the lab.

"Any update?" he said, straightening a silk tie.

"You look smart," Mirin said.

"I'm doing that interview tonight with Lucy on the early evening show. Whetting the public appetite about our wee man here." David said the 'wee' with emphasis, as though making sure he had the pronunciation right.

Mirin noticed Portia tense at the mention of Lucy's name. She looked even worse than she had done the day of the excavation: paler, thinner even, and she hadn't had much in the way of fat to lose as it was. She looked tired and sick. If she looked like that tomorrow, Mirin thought she would send her home.

David, in his tailored suit and a paisley-patterned silk tie, which was something of his trademark, sidled up to the lab table. "Those markings, they're not typical of a bog body, are they?"

"No. It's unusual if it's an Iron Age body. Bodies have been found with leather bracelets, small items of metal jewellery, and even intricate hairstyles, but never with tattoos as elaborate as these," explained Mirin.

"Fascinating!" David said, finger on his lips, mulling the implications over. "They look like a written text."

Mirin took off her lab coat. "We think they might be, but..." Mirin hated to speculate like this, and realised the camera was still recording in the room.

"But what?" said David.

"I'm going to check them with a colleague, Jenny Mordaunt, but Portia did some initial checks."

David turned to Portia expectantly. Still hunched over the boy's body, carefully removing peat from around his legs, Portia didn't look up. "It doesn't appear to correspond to any known script. Some of the signs look similar to Jiahu symbols. Others are like the markings on the Dispilio tablet, and some resemble the Vinča symbols."

"But that would mean..." A smile quirked at one side of David's mouth as he realised the potential implications, and that he would be the one to deliver it on national television. Portia and Mirin exchanged looks. Rain hammered on the windows of the lab.

"Like we said, we don't know anything at the moment," Mirin cautioned.

"If this were true," David seemed to say as much to himself as to his colleagues, "that would make the boy not from the Iron Age but from the Neolithic. He'd be the oldest bog body ever discovered, in a remarkable state of preservation, and with the earliest and most complete indications of writing tattooed on his body. He would rewrite prehistory. This could be even more significant than we first thought." The possibilities glittered in his eyes.

"David," Mirin said firmly, snapping him back from the fantasy he was inhabiting. "We need to be cautious. These are early days. This could be a hoax for all we know. The very fact that he appears to have writing on his body from the earliest known writing systems, from the Middle East and China, means this body has no business being here. Things don't add up."

"I know, I know. But you're being too pessimistic. If it's true, this rewrites history."

"David, please, this is serious. Don't go on tonight and make claims which we might regret later. We don't yet know what we are dealing with."

David considered Mirin for a moment, straightening his back and tie simultaneously, an affectation Mirin thought he might have cultivated over the last twelve months in his TV career.

"As head of department, I think I will exercise my judgement as to what will be to our benefit and the university's."

"Fine." Mirin pulled on a coat and satchel. "I don't have time for this now." The rain pummelled the windows.

"Where are you going?" asked David.

"I need to get home," Mirin said, heading for the door.

"But what about the body? You're not done here."

"Portia's perfectly capable of handling the rest."

"Who goes home early from *this*?"

"I do." She fixed her collar and buttoned up the front of her raincoat. "Now, if you don't mind, I need to get home to my boy, the one at home, not this one on the table."

Portia and David exchanged glances. David was about to say something when Portia began to cough, hacking deeply. He made towards her, but she held up a hand.

"I'm fine. You go. Enjoy your television programme with Lucy." Another coughing fit ended their discussion.

David opened his mouth, but in that moment he surprised himself: he didn't know what he wanted to say. Instead, he turned and left Portia alone in the lab with only the boy's body for company.

16

THE HEAVY PLASTER on his arm made changing gear uncomfortable. Dip shifted awkwardly into second and drove around the accident, which was clogging the middle lane of the motorway. He tried not to rubberneck, but there was a confrontation: a uniformed officer between two men who were both soaked to the skin and looked ready to kill each other. The policeman in Dip thought about pulling over to help, but the urge to push on was greater. It came from that same place, the part inside a fireman that runs into the building *towards* danger. They were all lifeboats sailing into the storm against the pounding rain. What he knew was coming made a roadside brawl look like nothing more than grey clouds on the horizon.

Streetlights fought against the dark, shrouding the city. Their lights blurred in the torrent of rain, whipped through the air by the growing wind. Dip's small Ford Fiesta was buffeted as he pulled off the motorway into Glasgow city centre, the wind howling through the funnel of the motorway. Cars beeped at one another, as if there was a frantic need to get out of the city. They rushed through orange lights at the maze that was the intersection at George's Cross, causing further backups and more angry blaring of horns.

Dip hunched over the wheel, sailing into a stormtide that pushed back so hard it was a physical effort to hold the car in place.

Two bowls of pasta steamed in front of Mirin and Oran on the kitchen table. The small TV set on the kitchen counter showed a weatherman explaining that it was raining, as the wind creaked the windows in their frames and rain thrummed the panes. No shit. The storm had been unexpected, catching them off guard and weirdly localised to the Glasgow area. The red-headed weatherman zoomed in on the animation of a circular storm squatting over the city.

Mirin ruffled Oran's wet hair and took her seat. They'd both got soaked on the walk home. She had put him in a hot bath as soon as they got in, and then they both changed into their pyjamas. Mirin blew on her pasta and Oran did the same, aping his mother. She saw mischief in his eyes and stuck out her tongue. Oran mimicked her before taking over the game. Shovelling in a fork full of pasta, he chewed a few times and then opened his mouth. Mirin feigned disgust and then copied, showing the half-chewed gunge in her mouth. They both snorted, straining not to spit out food with full-blown laughs.

"Look, Mummy. It's Uncle David." Oran pointed at the television, pasta falling off the end of his fork.

David looked immaculately dressed, sitting confidently opposite Lucy Walker. Legs crossed at the knee, he leant on one elbow resting on the edge of the sofa, barely able to control the smile touching the corners of his mouth.

Portia carefully placed the boy's severed hand near the arm it was cut from. The arm was positioned on the underside of the boy's body as he lay foetal on his side.

Portia took photos from several different angles, checking the images on a small LCD screen. She turned off the video camera, as it had been filming for several hours now, and took out its memory card. Armed with the video card and the still photographs, she went to the other side of the lab to download the material onto the university's server.

The angry cough sputtered through her ribcage again. Portia hacked into her forearm until it passed, and then removed her latex gloves to work with the computer. Peeling the second glove from her fingers, Portia was hit by a powerful wave of nausea, barely managing to grab the bin under the lab bench in time. She threw up into it, and a thought that she might be late for her period crossed her mind.

Things began to whirl in Portia's head: David, that bitch Lucy, her PhD. It'd all been going so well. She'd carefully built this future, like an intricate glass house. Now, it seemed like it could shatter at any moment.

If she was pregnant, could she keep studying? Could she change direction and stay involved with this new, potentially career-making project? She should be elated about being involved. She could write a PhD that would far outstrip any of her colleagues because of her unique access to the boy and the story: it could be a gateway to an academic career at a time when jobs were nearly impossible to get. But a baby could fuck all of that up.

A part of her was happy about the possibility of a life growing inside her. She had always thought she would have children at some point. But she was also eighteen months into her studies and had the same amount of time left with funding. Topping it all off she felt awful, which was probably clouding her judgement. Another tide of nausea rose from her belly.

A rumble of thunder sounded in the distance, briefly cutting across the tick, tick, tick of the rain counting down at the basement windows. The lights overhead flickered, and on the lab table behind Portia the middle finger of the severed hand began to twitch.

DIP FINALLY MANAGED to pull onto the bottom of Woodlands Road, joining the edge of the city centre to the West End of the city where the university was located. The wind had grown even angrier, battering the car as it drove past the bric-a-brac parade of organic food shops, coffee bars, pubs, and antiques shops, all topped with tenements populated by students or the affluent residents of the West End. At the top of Woodlands Road, Dip should have turned right at the small roundabout to head to his parents' restaurant. It would have been the start of the evening dinner service. He should have dropped off Jackie Chan and helped his mum out in the kitchen, maybe grabbed something to eat himself.

Instead, Dip turned the car left and up into the heart of the university campus. A couple, probably students, though it was difficult to see because they were so wrapped up, were thrown against the side of a building. He'd have thought they were drunk were it not for the atrocious weather. The car was about to reach the traffic lights at the top of the road when a piece of masonry fell from a church at the side of the road. The stone plummeted towards the road and smashed three feet from the bonnet of his car. Dip hit the brakes, skidding to a halt.

———————

PORTIA DRAGGED the files across the screen until they reached the icon of a cloud, where she dropped them. The video and digital pictures disappeared into the ether.

Portia's nose was running, and her head pounded in heavy, pressuring throbs. She was going to go home, just as soon as she repacked the boy in the peat that had held him in suspended animation for aeons. She wished she could just leave it and go home to lie down. Maybe everything would feel better tomorrow. Maybe she needed a few days off to get over whatever this was. *Yeah,* part of her mind said mirthfully. *Lie down for the next nine months, and then kiss goodbye to the next eighteen years of your life.*

The storm had been affecting the electricity in the lab for the last hour. She was glad to get the files stored safely in case the power went out.

As if her thoughts had triggered it, the lights snapped off. Behind her, in the cover of darkness, the hand moved.

MIRIN HAD to turn down David on the television once he began to talk about the discovery of "an as yet unidentified script of writing, which could date back to the very invention of the written word." She and Oran had finished eating anyway, and Oran wanted to show her something he'd drawn at school today. He'd hurried off to his school bag and returned with a sheet of paper and presented it to her proudly at the table.

"Wow, this is great," Mirin said. It was what she said of his pictures, and she loved them because they were his. "Shall we put it on the fridge?"

"No, look, Mummy. It's a picture of you."

She looked at the image again. Oran clearly wanted her to take this seriously. The figure of a woman, with hair a caricature of her own, up in a ponytail, stood on a bridge with a boy. "Is that you and me on the Squinty Bridge?" It was the name given to the bridge by the people of the city rather than the grander 'Clyde Arc' which was its official name. The bridge was unmistakable, with its sail-like steel support arcing over the Clyde like a rainbow drained of all colour, joining the north of the city to the south at Ibrox near to Rangers football ground and the headquarters of the BBC.

"That's not me," said Oran, his brow furrowed, as if that should be obvious. "It's the boy."

"What boy?"

"The boy you found in the bog, Mummy."

At first, Mirin marvelled at his imagination. Then she thought about how this could be connected to the past year, and Oran's very real encounter with death. Maybe it was a way for him to normalise what happened to him, making death a part of the everyday? Children were much more adaptable than adults in that way. She smiled again, making a pantomime of really looking at the picture. "Well, I think it's brilliant," she said, pulling him in to kiss the top of his head.

PORTIA TUTTED at the failing electricity and looked for her phone in her bag. Bending down under the workbench, she began to feel for it in the dark, her eyes not yet accustomed to the light. Crashing waves of blood pulsed in her ears. Then through the tumult of her cranial tempest she could have sworn something dropped onto the lab floor, something as muted as a boat slipping its mooring.

"Got you." Portia pushed the button at the side of the phone, illuminating the screen. There was a torch app somewhere on the device, but Portia could never remember where.

The sound of bare feet slapping swiftly across the lab.

Portia froze, every muscle in her back and arms tightening. She became acutely aware that she stood in the dark, alone, or seemingly alone. Her hands began to shake. She listened. There was only the storm.

Breathe, she thought. *Think this through.* It was unlikely someone was here, but if they were, it was probable they would struggle to see in the dark just as much as her. All she needed to do was slip out of the room unnoticed.

Moving toward the door, as silently as her now seemingly poor choice of footwear would allow, she used one hand to steady herself against the wall. Her eyes were beginning to adjust to the gloom, forming nonsense shapes in the blackness. No. Not nonsense. Something was *moving.*

It could be Chin, a desperately hopeful part of herself thought. She knew it wasn't. He'd left an hour ago and was not the practical-joking type. It could be a cleaner, but that did not explain the protracted silence, the furtive movements, and the sheer unease she felt building in her chest. Although, funny thing, her headache had gone, replaced with a laser-clarity that was almost uncomfortable.

A voice came from the dark, spoken in a wet whisper:

"Bizi izan hil. Uswe txar den."

DIP CRUNCHED THROUGH THE GEARS, barely able to see the road in the torrent of rain. The small car's engine revved and its wheels spun in the surface water running down the hill. He sped up the steep incline, the old car whining in complaint, past the gothic edifice of the university's main building at the heart of the campus. The Gregory Building was less than a minute away. He leant forward over the wheel, wiping away the mist forming on the windscreen. Dip heard the crack so loud he flinched, as though it was a rent of thunder immediately over his car.

The car veered in the wind again and Dip fought to keep them on the slippery road. Jackie Chan whimpered from the passenger seat. And then Dip slammed on the brakes to the sight of a huge horse chestnut tree falling in front of him in slow motion. The roots tore from the ground, like the rigging ripping from a falling mainsail. Dip's forearms strained, arms locked, bracing. The canopy descended on the road. Dip heard the banshee screeching of his own brakes as he skidded toward the branches of the fallen tree, losing all control of the car.

PORTIA LUNGED FOR THE DOOR.

The slaps of bare feet moved quickly in the shadows. She still couldn't see what was there.

Throwing caution to the wind, Portia threw her phone forward, the bright screen casting light into the shadow. Panting heavily, hands still shaking, she edged in the direction of the door. The phone began ringing unanswered. A tray of instruments clattered to the floor when she backed blindly into them. Tripping on something under foot, she twisted her ankle, stumbled, but kept herself upright and the light held aloft, searching the dark in skittish, quivering sweeps.

The rain thrummed impatiently, the metallic ionisation of the storm palpable, like the copper-sweet taste of blood, hanging in the air.

The voice came again from the blackness. "Guzti hil pentsatu-bait. Zorrotz ni."

Frantically, Portia turned the phone towards where the voice had come from. The light fell on the examination table in the middle of the lab, giving her some bearings, but all elation was quickly quelled: there was nothing there.

There was only a heap of earth on the examination table. At its centre, an empty hollow was left in the peat where the body of the boy should have been lying on his side.

He emerged from the darkness. And with him came a terror looming behind him in a tidal wave of blood. That great crimson tide followed in his wake, pulled through time with him. It churned and chewed through everything before it, everything but the boy. The wave of fear hit Portia and in the whites of her glaring eyes, every slight festered, every injustice magnified, and every trauma was relived. Faced with it all, Portia was left with the only two options the hunted have.

It was then Portia thought of the flint knife lying behind her on the workbench. The black blade was wrapped in its plastic evidence bag, but it was still as sharp as the day it was made. Why the idea came to her then she would never know. There was no time to question her thoughts. Only to act. The wave of fear was dragging her under, subsuming consciousness. The knife was her only chance. She knew it more certainly than she had ever known anything.

Portia made for the blade. Just a few feet away. But the boy was already there. With lizard-like speed, his hand caught Portia's wrist. His grip was as cold and damp as the grave and the feeling of wrongness crystallised her fear, hardening in her veins, so that movement was impossible.

Portia did not want to, but she could not help it: she looked into his eyes, eyes which should not have been open, staring out from the face of the boy that should not be alive. They were dank pools, infinitely deep and infinitely dark.

There, in the blackness of his gaze, there was an event horizon over which the crimson wave crested. As she reached it, a scream left her throat that was swallowed by the storm.

PART II

"Man produces evil as a bee produces honey."

William Golding

"Insanity in individuals is something rare – but in groups, parties, nations and epochs, it is the rule."

Friedrich Nietzsche

1

EDDIE BURNS seriously considered not going into work that morning, but he needed the money. Last night's storm was an absolute stinker. It kept him up half the night. It was all over the news in the morning. *Jesus*, he thought. *This is Glasgow. When is it not pishing with rain?* But he dragged himself out of bed because he knew he was on shift with Annie Brown. He didn't even try to contain his erection in the shower. And he made sure to put on extra aftershave.

As it turned out, the storm was a whole lot of fuss about nothing. The underground from Ibrox was running as normal. The streets were a little quieter, and there was still some debris from fallen trees clogging paths and roads. But the clean-up crews were already out clearing up, probably getting time and a half, the lucky *bawbags*.

There was an eeriness to the quiet on Eddie's early morning trek to the station. He ticked off the stations in his head, rattling through them, encased in the brown and orange carriage of a Glasgow underground train. The familiar earthiness of the underground pervaded. He got off at Hillhead station, and let the escalator carry him to the surface.

It was his lucky day. Annie Brown was walking up to the Gregory Building right when he appeared up the steep steps from the back of the building, which led up from Ashton Lane, where all those stuck-up, lazy students spend their loan money on beer in poncey bars lining the cobbled lane. Annie had her hair tied back in a high pony-tail and was wearing black-rimmed glasses with her cleaner's uniform. But Jesus, he could see her tits from a hundred yards. Eddie would have laid money on them being fake. She was probably in her late forties, barely over five feet tall, but Annie's rack seemed to defy gravity. She gave him the lukewarmest of smiles when they met at the front door, fumbled in a bag for the keys, and unlocked the door.

"Didn't know we were on together today, Annie."

"I can't catch a break, Eddie," she said, taking off her heavy coat.

"Aw, don't be like that, hen." Eddie tried not to stare at her tits. *Oh Jesus,* he thought. *I can see her nipples.* "I can tell you're pleased to see me."

"Shut it, you *wee* prick." Annie caught his gaze and hurried off purposefully to the store cupboard where they could stow their things and collect the necessary tools to begin cleaning the building.

The store cupboard was cramped. Annie hung up her coat. Eddie made sure he was right beside her doing the same thing, his arm brushing against hers. Loading up her trolley with all the equipment she needed, Annie bent down to shove rags and a window spray in the lower compartment when Eddie brushed against her backside, his hand clearly lingering at the cleft between her buttocks. Clenching defensively, she stood bolt upright.

"Get away from me, you *bawbag*."

Eddie put his hands up defensively, his face a picture of innocence. "What, hen?"

"You know what, ya *wee* prick."

"Fuck's sake, Annie. Are you on your rag or something?" Eddie grinned, the gap beside his two front teeth making a grin like a tuneless piano.

She tutted and roughly grabbed the trolley, pushing it past him, deliberately running over the toes of his boots.

"Good job I've got steel toecaps on," Eddie called after her. Annie said nothing, but flicked the finger over her shoulder without looking back. Eddie watched her push the trolley down the corridor, savouring the look of her behind. She might be a good ten years older than him, but God, he would love to have a go on that. *She just likes to play hard to get*, he told himself.

Eddie took his time loading his own trolley. They had all day together. He'd have plenty more opportunities to get close to her. And it wouldn't be that long until Christmas. There would be the work night out, a few drinks, a little something extra to go in her drink. Annie Brown would find Eddie Burns irresistible then. This plan had Eddie even harder than this morning's shower when he heard Annie scream.

It wasn't a short scream of fright, as though Annie had seen a rat. It was a long, protracted scream, piercing and high-pitched, like in one of those slasher movies where the blonde gets a knife in the gut and blood overflows from her gaping mouth. Eddie liked those movies. But Annie's scream was real and startled Eddie from his daydream. He dropped the bottle of bleach he was holding and sprinted into the corridor, bouncing off the wall.

Annie's first scream had transformed into a continuous ululation of terror. Eddie's boots squeaked on the polished floor like the pulses of a heart rate monitor before cardiac arrest. The screams were coming from the labs. Reaching the doors, Eddie pushed down on the handle and yanked them open. Thoughts of a burglary or maybe an assault in progress filled his mind. He burst into the lab to find Annie, arms rigid by her side, fingers splayed, eyes wide (and still screaming), looking at something on the other side of the room. Eddie could not see what it was at first. The door and lab benches obscured his line of sight. Annie was still screaming, which was surreal. The screams didn't stop. He'd never heard of someone doing that.

"Annie!"

Her eyes were peeled wide and he could see the back of her throat. But he'd broken some spell. Annie was no longer looking at what was causing her terror, and so her screams began to calm, chest rising and falling. Arms still rigid. Fingers still stiff and splayed.

Eddie held up his hands to show everything was okay, that he wasn't a threat. Annie slowly focused in on Eddie. As much as she didn't like Eddie, she knew who he was.

As Annie calmed, Eddie let his eyes wander. At first, the lab didn't look as though it had been disturbed, but as his gaze reached the other side of the room, he could see signs of a struggle. Instruments on the floor. Something glass had smashed on the institutionally-bland, age-worn tiles. Some of the lower brushed-steel storage cupboards were dented. Then Eddie saw the blood. There was so much of it. Thick, sticky pools of dark red. Smears of it on the cupboards and surfaces. There was also a body. It lay slumped against a set of cupboards, like a passed-out drunk. Long red hair fell over its face. Skeletal-thin arms hung loosely by its sides, palms up, deep slashes criss-crossing the wrists and upper arms. Next to her lay an odd-looking knife, with a black blade, reflecting the light like chipped glass. Eddie liked knives and collected them, but he'd never seen one like this. It looked old, like some kind of caveman's knife.

The sight of all that blood and violence didn't scare Eddie. Far from it.

"Call the police," he told Annie, stepping forward gingerly. Normally, Eddie wouldn't want anything to do with the pigs, but they had their uses, and this was definitely one of them. Annie stood frozen, unresponsive.

"Annie!" he shouted, causing her to jump. "C'mon, hen. The police. Phone the police."

Annie nodded slowly, her hand trembling into the front of her cleaner's smock where she kept her phone.

Eddie was careful not to step in the blood. There was a long trail of it smeared across the floor, as if the girl had tried to escape and then fell in a heap, unable to fight any more. The blood pooled around her hips. The room hummed, vibrating with an excited energy. The aftermath of the violent assault in front of Eddie was disgusting, but still he grew in his trousers. The feet of the girl lay splayed, and Eddie crouched down between them, peering closely at her.

Somebody fucked you up good and proper, hen, he thought. This close, he could see the white-yellow subcutaneous fat showing through many of the slashes in the girl's arms. Eddie thought he knew who she was, although he didn't know her name. She was some posh English bird. He'd noticed her during the course of his work, but she hadn't ever really noticed him in return. No one ever did.

Eddie liked redheads. Annie was auburn, which to Eddie was more than ginger enough. This one was flame-red, younger than Annie. In her twenties, although it looked to Eddie as though she had let herself go before she got fucked up. She had a starved look. He reached out his hand to check it was actually the posh tart. His fingers touched her flame-red hair, which was the only thing about her that still looked full of life. The rest of her skin looked as drained white as marble. The hair was soft to the touch. Slowly, Eddie's fingers found their way to her head. She still felt warm. The possibility that whoever did this was still here occurred to Eddie, but then maybe she did it to herself?

Annie was on the phone talking too fast, stuttering through crying gasps, trying to explain.

Eddie tilted the red-headed girl's head back. The flames of her hair fell from her once-beautiful face. Her cheekbones were elegant, and she had a delicate nose, peppered with freckles. But the face was now cut and bruised. One of her eyes was closed completely like that of a boxer in the later rounds of a brutal match. He looked in wonder at the massacre. It didn't repulse him. In fact, his member was now straining against his trousers. He felt a sense of power and exhilaration.

Right up until the girl opened her eyes.

The green irises grew as her pupils shrank to pinpricks. She took a huge gasp of air and began to shriek. Eddie fell backwards, bumping into the examination bench in the middle of the lab. Annie dropped her mobile phone. It clattered to the floor. She stumbled against the bench, putting a hand down for balance. It plunged into black peat. The cold sensation turned Annie's stomach. Her eyes fixed on the body of the young boy lying on his side, as if asleep, his severed hand resting not far from the arm it once belonged to.

Annie fell to her knees and shook uncontrollably.

2

"Forensics already there?"

DCI Connie Shepherd looked to the Gregory Building, a short way from her crime scene on University Gardens, sitting on the corner of Lilybank Gardens about fifteen feet below and two hundred yards away. She took off her jacket. Considering it was autumn and there had been a storm last night, it was unseasonably clammy.

DI Stuart Blair pulled his head out of his notebook. "Aye, they just arrived."

"That's the archaeology building, isn't it?"

"Buggered if I know, boss. Why? What you thinking? Little inter-departmental liaison?"

Connie had worked long enough to know the universe will randomly throw things together in something that looks like a pattern but is in fact just that: random. But either by nature or train-ing, coppers are a suspicious lot, and coincidences bug the hell out of them, because true coincidences were as rare as happy endings in Connie's experience.

"Aye, let's see if we can lend a hand," she said, stooping under the police tape cordoning off the bottom of the alley they had been working as a crime scene.

There was quite a crowd gathering around the corner of Lilybank

Gardens. It was blocking traffic and as soon as the two uniformed officers cleared the road another couple of people would join the gathering. Like a gelatinous organism, the crowd would ooze back onto the pavement, jockeying for position.

Connie and Stuart jostled their way to the front. It was strange. Usually when the police tell people to bugger off, all but the hardened journalists and weirdos obey. Not this crowd. They weren't rude but neither were they really listening. Connie and Stuart flashed their warrant cards and the two uniformed officers on the front doors allowed them in. It was even hotter inside the Gregory Building, the kind of stifling heat common to institutional buildings which set the temperature at some centralised location, either on full blast or completely off and is entirely insensitive to the actual environmental conditions.

"Boss, aren't those the archaeologists from the site up in Stirlingshire?"

"Aye, they are."

Professor Mirin Hassan was stood calmly answering questions from a detective in a grey suit, while Professor David Hamill looked agitated. His usual polished, smooth demeanour had gone, along with that trademark smile. Connie had seen him on television last night waxing lyrical about startling new findings regarding the body they'd found in the bog.

This was delicate territory. This wasn't a homicide, otherwise she would have known about it and known every detective working the case. But she didn't know what it was, and coppers from other departments don't like colleagues blundering onto their patch uninvited, no matter how much inter-department, inter-agency cooperation was pushed. She didn't know the detective questioning the archaeologists. He clocked them walking up out of the corner of his eye. Connie knew that look. The face gave nothing away. The eyes registered them, made a mental note, and then went back to the task at hand.

"Sorry again. When did either of you last see her?" the detective asked.

"Five o'clock, I suppose. I had to get home. David had a TV show to get to," Mirin explained matter-of-factly.

"Professor Hamill?"

"What? Look, is she alright?" Professor Hamill looked over the officer's shoulder into the lab.

Mirin answered for him. "David left here at five and was on a live television show at the BBC shortly after. I'm sure you can check that."

"And you, Professor Hassan, were at home by yourself?"

"No. I was with my son."

The interviewing detective scribbled something on his pad before lifting his head along with his eyebrows to the two unknown detectives in his presence.

Connie took her cue, offering a hand. "DCI Connie Shepard. This is DI Stuart Blair. We were finishing off working the homicide scene across the road. Just wanted to make a friendly enquiry, in case there was any potential crossover."

"DI Tony Jackson, ma'am," the other officer said, returning the handshake. "We have an assault of a Portia Harrington-Wright, twenty-three years of age. A PhD student working late last night. Seems she was attacked with a weapon in the lab downstairs at sometime between 6:00 pm, when the security guards last checked, and 6:00 am this morning when two cleaners found her. She's been transported to the Royal Infirmary. She's in intensive care. Sound like there's a connection?"

Connie fished a business card out of a pocket and handed it over to DI Jackson with a noncommittal shrug. "We met the victim a few days ago at another murder scene, and now I'm working a second murder scene across the road from where the victim works."

DI Jackson took the card, gave it a quick inspection, and pocketed it. "That would have been the multiple murder case up in Stirlingshire?"

Connie nodded.

"So, you've met the professors before as well?" DI Jackson enquired, indicating Mirin and David.

"Aye," confirmed DI Blair.

"Quite the coincidence," commented DI Jackson.

"What's that supposed to mean?" blustered David, running a

hand through his hair and scratching the back of his head repeatedly. "You can't think we had anything to do with this?"

"That's not what anyone is saying, Professor Hamill."

Not bad, DI Jackson, thought Connie. He was calm and unassuming, around five feet eight, with black hair that had begun to prematurely thin on top.

"Like you academics," Jackson went on, "coppers notice patterns and we tend to get a wee bit interested in them. That's all they are until we have evidence to say otherwise. Sometimes a coincidence is just a coincidence." He smiled, putting David at ease. Connie noticed Professor Hassan seemed to be taking it all in, detached, like a good copper herself. Maybe she didn't believe in coincidences either. But *why* was what interested Connie.

DOUGLAS WALLACE STOOD with the camera in his hands for the second time this week, looking at the hand. It seemed different to him now, somehow more alive, plumper. The boy was perfectly still, eyes closed. Douglas had seen the face once before, when the boy was still buried in the bank of peat.

"Earth to Douglas." Douglas snapped out of it. John Gillespie was running this scene and wanted his attention. "Are you finished there, Doug? I need you over here."

Douglas resisted the urge to touch the boy's hair. He didn't know what had come over him, but his heart pounded in anticipation. There was a feeling in the air. He felt like a boy himself, about to go and watch Celtic play at home against Rangers. The crowd chanting and moving in unison, like one huge organism of one mind, one passion. It was like war. It was like...

"Doug, something wrong?" John broke into his thoughts again.

"Sorry. I was just wondering if I'd brought the spare SD card for the camera," Douglas said, walking over to John.

Douglas had never really liked John, a Partick Thistle supporter, who... He wasn't sure exactly why he didn't like him. It was just one of those things. They were colleagues. Neither had ever tried to be more than that.

"I've a spare card if you need it. Make sure you get shots of everything." John indicated more blood splatters. "Family good?"

"Never better," said Douglas. "They were all over for dinner the other night."

"That's great," said John. "Mary's back, is she?"

The camera clicked and Douglas checked the image. "She's at home in my kitchen as we speak."

"That's brilliant, Doug." John didn't realise Douglas meant that Mary was dissolving in a plastic barrel.

"Isn't it?" smiled Doug. "You and Gillian should come around for your tea one night." Click, click, click went the camera.

"Sounds like a good idea, Doug."

3

"WHAT ARE WE GOING TO DO?" David looked lost, standing out on the street with Mirin and the other members of the department who'd not yet gone home.

"You should go and see her," said Mirin.

"I don't think that's wise. It wouldn't be appropriate."

"David." Mirin put a hand on his arm. "She'd want to see you."

David pulled his arm away. "I don't know what you're talking about."

"David, seriously?"

"I've no idea what you're implying. If you think you're going to use this to besmirch my good name, and take over from me with this find..."

"That's what you think of me?" Mirin cut in. "Don't judge me by your own standards."

"Don't give me that." David's voice had risen to match Mirin's. "I've known you long enough. I remember the old Mirin. Don't tell me the ambition has gone. You used to live at work. And now you're back and a changed woman. Saint Mirin's gone through hell and now..."

Everyone was looking at them.

"David, stop!" Mirin tried to bring his attention to where they were. He took another breath to keep going, running his hand through his hair and only adding to its manic, unkempt appearance. The man in the spotlight can't always see the crowd, but now he could. All those eyes staring at him and not with the adoration he was used to. He straightened his back and pulled his suit jacket straight with a short tug at the hem and exhaled.

"I... I... I need to organise alternative arrangements for the boy. The Hunterian Museum in the main building may be able to help us. They should have the necessary storage facilities until we can get the lab up and running."

David walked away before Mirin could say anything more.

There was nothing else to do today. Mirin wanted to go and see Portia in the hospital, but she suspected that Portia wouldn't get much from a visit from her. She felt a duty of care for Portia, but it wasn't emotional.

Mirin went to a counsellor, but she preferred to find things out for herself in books. That was her default mode, the autodidactic of academic life. Mirin knew where she stood with books. She had dedicated most of her life to studying them. She had read about grief, looked up the most recent research on the subject, systematic reviews, the best large-scale evidence and case studies and the recommended courses of treatment. When her emotions had come crashing in, she sought refuge in rationality and had begun to understand her condition. From what she'd read, a sense of detachment was not unusual as part of the grieving process. It could go on for years. It might never stop. It wasn't that she couldn't feel. Instead, feelings came through a filter or a buffering zone, which was her rationalism. Ironic that rationality could be an emotional response.

David had gone, lost in the crowds of students and staff who swarmed over the campus like ants. There was nothing more for her to do today. She could work at home, and pick up Oran early, when the school bell went at three o'clock.

"Professor Hassan?"

Mirin turned around to be presented with a face that was familiar, but which she couldn't immediately place. The accent was Glaswegian, and the voice sounded familiar. Despite a rough beard, he looked gaunt, with large bags under his brown eyes. The gauntness reminded Mirin of Portia more than anyone else, although David had that similar look today as well. Then it hit her.

"Constable Bhaskar? What are you doing here?"

"Could I have a word?" Dip said.

She walked over to him, standing apart from the crowd.

The constable, in civilian clothes, checked around furtively to see that no one was listening.

"Is there another murder?" Dip asked, gesturing to the Gregory Building.

"No, thankfully. But Portia, the young lady who was with us at the excavation in Stirlingshire..."

"The redhead?"

Mirin nodded. "She was attacked in our department last night."

"Will she be okay?"

"She was badly injured but she's in the best hands now." There was an awkward silence. "Is there something I can help you with, Constable? I'm a little surprised to see you."

Dip seemed to force a smile. "I'm in town visiting my parents and, well, actually, I want to apologise for how I was at the scene the other day. I can't imagine what you must think."

"You've nothing to apologise for."

"That's very kind of you."

"But you didn't need to come all this way for that." Mirin felt sorry for the constable. He looked so tired and lost. She remembered that look. She had seen it in the mirror many times in the last year.

Dip pushed his hands into his pockets and looked at his feet. "I know. There was something else. It was about the boy." He gestured to the Gregory Building.

"Shouldn't you tell your colleagues?"

"No, it's not about the murders. I keep thinking about him and thought maybe you could tell me something about him. You never know, I might even remember something that could help you." He forced another smile.

He looked so piteous, Mirin thought. "They've sent us home for the day. I was just about to get a coffee. You're welcome to come along."

4

ANNIE BROWNE SLEPT on Eddie's bed. The sheets barely covered her, the curve of her back gliding down to the cleft of her buttocks, rouged from Eddie's hands. Her body had been everything Eddie had hoped and more, but as he looked at her now, she seemed her age. Despite the fact that he could tell she'd had her crow's feet filled, and her lips slightly enhanced, she was a woman fighting the aging process. Until today, perhaps, she had been winning. But in the breath of a scream Annie had given up, in more ways than one, which had been to Eddie's advantage.

He had been the wrong guy in the right place at the wrong time for her.

Whereas Annie had lost, Eddie had never felt more like a winner. He stretched and got out of bed. They had gone at it like animals until Annie was exhausted, collapsing. But Eddie's dick was still hard. He looked at himself in the mirror, inspecting his body, now covered in scratches and bite marks. He'd never felt so confident and certain in himself.

Their clothes were strewn all over the bedroom amongst the usual mess. Eddie's mum would have called it a *midden*, the old bitch. Annie and he had practically torn the clothes from each other when it finally kicked off between them.

After they found the body, Annie had been in shock. They had been given the rest of the day off by the shift manager, Fat Martin. Typically, he was a useless lump of lard, but the fat bastard had come through this time. In a big way. Eddie flexed his hard-on at the mirror and let out a guffaw.

Playing the White Knight, Eddie said he'd see Annie home. And from that point on, for the first time in his life, everything went as planned and he got everything he wanted. Guiding her to the tube station in the opposite direction from where she lived, Annie didn't say a word. She sat shivering like a small animal with his arm around her while they rattled under the city. They got off at Ibrox and walked to Eddie's flat. He offered her a drink to calm down, and she had agreed with a silent nod. Annie sipped the over-sized measure of Bell's whisky from a tumbler Eddie had barely washed. When she was done, Eddie offered her another, and she polished it off in one.

Eddie had never had much luck with women in the past. They were a complete enigma to him. But today there had been something in the air. He felt it like an alcoholic buzz, only Eddie had been clear-headed: crystal clear and uninhibited. No complaint had been forth-coming when Eddie slipped his arm around Annie's shoulders. He let his hand roam up her thigh, meeting no resistance even as it swept to her crotch. She turned and looked up at him with glassy eyes, still full of fear. He understood something then. It was the fear that was driving her to this, to him. The death-fear that had triggered some-thing primal. In turn it had triggered something sadistic that burned deep inside Eddie. He had kissed her with cannibalistic force, and they had torn into each other.

When they had finally finished, Annie slept, exhaustion curling her up in a ball among Eddie's dirty bedclothes. But Eddie couldn't sleep. He was buzzing with too much energy for that. Ideas whirled in his mind, and with them Eddie felt a compulsion to move and almost sprang from the bed.

The wardrobe was falling apart. The doors clung on with twisted hinges. Eddie opened them wide and reached under the screwed-up jumpers and sweatshirts on the top shelf until he found what he was looking for. Sliding the box from the top shelf, he caught the weight of the old army surplus khaki tin. Taking it back to the bed, he flipped the two latches at either end of the box. With reverence, Eddie opened the lid. Inside lay his treasures. He'd inherited a couple from his grandfather; one, he'd won in a bet, but most of them were bought online, paying over the Dark Web.

Inspecting the medals, Eddie held them up against his bare chest and moved his body around in the mirror, admiring how they looked. Then he carefully put them back and picked up the 1940s German bayonet, slightly tarnished but in good condition. Eddie would regularly tend the blade, keeping it well oiled. He felt its heft in his hands and gently caressed its shaft before resting his finger on the tip. Lastly, he picked up the red armband, admiring the insignia. He looked at it with a certainty of mind, that some things in the past had been just plain right, even if they were rejected by most. Eddie thought about the shitty job he had to do and how much this city had changed since he was a boy, full of all those faces from foreign places, the university especially. He slipped the armband on, the black swastika shining against the white circle. He admired it in the mirror, like a soldier who had graduated and was ready for the real war now. No more games. No more pretending.

In her sleep, Annie moaned in distress. Eddie walked around the side of the bed still wearing the swastika, bayonet in hand (jutting forward like his penis) and looked down at her buttocks. A feeling of power, that he could do anything, that he must do something, coursed through his entire body.

Annie moaned again, beginning to weep in her sleep. Eddie climbed between her splayed legs, spat on the palm of his hand, and prepared to wake her from her nightmares.

5

THE GOTHIC SPIRES of the university's Gilbert Scott Building loomed above them, the thousand-eyed mullioned windows staring out gravely over the city, as Mirin led Dip to the staff cafeteria. Faculty and students walked with purpose, worried looks on their faces. Two deaths and a third brutal attack in as many days on campus had set people on edge. Uniformed officers patrolled the campus, their yellow high visibility jackets standing out in the crowds like searchlights.

Mirin ordered them coffee and guided Dip to a corner.

"You looked tired, Constable."

Dip gave her a wan smile. "Just call me Dip. I'm on sick leave. They think I'm nuts."

"Maybe you are. It's a question of degree," Mirin said, blowing on her coffee.

Dip sat up, looking at Mirin through rings of dark shadows. "I've barely slept."

Mirin put down her coffee cup. "How can I help you? What do you want to know about the boy?"

"Whatever you can tell me. I keep thinking about how his throat was cut with a knife. The image keeps playing over and over in my head."

Mirin froze and then slowly put down her coffee. "How do you know about that?"

"About what?"

"That the boy's throat was cut." Mirin had lowered her voice, not wanting the macabre turn in their conversation to carry, particularly given recent events.

Dip didn't say anything straight away. He looked to be searching for an answer.

"Someone on the investigation must have told me," he said finally.

"You said you were on sick leave. And how do you know a knife killed him? Only a handful of people know that."

"I just assumed."

"Which bit?" Mirin said, growing suspicious.

"I don't understand." Dip looked like he was trying too hard to be casual.

"Which bit did you assume: his throat being cut, or that the murder weapon was a knife?"

Dip let out a sigh and nodded. "Okay, you're right. No one told me about any of it. And I don't want to lie to you. Honestly, I don't think we have enough time. But before you leave thinking I'm just some crazy stalker, I also know the knife is a stone knife made of black stone. Obsidian, I think it's called. And the boy has markings on his skin. Tattoos, I think."

"Is this some kind of joke? Who put you up to it? It's not funny given the circumstances," Mirin practically hissed, trying to keep her voice low.

"It's not a joke. I'll tell you how I know, but first, didn't you ever think about how the boy was found amongst all that death?" Dip said.

"That was terrible, but I don't see what that has to do with..."

Dip interrupted her. "And you haven't thought about how the deaths have followed him here?" Dip indicated the university around them.

"But I don't see how that has anything to do with a boy buried for God knows how long in the ground." Mirin was preparing herself to leave. She was trying to be kind, having had her own brush with trauma, but she didn't need this, not with Portia lying in the hospital and the media attention on the boy. All she wanted was for things to get back to normal.

Dip hung his head, as though he knew he had lost her. As Mirin put her hand on her bag ready to go, Dip spoke.

"Everyone thinks I'm traumatised. The truth is, I'm sure I would be if I didn't know there was a reason for those people's death. I knew them all, the eco-protesters, every one of the road crew, and that's just it." He leaned in. "They were good people. Ordinary people. And then one day they just decide to kill each other with their bare hands? And I don't just mean a drunken punch-up. I've seen plenty of bar brawls in my time. No. They pounded each other's heads in, and that's not an exaggeration. They literally destroyed each other until all but one of them was dead, and he gave me this before he died." Dip held up his broken arm. "People don't just do that. We all have our faults, our secrets, and our little prejudices. But this? This was something else. Something bigger kicked them off."

"Alcohol? Drugs?" offered Mirin, her hand still on her bag.

Dip smiled weakly again. "The toxicology report says there were only minor traces of cannabis in a couple of the protesters and one from the builders. But that's it. It wasn't booze, and it wasn't drugs. The only thing out of the ordinary at that crime scene was the boy. And he was also present at or in the vicinity of the two other violent crimes here."

Mirin was about to open her mouth, when Dip held up a finger to stop her. "And I'd probably agree with you. I'd say it was just a coincidence, or maybe we're missing some vital clue, if I hadn't seen what he can do. If I hadn't felt it, right in here." He tapped his temple.

"But how?" said Mirin. "And why you?"

Dip took a deep breath. "Because I touched him. I touched his hand."

"What?" Mirin said.

"It was like drowning, but not in water. When I touched him I felt sick, so sick. But it was what came with the sickness: an onslaught of memories and emotions. That is what I was drowning in. Small things I hadn't thought about in years. A girl I'd cheated on in high school. A lie I told my parents. A test I cheated on at university. Every one of them and dozens, hundreds more came rushing into my head. Each little misdemeanour suddenly made me feel what a terrible guy I was. It started to rain. As the raindrops hit my face, I felt myself surface from the onslaught of memories. But the guilt remained. At first, I put it down to shock.

"Eventually, I found my phone and called it in. I finally got home..."

Mirin sensed there was a part of the story left unsaid here, but she didn't press.

Dip gave that tired smile again and went on. "I dragged myself upstairs to bed, but I needed a shower. When I stepped under the water, it came to me."

"What 'came' to you?" Mirin said, her hand letting go of her bag.

"I had a vision, I suppose you would call it, but it was more than that. I *was* the boy. I saw his death, or rather I lived his death through his eyes. I... He was filled with hatred... walking through some ancient bog surrounded by mist and fog. I came across a young woman chanting on her knees, holding a black flint knife to her chest."

Mirin made an involuntary sound.

"What?" Dip said quizzically.

"That's how you know about the knife?"

"Aye. Like I said, it was in my vision. I felt intense rage at this woman, at her people, at *all* people. And as I approached her, they sprang from the bog, surrounding me. Two men on each limb. Still, they could barely contain me. They pushed me into the water of the bog, and I felt weaker but still too strong for them. Then the woman slashed my throat with the black knife. As the blood drained from my body, they tied a heavy stone to me, and threw me into the deepest part of the bog. I tasted the stagnant water, felt it fill my lungs, saw the light of the world fade away. And then I woke, slumped in my shower."

Dip leant across the table. "I *knew* he was back. We've released him somehow."

"You must have read our report to the coroner," Mirin said coolly.

"I haven't read any report. I'm on sick leave, remember?" He held up his broken arm again.

Mirin weighed him up. He felt intensely scrutinised in the same way he had during his early days on the force, suffering under overzealous drill instructors.

Still, he waited.

"How else would you know about the knife and the boy's throat being cut?" Mirin thought out loud.

"Nothing I say is going to convince you. It wouldn't have convinced me either." He looked around the cafeteria at all the faces, young and old, engrossed in conversations. They all looked oblivious.

"I guess seeing is believing," Dip said, and finished the last of his coffee in one gulp. He wiped his stubbly mouth with the palm of his good hand, before giving the professor another of those defeated smiles.

"Thanks for the coffee, Professor Hassan. I'm staying in Glasgow at my parents', above the Indian restaurant on Park Road." Dip scribbled a number on a scrap of paper from his pocket and slid it over the table to Mirin. Then, picking up his coat, he said, "Just in case something changes your mind. I hope it won't be too late."

6

TOMMY POPPER WIPED the sweat from his brow. The day hadn't started off too badly. A balmy autumn morning quickly turned muggy. The heat and the closeness grew worse as the day dragged on. By the time he got to work, he was uncomfortable and grouchy. Just as well he was down for the night shift. It meant he had the run of the place. He could do his rounds and there was always plenty of time to drink tea and finish his book without the interruptions of the day job. He savoured being alone with the quiet of the night. If only it wasn't so hot.

There was another bonus in addition to the solitude. Tommy didn't have to get it in the ear from Mrs Popper. Oh, how the *wee* witch liked to complain about the number of shifts Tommy had to do. Tommy wasn't entirely sure how exactly she expected the mortgage to be paid or for food to be put on the table if he didn't go to work. It wasn't as if a guy pushing sixty, with barely any qualifications, had his pick of jobs. Tommy would have loved employment that involved lying around on a velvet sofa, while lackies massaged his bunions, and he counted all the money they were paying him for doing nothing. Alas, he was yet to find such an opportunity. However, there were plenty of jobs around as long as a man didn't mind getting stuck in, doing something a bit dirty, or working unsociable hours. So, night shifts it was for Tommy, he thought to himself, wiping more sweat from his forehead. For some reason the heat hadn't dissipated with nightfall. Tommy hadn't felt this hot and uncomfortable since the week in Benidorm about fifteen years ago when the air conditioning broke on their summer holiday. Tommy had avoided ridiculously hot places ever since, much to Mrs Popper's annoyance.

The campus was quiet, apart from the usual pockets of noise that came from the Stevenson Building, housing the university's sports facilities, and the two student unions, one at the bottom and one at the top of University Avenue. But, of course, only one of the unions was open. The Queen Margaret hadn't got back to business since that horrible incident a few nights ago. Tommy thought about what the world was coming to when something so grisly could happen between students on the university campus. Sure, the kids might be annoying, and occasionally stuck up, but most of them were pretty good kids and as soft as feathers. They didn't have the edge of the kids he grew up with, or the ones he and Mrs Popper had produced, more used to street fights than money.

Tommy did his usual walk up the back of the main building, taking a moment to enjoy the view spreading out over the rest of the city. The towers of the Gilbert Scott Building sat atop Gilmore Hill, which stood above the rest of the city. A bed of orange lights spread out below Tommy like a field of fireflies. He loved the city. He couldn't imagine living anywhere else. Glasgow born and bred, even if his parents were Polish immigrants who came over at the end of the Second World War. He took a deep breath and checked his watch. He'd better finish his rounds.

He strolled around the perimeter of the main building, checking the entrances were locked, gates closed, nothing untoward. Tommy circled back up from the corner of University Avenue and crossed onto the other side of the road. This bit of the hill was steep, and sweat started to drip down his face, making his moustache itch, and his breathing laboured. At the crest of the hill, he turned up to the library with an even steeper incline, but it was only a short distance before he veered off into the back streets that ran behind the town-houses on Lilybank Gardens. These were vulnerable to break-ins and needed checking, and on the other side of the alley were the back service entrances to the library. Further down from that, he would get to the back of the Queen Margaret Union, near to where the two students were murdered. Tommy intended to double-check these back alleys because he would bet some *bampot* would have already worked out this was a vulnerable target given the recent crimes.

A bat swooped, dipping into the haze of nightlights and then vanishing.

Another did the same. And then another. Tommy stopped, looking up. More bats were hunting overhead. He had never seen so many. Filling up the spaces in between them were clouds of gnats, a great swarm of them. *The heat must have woken them up*, he thought. *They think it's spring.*

Eyes still on the sky, Tommy tested the rear exit to a store at the back of the Queen Margaret Union. Out of habit, he was anticipating the catch in the bolts. It never came. The double doors swung inward with a metallic clunk. Tommy regained his momentary loss of balance and took the torch from his belt. Turning it on, he followed its beam into the dark, moving a sweaty hand along the wall, looking for the light switch.

"Feck's sake," he muttered.

Under the noise of his own heavy breathing, a quiet rustling caught Tommy's attention. As he swept the torch beam around the room, the double doors clicked shut behind him. Only the narrow disc of light emitted by his light illuminated the room. Beyond its perimeter, all was formless black mass. A realisation dawned on Tommy. The sound he could hear were the bodies of millions of flies crawling all over each other. He swept his light down.

They covered the floor. As he took a step, he felt them pop underfoot. They covered whatever boxes and furniture lay in the storeroom, and they crept up the walls like a fungal growth recorded on a time-lapse camera.

Heart racing, a twinge pinched in Tommy's chest, a sharp, constricting ache. He bit down hard on the pain, but his panting only increased. If it was hot outside, it was a sauna in the storeroom. His shirt was wringing wet. Sweat dribbled down his red, puffy face. He slapped the wall, frantically trying to find the light switch. He kept his torch trained on the mass of black, glinting insects.

The heel of Tommy's shoe found a box on the floor, and he stumbled. His other foot stamped on the corner of another cardboard box. With stuttering backward steps, arms pinwheeling, he fell heavily on his backside, pain shooting through his chest.

Disturbed, a pall of flies rose, an angry buzz vibrating the hot air. Tommy could feel them brushing his face, hard-bristled bodies prickling his skin. Instinctively, Tommy closed his mouth despite his hyperventilation, pressure growing in his head. The insects crawled into his hair, their legs itching his scalp. He gave a strangled cry through closed lips, pain still pinching in his chest. Shaking his head and rubbing his hands through his hair frantically, Tommy tried to rid himself of the infestation. But the more he struggled the more they seemed to swarm him, settling on him in a living blanket. They began to find their way under his clothing, down the collar of his shirt, at the cuffs, under the hem of his trouser legs. And then they were trapped between sweaty flesh and damp clothes.

Scrabbling on his backside Tommy disturbed more flies and whimpered through lips clamped shut. He turned to his hands and knees, risked a breath, and flies, God knew how many, darted into the open space. The unnatural texture of them on his tongue and gums and teeth made Tommy wretch. He tried to spit them out.

The flies whirled around Tommy, a black mist. As he struggled to his feet, trying to find a wall to support him, he bumped his forehead, drawing blood.

The night watchman knew there was a door somewhere, but the darkness and his disorientation gave the illusion of a doorless room. Tommy could feel flies beginning to explore the shell of his ear and his nostrils. He pushed as hard as he could, thinking he might have found the door and it would give, but he only met concrete. Stepping to his left, he pushed again, not knowing whether the pain in his chest was just panic or a heart attack. Again, there was no escape. He felt a fly buzz in his right ear. He screamed again through tight lips, wildly shaking his head from side to side to dislodge the insects. He took a third step to the left and threw his entire weight behind his hands once more. The doors gave a little but wouldn't open. Panic now driving his every move, he tried again and got the same response, and then realised the doors opened inwards. He fumbled for the handles, found one, and yanked.

The door burst inward. Tommy barrelled forward into the alleyway. A plume of flies escaped with him, ascending to become dinner for the bats, before the doors shut behind him automatically.

There was still a fly buzzing in Tommy's earhole, loud against his brain. He screamed out loud now, shaking his head, brushing every part of his body and face. The fly buzzed angrily in his ear, creeping deeper. Tommy managed to get his little finger inside the hole to scoop out the fly. The buzzing stopped. He couldn't feel anything. *The fly must have got out*, he thought with relief.

Tommy lay down on his back, looking up into the night sky, panting. The pain in his chest subsided. He caught his breath. He was alright. The panic of a moment ago replayed in Tommy's mind. As the bats gorged themselves above him, a smirk crept across his face. Slowly at first, an idea took root. Then it bloomed quickly. A huge grin spread across his features, still bearing fragments of crushed insects. Tommy let out a bark of a laugh that rang and rang, seemingly unable to stop, into the night.

7

THE FLIES WERE DYING off everywhere in the chill of the morning. They covered cars, windowsills, and doorsteps. They crunched underfoot on the pavements and roads and formed desiccated blankets on the frosted grass. Millions of little bodies frozen from a miniature alien cataclysm.

DI Stuart Blair wafted sluggish survivors from around his face. They were slow in the cold, holding on to the last vestiges of life. "This weather is *fecking* weird, eh, boss?" A storm one day, stifling heat the next, and now a cold snap.

Flies had settled in DCI Shepard's auburn hair as they left the police station. She ruffled them from her head.

"*Aye*. Let's get in the motor," Connie said, hurrying to get out of the haze of dying insects.

Stuart jumped in. The car started up with a turn of the key and they were hit with a hail of half-alive but mostly dead insects, blown through the car vents, left on because of the previous day's heat. With cries of disgust they quickly closed all the vents and shut off the fans.

It wasn't raining but they drove with the windshield wipers on, clearing the fly carcasses with jets of water and sweeps of the wipers.

The detectives found their way to the crime scene, parking up at the foot of the flats in the Finnieston area of the city, lying below the university, and cornered between the M8 motorway and the River Clyde.

Dismounting their vehicle, Stuart clocked three children, perhaps aged between nine and eleven, who should have been in school, lurking in a tunnel leading through the ground floor of one of the blocks of flats opposite. They jumped back into the shadows, pulling up their hoods shouting "Pigs" and running away.

"Children are our future," Stuart grinned.

"Best be nice to them then," Connie said, burying her hands in her pockets against the cold and looking up at the block of flats. "Tenth floor?"

"*Aye*, boss."

Uniformed officers were already taking statements from neighbours. Stuart caught a glimpse of Connie's face as they rode the lift. It was as unreadable as ever. She had a reputation with some of the guys for being cold. They called her the Android, which was kind of a backhanded compliment. But Stuart knew better.

There was a case a couple of years back, a bad one. It had affected Connie. Stuart didn't know why. They ended up in the pub having finally charged the right suspect. A newspaper from when they'd made the arrest had been abandoned in the booth they took. 'Broken Biscuits' the headline read. Quite poetic for the *Daily Record*. The family had the name McVitie, like the biscuit manufacturers. Turned out it was the mother, Carol, who'd killed her two children, eighteen months and three years old. The husband had tried to take the blame, but it was Connie who didn't believe him. It came out in court later he was covering for his wife, prepared to go to jail as a child killer because he knew his wife was suffering from postnatal depression. She only served a year in jail at least. Where she'd ended up after hanging herself, who knew?

Stuart had got them two pints, heavy for him, lager for her. Connie didn't want to talk about the case. She deflected, asking questions about Stuart, what he was like as a boy. He told her about boxing, about nearly making the Commonwealth team for Scotland, about nearly messing up at school, about nearly being most things and then nothing. Stuart could get a little morose with booze.

"Nearly missed this one too," he'd said, referring to the case again. "If it wasn't for you."

Connie's eyes were wet, like glistening green pools, sad and deep. She didn't say anything and took a gulp of lager instead.

"Fucking kids though, *eh*? I mean, how can some..."

It was the first and last time he'd ever seen Connie cry, or show any emotion for that matter. She wiped the tear away with her sleeve and swallowed the last of her pint in two huge gulps.

"My round," she said, standing up.

They never mentioned it again.

Stuart knew there was something else making her emotional about the McVitie case. The guys were right: she *was* like an android. Clinical. Efficient. Smarter than the rest of them put together. So whatever was bugging her must be big. Stuart was proud to work under her and wasn't about to go digging around.

Connie had laid two more pints in front of them and they started talking about their other cases. Her eyes were dry, and her face was unreadable again.

Stuart played this memory over until the lift lurched to a stop and they stepped out onto a communal landing which Stuart noted *didn't* smell of piss for once. The block had been recently spruced up by the council, and some of the tenants owned their own flats. Most of the residents were hard-working, low-income families. *Most of them*, Stuart thought, remembering the kids in the tunnel.

A young constable stood sentry outside the flat. They showed their warrant cards. The constable tipped his hat with a polite "Ma'am" to Connie.

"Jesus!" Stuart flinched at the smell: blood and loose bowels.

The two detectives went room by room. They had a routine and would compare notes later. There was broken furniture, three bodies, all violently assaulted peri- or post-mortem. The sheer amount of blood suggested a lot of it was done perimortem, the heart still pumping it all over the floor and across walls.

"This is the wife," said one of the constables, an older man with years of street experience worn into his face.

Stuart watched Connie crouch on her haunches, getting as close as she could without disturbing anything. The scene was fresh, and forensics were on their way. The wife's eyes were open, gazing with all the life of a mannequin.

"What do we know?" Connie asked, standing up.

The constable looked at his notes. "Neighbours said they heard a disturbance around five am this morning. By the time a car got here they were all dead. No sign of the attacker."

"Is there a husband?" asked Stuart.

The constable looked at his notes, flicking back a page. "A Tommy Popper. Fifty-nine. He was on night shift at the university last night. He was due home around six. They were happily married, apparently. The other two bodies seem to be the children, grown-up ones at least."

Stuart always asked the basics for Connie, letting her filter all the information. "Any neighbours see him?"

"No," said the constable. "I checked with the university. No one saw him at the end of his shift either. Seems he may have left early."

"Naughty boy," Stuart said dryly.

Connie walked out of the room and into one of the flat's bedrooms where they'd found the body of a young man in his late teens.

Stuart was going back over the timeline, asking about routines, any details the uniforms might have noticed in the flat or outside, when there was a muted thump. Stuart thought maybe Connie had tripped on something. Both coppers paused, listening, sensing something was off. In these blocks of flats, sound could travel through the walls and down ventilation shafts. Stuart had grown up in ones like these, before they were refurbished. And as a child, he would hear all his neighbours' business through the walls.

"Stuart!" It was a strained call, barely audible.

Stuart sprinted for the door, crashing into the tight hallway. He navigated by sound, rushing into the bedroom where a fat man sat astride Connie's chest, pinning her with his weight. He was raining down punches at her head. Connie had managed to get her forearms up in something like a boxer's shell, but punches were getting through.

Stuart dived at the assailant, tackling him clear. They rolled and Stuart ended up on top. He felt nothing but rage, a pure white rage. He gripped the fat man's sweaty hair in the fingers of his left hand, and with his right he punched the fat man repeatedly in the face. There were voices far off, shouting.

Stuart quickly opened up the fat man's face, the left eye bleeding above and below the cheek. The nose was squashed beneath his fists. Blood and a tooth flew from the fat man's mouth. Then Stuart was being pulled off by two uniforms and Connie was shouting, staggering against a chest of drawers, dazed and with a fat lip, a bloody nose, and an eye already beginning to swell.

"What are you doing, DI Blair?" Connie said, managing the tone of a superior officer while holding her eye. Blood ran from her nose.

Stuart stopped struggling, realising he'd lost control, that maybe he would have killed that man if there hadn't been someone to stop him. What the bloody hell was he doing?

He didn't know.

8

THE RESTAURANT HAD PUT the tables out again in the morning, thinking they'd get the same heat as the day before. The bloom of insects from the previous evening meant that no one wanted to eat outside anyway. People had crammed into the little Italian, sweating in the closeness of the strange autumn. Tips had been down, and several arguments kicked off between patrons and staff.

Today was a different story. People stayed away. Maybe because of the cold, or maybe because the erratic weather had begun to unsettle them.

Simon couldn't wait for the shift to be over. Derek, the manager, was being a dick. The staff were lazy and had their hands in the till as far as he was concerned, although Simon was sure he'd seen Derek skim from the tips numerous times. But Simon needed to keep the job to help pay for university. He laughed at the thought. Paying for university seemed like a euphemism, a Sisyphean task that would last a lifetime and beyond, and maybe he *would* be working in a restaurant for the rest of his life, earning minimum wage with letters after his name. Derek had a degree in law, after all. The manager hovered like a morose portent of the future awaiting Simon.

No one had sat outside all day, so Derek gave Simon the job of cleaning down the tables and chairs with soapy water and then packing them away.

The washbasin of water sloshed over on the pavement, soaking his feet. The water quickly cooled, and his socks were wet through so that his feet now squelched. Simon shivered against the cold. It was hot inside and so he only had his white short-sleeved shirt. The thought of going back in for his coat crossed his mind, but Derek glared at Simon from the till, gesturing stiffly at the tables. A billow of white marked his sigh, and he got to work.

The sponge needed regular cleaning as it clogged with flies. *Gross.* After washing one table and a chair, with four more tables and nine more chairs to go, he already needed to change the water. Simon wrang out the sponge when a large hailstone the size of a small marble hit the far table. He saw the little white ball of ice bounce off down Byres Road. There was a *tick* noise as another struck the table. Then several more in quick succession. Simon looked into the sky, still crouched over his basin.

A blow hit Simon's shoulder, hard as a fist. He stumbled, sprawling over the wet table. More hail fell, drumming loudly. Some were the size of ice cubes, others as big a small fruit. A second blow hit Simon in the small of the back and he cried out, flinching.

The ice fell in thunderous missiles. A cold block as big as a tennis ball struck Simon's forehead, felling him to the ground. He tried to stand to reach the restaurant door, but all the air left his lungs when a chunk of ice struck his spine. Gasping like a beached fish, Simon covered his head, but the hail kept pummelling. The noise swelled, drowning out Simon's weak cries for help. Car windows shattered. Alarms wailed.

The roaring filled Simon's ears until a hailstone the size of a house brick struck him cleanly on the temple, and Simon heard no more.

9

AFTER THE BIZARRE weather of the last few days, a typically fine Glaswegian rain had settled over the city as Mirin walked into the hospital holding Oran's hand. Royal Infirmary swallowed them up, its stone exterior stained with mottled patches from the city's pollution.

They scanned the boards together. "Can you see it, poppet? We're looking for Special Care."

Biting his lip, Oran looked intently at the sign on the wall. "There," he said finally, jumping up and pointing with his free hand, not quite reaching the letters.

The lift doors closed behind them, and they began to ascend with a small lurch. Mirin hadn't been in a hospital since... She didn't want to think about it. Looking at those memories was too painful. They weren't here for that. Portia didn't need her crying, and neither did Oran.

"Mum," whispered Oran, tugging at her hand.

"What is it?" She bent down, mirroring his conspiratorial whisper.

"It smells funny in here." Oran had put a sleeve over his nose.

A doctor, stethoscope hanging around his neck and stubble developing from a shift that had gone on too long, gave him a disapproving look.

"That's what hospitals smell like, darling."

Oran leaned in closer so the doctor couldn't hear. "It smells like when Daddy used to put bleach down the loo after he had a poo."

Mirin couldn't help but laugh, and the doctor shot them another look of disapproval. The elevator arrived and they stepped off. Medical staff walked with purpose in different directions. A few patients hobbled around in night clothes. Relatives lingered in small groups. They found a nurse at a desk and asked her where Portia's room was. Then they were standing outside a small private room with a heavy beech door. Portia's name was written in a wipeable marker on a small whiteboard.

"Are we going in, Mum?" Oran asked, looking up.

Mirin took a deep breath, holding back the memories, and opened the door. She had to hold back a gasp. Portia's naturally pale complexion had been drained of the tones of pink so that she was sallow and grey. Her cheeks had sunken in, and the dark rings around her eyes were made darker by the vacuous eye sockets. She looked like a living skeleton. The only thing about her that seemed alive was her flame-red hair, splayed across a pillow. It looked even more vibrant against her deathly pallor.

There were signs of physical trauma: the cracked lips, a gash held together with stitches; the swollen eye, a purple bruise beginning to turn shades of green and brown. Her neck was wrapped in gauze. But the worst of the cuts were covered by heavy bandages, binding her arms and hands like a partially uncovered mummy, Mirin thought with sad irony.

A heart monitor bleeped, marking time.

Oran whispered again. "She's sleeping."

"We'll wait a little while. Hop on that seat over there." Oran ran over to the armchair, covered in a pink, institutional, wipe-clean vinyl. He threw off his coat and clambered onto it, swinging feet that barely touched the ground.

Mirin placed a small bouquet of flowers on the bedside cabinet. Other people had sent flowers too, large bouquets from her family in England and cheaper arrangements from student friends. Mirin read some of the dedications, feeling nosey for doing so, reminded of condolences she had received.

They'd been given the go-ahead to come in once Portia had been transferred from intensive care after a few days. Mirin understood that Portia's family had already visited and were staying in a hotel nearby. She checked all the bouquets. There were no flowers from David. He'd been aloof and had barely spoken to Mirin since Portia's attack. He arranged alternative lab space for them, sending Chin down to the Medical Faculty. The Hunterian Museum in the main building came through and were more than happy to help store the boy's body and also let them do their work, bringing up the necessary equipment, much to the annoyance of the guys in the estates department. However, David's arrangements meant they'd be working in public, as a living display, within the vaulted space of the main hall of the Hunterian Museum. Mirin had tried to protest and make clear it wasn't appropriate. But David had the vice chancellor on board and, of course, Lucy Walker at the BBC. It was going to be great exposure for the university, "and your career," Mirin had added. To which David had spat that she had always been jealous of him and that maybe she wasn't seeing things clearly. They left it on bad terms for the second time.

Portia let out a quiet moan.

"Portia, it's me. It's Mirin."

Her eyelids slowly blinked open and she turned her head to look at Mirin. A weak smile played on her lips.

Her eyes fell on Oran sitting in the chair swinging his legs, his black curly hair tousled around his face. And then she looked back at Mirin and began to struggle. Unable to speak, Portia made desperate groans. Her bandaged arms reached out defensively in front of her while her legs tried to push her away up the bed. The alarm on her heart rate monitor began to sound.

"Portia, it's okay. It's Mirin. You're safe." Mirin urgently pushed the alarm button above the bed.

Portia's eyes bulged in their sockets. Her strangled groans only increased in intensity. The door of the hospital room burst open. A doctor and two nurses ran in, and began to try and calm Portia as Mirin backed away.

The doctor was preparing a sedative, while the nurses held Portia with firm hands and soothing words, when DCI Shepherd and DI Blair appeared in the doorway. DCI Shepherd looked between Mirin, backed up against the visitor's chair in the corner of the room, and then to Portia struggling, crying and grunting like a terrified animal. The doctors administered the sedative and Portia's cries subsided quickly. Corded muscles in her wasted arms relaxed, and she fell back into the netherworld of sleep.

10

THE NEW MOBILE cooling unit from the Faculty of Medical Sciences had only cost David a couple of favours, one of which was to let old Harry Reid appear as a 'specialist medical consultant' in the documentary.

The cooling unit was designed for special incidents: terrorist attacks, viral outbreaks, exotic disease cases and the like, for which the Medical Faculty's tropical disease unit had won a grant. The unit itself was like a giant steel sarcophagus, measuring eight by five feet, and would enable them to keep the boy in a temperature- and climate-controlled environment in their new workspace.

The Hunterian Museum, located on the fourth floor of the university's main building, consisted of two rooms. The first was a smaller reception area through which the elevator granted visitors access to the museum. The room contained carved reliefs from the Antonine Wall and fragments of Roman pillars, all behind an exhibit sign proclaiming 'Rome's Final Frontier.' Beyond this lay the museum's main hall and David and his team's new workspace.

The cooling unit had been placed in the middle of the vaulted hall. The skeleton of a plesiosaur had been moved, and two of the central display cases removed to make room for their work area, which had been cordoned off by moveable brass balustrades linked with red ropes. Tomorrow, they would go on display.

David's whole body tingled. He could not wait to discuss the possibilities over dinner with Lucy Walker tonight.

He gave the boy one final inspection and closed the heavy brushed-steel lid of the storage unit. Its hydraulic hinges hissed. David locked it with the two heavy clasps, and unseen mechanisms clunked. All the readings on the LCD screen were as they should be, and the run of complex electrical cables all appeared correctly attached.

David took one last look; he was well satisfied with the theatre of the space. The high mullioned windows. The cases of fossil hominid skulls, dinosaur eggs, trophies from indigenous peoples, and insects pinned to white panels within glass display cases. The mezzanine overlooking them contained many of James Hunter's surgical and anatomical specimens, dismembered and floating in formaldehyde, or preserved with resin. Yes, this would be a fine setting for their work. It evoked the grandeur of the institution and the romance of discovery. David breathed in and let it out slowly.

His handmade Italian shoes echoed as he left for his dinner date.

The hall lay in a meek gloom of security lights, and the fine persistent rain continued to fall over the dark city. Then the first caw of a crow broke the silence.

The two clasps on the sarcophagus clicked, first one and then the other, reverberating through the vaulted hall. The lid hissed when the seals released. Phosphorescent green light shone through a seeping white mist that flowed from the casket. Oozing down to the floor, the mist spread, creating a vaporous blanket, slithering between display cases and sneaking into corners until it filled the hall.

A glass case of butterflies and moths, all delicately pinned through the thorax, began to flutter their wings. A dismembered hand, a bleached gash through its palm, flexed bloated fingers. In its glass tomb, a deformed fallow deer faun, with one head but eight limbs, kicked spasmodically. A human foetus, forever in its fifth month within its mortified mother's womb, stirred.

The sarcophagus lid rose. There was a rustling and scratching of hundreds of tiny feet, finding their way through the walls and beneath the floorboards. Called. They came before their master.

The stump of an arm sought the edge of its tomb. Slowly the rest of its form woke, rising from the aphotic slime which had ensnared it for millennia.

A large mullioned window behind the Antonine Wall exhibit cracked when a crow struck it, as many more of its brethren cawed to their lord.

Sitting up, the boy opened his eyes. He looked down through black orbs at the stump where his hand should be. The severed hand twitched to life, a nocturnal animal crawling through mud. It turned, presenting the severed wrist. A fine gossamer grew between hand and stump, thicker and thicker, until the arm was once more whole. The boy hopped down soundlessly from his casket, flexing his fingers, slowly inspecting it.

Rats swarmed through the low fog over the hall, gathering before the casket as though at an altar. Standing on their hind legs, their black eyes gazed awestruck upon their master.

The cawing of the crows grew to a crescendo.

The boy walked through the hall. He was a gardener, and tonight he would plant more seeds. He could feel those he'd planted already, crying out from their dishonest souls. All their petty fears and desires crouched shivering in their minds.

The tide of vermin followed, and doors unlocked before him. Lights choked in and out of existence in their wake. Under the cloisters they marched until the final two great oak doors yielded before him, and he walked through the stone portico to the world beyond. Below, the city spread out in a blanket of caliginous orange lights.

On the slated roof, high above, hunched thousands of crows.

Raising his arms, his minions scurried off into the dark, bearing his seed with them. The harvest was near.

The reaping would be glorious.

11

GLORIOUS SPICES FRAGRANCED THE AIR. The smells transported Dip back to his childhood: his mother passing him crispy pieces of pakora batter, huge vats of sliced onions simmering with their sinus-stinging smell, piles of crushed garlic and chopped coriander ready to flavour the various dishes his family were preparing. He remembered his uncles with their smooth forearms, the heat of the tandoor oven burning away any hairs. Leftover naan bread for breakfast, warmed and brushed with ghee and topped with marmalade.

The comfort of those memories only deepened the worry Dip felt. The boy squatted in the dark at the back of his mind, lurking amongst the shadows of his fears.

Dip had slipped back into family life, helping in the kitchen, deflecting questions about when he'd get married, bearing his mother's prideful way of announcing him as "my son, the police officer" to customers. Dip still hadn't slept well and welcomed the frenetic life of an evening dinner service.

They had been fully booked, as if it were some holiday period. Everyone was eating and drinking more than usual, which, as far as Dip's parents were concerned, was good business. There was laughter throughout the evening, but on several occasions, that same laughter erupted into angry words. Dip was used to the foreshadowing sounds of conflict. He'd grown up in the restaurant, a little brown boy in a sea of white patrons.

That young man had trained to be a police officer in Glasgow before moving to the quiet of Stirlingshire. But even farmers in country pubs drink too much to alleviate stress. Dip would appear from the back, point out he was a police officer, and with calm certainty de-escalate confrontations. Their friends would help and before long the same person either left or began to cry. Such things would typically kill the mood in the restaurant. Conversations would become muted, less wine would be bought, people wouldn't order dessert and leave as quickly as possible. But not that night. The quiet would be replaced by a throng of laughter and engrossing discussions. When couples kissed, they did it with passion. Men slapped each other on the back, or slung arms over each other's shoulders.

"Bloody strange night," Dip's father said, smiling to himself. He was tallying a huge bill for one of the last tables. Dip polished glasses with difficulty, his cast requiring him to pin the glasses between his forearm and chest, while the other hand worked the cloth. The restaurant was finally emptying. He'd been trying to think all night what it reminded him of. The thought hung in the back of his mind along with the boy.

A man approached, his face glazed with the happy muzz of alcohol.

"Brilliant food," the man slurred. His accent connected the dots in Dip's mind. He was Irish. "Best night ever." The Irishman leaned on the bar, his elbow nearly slipping off.

"Are you celebrating something?" Dip's father asked, handing him the huge bill. The man didn't look at it and handed over his credit card.

The Irishman contemplated the question with a high degree of seriousness before concluding "No" with a surprised cheer to his voice. "The notion took us, like we needed to, you know?"

"There's nothing like a good party," Dip's father said, passing back the card machine.

"You're not wrong there." The man put in his PIN and looked back at his group of friends. Dip read his face. The smile wasn't so broad any more. It had evened out and his gaze was directed not at any place, but at a time. A recollection of those good friends still sat at the table.

The Irishman took the receipt and for the first time looked at the price and nodded. It was apparently a more than fair price for whatever he thought he was getting. One last look at his friends and he opened his wallet again. Taking out the entire wad of notes, he pressed them into Dip's father's hand. "You know, you can't take it with you." He smiled wanly and turned back to his friends, who were all putting on their coats.

Dip's father looked down at the money. More than three hundred pounds lay in his hand.

The Irishman and his friends left, climbing into a waiting taxi outside. Dip remembered an old university friend then called Connor. They were still close. Connor's father had passed away in the second year of university and Dip and their other friends had gone over to County Offaly with Connor for the funeral. The afternoon and night had been one of the most wonderful parties he'd ever attended, full of music, food, drink, laughter and crying, singing and dancing. But, of course, it hadn't been a party.

It had been a wake.

12

THE DAMN RAT WAS ELUSIVE. Connie stalked it with the big volume in her office, a textbook entitled *A Foucauldian Interpretation of Modern Law* she still had from the MA she'd completed six years ago. Connie enjoyed academic work mostly when there were clear outcomes. She liked to solve the puzzles, collect the evidence, and make a conclusion. Theory never floated her boat, and as such this seemed like an excellent practical application of this book. *Evidence and Proof in Scotland* was much bigger. However, Connie liked that book. It had notes in the margins and sections underlined. She wasn't about to bludgeon a rat with it.

The whole damn station was infested with rats. It had caused a small riot in the cells when they appeared last night. Two men and a woman had been transferred to accident and emergency and half a dozen others had minor injuries. The commotion distracted the turnkeys and the sergeant in charge, and they had found a young man hanged in his cell. He wasn't considered a risk, only in for some minor drunk and disorderly offence involving him breaking up a fight. He was about to be released when they found him strangled with his own belt, something he should never have been left with, but which was overlooked when the infestation took hold.

Exterminators had been called but, as yet, they had not turned up.

Apparently, the police station wasn't the only place suffering a rat infestation and they'd be some time. Small teams of probationary officers had been mobilised as *ad hoc* rat catchers. However, they were proving ineffective at killing them. They were better at displacing the rodents to other parts of the station. The Chief Super had ordered everyone to "conduct yourselves like Her Majesty's Constabulary, regardless." He was already in a bad mood, and Connie felt from his tone that the recent spike in violent crime and murders was somehow her fault.

When the rat made a break for it along the wall behind the desk, Connie pounced, dropping to her knees and slamming down the textbook. A mocking squeak signalled Connie's failure. The rat disappeared behind a filing cabinet, and a knock came at the door. She blew a lock of hair from her face as she stood up still brandishing the textbook. One of her detectives, Kenny Strachan, poked his head round the door.

"Boss?"

"Rat."

Kenny nodded. He was one of Connie's younger detectives, slim, black hair and relatively unassuming. He'd made the rank last year. Time on his side and bright, he could go far.

"What is it, Kenny?"

"First, the Super wants to see you with HR about DI Blair's disciplinary meeting."

"And second?"

Kenny spotted the rat sneaking out from behind the cabinet, tipping off Connie to its whereabouts. "I did the background digging on those academics you were interested in."

Connie crept around the back of her desk, edging along the filing cabinet, brandishing the full weight of postmodern theory. She indicated for Kenny to continue.

"Nothing much on Hamill. There are rumours he was in a relationship with Portia Harrington-Wright. Also, a rumour he had an affair with Hassan."

Connie sprang, throwing postmodern legal theory with all her might at the rat. The animal darted from its spot against the wall and ran for the door. Kenny jumped with revulsion as the rat scurried over his polished black shoes and out into the corridor. The cover lay ripped from Connie's textbook. She examined it before dropping the cover and its verbose pages in the bin, theory not matching up to the test of practice.

"Rumour? What kind of rumour?"

"Seems pretty solid. A couple of their colleagues mentioned it. It was a while ago, but..." He left the conjunction hanging.

"Anything else?"

"Yeah. Professor Hassan has recently come back to work after a long period of absence."

"How long?"

"A year."

Connie raised her eyebrows questioningly.

"Family tragedy. A boating accident. Didn't handle it well." Kenny handed over a printout of his report.

"Is that something you're supposed to handle well?"

"Suppose not, boss. Although the word 'breakdown' came up a few times."

"We got all this from rumours?"

"Of course, boss. People love a good rumour."

"They certainly do. And what do you think about those rumours?"

Kenny gave a little non-committal sideways twitch of his nose, as if rumours were foods one could never quite trust smell of. "Might be a motive in there. Love triangle? Hamill's alibi checks out. But maybe a younger model moved in on Hassan's turf? I spoke with Tony Jackson, working the Harrington-Wright case. He and I used to do the beat together."

"I met him at the scene," Connie said.

Kenny nodded. "He says there's no physical evidence of Hamill or Hassan performing the attack. The knife is clean of their DNA and prints. But Hassan, well, she's got two major problems. The first is she knows more than enough to clean a crime scene, far more than Hamill as I understand things. How did their colleagues put it? Ah yes. Professor Hamill is not much of an applied archaeologist. That's not a compliment, as I understand it."

"And Hassan's second problem?" Connie prompted.

"It seems..."

A scream interrupted Kenny. He ducked out into the corridor. Connie got up from perching on the front of her desk.

"Boss." Kenny called back through the open door. "It's kicking off in one of the interview rooms."

Connie ran out after Kenny, the sounds of a struggle drawing them. DI Blair, the archaeologists, and the growing list of ongoing murder investigations in the city would have to wait their turn.

13

IT WAS ONLY nine thirty in the morning and people were already in the Hunterian Museum to see the body of the boy. The university had set up a cordon of red, which only added to the impression they were part of a circus show. David played the ringmaster, dressed in a white lab coat over his herringbone shirt and silver cufflinks.

Despite it all, Portia occupied Mirin's thoughts. Portia was, or had been, bright, good at her job, enjoyable to work with and teach. She was, or had been, full of life. But now she seemed to have wasted away physically and emotionally. Mirin felt a duty of care towards her, not just as her former PhD supervisor, but as someone who had insight into the effects of a traumatic event.

Camera phones flashed, distracting Mirin from her thoughts.

Occasionally a guard would come over and ask people not to use their flashes.

This was Mirin's first chance to work on the boy again since they moved him to the Hunterian after Portia's attack. They would most likely be allowed back in their lab in the Gregory Building again later in the week, but looking at David enjoying himself, Mirin suspected they would be here for much longer than that.

Mirin was occupied with checking the equipment, which she knew annoyed David. It wasn't that she didn't trust him - he had a lot at stake after all - but Mirin knew where David's talents lay, and they weren't in the technical and practical aspects of biology and biochemistry.

The crowd of people were becoming restless to see the boy, for the moment still encased in his steel sarcophagus. David was placating bystanders with selfie-pictures on mobile phones and telling them what they knew about the boy so far. He'd taken to calling him the 'wee man' as of this morning. Mirin had shrugged it off, mentally conceding that the boy would need a moniker at some point, at least for the media. Mirin was trying her best to avoid Lucy Walker and her whole film crew. They'd set up fixed cameras. One camera roamed free with a sound guy, and the whole investigating team had to wear lapel microphones.

Chin didn't like the limelight either. He was even more withdrawn and quiet than usual, if that was possible. Keeping his eyes cast down, he ran through a chemical spectral analysis of samples on a computer terminal. Mirin called him over to help with opening the boy's storage unit. They were in position when David pushed in, clasping Chin firmly on the shoulder.

"It's okay, Chin. I'll help Professor Hassan with this." David let his voice carry for the benefit of the crowd and Chin shuffled back to his computer without a word. "Shall we give them the big reveal, Professor Hassan?"

Mirin suppressed a sigh.

The metal clasps released with a satisfying *clunk*. The seal around the lid of the enormous steel case sucked briefly as they pulled up, and then it gave with a gentle hiss, mechanically-assisted hinges opening in a yawn. David looked down at their prized artefact with a satisfied smirk. However, the same look was not on Mirin's face. Quite the opposite. Her expression first flared and then hardened to a scowl, knitting her eyebrows.

Still aware of their audience, David said under his breath, "What is it?"

Mirin couldn't believe it. Of course, they still didn't know for sure that the boy was as special as they thought he might be, but this... this was cavalier to say the least.

"His body has been moved," she said coldly.

"Impossible." David shifted, examining the boy.

The crowd of people bustled, trying to hear what was being said, craning their necks to see what the bog body from the news looked like in the flesh. David saw Lucy Walker wave to one of her cameramen to get in a better position.

"I am not mistaken." Mirin's tone was firm, barely concealing her fury. "He's not in the same position. *Look!*" She pointed with a latex-gloved hand. "He has been moved more to his back and the separated hand has been shifted closer to the arm."

David looked more closely. "I..." He hesitated, unsure, his fingers lightly resting on the edge of the steel case. "Well, this is unfortunate. He doesn't appear to be damaged."

The muscles in Mirin's jaw clenched. "Unfortunate" was not the word she would have chosen: careless, unprofessional, irresponsible... But David was moving on.

"On a positive note, we can now see more clearly the proto-writing ideographs. Which is fortuitous considering Jennifer is joining us today. Ah, speak of the devil." David gestured over the heads of some of the assembled onlookers, down the hall of the museum's vaulted hall. "Professor Mordaunt, please join us. Your timing is perfect."

Jennifer Mordaunt was a big woman, nearly six feet tall and broad of hip and shoulder. She wore a beige Pringle sweater and ivory silk blouse. Mirin had known Jennifer since her undergraduate days, when taking the professor's comparative philology classes, studying the writing systems of antiquity and older, such as the early symbolic systems from which it was thought the more complex writing systems of Babylonia, Egypt, and China had developed. Jennifer looked awkward, walking with a shuffling gait. She was not used to having so many eyes on her, unless she was in the comfort zone of a lecture hall. Even then, she would make little eye contact with her students. Public attention wasn't something she sought, or evidently expected to see today.

"Let the professor through," David said, cheerfully returning to his role as ringmaster. The crowd parted and, head down, Jennifer

Mordaunt passed through, a security guard unhooking one of the velvet ropes for her. "Wonderful to see you, Professor Mordaunt." Jennifer did not look at David. She walked up to Mirin and offered her hand. Mirin shook it. It was gentle, despite her size, and soft with her index and middle finger stained yellow.

"Hello, Mirin." Jennifer began to cough, a rasping, phlegmy sound. "How are you?"

Mirin was still angry, but Jennifer had taken time out of her day. She was a senior academic, a leader in her field, someone who'd built a life out of studying esoteric dead languages; she was little interested in anything else. Those facts were calming and reassuring. Jennifer was a professional and Mirin could work with that. "I'm well. Thank you for taking…"

"You said the body had indications of proto-writing?" Professor Mordaunt asked, eyes already glued to the tattooed symbols.

"Yes," said David, inserting himself into the conversation. "It appears quite remar…"

Jennifer turned her back to David, addressing Mirin. "Have you dated the specimen yet?"

"Our research fellow, Dr Chin Zhau, is waiting for carbon-14 results." Mirin indicated Chin working at the computer terminal, his posture as uncomfortable as the old philology professor.

Jennifer leaned over the body of the boy, pushing her glasses up her nose and squinting, turning her head to read at the correct angle. Mirin handed her a face mask. Jennifer held it over her mouth and leant closer. Slowly, she inspected the various tattooed markings decorating the boy's body. "Jiahu," she whispered to herself.

David couldn't hear. "What was that, Professor?"

"Like the Tărtăria here, but similar to the Dispilio Tablet here. Elements of Vinča." Jennifer fell silent. The crowds were still straining to see. Mirin waited patiently, not wanting to rush her colleague and former teacher. Finally, the elderly professor straightened up. "What are your thoughts, Mirin?"

"We are thinking these are…." Jennifer held up a hand, stopping David. David closed his mouth and then blushed before adopting the posture of someone listening intently. The man should have been an am-dram star.

"Portia, our research student, had compared them to various proto-writing systems. But..." Mirin trailed off.

"But?" Jennifer looked expectantly at Mirin.

"She was the student who got hurt," David answered from behind.

"Hurt?" Jennifer shook her head. "Violently assaulted. Words matter, Professor Hamill. We should use them accurately. So?"

Mirin continued, while David tried to hide gritting his teeth. "Portia noted there were some similarities between them but also differences."

Jennifer looked pleased with her former pupil's answer. "Your student was right, in part. There are similarities but more than that..." Lucy Walker was anxiously hissing in her soundman's ear, asking if he was getting any of what she was saying. The professor went on: "There are similarities between the fragments we know of: the Vinča and Jiahu symbols, and the examples we have from the Tărtăria and Dispilio Tablets. However, 'similarities' may not quite be the correct word. It doesn't quite carry the exact meaning. It is not that these different symbols from different parts of the Neolithic world share similarities with what you have here. This is no piecemeal script, cobbled together from combining other sets of symbols. No. Instead, it looks to be, although I'd need to study it in more detail, a unique and coherent system, with more symbols than any scripts we currently know. The differences between the other known symbolic systems, orthographically speaking, are blended out. This might suggest this specimen exhibits a cognate system of symbols from which the others were derived. And therefore?" She left the possibility hanging for her former student.

Mirin thought, pinching her brow at the implications. "And therefore they *do* have a relationship with it." The professor gave Mirin a satisfied look, raising her eyebrows, expecting a more comprehensive conclusion. "It's older..." Mirin said, "and more complete."

"It would appear so..." Professor Mordaunt began.

"This is wonderful," David said, clapping his hands. He turned to the crowd again. "Once again, the Wee Man has provided..."

"*But*..." Professor Mordaunt raised her voice uncharacteristically, silencing David. "...but it will take a lot of additional patient, *scholarly* work before we go off half-cocked and make fools of ourselves. Would you send me detailed photographs when you can? I assume you'd like me to work on this?"

"Of course, Professor," Mirin said. "And thank you."

14

Mɪʀɪɴ sᴀᴛ with Oran in a cafe on Byres Road, in the heart of the city's West End, at the edge of the university campus. School and work were over, and so Oran drew while she drank her coffee. His doodling was something she never would have let him do a year ago, work being too important. Now she looked at him in a daze of wonder, at this life growing in front of her. Mirin had never had a great relationship with her own family and still barely spoke to them now. They came to Omar's funeral, but she had pushed them away and they hadn't resisted. It wasn't that they didn't love her or she them, but there had always been a distance in their home, an emphasis on professional life and school. "You are all too English," Omar used to tease her. "So polite, yet so alone."

Mirin was thinking this, sipping her coffee, when two things happened.

Firstly, the police constable Hardeep Bhaskar walked into the coffeehouse. He still looked terrible, drawn and even more tired. Mirin didn't call his attention. However, once he had picked up a coffee, he saw them on his way out. He had that policeman's way about him, in that he wasn't afraid of introducing himself to people. Dip asked how she was and whether she had thought about what he'd said.

Mirin didn't want to say. Yes, she had thought about how random events often congregate and humans tend to look for patterns and that that was probably an evolutionary response to the randomness of the natural world. But as Mirin considered this, faced with the dishevelled man, another thought surfaced.

A black blade, glinting dully.

The knife: she *still* couldn't explain how Dip had known about it. True, now it was in police custody as part of the investigation into Portia's attack, where someone with Dip's contacts could easily access it, but that wasn't the case when he first told her about it.

"I'm still thinking," she said. She thought about asking him to join her. There was a silence between them.

"Look," he said, "I'm still staying at my parents' while I'm in town."

"The Shish Mahal, on Park Road, isn't it? I love that place. My husband and I used to go there all the time."

"Well, then maybe time for you two to revisit it?"

Mirin's face saddened a little. She was used to this now, or at least familiar with it. Uncomfortably she said, "I'm afraid he passed last year."

"I'm sorry to hear that."

"It's okay." It wasn't okay, but that's what Mirin always said. There was a script she followed. Sticking to the script was important. Deviation could lead to... she knew where. She and Oran were making a new start. They didn't need to dwell there any more. "It's hard and life goes on."

"That it does." Dip smiled softly, not showing any of the discomfort Mirin felt. "Well, I'll leave you to your day. Here's my number. If you want to chat or hear what else I have to say, call me."

Dip pulled on a woollen glove; the weather had turned cold again. He was about to leave when the second strange thing happened: a murder of crows landed outside, surrounding a solitary pigeon. They perched on the cars tightly packed along the road. Dip stopped at the door. He and Mirin were watching the same thing.

The pigeon tried to take off and one of the crows from a car intercepted its take- off, knocking the pigeon back to the ground. That crow returned to its perch. Another crow shrieked and cawed, landing on the pigeon with its talons, pinning it to the ground. The crow then stabbed its long grey beak into the pigeon. The grey bird struggled, flapping its wings uselessly. This provoked a frenzied attack from the crow. The more the pigeon struggled the more the crow stabbed its beak down. Red stained the grey feathers. Scarlet flesh was exposed to the air, and still the crow attacked. Its murderous cohort called in excitement, hopping and flexing their wings. Three more crows joined the assault. Between them, they tore the pigeon apart, severing the head, pulling off wings, opening the belly and snapping at the organs. The whole attack took less than a minute. Only feathers and red streaks were left when the crows flew off carrying what was left of the carcass.

Mirin found herself squeezing her coffee cup. Her other hand had instinctively reached for the back of Oran's chair, protecting the child, who sat drawing obliviously. She turned to Dip not knowing what she would say. Dip's face was impassive, as if he had observed nothing out of the ordinary. He opened the door and walked into the street. He looked briefly at the red on the pavement, took a swig of his coffee, and walked out of sight.

15

AFTER THE COFFEE SHOP, Mirin and Oran found their way home. She bathed him. They ate dinner together and curled up to watch some programmes on her iPad. All the while she had been distracted. During her night's sleep the image of the knife lingered, as did the horror on Portia's face and her awful physical condition. Mirin had suspected Portia and David might be having an affair, which was completely against university regulations, but David had shown little interest in the poor girl since the attack. Then there was how the constable had known about the knife. The attack across the street from her department. The unusual weather. The last hailstorm had killed one poor boy, a student at the university too, and injured many others. However, the weather had returned to the normal *dreich* Glaswegian offering in under twenty-four hours. Such events weren't outside the realms of possibility but pulling them all together, was that a flight of fancy? Mirin couldn't tell. Another thing gnawed at her as she put Oran to bed, tucking him in and kissing his forehead.

Mirin thought about it all night, and it occupied her thoughts as they readied themselves for work and school. The boy, the Wee Man as David had now named him, had been moved. David denied responsibility and vehemently claimed the boy had been in his original position when he checked and shut him away for the night.

There had been a problem with the power the night before in the university and there were faults with the security cameras, not only in the Hunterian Museum, but throughout the building. In fact, it seemed to have affected several circuits from the back of the quad in the main building all the way up to the Hunterian. Was the body of the boy a common denominator or a mere coincidence? How many other objects or people could be put in association with these events that they weren't aware of? Probably many. Correlation does not equal causation, let alone that it would imply something preternatural, beyond the realms of possibility and into the lands of fantasy.

Lastly, there was the boy's amazing state of preservation. Apart from the severed hand (but without the digger he would never have been found), his body was an exquisite specimen. There were other examples of well-preserved bog bodies, of course. But most were damaged or partial specimens in some way. The Tollund Man was perhaps the best example of a complete specimen. He, like the boy, looked as though he was sleeping peacefully, but gruesome injuries, not least the ligature around his neck, told another story.

Today they were X-raying the boy's body. David's influence had once again paid off and he'd arranged for a mobile X-ray unit delivered to the Hunterian Museum. None of this was cost-effective, but the university powers that be didn't seem to mind. Far from it. David was using his expertise at garnering media and public attention. It would probably mean further grants and increased student numbers, a raising of the profile of the university worldwide. Mirin knew that David was fielding media calls from all over the world: China, America, India, Russia, Brazil, and many more. The university head even transferred the vice chancellor's personal assistant to aid David with the additional communication obligations.

All these things played on Mirin's mind on her walk to work. She was so distracted she even turned up at the Gregory Building at first out of habit, and then realised she wasn't working there right now, turned heel and headed for the main building.

It was still difficult to get used to working in such an open space, let alone one filled with so many bystanders watching them as they worked, a film crew recording everything they were doing, and Lucy

Walker asking for interviews with David and occasionally the other members of the team.

Chin was already setting up the X-ray with the help of a technician from the Medical Faculty, when Mirin, putting on her white coat, joined the team. Today they would get their first look at the internal structures of the boy. They had an MRI scan lined up, but the X-ray was the first tool in their exploration of what lay beneath the tattooed skin on their sacrificed boy.

Chin and the technician took the pictures, sliding the machine down the body and then from the side. The results would be in relatively quickly, one of the advantages of X-rays. Moving the machine out of the way, David and Mirin returned to the body. She wanted to take a look at the wound on the boy's throat and required David's help. She didn't notice Lucy Walker and a cameraman paying particular attention. The constant presence of the camera crew had become a familiar thing, and like an annoying noise or a bad smell, they had drifted into the background.

David helped gently lift the boy's chin. "It's a very clean cut," he said.

"Flint blades can be as sharp as a modern surgical scalpel," Mirin said.

"Why do such a thing to a young boy?"

It was a very good question. "Sacrifice is certainly a possibility," Mirin said in a low voice. "Ritual killings are common in the bog bodies of Europe. Not so in the North American examples."

"But of children? I'm right in thinking that is much less common?"

"It is unusual." Mirin measured the injury. The words prompted something in her. It stumbled out, like a confession. "I bumped into Constable Hardeep Bhaskar the other day."

"The unhinged policeman from the nature reserve?" David said quizzically.

"He came to talk to me after Portia was... Actually, he phoned me first, after the student attacks on campus. And then I bumped into him again by accident in a coffee shop yesterday."

"I'm surprised he's not sectioned with that kind of erratic behaviour," David said.

Mirin couldn't decide whether the look of concern on his face was for her or the constable. "Erratic behaviour often has its own internal logic. He has a theory."

"A theory about our Wee Man?"

Mirin took a deep breath. "Have you thought about all the strange things that have been happening? The highly unusual weather. The deaths and violent attacks on campus. Electrical faults in the building the other night, the same night that the body appears to have moved. And you yourself said that you locked the storage unit and he was as we had left him. The news is full of stories of murders and assaults."

"Mirin, what are you getting at? You don't think..."

"I'm laying out the facts." She leaned in closer. "Constable Bhaskar suggested to me that it was connected with *the boy*."

"You mean somebody is trying to obtain our artefact for their own benefit?"

"No, he meant the boy *himself*, that the boy is exerting some..." God, was she really going to say this? "...influence."

The worry evaporated from David's face, and he laughed. "Oh, very good," he said, bringing himself under control. "The constable is in a more worrying mental state than I first thought."

Mirin wasn't laughing along.

"You're not taking him seriously, are you?" David asked.

Mirin hesitated.

Unlike Mirin, David always knew when he was on camera and when he was in public. He lowered his voice somewhat. "Are you okay, Professor Hassan? This has all been very stressful." He indicated the circus around them. "It's a lot of pressure, a lot of responsibility with a find as potentially important is this. And you've recently returned to work."

"I didn't say I *believed* him. I'm fine. This is my area of specialism. I was merely..." Mirin didn't know what she was really saying. Was she starting to believe the constable?

No. She didn't need to give David any reason to take this away from her. She needed this, to be back at work, to be doing something important. It was good for her. Mirin couldn't just shut herself away in her flat again.

David waited for an answer.

"I thought I'd let you know what he was saying," Mirin said a little weakly.

"Mirin," David began, hand on her shoulder, and lowering his voice even further to a whisper. "I'm saying this to you as a friend. You don't need someone like that in your life right now. And we..." David opened his hands, indicating the significance of everything around them, "...certainly don't need such..." He was clearly searching for the right way to say it. "...unstable thinking. Stay with the facts. Especially with all this attention on us."

"You're right. I was just thinking aloud," Mirin said and turned her attention back to the wound in the boy's throat.

16

Every day felt better than the last, until today. Today, Eddie felt perfect.

He saw it all so clearly now. The world and his place in it made sense at last. His whole life he realised he'd lacked meaning. He'd been directionless and without purpose. But that had all changed.

Eddie had been a busy boy, and it was all coming together. Learning, which had been something of a mystery to him in the past, now came easily. The words didn't move on the page when he tried to read them any more, and one idea led to another and another smoothly and pleasurably.

Using a VPN and an onion browser to maintain his digital anonymity, Eddie had gathered what he needed from the dark web. He'd experimented a little with it before: a friend had shown him how. He'd used it mostly for buying weed, some Nazi memorabilia, and the kind of pornography too hard to make it onto the ubiquitous free sites. Now, he was going far beyond that.

The little knowledge he'd had became a springboard for rapid evolution. He pulled the information together from chatrooms, threads, and a little experimentation of his own, until acquiring the things he needed was child's play. The job was completed with the occasional trip to a hardware store - using Annie's cards, of course. He was careful never to buy things from the same place. That might raise some red flags, and Eddie didn't want that. He didn't want anything to spoil the surprise.

He sat on Annie's bed in only his jeans looking at a laptop. Annie lay naked beside him. What a time they'd had. They'd been inseparable. It was funny: Eddie had desired Annie so much before, but after the initial honeymoon of a couple of days, he realised he was just using her. Not that it bothered him. It hadn't stopped Eddie wanting to have sex with her, even though Annie had let herself go in the short time since they got together, a matter of only a few days. But the sex was good, really good. Not that it was passionate or loving. Rather, Annie let him do whatever he wanted to. Occasionally, Eddie thought that Annie's consent hadn't been particularly explicit, especially for the rougher stuff. But then again, she had never complained and never said no. In fact, she hadn't said a word, not ever. Eddie liked Annie that way.

After their first day together, Eddie decided they better move to Annie's place. He had plans and having access to Annie's flat and an internet address that wasn't associated with him would be very useful. Annie hadn't complained. She walked silently, not shrugging off the arm he put round her. She didn't even complain when he felt her up on the underground in front of everyone. He'd grabbed her crotch and idly played with her breasts. Annie stared glass-eyed out of the carriage window across the aisle. Eddie grinned his gap-toothed smile and people looked away, tutting. A mother turned her child's head away, covering their eyes. Eddie knew what they would do. Nothing. Pathetic, self-righteous scumbags.

Once ensconced in her flat, Annie never went out again. She remained silent, lying in bed or on the sofa, unless Eddie made her move. That suited him. He made an excuse for her at work and came and went as he pleased. Eddie went through all Annie's things. He relished exploring the strange secrets of her feminine world, particularly enjoying the underwear drawer, making Annie put on the nicest of it, before he'd rip it or cut it off her with one of his knives. He was a puppet master, living out a lifetime of fantasies in different rooms of the flat, each time seeing how far he could push things. And he found he could push things very far.

Eventually, Eddie found a diary and read it. He'd been mentioned, not in any favourable way, and punished her for that the next time they made love. The bruises on her neck and buttocks were a dark purple as a consequence.

Annie Browne's credit cards proved extremely useful for other things as well. Eddie treated himself to a new Glasgow Rangers football top, a pair of trainers, and some aftershave, which had become more important in the last day or so.

Eddie stretched out, yawning away the effects of the glowing screen and closed the lid of Annie's laptop. He really did feel tremendous. The only thing that had been a little odd were his dreams. They were filled with images and experiences he couldn't understand, even with his newfound intellect. However, Eddie had always liked horror movies, and his dreams played like the worst, or rather the best, slasher movies. The death and carnage were of biblical proportions, fuelling his own ideas. Swathes of people set against each other, killing in the most brutal ways. Plagues and pestilence ravaging ancient lands. The ineffectual building of huge stone monuments. The felling of great forests, which grew into endless fields of bowing yellow grasses watered by showers of blood, until the grasses drowned in pools of red when the crops became battlefields. So many crows feasted on the dead that when they took flight, they blotted out the sun, casting a shadow which swept across the land, a shadow in the shape of the monster, a monster in the shape of a boy, with curls of silken black hair, nut-brown skin covered with markings, and eyes into which Eddie fell.

Eddie loved the boy. Not in a gay, paedo way. Like a brother or a father. Not Eddie's father. He had been the king of all *jakie* scumbags. More like the father he'd wished he had when he was a little boy, crying with a black eye and a broken wrist. This was a little surprising for Eddie, on account of the boy being foreign. He looked like a Muslim or something. From that part of the world anyway, the

Middle East or somewhere. Anyway, they were only dreams. Whenever he woke, Eddie felt better than the day before. Then each day the idea of what he wanted to do became clearer. Like with the vengeful boy in his dreams, reaping death and destruction wherever he went, there was some payback coming people's way.

Eddie got up from the bed, looking down at Annie lying motionless, her blank eyes staring at the ceiling. A bite mark on her cheek was red and granulated against the white, drawn skin of her face. He thought maybe they could do it again, for old times' sake, even though she looked like death. Her fake breasts had become somewhat preposterous now that she'd lost so much weight. Ribs and pelvis bones showed through her thin skin like a concentration camp victim. Her face had become incredibly skeletal-looking. Her hair was greasy and unwashed. And the smell: she was more than a little ripe, hence the need for aftershave. But there was no point telling her to wash any more.

Eddie put on his uniform. He had to get going for a shift at his second job, a cleaner at Ibrox football stadium for Rangers FC. They had a big game coming up with the local city rivals Celtic. And the Old Firm game was part of Eddie's plan. All those people trapped together in an enclosed space, sitting across from each other with natural hostility. He packed some of the things he needed into his holdall. The other stuff would be arriving soon by post to his own flat.

Before he left, Eddie thought he'd better leave things with Annie in a way that wouldn't mess with the future. He rounded the other side of the bed, her vacant eyes looking up at him. He shrugged off his erection, and then flicked open a large storage bag he'd bought from IKEA. Placing it on the floor next to the bed, he picked Annie up. She had already begun to stiffen. He folded her a little bit at the hips and knees, rigor mortis in the early stages, and dropped her corpse into the storage bag. With a bit of effort Eddie manoeuvred Annie's limbs so that she lay on her side, balled up. Then he stripped the bed of the blood and faeces-stained sheets, stuffing them around her. Finally, he opened two boxes of washing powder and, with one in each hand, showered the contents over Annie's body. Zipping shut the bag, Eddie gave a small grunt of effort, lifting it into the bottom of Annie's wardrobe. Then he made a cup of tea in a thermos flask from one of the kitchen cupboards and left for work, locking Annie's flat door behind him and posting the keys through the letterbox.

17

A HARD FROST crystallised on everything in the clear evening, covering the city in a film of sparkling white crystals, shimmering like stars. Professor Jennifer Mordaunt lingered for a moment on the steps of her department at number twelve University Gardens. Lighting her fifteenth cigarette of the day, she dragged deeply.

She had never felt this excited at any point during her career, and it spanned nearly forty years. She thought ruefully how something so tremendous could come along right at the end of one's career, right before she was due to retire. But retirement for academics like her was an opportunity to finish things that had been put on hold, since the weight of administration and faculty meetings had left little to no time for anything else. She had made some not insignificant contributions to her field, however. But every academic dreamed of making that one stellar discovery. Something that would leave their star forever in the academic firmament.

Jennifer blew clouds of smoke into the night. They billowed spectral white, evaporating into the orange-hued blackness of the streetlights, like spirits dissolving into the world lying just beneath what they could perceive. The past was like that spiritual world, always there beneath the layers.

Mirin, a very talented pupil in Jennifer's estimation, had sent over the photographs and they were more than she had hoped.

With each inhale of her cigarette, she let her mind wander in the swirl of the exciting discovery. Mirin was a part of those thoughts. It was so sad what had happened to her former student. She had attended the funeral and wondered how someone came back from something like that.

Jennifer had never had any family herself, no husband nor children. She had a mother still hanging on at ninety-three in a Lanarkshire care home. Jennifer tried to go and see her at least twice a week. However, tonight Jennifer had stayed late. For once, it wasn't to get through some committee paperwork but to work on the most amazing discovery of her career.

She had printed out the photographs and laid them over the large table in the office she used for seminars with small groups of undergraduates. Around the edges of the table, she had arranged images of the known proto-writing scripts from the Neolithic era. There were very few examples, and they were geographically and chronologically separated, often by thousands of miles and several millennia.

History is often attributed to the dawn of writing, when ideas and stories became fixed in a written record, but that was not the case as far as Jennifer was concerned. Writing began much earlier than the alphabet. All the complex ideographic writing that preceded it was generally thought to have grown out of basic symbolic systems that worked like mnemonic memory devices for largely illiterate cultures. However, what Mirin had provided Jennifer would turn that completely on its head. It would push back the origins of writing; how far, she did not yet know. What's more, the tattoos on the boy's flesh appeared to be a comprehensive script, with all the internal structural markers of a functional writing system, not mere mnemonics. A foundational script from which all the other fragments may have originated. All this, Jennifer felt confident of already. But there was *another* potential insight.

She hadn't mentioned it to the others, partly because she wasn't confident of it yet. But with modern computational linguistics, allied with some of the similarities found in the new script with symbols in

Ancient Sumerian and even Egyptian hieroglyphs, Jennifer held out hope for a partial or perhaps even full *translation*. This would shed unprecedented light into prehistory. At the very least, it would likely say something of the boy's culture and the beliefs of his people. Perhaps it would give a clue as to why he was so brutally killed. The archaeologists would disagree. They tended to downplay textual evidence. *We all have our epistemological biases, not least myself,* she thought wryly.

A crow cawed as Jennifer stubbed out her cigarette in one of the steel ashtrays at the top of the departmental steps. She walked down the steps. Another crow cawed, this one sitting on the bonnet of a car.

"Don't look at me like that, Mr Crow," she said, amused.

Three others appeared on the wall to her left. She walked through the carpark and another crow landed on the pavement in front of her. Then another on the roof of a car behind.

Jennifer turned her collar up against the cold and walked on, expecting the crow on her path to fly off when she approached. It did not. Instead, it hopped back a yard, staying in front of her. Another fluttered down to join it.

More crows cawed from the guttering on the second storey of one of the terraced townhouses lining University Gardens. They looked like dozens of gargoyles, leering from the ramparts. Jennifer didn't scare easily, but she couldn't help but feel *hemmed in.* More hunched black figures joined the group, surrounding her.

"Shoo!" The old professor kicked at the nearest crow with her flat leather pump. The crow pecked at her foot. Jennifer took a sharp intake of breath at the pain. The crow opened its grey beak, screaming. Jennifer looked around, searching for an exit, between the cars, back up the other way, even through the bushes. With arthritis in both knees and a hip that needed replacing, she hadn't run in years. The crows were everywhere, stretching out their wings, hopping on their gnarled claws, their talons scratching the roofs of the cars.

The cold air caught in Jennifer's throat. She turned, nearly tripping over the crows at her heels. She cried out as they began to peck at the puffy flesh of her ankles. The professor staggered with pain and felt the blow of something weighty land on her shoulder. Then hard, stabbing points ripped into her coat.

She turned her head only to see a faint glint of orange in two black pearls, set into a feathered head. Its beak gave the impression of a knife being unsheathed in the moonlight. The grey blade stabbed towards Jennifer's eye. She flinched. A gash opened up in her wrinkled cheek. Her cry came out as a whimper. She brought her hands up to protect her face.

Excited cries rose into the night as a murder of crows descended on the professor. Jennifer screamed and writhed as they tore through her clothing and then her flesh.

As her screams filled the darkness, they became a language of their own, one the crows knew so well.

18

IT HAD BECOME ALMOST ROUTINE. Mirin would hear the shuffling in the lightness of her sleep. Little feet padding across the floorboards of their apartment. Then her bedroom door would open, followed by the few steps to cross the short distance to the bed. She would feel the weight of him climb up on the mattress tentatively, before hurrying to get under the covers beside her. Mirin would open her eyes to Oran's beautiful face inches from hers. The smoothness of his skin. The fullness of his cheeks. Large almond-shaped eyes like his father's. The same hair too: dark, abundant curls hanging loosely across his smooth forehead and full, childish cheeks.

Tenderly, Mirin moved the locks from his face, tucking them behind his ear.

"What is it, my love?" she whispered.

"Bad dream."

"About Daddy?"

"No, Mummy. That would be a good dream. There were frogs."

"Frogs? That doesn't sound like a scary dream. Ribbit," Mirin said, making her hand into a speaking frog's head that then tried to tickle him under the armpit.

Oran closed his eyes, pulling the duvet around him. "They were falling from the sky, and people were being horrible to each other."

"Because of the frogs?" Mirin said lightly, giving up on the game and resting her hand on his back. She had felt an uneasiness since her meeting with Constable Bhaskar in the coffee shop. Or maybe it had started before that? Maybe what happened to Portia had made them all a little uneasy.

"No, not because of the frogs. Because of the boy," Oran said, yawning, already closing his eyes.

The hairs on the back of Mirin's neck stood on end, a cold wave prickling across her skin, a lurching feeling dropping her stomach.

"It was only a dream," she told him, but it felt thin and weak.

Oran burrowed down beneath the covers.

A wet thud hit the sash window of the bedroom, and then another, like corn beginning to pop in the microwave.

Oran covered his ears, closing his eyes as tightly as he possibly could. A pane of glass in the bedroom window cracked. Mirin sat upright in bed. The thuds were coming quicker, hitting windows, walls, pavement and road. Alarms wailed from parked cars, amber flashes from the hazard lights strobing through the drawn curtains.

Mirin rushed to the window and pulled back the curtain wide with a sharp tug. She was not alone. All along the street people had got out of bed, some turning on their lights, framing them in their windows. Like her, they looked into the street or up into the sky with disbelief, trying to understand how what they were seeing was possible. Still the wet thudding continued, growing more ferocious, coming on faster and more aggressively.

Another impact made Mirin's bedroom window shake. The crack in the glass grew into a jagged line running down the length of a pane, followed by a streak of blood oozing from the body of a small frog.

They fell relentlessly, of all different sizes. Many died on impact, organs spilling from their soft bellies. Some survived, dazed. Mirin could see them hopping around in the street, on top of cars and window ledges.

A large toad, its back dark green and covered in rough nubs, struck Mirin's windowsill. It rolled, dazed and dying, a tear on its underbelly spewing something white and pink. On broken legs, it pushed forward weakly, finding little purchase on the stone sill slick with its own blood. Mirin stood in perplexed horror, eyes fixed on the toad. It reached the glass. One webbed limb slapped against the pane, as if beseeching her. Its dark eyes reflected only bewilderment back at Mirin; Oran whimpered behind her.

Mirin retreated from the fractured view of the window, and the impossible amphibian rain. She fled to the bed and gathered up her son, rocking him, while they waited to wake up, because this must be a dream.

All of this must just be a bad dream.

19

THE CROWS GORGED on the bodies of the frogs and toads. Their huge beaks tore at the flesh, stretching it until it tore.

DCI Connie Shepherd watched the myriad of hunchbacked forms glut themselves, their harsh cries grating against her ears.

A young female constable stood close by. A white tent covered the place where the body of Professor Jennifer Mordaunt had lain.

"What shall we do about them?" the young constable asked, eyeing the birds nervously.

Connie looked across the road to where the other double homicide had taken place not a few weeks ago. A little further down led them to where the assault of Portia Harrington-Wright had taken place. *Killer crows and a rain of frogs. Jesus.*

"I've got a feeling we should arrest them," Connie replied. The young constable clearly couldn't tell if her senior officer was being serious or not.

The security guard, Tommy Popper, had worked here too. *That's a lot of coincidences,* Connie thought to herself. *And all of it centres here. But is that really the thing tying it all together, or is it something deeper?* Of course, it might not tie together at all. In a weird way, that would scare her more.

Raining frogs, murdering crows, a plague of insects, rat infestations, gales, hailstones, winter heat waves. And behind it all a city-wide murder spike, with its epicentre here at the university.

"It's so sad. She only had a mother at an old people's home. What a way to go." The young constable broke Connie's fanciful line of thinking. The constable had been there since the middle of the night. She and her partner were the first to the scene. Connie was playing catch-up, which was an all too familiar state of mind at the moment.

"Remind me, what's your name?" Connie asked.

"Debbie. Debbie Stewart, ma'am."

"Do you know why the professor was working late, Debbie?"

"I think so, ma'am. I can show you." The young constable opened the front door.

The department had a dark ground floor, oak panelling, with graceful pre-Raphaelite figures carved into the architraves of the doorways. An ostentatious and redundant fireplace dominated the reception hall with a huge notice board hung above it.

The constable led Connie up the staircase. A glass roof above them flooded the stairwell with light. They climbed up creaking steps through two floors, each with numerous large dark-oak doors facing the landing. Professor Mordaunt's name plate signalled her office, along with a laminated sign, presumably for the benefit of under-graduates, which read 'Please knock.' There didn't seem any point any more, and so Constable Debbie Stewart opened the door and Connie followed her inside.

The room was large, perhaps over twentyfeet square. Two of the walls were covered from floor to ceiling with bookcases, probably added in the 1970s. The shelves were made of a utilitarian, hard-wearing plywood, varnished in a failed attempt to make them look presentable, but which only succeeded in jarring with the rest of the room, which had been crafted by the Rennie Mackintosh School of Art. Every space was jammed full of books. Along with the obscure pastel prints on the walls, an untidy desk with a computer hidden amongst piles of more books, papers, folders, pens and papers, it was pretty much as Connie imagined a profes-sor's office to be.

In the centre of the room sat a large table. It was covered in photographs and printouts with strange markings all over them. Debbie led her detective chief inspector to the table, gesturing.

"It seems the professor was working on some kind of translation connected to that bog body we keep hearing about on the news. The Wee Man? That's what they keep calling him now, I think."

The papers weren't merely strewn over the table. There was an order to them. Connie recognised the habits of a person working on a puzzle, trying to put all the pieces that didn't seem to fit together into their correct order. Around the edges lay mostly white printouts with black and white symbols on them. Some of the symbols were highlighted with circles, or connected by lines drawn in blue and red pen. There were annotations and question marks and supplementary comments next to certain symbols in the professor's handwriting.

In the centre of the table were high-resolution colour photographs of the bog body. Connie hadn't seen it with so much detail. It was so well preserved it could have been a body found at one of her crime scenes. In fact, it *had* been a body from one of her crime scenes: the coincidence of all coincidences.

Walking around the table, inspecting the papers, Connie noticed a few emails printed out and placed among the photographs and pages of symbols. A name jumped out at her, affixed with the university's gu.ac.uk: *Mirin Hassan*. Moving the papers aside with the tips of her gloved fingers, Connie read through the emails. They were short and polite messages to which the high-resolution photographs were attached, asking Professor Mordaunt to work on a possible analysis of the symbols after her initial inspection of the body.

There she was again: Mirin Hassan with a relationship to another victim. And there it was again: the problem of all those coincidences. Coincidences that kept stacking up with a common denominator.

A hard, pointed tap came at the second-floor window. Connie and the young constable both jumped. A large crow stood on the other side of the glass, hitting it with its beak. Connie frowned, as much at herself as the crow.

"It's creepy that there are so many about, isn't it, ma'am? The crows, I mean. I suppose it's the frogs that have attracted them all," Debbie said.

"It wasn't raining frogs when they attacked the professor," Connie replied, unable to stifle a high-pitched laugh.

The frogs and toads had been given an explanation on the morning news. Connie listened to the radio on the way to the scene this morning. Similar instances had occurred previously involving amphibians and fish. They got scooped up in tropical cyclones and transported great distances away from their point of origin. Then, when the weather system runs out of steam, the animals are precipitated on the land below. The journalist had talked about how some of the biblical stories may have been similar examples, translated by primitive minds into supernatural events, when in reality there were perfectly rational, scientific explanations.

Apparently, this case of raining amphibians was of particular scientific interest, given how far north in the world it occurred, Scotland not being known for its tropical weather conditions. This was then discussed in connection with the other recent unusual climatic conditions, in particular the bloom of flies following the micro heatwave they'd had and the killer hailstorm. Exactly what the origin of all the frogs and toads was, they had not yet decided. Climate change was the most likely explanation. Connie failed to see how melting polar icecaps had created hailstorms, heatwaves, and skies filled with raining amphibians, but then she was no ecologist.

"What now, ma'am?" Debbie asked as they left the department.

"You can knock off now."

"I meant about the professor, ma'am."

"It's not a murder. It's an animal control problem." Or at least, that was the rational explanation.

20

DIP'S MOTHER handed him a clean, folded towel and pushed him through the door of the bathroom, shutting it behind him. He bet she was hanging on to the handle to make sure he didn't try to leave. She knew what was best for him.

Dip turned off the taps filling the bath with hot water and carefully undressed. He had a plastic bag, inserted his hand into it and proceeded to tie electrical tape at the bottom of his cast, attempting to give it some waterproof protection.

Steam clung in gyring wisps to the surface of the bath, spectres guarding the membrane between two worlds. Dip tested the temperature with his good hand. It was hot and soothing. The water felt almost too warm as he stepped in, lowering himself slowly. The cast on his left arm made gripping the edge of the bath a precarious task. Sat in the middle, knees drawn up, Dip drew large breaths, preparing himself.

He had tried to avoid it, but the more he did, the harder it was to keep from his mind. And so, when his mother, a force of nature incarnate, began to complain that he wasn't taking care of himself, she hustled him up the stairs, already running the bath like he was eleven again. Dip had surrendered to the idea. He'd been washing in a sink for more than a week, afraid of the water, knowing its power, fearing what it might show him. His fear was born out of experience, from the visions of that first night at his cottage after the massacre. But things were getting worse: the weather, the killings, the violence. This, then, was something he must do. Dip needed to see what he knew only the water could show him. He needed to enter another world, and maybe even then it still would not be enough. What could one man do if no one believed?

Gulping down one last breath and holding his nose with his good hand, he squeezed shut his eyes.

He sank beneath the surface of the water and into another world.

The moment his head was submerged, the last of his dark hair slipping beneath the surface, Dip was falling, dissolving. He felt himself compress into a point of view rushing back through time. Countless images, sounds, smells, and sensations accelerated through his perception, as if he was carried on the crest of a tsunami. Finally, he came to a halt, and he was no longer Hardeep Bhaskar, no longer in a bath in his parents' flat above their restaurant in Glasgow. He was someone else, in another place and another time, and he would bear witness.

21

Tᴋ'ʟᴏ, Bear Paw, led his troupe through the trees, while Ts'sha sang the dreaming songline as they walked. The spring rains had stayed longer than usual this year, soaking the ground. It was no matter to Tk'lo's tribe. They moved with the herds of deer and oryx, and while the berries, nuts, and tubers they gathered were much fewer, the game turned fat on the lush grass. The rains disguised their scent when hunting, and the rivers and streams swelled, carrying all the food they could want, so that the smell of smoking fish marked their camp from miles away in a favourable breeze.

From the woodland they now walked through mushrooms burst from the ground in pockets or covering wet, rotting stumps. They would pick them on their way back. Now, they had food and hides to trade with the grass eaters and milk drinkers.

Grandfather Ulv'ts, Wolf's Tail, told Tk'lo stories that the farmers had once been part of their tribe long shadows ago. Their songs led on from his tribe's, and as a boy Tk'lo had learnt the song, giving him passage in their lands and knowledge of their tongue, their history, and their ways. Curiosity filled Tk'lo's belly in anticipation of these strange people he only remembered from childhood. His own tribe tended the fruit trees in the forest and glades, clearing out saplings, cutting down older trees no longer fruiting, and thinning the fruit on bountiful trees to ensure a better crop when they returned from their wanderings. They would always leave tubers in the ground, never taking all of them and often putting back the best ones for the future. But this was just as they would thin the herd of weak ones, as well as killing and honouring an old buck or bull no longer able to have healthy offspring.

Tk'lo's tribe tended and took what they needed, moving with the flow of the river and the winds of winter and the rutting of spring. Whatever they needed would be there when they returned, as sure as Sol'nar, the Great Fire, rose each morning, and Muk'nor chased him out of the sky each night. It had been this way ever since the Dreaming Time.

But to stay in one place, Tk'lo couldn't fathom. The milk drinkers ate few things, and their harvest could be great or awful; they remained at the mercy of the land, rather than moving with it. Two things drew Tk'lo to the village then: his curiosity to see these sickly folks and sing a song he had not sung in many long shadows, and the thought of the waterlogged ground that would not favour the grasses they cultivated. They might trade some of their tools for dried fish, venison, or oryx meat.

Even before Gn'la, Little Fox, came running back through the woods as quietly as his spirit animal, Tk'lo sensed the change. The forest's noises were only of the hunters. Those that could burrow or flee had done so. But the crows flitted across the forest canopy, their cries disturbing the air. Tk'lo had heard such confusion before, when they'd come across a full hand of horses trapped in a bog. A foal must have become stuck in the quagmire, and its mother would not leave her child, sinking deep as she stamped anxiously, trapping herself alongside her young. Only a stallion was alive when they came upon the horses, screaming as crows ate him alive.

Tk'lo's father, Tk'la, Little Bear, ran his stone blade across the horse's neck, blood flowing hotly over his hands during the singing of the horse's dreaming song - *horse, who made the wind from his swiftness and thunder with his hooves.* Now his spirit was free. The crows barely moved. Dead, alive: it did not matter to them. Their eyes blinked between the worlds of the living and the dead.

Little Fox panted, bending over with his hands on his knees.

"What is it, Gn'la?" Tk'lo asked, offering a bladder of water.

Gn'la forced himself upright, his eyes wet, and in a broken voice he said, "Their song has gone."

This made no sense. "What do you mean, Gn'la? How can their song have gone? You mean you have forgotten it, little brother. I will teach it to you again." Even this forgetting was strange but not unheard of, although usually it would be in the old folk, at the end of their days. Even they rarely forgot the songs. The songlines had always been, sung into existence at the end of the Dreaming Time by all the spirits when they awoke into the world. All the world was a song. All the world was memory.

"No!" Gn'la's voice was frustrated and angry. It was not his way. "There are no songs left there." He pointed back over his shoulder to the lands of the milk drinkers and grass eaters, which lay beyond the edge of the forest, and the water fell from his eyes.

The edge of the forest came too soon and what Tk'lo saw made his heart break.

They looked out over the land, where their songs ended and the Göbek songs should begin, but Gn'la was right, there were no songs here. It should have been a place where the forest thinned for many miles, turning gradually into rolling hills of grassland, with copses of wild fig and apple trees. Instead, the land had been stripped, and lay rotting in the damp of the long rains. The stench of mould caught in their noses as they walked lost in silence.

There was no song to guide them; all memory had been wiped from the earth. They did not belong. They pressed on into the strangeness, pulled by Tk'lo's curiosity, which had been amplified by the dark spell of this place.

When the edge of their world became a thin line in their eyes, Tk'lo told Chok Bha, Grey Eagle, and Nasta, Thin Clouds, to mark this place with a pile of stones so that they could find their way back. Both Nasta and Chok Bha were not happy and said they should return to the songs of the forest and their own lands. Gn'la's eyes said as much, but his little brother would not disagree with Tk'lo. He would be the leader of the tribe one day and was already a wise one.

"A little farther, brothers," Tk'lo said, and they walked on into the growing nightmare.

The land began to change. At the edge of the forest the songs had gone. Great boulders had disappeared, trees were felled and even their roots removed. The grasses had been turned over so that dead long-stem crops of the milk drinkers rotted on the ground, as on a festering deathbed worried with flies. But there were echoes of the land's songs still there. A hill was a hill, even when ravaged of its life. The whisper of its song was there but drowned out by the squawk of carrion eaters flying overhead, all flying in the same direction, the direction in which Tk'lo felt compelled to walk.

Now even the land changed. The hills had been moved. Tk'lo's troupe stopped in its tracks, looking around themselves and to one another for an explanation none could give. It was as if the earth had been lifted and moved by a great spirit from before even the Dreaming, before the time of songs, from the place of nothing: a black, silent abyss. It filled Tk'lo's heart with a dread he remembered, not from his world.

He had seen this place before.

It was from his *ikkalo,* when he drank the tea of many dreaming mushrooms, and hung in the hut suspended by the eagle's claws. He turned hanging in an endless, cleansing pain which cleared his mind of all but anguish so that the vision might be a true and dangerous joining with the spirits of the dreamworld. In this way Tk'lo gained the knowledge to become a man.

In his vision he saw this, an unbelievable place where a greedy spirit had passed his claws through the soil, gathering up a great hill on which many thin and sickly people hauled enormous, smooth and unnatural rocks into place. They placed them in circles and carved animals and other images into them, as Tk'lo's people might carve wood. The great spirit, black and fat, with huge mothering breasts, heavy with milk, forced the people to drink from its teats. As they suckled, they grew thin and sickly, but craved more. The cycle was endless. The people would pull more rock to the unnatural hill and willingly join the queue to be fed from their lizard mother. They had forgotten their songs. They knew only songs which the black lizard taught them, which were not the songs of their land and the animals and plants. They had even forgotten the song which sang their own tribe into being. They no longer knew who they were.

The unnatural hill from his vision rose from the earth in the distance. Above it circled thousands of black-winged crows, their cries growing deafening the nearer they came. Nasta wanted to run now and follow the piles of rocks back to the forest, but Gn'la, brave and loyal Little Fox, caught him by the arm and shook his head.

Many cattle lay dead and rotting around the hill, bones pointing through skin torn at by scavengers. Among the dead lay things once human, but now their soulless eyes stared blankly from gaunt faces as they moved across the corpses, sluggish as insects.

A great number of people had gathered, perhaps all the tribes of this land and lands beyond, from ones Tk'lo had not learned to sing. All were weak and sick, their eyes sucked into their sockets. Some pawed at Tk'lo and his brothers, though what they begged for, Tk'lo didn't know. They shrugged them off, climbing the hill, weaving between crowds and standing stones.

The crows swirled overhead, mirroring a black storm cloud centred on the hill. They rained shit onto the heads of the people below. The smell of death pervaded everything, acrid and fermenting. The wall of people was thick now, and with their strength Tk'lo's troupe pushed their way through to the front.

They should have listened to Nasta and run back to the forest without looking over their shoulders. But even if they had fled, Tk'lo would still have stayed. He had seen this moment in his dream.

They faced a great circle, rimmed with standing stones the height of four men. In the centre of the circle, another unnatural rock was laid flat. It was as long as two men and stood at the height of the waists of the three who gathered around it, their white furs stained crimson. The three stood in a pool of blood, which lapped at their calves. With eyes cast down, two more men waded through the pool of blood from the edge of the circle. They lifted a body from the stone, and one of Tk'lo's troupe stifled a scream that drew no attention among the others wailing around them. It was a child's body. A girl. A bud far from blooming. Her throat had been cut and her blood let over the stone.

How many children... Tk'lo did not allow himself to imagine.

Crows spiralled. Another child was brought forward from the circle's edge. This time a boy, his hair black and curly, with a face that could be mistaken for a girl at first sight. He did not struggle, but he cried and called for his mother. Tk'lo knew this word. Why he could not say, but in his belly, he felt it, a deep sickening burn: this was the last child of the Göbek tribe. They were giving him to the black lizard for next year's harvest.

Snot and tears ran from the boy's nose and eyes. His face was contorted. The three white-furred men awaited him, the shortest of them holding a black knife, a thing Tk'lo had never seen but heard of in darker songs. It was made from stone and glinted like a sky from before the Dreaming Time, when no stars lit the heavens.

The others surged forward. Though they were outnumbered by so many, these were sickly, songless fools.

It was Tk'lo who signalled for them to hold. His fingers curled into a fist at his chest.

The boy's cries became the guttural whine of a terrified animal. He tried to dig his heels into the ground, leaning back between the men who brought him on, and he jerked in the vice of their grip. Beneath his feet, under the sea of congealing blood, the dirt was soft and pliant. There was no grip; there was no reprieve.

The crying became a piercing wail. The crows grew more excited, swirling faster and faster. Above them, the clouds had darkened, forming a spiralling tumult mirroring the path of the crows, the stone circle, and the people: a tunnel between the earth and some other place. Thunder pounded overhead, as if all the horses of the earth were fleeing this place, back to the Dreaming Time to be forgotten by the people. Tk'lo and his brothers began to weep as the boy was lifted struggling from the red pool.

"Na! Na! Na!" he screamed.

The heavens opened. Thunder rolled. Crows screamed. A mother let herself be pushed away by the eddies of the crowd. And Tk'lo and his brothers' tears were lost in the pouring rain. Heavy droplets, warm as fresh blood. Two of the three priests held down the boy.

The third priest, black knife raised above his head in one hand, the other, pulling back the head of the boy by his hair.

"Na!" the boy whispered hoarsely, his eyes wide and staring wildly at the black blade.

A blinding flash of lightning blazed above their heads, green and phosphorous. Thunder snapped, ringing in their ears. The people of the circle screamed and ducked beneath their Black Lizard God, who licked his hungry lips.

"Na!" mouthed the lips of the boy, his throat robbed of all sound.

The priest brought down the knife in an arc, a sweep practised in a thousand sacrifices. The blade slid through the flesh of the boy's throat as a spear might slice through the water to the salmon below. A great crimson gout sprayed forth, soaking the three priests. The black clouds overhead clapped once more, and a fork of green lightning connected heaven and earth. All was black.

Tk'lo knew then he was staring into the time before the Dreaming. It was a night without stars, though swirling colours appeared to dance across the blackness like the cooked fat of animals swirling across the surface of the stream. A great aching in his heart twisted in Tk'lo's chest, and a ringing grew in his ears. This was not the time of Dreaming. This was not part of his vision.

Weak moaning reached his ears, and Tk'lo let out a groan of his own. He had fallen somehow and was lying down on a peculiar surface: soft in places, hard in others, smelling of burning hair.

Tk'lo opened his eyes and forced himself up onto his knees, hands touching the bodies that lay all around the stone circle beneath the great monoliths of stone. He clutched the pain in his chest and got to his feet while the others lay unconscious around him, as if a great wind had flattened a meadow of tall grass. Smoke rose from the fallen bodies, and in the centre of the circle the three priests lay face down in their bloody pool.

Tk'lo looked for the body of the boy. The black clouds still hung heavily, turning slowly over the circle of stone. But the crows were no longer in flight. They roosted atop the great rocks, looking inward.

And then Tk'lo saw him, lying face down like the priests, only the back of his head visible above the surface of the deathly pool.

Tk'lo was filled with unbearable sorrow, dropping again to his knees and weeping. His brothers stirred. They would leave now, and never look back to this place.

The crows above them began to squawk angrily. A small ripple from the centre of the pool began to spread its way slowly to Tk'lo's bare feet. Then another ripple, larger, drew Tk'lo's eyes. A twitch. An impossible one. Tk'lo squinted, shaking his head. But he wasn't dreaming it. The boy was moving.

Tk'lo had killed enough animals and other tribesmen in war parties to know that animals moved after death. His grandfather had told him it was the soul struggling to leave the body and earn its right to return to the churning of heaven's river. Whether it was for the passing soul or from fear of this place, Tk'lo began to sing his tribe's dreaming song, the only song which made sense in this place without music, without life.

A larger ripple emanated from the boy. Tk'lo wanted to run, but his legs would not move. Heart pounding in his chest, he wanted to grab the flint knife secured in the waist of his furs, but he could not move other than to sing, words tumbling quietly from his trembling lips. The boy twitched more violently, as if shaking off his soul, letting it float to the churning heavenly waters above so that it would burden him no longer.

Slowly, the boy rose from the red pool, stained with the blood of a thousand sacrificed children. His eyes opened. He no longer looked afraid. His stare was as blank and hard as the stones that encircled him. His long eyelashes were heavy with crimson droplets, framing eyes which had become as black as the flint knife used to cut his throat. Slowly, the boy's eyes turned upon Tk'lo.

Tk'lo vomited, nausea sweeping over him, a feeling of something unnatural and guilt and fear. The boy tilted his head at the tribesman before turning away as if Tk'lo was little more than a small flower in the forest. The boy reached the edge of the circle on the other side and glanced over all the fallen people. The crows stood, sentinels hopping agitatedly from foot to foot awaiting their orders. The boy raised a hand to the fallen people and walked away.

The shrieks of the crows pierced the air as they took flight. They fell from their roosts upon the bodies below them. Screams went up from those who were still alive.

Tk'lo beat away the attacking crows, the song still upon his lips, as if it was that and not his physical effort that would keep them alive. He shook his brothers, rousing them from their stupor. They moaned like sleeping children. The crows continued to attack. He struck his brothers, again and again, until they woke.

Tk'lo dragged them from that place. Behind them, the crows gorged.

They ran back to their homeland. Tk'lo called his brothers to sing them back into the forest, back to their songlines, back to their memories, back to life and as far away from the boy and those people as they could.

22

THE WATER WAS COLD, and Dip still had the dreaming song lilting in his mind when he became vaguely aware of other muffled noises. Noises from this world. They were like the low vibrations of a train coming from deep within a tunnel, growing louder. He had the sensation of small bubbles drifting across his skin, tickling as they ascended. And then light, thin and startling, and more noise: urgent, panicked. Distorted shapes loomed above him. A flurry of movement, the surface of the water was broken. An arm looped under his neck, another beneath his armpit, and Dip was hauled bodily from beneath the water of the bath.

Air struck his face, and the trance was broken. He opened his mouth, gasping, sucking in the breath of life. His mother and father were crying, holding their son close, sobbing and kissing the side of Dip's head. Dip still clung to the side of the bath with his broken hand. Looking into his mother's weeping eyes, he felt so sad: the song of Tk'lo and his brothers was leaving him, evaporating like a dream.

23

MIRIN AND ORAN curled up on the sofa. Mirin ran her fingertips over the surface of the card in her pocket, the one Constable Bhaskar had given her. She had her other arm around Oran's shoulders as he snuggled against her. She played with the wet curls of his hair, drying after his evening bath. Oran drew on the glass screen of Mirin's tablet, whilst the TV spoke to itself in the background.

Mirin stared blankly at the fireplace. It didn't work. It never had. It was just for show, with an ornate surround and Victorian tiles still in place. Pictures of Mirin's little family lay on the mantel. Oran as a baby between her and her beautiful Omar. A picture of Oran playing in the park, kicking up piles of autumn leaves as a toddler. And the last picture, the most recent, taken only months before Omar's death, a posed picture they paid a professional to take. Oran perched between the two of them, his parents leaning tightly together behind him, their smiles fixed. The similarities between Omar and his son were striking, even with decades between them. It was in the smile, in the way their eyes creased and the whole face radiated happiness. Mirin looked at her own. It seemed forced in photographs, always a little too serious, as though her mind was elsewhere.

David Hamill said, "Thank you for having me."

Mirin came back from her daydream to see her colleague on the

TV again. Her fingers closed around the card in her pocket. Lucy Walker smiled at David. They sat opposite each other. She with her long, elegant legs crossed, a set of papers held in one hand, silver ballpoint pen poised between thumb and forefinger in the other. David leant nonchalantly on one shoulder, every bit the public intellectual. Lucy's smile faded as the camera closed in for a close-up. She looked at her notes and then posed a question to David.

"Professor Hamill, it has been quite a remarkable week. People are worried, perhaps even a little scared. Following your discovery, we have had several unexpected and severe weather events. And a series of gruesome murders and violent attacks across the city and in particular around the university. *Your* university. In fact, I believe you knew one of the victims. She was a student of yours, wasn't she?"

David nodded solemnly. "Yes, a very talented doctoral student of mine."

Was? thought Mirin. *She's not dead.*

Lucy Walker went on. "Professor Hamill, you are a respected intellectual, a well-read man, a scientist. Is this all connected? Just what exactly is going on?" Lucy looked earnest, her head cocked to the side to metaphorically lend the public ear.

David nodded solemnly to show that he understood, but of course couldn't agree with where the questions were coming from. He knitted his fingers together, opening his thumbs as he began to speak.

"The weather has been rather unpredictable. And the police inform me there has indeed been a spike in violent crime and murders across the city. And, of course, these things have happened at the same time we discovered the Wee Man. It is quite natural for people to make connections and draw conclusions from the things that they see in front of them. Something we drum into our undergraduates at the university is that correlation does not equal causation. Let me explain. While two things might happen at the same time, it can appear that they are connected, when in actual fact it is mere coincidence." He gave a little chuckle. "In fact, many peculiar things correlate. For example, divorce rates have been correlated with margarine consumption, the age of Miss America has been correlated with murders by steam and hot vapours, or US crude oil imports from Norway have been correlated with drivers killed in collisions with railway trains. Patterns occur throughout nature. It can seem a little odd to those unschooled in statistics. These things are true nonetheless, but there is no causation between one thing and the other. Coincidences happen. They occur all the time."

"So, Professor, in your informed opinion, what *is* happening?" Lucy Walker asked, head still tilted and listening.

David took a breath, mirrored her head-tilt, and put a lock of his trademark foppish hair behind his ear.

"With the weather, we need look no further than the dangers of climate change."

Lucy Walker cut in. "But, Professor, some people have found it hard to believe that such extreme weather conditions, from a flash heatwave one day, to giant hailstones the next, could be attributed to climate change."

"Lucy, this is exactly what we have predicted will happen with climate change. It is not merely that the weather will become warmer. It is that it will become more extreme at both ends, and..." David raised a finger for emphasis. "...more unpredictable. Indeed, these huge swings between temperatures are the consequence of man's obsession with fossil fuels. I was speaking with Sir David Attenborough about this only last month, and he shares my concerns. We, as a species, cannot continue to consume without thought to replenishing what we take, because if we do, the things that we have experienced in our great Scottish city, here in Glasgow, will become commonplace. Indeed, there are some areas of the world where this is already the case. If you live in the Maldives, you have a very real chance that in your lifetime your entire nation will be submerged by rising sea levels. A modern-day Atlantean tragedy."

"You're saying this is just the natural and understandable result of changes in the climate?"

"Exactly."

"What about the murders and the attacks?" Lucy followed up. She made a face as if to say: *I know, I know.* "These are the things that people are asking, Professor."

David unlaced his hands, placing a finger on his chin as if in deep thought for a moment.

"Like the weather, human behaviour tends to be predictable at the macro but not the micro level. What I mean is, as terrible as everything that has happened is, statistics and history tell us that we do get these occasional spikes or statistical agglomerations. It is terrible and unfortunate, but it is merely a fact of being human. We are capable of both the sublime and the terrible."

Lucy nodded in serious agreement. "And there's just one other thing..."

"I know what you're going to say," David said, smugness smeared across his face. "You do ask the tough questions, don't you?"

"That is what they pay me for." Lucy mirrored David's conceit. "But I have to ask. The people want to know, could all of this - freak weather conditions and the violent attacks - have something to do with the Wee Man, *your* incredible archaeological find?"

They shared a hearty but polite laugh.

"He is a truly remarkable archaeological discovery. Every day the Wee Man seems to shed new light on our distant past. He is indeed very special. But not in a supernatural way. He doesn't have magical powers. He cannot change the weather. He cannot cause violent attacks. People are responsible for their own actions. What *is* remarkable about the Wee Man is his level of preservation." David leaned in conspiratorially. "Sometimes, I must confess, however, I *do* wish he would wake up. Spring to life. What a remarkable story he could then tell. When terrible things happen, people look for miraculous explanations, their minds will turn to the seemingly impossible to make sense of what they don't understand, what they can't bring themselves to accept. I'm no psychologist, but if I had to guess, I'd say that is what is happening..."

"Ouch! Mummy, you're hurting me." Mirin's hand had closed around Oran's shoulder, holding onto the boy as tightly as she could.

"I'm sorry, poppet."

"That's okay, Mummy. What are you watching? Was it scaring you?"

Mirin couldn't place the exact cause of her anxiety. David was definitely part of it. But was it jealousy? Did she envy his progression ahead of her, or how he was misrepresenting what they were doing? Possibly. But it wasn't simply anger she was feeling. It was fear as well. It included uncertainty and the feeling in her gut that something wasn't right. Proof, however, was something she did not have. She knew how ridiculous it all still sounded.

An idea struck her then. Portia: she might be the key. Of course, the last time she had been to see her, she was in a bad way psychologically, and maybe she still was. But the fact remained, she was the one that needed to be questioned. She had been with the boy when she was attacked.

Mirin remembered Portia's face: the look of pure terror seeing Mirin in her room. What had she seen? Why was she so terrified? Mirin would have to find out. She would have to follow the evidence, no matter where it might take her. That was a scientist's job.

"No, darling." Mirin ran her fingers through Oran's hair. "I'm fine."

Oran yawned.

"Are you tired, poppet?"

Oran cuddled against her chest, putting the tablet down and closing his eyes. "Would you sing to me, Mummy? Daddy's song."

"The Arabic song his grandma used to sing to him?"

"It reminds me of Daddy."

"It reminds me of him too. He loved singing that to you. Will you help me with some of the Arabic words?"

Mirin picked her way through the lullaby, Oran drowsily filling in the words she couldn't quite remember, going around in a circle, repeating the charm, until she remembered all the words. Oran had fallen asleep on her lap. Mirin continued to play with his hair, lost in the gentle rhythm of the lullaby.

24

DARK CLOUDS, heavy with rain, began to circle, forcing an ochre sun from the sky. Head down, Mirin hunkered into her coat and dragged herself to the museum.

Soon, she was inside and out of the rain. There was a lump in her throat from what she had to say to David. It was Friday and the university was deep into Candlemas term. The place should have been a buzz of activity, with students attending their final lectures before exams. Instead, it was quiet, as though it was the summer, when only a skeleton crew of staff rattled around the empty buildings. Each step Mirin took sounded hollow on her way up to the museum.

The lift doors opened, and the hallway was empty. The crowds had not arrived yet, if they would come at all. David was busying himself with preparations for unlocking the stainless-steel sarcophagus and looked up when he heard Mirin's steps. For a man usually so animated, always wearing the mask of an upbeat personality always on show, his face was blank and impassive, difficult to read. He gave Mirin a curt nod as she went to a side room to store her coat and bag, exchanging them for a white lab coat.

Chin was due to get the carbon-14 dating results. They were all excited to see just how old the boy was. If the boy was truly older than the Iron Age bodies, it would be an outstanding discovery. Therefore, Mirin had decided she would just have to come out and say it. There was no point in dragging out the day.

David was about to pop the latches on the sarcophagus. "David..."

One of the latches flicked open. From the other side of the hall, beyond some of the display cases and central exhibits, Chin entered from one of the back doors, hurrying up with the lab results printed out in his hand.

"He's here. Chin, have you got them?" In David's excitement, Mirin's call went unnoticed.

With his usual shy face and head cast down, Chin raised the papers in his hand, indicating he did indeed have the results.

"David..." Mirin tried again.

"Well then, what does it say?" David's voice bounced off the walls.

Chin didn't answer. He walked at his usual methodical pace, almost a shuffle, shoulders rounded.

Unable to wait, David started to walk around the sarcophagus to meet him halfway.

"I really need to speak to you, David."

"Can't it wait?" David snapped.

"It's about the boy. I need to talk to you about him. It's important."

Chin was still taking his time. Something appeared to occur to David. "Have you already spoken to Chin? Do you know the results? What are they?"

Mirin shook her head.

"Then what is it?" David said shortly. "What could possibly be more important than these results?"

Chin hung back at a respectful distance while his senior colleagues were in conversation. David fidgeted with his gloves and flicked a lock of hair from his face, waiting for Mirin to spill the beans on... whatever it was.

Now she had his attention, Mirin wasn't sure how she was going to put it into words.

"The boy... He... What I am trying to say is..."

His smug public mask came back to David. "Look, Mirin, I know all this..." He indicated the hall, the equipment, the boy. "I know it's been a big undertaking for you, what with everything that happened, and you with only one foot back in the place. But it's okay. You don't need to worry, Mirin. This is a find of a lifetime. It's going to mean big things for all of us. But I'll take care of the media side of things. That's my bag, so to speak. You'll be there with the research. The credit will be shared."

"No, that's not what I mean. I don't care about any of that." Mirin's voice was earnest. "I mean, yes, the research is important. But we should slow down. We need to take a minute and think. For God's sake, David, Portia was attacked in *our* lab. She nearly died. She is in hospital right now trying to recover from whatever happened to her. And what did happen to her? Honestly, David, can you explain that?"

For a moment David looked ashen-faced, and then his features hardened. "That's the police's job, not ours. Maybe it was a boyfriend or something. How am I supposed to know?"

"I thought *you* were her boyfriend."

David reddened; his jaw tightened. "How... dare... you." Venom punctuated every word.

Mirin couldn't believe it. After all this, he was still in denial.

"What happens in your private life is none of my business. But-"

"Oh, well, *thank you,* Mirin." The sarcasm dripped from each of David's words.

"There's something more important going on."

"What could possibly be more important than this?" David's voice had raised a few octaves.

"Did you ever wonder why Portia got attacked with the obsidian knife? Or why the boy's body had moved but there seemed to be no cause? Or what happened to Jennifer? Crows, David, crows killed her right outside her department. For Christ's sake, we could look out of the window and almost see where she was killed by a flock of birds, David. Then the frogs, the *fucking* frogs. Doesn't any of this sound a little strange to you? Something very fucking odd is happening around here and we seem to be the last people to see it."

David's eyes were wide and fixed on her.

"Can't you see something isn't right?" Mirin implored. "It all began when the boy was discovered, amid all that violence and killing, and it followed him here. I know it sounds crazy. I know what I'm saying sounds ludicrous, but..."

"No, it doesn't sound ludicrous," David said calmly. "It sounds *insane*. I expected more from you, Mirin. I once looked up to you as the cleverest among us, and the hardest working, and the most focused. But just look at what you are saying..." His voice shook with genuine emotion. "I've been too harsh. After everything that happened to you, it's been too much. I've been a taskmaster. I can see that now. Go home, Mirin."

Mirin was shocked, not even sure that she'd heard him right. "David, wait. What?"

"Go home, Mirin. As your head of department, I am formally suspending you. We can call it compassionate leave, if you prefer. You need to take care of yourself. We can talk later when you've had time to think things through. I'm saying this as a friend: you need to get some help, Mirin, some serious help. Now, please leave. I'm begging you."

Mirin looked between David and Chin, who kept his eyes firmly fixed on his feet. She could see there was no way to make David understand. As she walked away, her vision turned glassy and her walk became a run to gather her things.

David and Chin waited, the results in Chin's tightly clutching fingers still unread.

25

THE CLOUDS OVERHEAD had become dark charcoal smudges. They moved like snakes, gathering above the city, and the university was at the epicentre of the coming storm.

Mirin let the hill's incline carry her downwards, tears bleeding from her eyes. At the crossroads of University Avenue, the blaring of car horns did not even register with her. She pressed on, sobbing.

A TAXI DRIVER, with thinning grey hair and a belly from spending too long behind the wheel, got out of his black cab effing and blinding at another man half his size, sat in the driver's seat of a beat-up Ford Mondeo. The Mondeo man opened his car door, catching the taxi driver by surprise, and slamming steel into the fat taxi driver's legs and stomach. The taxi driver fell back into the road on his arse. Another car came around the corner from Gibson Street and missed running over the taxi driver by inches. Its own angry horn sounded as it swerved but did not stop.

"You fucking *bawbag*," the fat taxi driver shouted, pulling himself from the ground, his face now flushed red. Wisps of his hair, kept long to be combed over the bald spot on the top of his head, fell ragged about his face. He puffed out his chest, glaring at the little man with spectacles and a shaved head. The little man had, to the taxi driver's surprise, already got out of his car. Small as he was, he had set his feet apart, a stance of some kind, clearly familiar with physical confrontation.

The fat taxi driver was forming another barrage of expletive insults when the little man stifled the fat man's voice with an accurately delivered punch to his flabby throat. For a second time the fat taxi driver fell back on his backside. This time his hands went to his throat. He struggled for air.

While the taxi driver protected his throat, the little man kicked his unprotected groin. The full force of the football kick caused the fat man to collapse to his side, red and breathless. The little man wasn't finished.

A small crowd of people had stopped to watch, but nobody intervened. Some, like Mirin, continue to walk on as if nothing was happening. The little man took a step back and then ran forward and delivered another brutal kick: this one to the bulbous stomach of the taxi driver. The fat man was unable to scream, shout, or swear any more. All he could do was whimper like a pathetic animal. Another kick cracked ribs. He looked up to the blackening sky, trying to pull air into his lungs. He saw the black clouds. It was the last thing he would ever see.

———

IT WAS THE MORNING, too early to get Oran from school, as much as she wanted to. Instead, Mirin carried on down Gibson Street, past the parade of shops, where another argument between a shopkeeper and a customer had erupted. The customer threw a handful of chewing gum packets at the shopkeeper, who in return brandished a short rounders bat he retrieved from under the counter, causing the customer to flee, knocking into Mirin's shoulder as he barrelled out of the shop. She barely noticed. Things that would have seemed odd several weeks ago, terrible even, were becoming all too familiar.

She walked over the River Kelvin, turning left onto Park Road, until she stood outside an Indian restaurant. The rich smells of curry still filled the air, even though lunch service was several hours off. At first it seemed as if it was closed, and there were no lights on. She stood, half wondering why she came here, not entirely sure what she was supposed to do next.

Her reflection stared back at her, multiplied by the effect of the double-glazing, distorting her image and the world around her.

Before, with Omar, the world had seemed such a certain thing. And now she had survived one nightmare only to tumble into another even greater one. What would she do about Oran? Should they flee? Where would they go? Omar's family had wanted nothing to do with her. They had never approved of him marrying her, and she had never been close to her family. Her parents were distant and handled the death of Omar by staying away and saying nothing, justifying it as "giving her space". Mirin had not complained.

A figure came up behind her, dressed in a dark-green rain coat and a beanie hat, and for one glorious fraction of a second Mirin thought it was Omar because the man was of a similar height, and because perhaps, even after all this time, she still *wanted* to see Omar. Her heart leapt, but the illusion was shattered when the man spoke.

"Hello, Professor Hassan." The man's voice was a gentle Glaswegian accent.

Mirin turned and knew that it was Hardeep Bhaskar.

He looked cleaner than he had at their last meeting. He'd shaved and the shadows beneath his eyes were shallower. His eyes were the same though: the kind of eyes that didn't blink because they feared the intervals of darkness between sight.

"I think I'm ready to listen," she said, and there was a croak in her voice, like a dead thing revived.

26

DAVID NEVER THOUGHT a crowd of onlookers would become something he'd shy away from, but after this morning he needed to be alone. Retreating from the museum, David headed to his office in the Gregory Building. As he passed the lab, he felt a pang for Portia, but he buried it as soon as it arose. She was a lovely girl, but it was never going anywhere. It had been a lustful and fun fling, but God knows not something one would risk one's career over. He knew he should have gone to see her.; However, that would be a little too visible. Safely inside his office at last, David locked the door behind him.

"What are you looking at?" David snapped to the poster of himself on the wall as he began to pace back and forth.

"I had to suspend her," he muttered. "What choice did I have? It was for her own good. She was putting everything in jeopardy. And she's clearly ill. Yes, she's not got over the trauma of what happened."

An email to Human Resources was already forming in his mind. This was a similar process he used when generating potential monologues for the TV programmes. He'd lay down the audio after a long practice session rehearsing as he paced his office. However, unlike the BBC shows, this wasn't fun, and the strides weren't so relaxed. The pacing became shorter, turning every couple of steps, edging towards his office chair, like a penny spinning down a funnel trying to decide whether or not to give in to the gravity of the situation.

Switching on his computer, David opened his email, copying Kathy in HR's email into the address box, when his phone rang. He jumped. He was being ridiculous, riled because of what he'd had to say to Mirin. At that, another thought appeared: that Mirin had gone straight to HR and told them about his little liaison with Portia. *Shit.*

Still it rang. His answermachine would pick it up. David made the decision to ignore it. The phone stopped ringing, and relaxing a little in relief, he turned back to the email.

He had only managed to type 'Dear' when the phone rang again. It could be Lucy phoning to follow up on their big idea for the Wee Man. They had shared a dinner at her house. The wine had been red, and so had the shade of her lipstick. They had smiled, and circled each other with compliments, easing into talk of their aspirations for the Wee Man and for themselves. Excitement around the boy was already intense. There was talk of America, of worldwide streaming, of money and fame, so much money and fame.

The wine had flowed. They'd drank. They'd touched. Eventually, they'd done much more. David could still recall the smell of her and the soft silkiness of her legs, the raking of her manicured nails across his skin. The heat.

He remembered her sitting up in the gloom afterwards, lighting a cigarette. She'd passed it to David, who did not smoke but took it anyway and drew on the bitter embers. Lucy lit another and lithely straddled David, looking down at him as she smoked. She'd picked a fleck of tobacco from her lips, regarding him and then inhaled deeply on her cigarette. It flared red, a dragon's eye in the dark, and she'd arched her neck, billowing forth a great cloud of smoke into the air. Her beauty was consuming, her ambition intoxicating.

Still the phone rang. It was persistent, just like Lucy.

David tentatively picked up the receiver. "Hello. Professor David Hamill speaking."

"Professor, it's DCI Shepherd here."

"Oh, DCI... How can I help you?"

"I was wondering if you could put me in touch with Professor Hassan. I've been trying her phone all morning without any luck."

"I am afraid she's not at work today."

"Will she be back in tomorrow, or is there some other way I could reach her?"

"This is a little bit awkward, DCI Shepard. I'm afraid I had to suspend Professor Hassan. Not a few hours ago. Or rather, she is on sick leave. I think the stress of everything has got to her."

There was a brief silence at the other end of the phone which David felt the urge to fill. But then David remembered he had heard that was a cheap psychological tactic the police use to get people to talk more than they should, because the social pressure of silence works at a very base level of human psychology. Such cheap tricks were beneath David. He would not fall into such a trap.

"Could I ask," DCI Shepherd began, "why you suspended Professor Hassan?"

"Like I said, it was more for her own mental wellbeing. I think the pressures of the work we're undergoing had got to her. She behaved very erratically today. I think it might be the beginnings of a break-down. She has had... complicated grief before."

There was another brief silence. "Let me ask you another question, Professor Hamill, if you'd be so kind." Connie Shepherd didn't wait for David's agreement. "Could you tell me about Mirin's relationship with Jennifer Mordaunt?"

David relaxed a little. For a minute he thought the question would be about him.

"They were colleagues. Mirin had studied as an undergraduate and a little at master's level with Professor Mordaunt, I believe. They were maybe even friends or at least friendly as far as I'm aware. Professor Mordaunt was a highly respected figure in this university and beyond."

"There wasn't any tension between the two of them? No personal enmity or professional competition?" Connie asked, her voice unemotional.

"No, no, no. They were in entirely different departments. Jennifer, God rest her soul, was nearing the end of her career. In fact, she would become Professor Emeritus in the next twelve months, I believe. She could look forward to giving up teaching and administration and concentrate on whatever projects she wanted. She seemed excited, as excited as Jennifer ever really seemed. She was the archetypal quiet, introspective academic."

"Not like yourself then, Professor Hamill?" There was a light, playful tone now to Connie's voice.

David gave an equally light laugh in response. "No, not like me. Jennifer was old school, as my students would say."

"And what about Professor Hassan's relationship with her student, Portia?" Now it was David who paused, stiffening in his chair. "Professor Hamill, are you still there?"

"Yes. Sorry... I was miles away. So much on my plate at the moment. I guess you could say they were close. A mentor's relationship is typical for a PhD. But Portia was left in the lurch somewhat by the tragedy that befell Professor Hassan. And so, at least for the last twelve months, I was her principal doctoral supervisor."

"I see," Connie said, letting those two little words hang in the air. "And when Professor Hassan returned to work, that was...?" David could hear the rustling of paper as though someone was looking through their notepad. "Two weeks ago." Connie answered her own question. "There was no tension? No conflict from you having taken her PhD student?"

"No, no, no. I mean, for a start we weren't sure when Mir – I mean Professor Hassan – would return to work. Portia needed supervision. It would be a dereliction of duty not to support her. When Professor Hassan returned to work, we... Well, we haven't sorted it out quite yet, but it's pretty typical nowadays for a PhD student to have more than one supervisor, sometimes as many as three."

DCI Shepherd wrote something down at the other end of the line. "And there were no other sources of tension between yourself and Professor Hassan and Portia?"

David smelled a set-up. He had been interviewed many times on television, and reporters could be just as gruelling as police officers, if not more so, because they were not bound by the same legal codes.

"Oh, the usual, granted." He kept his tone casual. "The work is stressful. We're all excited about this discovery, and excitement can bring emotions to the surface."

"Workplaces can be very intense," the DCI said, as though she had not heard him. "Some people say we become closer with our work colleagues than our own family."

"Sad but likely true," David stammered.

"Was Professor Hassan in a relationship with Portia?"

A sudden pang of relief forced an involuntary laugh from David. "Portia and Mirin? Now that would be the talk of the university!"

"Sorry, Professor. Does that mean you're saying they *weren't* in a relationship? Just so I'm sure. As far as you're aware there wasn't any extracurricular relationship between Professor Hassan and Portia?"

"No, most definitely not."

"You sound very sure."

"Well, Mirin loved her husband very much. It was why she was away for so long." A sudden inspiration struck David. "But I guess we sometimes find physical comfort a way of coping with grief. We academics rule nothing out until it's categorically disproven. Thanatos and Eros, as they say."

"What's that?"

"Ah, it's Greek. I'm not an expert in that language or era, but the gods Thanatos, Death, and Eros, Sex, were strangely linked to the Ancient Greeks."

"I see." Those two little words again. "You've been very helpful, Professor Hamill. Just one last thing. It's quite silly really. But we have to follow up every lead. A number of people have mentioned your body. The Wee Man, that's what you're calling him now, isn't it?"

"That's right. What about him?"

"Well, there's a lot at stake with a find like him, isn't there? From what you've been saying on the TV and radio ever since he was found, I understand he is something of a one-of-a-kind. The sort of thing that careers are built on?"

"Yes, he is a very significant find."

"Well, with all the strange things going on, we can't rule out professional rivalry. Is there anyone you can think of who might want to get their hands on the Wee Man?"

It was David who paused now, thinking. His eyes lingered briefly in the email he had yet to write.

"Well, come to think of it, there is one person. I know I said it was stress, but the more I think about it, the more it just seems like she's the only person who could have done it."

"Professor, to whom are you referring?"

David took a deep breath.

"Mirin Hassan. I think *she* might just be the solution to all of this."

27

THE NURSE TUCKED in Portia's bed sheets. She had been on the same night shift for the last few days and Portia had learned her name was Tammy.

Tammy would say nice things to her, accompanied with a pitying look. No one had shown her a mirror yet, but Portia could guess what she looked like. The prickle of stitches irritated her face. The swelling in her eye and lips had begun to go down, but she still felt like tenderised meat.

But there was something worse than the physical pain: he had never come to see her. Friends had dropped by, but not David. Family had sent flowers and cards, but not him. Portia felt like a silly little girl: used, foolish, alone. And on top of all that, she thought she might be losing her mind.

It had grown dark even earlier than normal due to the gathering storm clouds. Portia could hear thunder outside. The hospital staff had been moaning about the weather. It affected the patients, creating an atmosphere of dread, of something about to break. The hospital was rushed off their feet. More serious assaults were backing up the Accident and Emergency Department.

The nausea had never left Portia. She felt permanently sick but couldn't throw up any more. The hospital staff would bring food, often mushed up, although recently they had tried more solid things: a cheese sandwich; an overcooked piece of chicken and vegetables covered with a thin gruel that passed for gravy. She had tried to eat, but the thought of it made the bile rise in the stomach, burning the back of her throat. One of the nurses, Susie or Josie, Portia couldn't quite remember, had admonished her for not eating, as if she were a small child. A psychologist turned up not long after that, talking in soft tones, and asking questions about eating disorders. She left a few leaflets and said she'd pop back another time, patting the bed comfortingly as a proxy for touching Portia.

They kept Portia on a drip, to keep her hydrated. But without eating, she shed even more weight. She was more skeletal than ever.

Portia turned her head to the window where the pall of black clouds churned.

A great clattering came from the hallway, a nurse or an orderly dropping a pile of steel bedpans. It drew Portia's attention to the other side of the room, to the bright lights of the hallway. A hubbub of life busied itself, running up and down the corridors and in and out a myriad of unseen rooms. It made her think of ants scurrying about a hive. Did they ever stop to ask if it was all worth it?

Thunder clapped, so loud the window in Portia's room shook, and unknown people somewhere on her floor screamed with shock and surprise. A low rumble followed, growling ominously from the heavens. Portia turned back to the window as a flash of lightning flicked from the swelling belly of the black clouds, forking to the ground. It was green, lighting up the entire city and Portia's room like a phantom presence. She was just thinking about how she had never seen green lightning before as the illumination faded, and something more substantial than a shadow seemed to move in the dark corner. Her heart quickened. It was the shape of something too familiar.

Portia kept her eyes fixed on the window. The acid burn rose in her throat. She shook, not wanting to look at the thing, standing where Mirin had stood, next to her boy, sitting in the chair, dangling his legs over the edge.

The lightning forked again, a green trident impaling the earth. The flash made Portia wince, flinching out of reflex.

Another scream came from somewhere down the hallway. From the shadows emerged the figure of a beautiful boy, *the* boy, his body covered in ancient language. His big almond-shaped eyes the glaucous colour of flint and looking straight into Portia's soul.

She was aware of the wounds to her throat, the damaged muscle preventing any sound escaping. The boy stepped into the light as a third fork of lightning blazed. He smirked, suddenly wraith-like, and Portia's pounding heart became a throb of agonising pain. She tensed, bony ribs flexing, unable to catch any breath, unable to scream, unable to...

The machine monitoring Portia's heart rate let out a flat, continuous tone, triggering an alarm. Shortly after, Tammy and two doctors ran into the room.

Tammy went up to the bed. She normally did not feel a personal connection to her patients. How could she when she had so many? But she felt unbidden grief at what had happened to Portia. The wounded, starved body had finally given up on her, it seemed.

Or had it? She looked into Portia's swollen eyes. There was a look there that told another story. Terror. Utter soundless terror. Tammy knew from first-hand experience that most people were scared to meet their end, but this was something else, something awful.

There was another flash outside. For a moment, Tammy thought she saw something in the shadows cast by the lightning. Then it was gone, and she willingly forgot it.

28

THE FIRST FLASH of green lightning that lit up the city made up their minds for them. Dip had listened to Mirin, over cups of spiced masala chai, as she recounted how she had tried to tell David. Mirin said that she didn't understand what was happening herself. That was when Dip was about to tell Mirin something important. He said he thought he finally understood something from what he had seen in his visions. But the lightning interrupted him.

Stepping out of the restaurant, it wasn't raining yet, but an oppressive and warm breeze had sprung up, buffeting them from all sides. They put their collars up against it, and side by side leaned their shoulders into the wind. Shopkeepers on Gibson Street pulled down their shutters. A bistro shooed out customers, who protested with offers of money and worried looks. In a bar there was the smashing of glasses and raised voices.

IF THE DAY had started terribly for David, having to send Mirin home, then it had ended wonderfully with that phone call from the police inspector. *We all get what we deserve,* he thought to himself, beginning to close down for the night. He had gone back to the museum once it was closed to the public. He sent Chin home. Feeling so much better, he was sad now that he had missed all the onlookers today. He'd said as much to the security guard who was doing his final rounds before clocking off. The guard had said that numbers had been way down today. Hardly anyone had dropped by the museum.

It was a little sad that the numbers were down. David had thought they'd be the big draw for much longer. On the other hand, he knew people were scared at the moment. The average person was just not able to rationalise what was going on.

That was kind of David's point in this world, or so he thought. His talent was to communicate with the masses, to bring science and education into their benighted lives. The Wee Man would help him take his message to more people than ever before. Maybe he'd become the new David Attenborough. Lord Hamill: that had a nice ring to it.

A green fork of lightning flashed through the high mullioned windows of the Hunterian Museum, followed by a clap of thunder. The storm, that was another reason people weren't coming out. Oh well, it'd pass. The boy had been preserved for millennia. He could wait a few days longer for the masses.

David pondered whether a move to London or maybe even America might be in the cards to take advantage of the additional media opportunities Lucy had suggested. Or perhaps he would just have a second home there, an apartment in Chelsea or Canary Wharf perhaps, and an LA pad with a swimming pool. The sky flashed green again; a crack of thunder made the walls of the great old building vibrate, and the lights overhead began to flicker.

David tutted. A little weather always seems to put a spanner in the technological, he thought. He'd better check the sarcophagus and its connections to the cooling unit. Luckily, it could survive a power outage for as long as forty-eight hours with its own internal backup battery pack. Nothing could be left to chance.

David picked up the papers Chin had printed out. Since he'd dealt with the Mirin problem, David had been able to savour the implications of the results. He had checked the numbers so many times, cross-referencing them against all baseline measures.

Samples had been sent with instructions to double-check, and both came back with the same result. The carbon-14 test proved beyond reasonable doubt: The Wee Man was the oldest bog body ever discovered.

All but the most jealous scientists would have to accept what they had found. He looked at the boy, lying at the bottom of the sarcophagus. He looked *alive*. A glow to his skin. David caught himself thinking that the boy looked even better preserved than when they first found him, as if he was regenerating. He laughed at the idea. Like something from an old movie.

David ran his hand down the results page one last time, tapping his index finger on the numbers, and shaking his head in mock disbelief. The carbon in the Wee Man's body dated him at over twelve thousand years old. The date was so old that the lab involuntarily ran a third test to triple-check. The one little fly in the ointment, from David's point of view, was that the other associated organic matter they sent had come out at nearly half that age, around six and a half thousand years old. It was still an incredible age, but down the line it might lead some to dispute the older dating. No matter, thought David. A little controversy, a little mystery, it would all add to the wonder of it. He could spin it out for years, decades perhaps, in countless follow-up programmes, to say nothing of the Neolithic script tattooed onto the body.

David slowly started closing the heavy-hinged lid that would return the boy to his stasis when the lift doors opened.

"We're closed for the evening, I'm afraid." David turned to give his best public grin. It vanished when he saw who it was in the flickering light of the hall. "Mirin! I don't think it's appropriate for you to be here right now. I've emailed HR and they're going to send you out a formal letter regarding sick leave. My mind is made up. There's no point in trying to convince me otherwise."

Dishevelled by the wind, collars still turned up, Mirin and Dip walked across the hall. Another flash of green, followed by a crack of thunder that felt directly over their heads.

"David, I'm not here about that. I want you to listen. I've brought..."

"That nutjob from the dig-site? I'm not listening to this. Now, you've got five seconds before I call security."

David's eyes were ablaze with anger. He stayed within the circle of machines and instruments, a magician within their sacred circle. A god growled overhead.

Dip stepped forward. "Professor Hamill, at least listen to us. You have to hear this."

"I see what's going on. You've talked her into this supernatural nonsense, haven't you? I should have guessed it when she said she saw you."

"David. You're a man of science. I've always said that about you, no matter what other people think. Please, look outside. When did you ever see lightning that was green?"

"Stop it, Mirin." Behind David, the steel lid of the sarcophagus began to slowly and silently rise. "It won't work on me. I am not a simpleton, one step away from believing in witchcraft and fairies..."

Mirin turned ashen. She pointed a shaking hand at the sarcophagus behind David.

David was shouting now, to be heard over the tumult. "You had your chance. We could have worked *together* on this. We could have shared the spoils."

From the steel sarcophagus, a green mist had begun to flow, creeping across the gallery floor. The mist reached David's feet, caressing his handmade shoes and the hem of his tailored suit.

"But now..." Whatever David's last words were, neither Dip nor Mirin heard.

There was a blaze of green. The building shook and the air exploded with a sound like a million trees cracking at once.

All three of them lost their balance. Dust and small pieces of plaster rained from overhead, falling into the mist which crept now towards Mirin and Dip.

This finally caught David's attention, as he struggled to keep his feet. He turned, mouth agape, believing that his prize possession might have been damaged by the release of some gas from the chemicals in the cooling system. He faced the sarcophagus, and the man who'd never been short for words failed to find any.

Lightning struck the spire of the building. More dust and plaster fell through the blaze of searing light. The power failed entirely, leaving the room lit only by the energy of the storm above and the dim lights of the city beyond. It was enough. At last, he finally believed. Too late. His mouth opened and closed like a fish dragged from its watery reality and thrown into a new one.

Dip placed a hand on Mirin's shoulder. He was backing out of the room, pulling her with him. She resisted, wanting to go to David. Dip could see the thought etched on her face and shook his head.

"David!" she shouted.

The lightning flashed, illuminating the shape of the boy, his eyes black and bottomless, standing before David.

"For God's sake, run!" Mirin screamed.

David did not run. He could not move, frozen to the spot, trembling. A hot, wet patch bloomed at the crotch of his trousers. The flow of urine spread down each leg, soaking his inner thighs before dribbling onto his shoes.

Dip dragged Mirin to the exit. She looked back one last time. David's body now obscured the shape of the boy standing before him. The building shook again from another lightning strike.

David screamed in pain, his back arching as he was lifted from the ground, rising slowly above the sickly green mist. The scream that left his throat was a piercing ululation. David's head thrashed. Then the screaming stopped, drowned in a wet, guttural choking.

A spray of blood left his mouth. His body began turning in the air, rotating around an axis through his abdomen.

The room went black. David's scream echoed in the dark.

"Come on, Mirin!"

Dip pushed the button for the lift with his broken hand as he held onto Mirin with his good one. By some miracle the power was kicking back into life, perhaps re-galvanised by another bolt. The lift was working again but came as sluggishly as it had always done, no matter how much Dip worried at the button.

The room was lit once more with a lightning strike. The glass cases along the walls of the gallery exploded, showering David and the boy with the emerald-green shards. The boy's black eyes met

Mirin's. His arm extended above his head. David was impaled through the stomach, the boy's wrist disappearing into David's belly button through a bloody orifice. Blood poured down the boy's arm and over his chest. The boy was smiling.

Moments later, David's body was hurtling towards them through the air. It landed with a sickening splat only feet away, spraying Mirin with hot blood. Mirin gawped. David's neck was broken, twisting his head to the side, and his lifeless eyes stared blankly at Mirin. The worst part, though, was the look of realisation on his dead face. The horror of *knowing*.

The boy walked toward them through the creeping green mist.

Dip frantically pushed the button for the lift. It still hadn't arrived. He looked left and saw a set of double doors. He prayed they wouldn't be locked. The fog slithered toward them with a mind of its own, licking at their feet.

"This way," Dip cried, pulling Mirin by the arm. They reached the doors in a few steps and Dip heaved with all his might, but they stood fast. Frantically he pulled again, rattling the brass handles. Still they did not budge.

The boy came on, mirth fixedly smeared across his face.

"Dip, hurry," Mirin said, backing into him.

The small sign above the door handles read 'Push'. Dip could have laughed if he wasn't running for his life. He pushed with all his might. They yielded, and together they fled down the stairwell.

29

Happy and contented in his work, Eddie Burns whistled to himself. There was talk of calling off tonight's game, with the police grumbling about the increased crime rate. But Eddie knew in his bones it would go ahead. It would take the end of the world to call off the biggest rivalry in football between the two Glasgow clubs, Celtic and Rangers, with all their history and competitive animosity. Plus, vital points were on the line tonight. Whichever team won would go to the top of the league and have bragging rights. When the go-ahead was finally confirmed, Eddie had only grown in confidence.

The pay at the football stadium, just like at the university, was crappy. But the work had never been so much fun. Not his actual work, of course. How could anyone ever learn to love cleaning toilets or picking up everyone else's crap? Eddie's extracurricular activities, however, put a spring in his step and a whistle in his mouth. The Sash was his particular favourite, though he was sure to change his tune when a supervisor was around. No point getting reprimanded and drawing attention to himself.

All week Eddie had been preparing. He brought what he needed into work and stashed it around the stadium where nobody would find it. Tonight was the night. The game was merely the setting for Eddie's plan. And like a fan in a chanting crowd, Eddie knew he was part of something much bigger than himself. He felt its power welling up inside him. He was its instrument. In fact, Eddie knew all the people of the city were a part of the great plan, only Eddie was special because he knew his role, while all the others were like a mindless herd. Eddie wasn't a dumb sheep. He had become a wolf.

There was still a little time before people started arriving. Eddie thought he could sense their anticipation, their energy: fathers and sons, groups of friends, gathered in pubs along the way to the stadium, and others trapped in slowly moving cars down the city's thoroughfares, or trundling through the underground. Poison in the veins of the city, all of them. Eddie took out a folded stepladder and a strip-light from the box, set up the ladder and had a look around, trying to appear casual. Not that anyone would suspect him. He was plain old Eddie, remember? He left the light at the foot of the ladder and climbed to the top. He'd already checked the devices under the Govan and Broomloan Road stands. There was plenty of time to check the other two and make sure all the things needed for tonight's event were in place. This third device was well hidden beneath the concrete frame of the stand above, on top of a bookie's booth. The timer and the wire connections were in place. The other devices were smaller, and more exposed out in the open, but he had disguised them well. This bomb, however, was much larger and the bookie's booth gave it the appropriate cover to do the damage he needed it to do. Eddie synchronised his watch to the timer on the device, and, happy that everything was in order, he whistled his happy tune, climbing back down the ladder.

30

Dɪᴘ sᴀᴡ Mirin barrelling through a set of heavy wooden doors onto the lush, carpeted landing. He wasn't far ahead of her, descending a wide staircase, grand oil paintings of forgotten university professors and patrons rattling on the walls.

Dip paused, grabbing the banister for support, looking back up through the balustrades. He could see the eerie glow preceding the fog. Hairs prickled on the back of his neck. Mirin was at the top of the stairs now, backing up until she bumped into another set of double doors, pushing them ajar. The fog oozed forward, the preternatural light casting green shadows across Mirin's bloodied features.

"Come on, Mirin!" Dip shouted desperately. A cold sweat soaked his shirt. He felt *them* before he even heard them. It was as if they were crawling over his skin already. Thousands of tiny paws, each with five sharp claws, scurried through the fog. Their backs formed an undulating furred tide. Mirin fell through the door. It closed heavily on a spring-loaded hinge, trapping her ankle.

The fog, with its writhing mass of fur beneath its surface, sped closer. Mirin turned her ankle and pulled. The fog was almost upon her, the skittering claws and excited squeaks approaching like a wall of solid noise. Mirin yanked her foot free and the door closed. The wave of rats clattered against it, tumbling back on themselves, like a wave meeting a cliff-face.

The stream of rats emerged from the fog onto the red-carpeted staircase. They were nearly on top of Dip before he could react. The rats at the head of the pack leapt from the steps above Dip. He covered his head as he turned and started to run. The rodent bodies unsteadied him, but Dip kept his feet. He ran down the steps two and three at a time, rats hanging from his clothes by their claws and teeth. He slammed into the wall at the turn of the stairs. Several rats on his back were squashed like toothpaste tubes. One more flight of stairs to go before he could enter the cloisters.

Taking the last five steps in one leap, Dip landed heavily and fell to one side. He got to his feet, the swarm reaching the bottom of the stairs, the green fog not far behind them. Lurching, stumbling, using his hands as much as his feet, he fled, like an ancient version of man, running from the nightmares lying beyond the safety of the campfire.

A heavy pair of double doors confronted him and he lowered a shoulder to charge them, but as he drew close, they opened of their own accord. Dip barely kept his balance. The cloisters were murky, lit either side by streetlamps. The east and west quadrangles still had some power, but other areas were out. Dip was drawn towards the light, turning left. He sprinted for the stairwell he knew was tucked in the corner, not risking a look back. He could hear them and still feel them on his skin. He wanted to be sick, but he wanted to live more.

Reaching the final stairwell that would deliver him to the ground level at the front of the university, Dip used the banister to take as many stairs as he could at one time. His body felt bruised, and his fractured arm throbbed with an unhealthy pain. The light of University Avenue shone beyond the wide stone arch ahead. Dip cried with one last effort, pumping his legs and arms, lungs burning.

Bursting onto the road outside of the main building, Dip saw that the pedestrian access to the main gate ahead still lay open. The security guards must have left it open. Or perhaps they'd been killed before they could lock up? Dip didn't know or care. He kept running, never breaking his stride. When he reached the gate's intricate black ironwork carrying the university's motto, *Via Veritas Vita* – the way and the truth and the life – Dip spun through the pedestrian entrance, grabbing the ironwork with his good hand, catapulting himself down the hill.

Now, he could risk a look back. He brought himself to a halt, panting and sweating, looking into the darkness.

There was nothing there. No fog, no rats, no boy risen from the dead. And there was no Mirin either.

Dip swallowed back his nausea. Only a weak green flash illuminated the black clouds overhead. The thunder sounded distant and insignificant. He waited and looked into the portico at the base of the gothic building. He thought about going back, and turned full circle on his heels, pulling his hair, growling through gritted teeth. He looked up and down the hill and then back into the building. Then Dip remembered: Mirin had fallen through the doors. They would probably lead to another landing and a different set of stairs at the other side of the cloisters. If Mirin had kept running as Dip had, more than likely she would have emerged at the back of the building with the small car park that looked over the city. If she'd got out, that is where he would find her.

THERE WAS A SCREECH OF BRAKES, and the flash of chrome and blue paint skidded into view. Mirin hit the front wheel-arch of the car, and her momentum carried her forward onto the bonnet, knocking the wind out of her. Her forward momentum halted, and Mirin rolled off the front of the car. White headlights cut through the night. Mirin heard car doors opening, the engine idling in the background. She wanted to move, give warning to the driver, whoever it was, to get running. The rats were coming, and their master would not be far behind. But there was no air in her lungs.

"Professor Hassan, we've been looking for you."

Mirin recognised the voice, but with adrenaline surging through her body, couldn't immediately place it. A strong pair of hands lifted her from under the armpits. She scrambled against the grip, fighting.

She needed to get Oran and run as far away from the city as they could. There was no fighting this, but maybe they could outrun it.

"Jesus! She's covered in blood." This was a man's voice from behind Mirin. Again, it was vaguely familiar.

"There's no need to run, Professor Hassan. We only want to talk." Mirin's eyes focused on the slender woman in front of her wearing a knee-length raincoat. At last Mirin recognised DCI Shepherd.

"You have to run. Now!!" Mirin tried to break free again, but the man behind her, who must have been DI Blair, had a firm grip.

"Now, now, Professor Hassan. Calm down. We will not be running anywhere," DI Blair growled.

Mirin scanned the dark portico behind them. There was no mist, nor rats, nor any sign of the boy. Her breath returned, heavy and laboured. Mirin calmed a little, her eyes searching DCI Shepherd's face. The policewoman stared at her passively.

"Where did the blood come from, Professor Hassan?"

Mirin looked down and saw the sprays of red across her coat and trousers. She brought a hand to her face. Her fingers came away sticky and red.

"David," Mirin whispered.

"David Hamill?" DCI Shepherd checked. Mirin nodded. "Is he dead?"

"Yes." Then Mirin sobbed. She could not hold it back. She would have fallen to her knees, but DI Blair had a hold on her.

"Show me where, Mirin," DCI Shepherd said softly.

31

THE OLD HOMELESS LADY, Mary, knew it was match day and was on her way to the underground station on Argyle Street. It was a productive spot, especially on game days. Mary did particularly well. She was old and dumpy and "a wee bit dotty" as she often put it. She kept her hair as neat as it could be, grey and straggly though it was. She liked to tie it back with an elastic band and hide it under a thick blue woolly hat, whatever the weather. Lots of people seemed to know her name, especially on match days. She enjoyed the minor celebrity; she could stop and chat to people. They'd buy her cups of tea or coffee. The ones that knew her really well got a hot chocolate and a doughnut and put a few pounds in her hand. A five- or ten-pound note wasn't uncommon, especially when they were drunk. They'd tell her that she reminded them of their granny or their favourite old auntie.

Mary knew a man who said he was a dentist. She'd often see him on a match day, and he always tried to give her his business card and told her to come in for a check-up. Mary would take the card with a chuckle, and then deliberately talk a little too fast to be understood, mumbling her words. No matter how nice he was, there was no way she was going to a dentist with all those needles and drills and chemical smells.

The underground station on Argyle Street wasn't very far away, as Mary waddled under the Heilanman's Umbrella, down the long, wide tunnel under Central Station. Giant steel girders ran overhead, supporting the railway tracks. Along either side of the tunnel were rows of shops, cafés, fish and chip takeouts, and tattoo parlours, with a wide path running between them. It formed a natural shelter from the harsh elements, where many of the city's homeless people congregated for the night. Mary was halfway through the tunnel when the football chants sounded in an exultant groan, bouncing down the long tunnel.

A group of football fans walked under the umbrella, in the green and white hoops of the Celtic. They were halfway through the tunnel when another small group of Rangers fans in red, white, and blue tops entered the tunnel from the other side, singing at the top of their lungs.

The Rangers' chants provoked the Celtic supporters into their counter-chant even before they had seen where the opposing fans were. The Rangers supporters heard the Celtic fans and increased their volume. In turn, the Celtic fans did the same, and both groups slowed their pace.

Mary looked for a safe place. Unable to find one, she kissed the head of the pigeon in her hands.

"Go on now," she told the pigeon, throwing it into the air. It took flight, pounding its wings out of the tunnel and into an oppressive charcoal sky crackling with latent power. The bird called back to her as it flew away. It told Mary to flap her chubby wings and hide from the crows. Mary smiled wanly at the silly bird, but she wished so much that she could fly.

Mary hugged the shopfronts and doorways. When the chanting turned into shouts, and the men began to swear, and the other people walking through the Hielanman's Umbrella started to give the two groups a wide berth, Mary shrank into a shop doorway.

"Come on! Come the *fook* on!"

"Oi!"

Feet moved quickly across the pavement. There was a pregnant pause followed by shattering glass. Blue and white lights flashed, reflected by shop windows. The police car's alarm silenced the supporters. Two more policemen entered the Hielanman's Umbrella from the other direction on foot. A riot van would not be far behind them.

Mary slipped from the doorway and passed unnoticed behind the policemen as they dismounted from their car, their hands instinctively checking that they had their side batons and pepper spray. She didn't look back, shuffling across the large junction to take her place outside Saint Enoch underground station, where the escalator descended.

There weren't the usual happy faces at a game. People moved quickly by Mary, many avoiding the underground. A young woman stopped, furtively checking up and down the street and reached into her coat pocket, producing her purse. Still looking around, the young woman took out a handful of change and pressed it into Mary's gloved hand. Mary wanted to pull away. She didn't like people touching her. But this lady seemed kind, if a little scared. Mary knew why: the birds had told her.

"Have you got somewhere to go, love? Get in somewhere safe, okay?"

Mary chuckled and nodded and did her usual trick of speaking too fast. The young woman looked over her shoulder and then hurried off up Buchanan Street.

Somewhere to go, thought Mary. *I live on the streets: I am home. The young 'un's right though. Best not stay too long tonight.* She'd aim to get enough for something to eat and maybe a hot chocolate, and then find somewhere to hole up for the night.

"Crraah! Stupid Mary," one of three crows said, standing on top of a bin. The other two sniggered behind it. "There's going to be some fun tonight," the crow went on, while Mary tried to ignore it, smiling her toothless smile at passers-by. A young man, with hair sweeping across one eye, and tight jeans that made his feet look like a clown's, barged past Mary as if she wasn't there. The old lady fell heavily on her behind and the crows burst into a great peal of laughter.

"Might as well stay down, Stupid Mary. It'll make it easier for us to eat your eyeballs. Might as well do it sooner rather than later," the crow squawked. Its two fellow crows laughed and nudged each other with their wings.

Mary's hip hurt a great deal as she got to her hands and knees, joints cracking with age. Someone else, hurrying without looking where they were going, knocked into Mary again. She cried out as she spun, hitting the ground again, this time face-first.

The crows hopped down from their perch, shrieking with laughter.

"Stupid Mary," the crow repeated, cocking its head. "You might as well *stay down.*"

32

"You have the right to remain silent..." DI Blair took the cuffs from his coat pocket and clicked them around Mirin's wrists.

David Hamill lay on the floor of the museum. The sarcophagus was open, empty of its prize. The hall was shrouded in blackness, shards of glass everywhere underfoot. She had called for a team to secure the room. The control room had tried to say there weren't any teams available, especially with the game on tonight. Connie had pulled rank, demanding they send squad cars to get here soon as they could.

The hall was graveyard silent. Butterflies and beetles, stuffed freakshow animals, and a flayed dinosaur stared blankly at them, as though the living were trespassers here.

Connie inspected David's body. His neck appeared to have been broken and there was a tremendous amount of blood. A gaping wound sat just beneath his
ribcage.

"Where's the weapon, Mirin?"

Mirin didn't take her eyes off David. There was horror there, mixed with disbelief. Connie had seen it too many times. Murderers unable to accept what they had done. It was partly the shock, but for many it was bound up with the breaking of one of the greatest social taboos. A cognitive dissonance sets in that won't permit them to admit what they've done, even to themselves. That's what interviews were for, to break down the barriers to the truth. It was often portrayed as a cat and mouse game on the TV, and it could be. But just as often Connie found it was about helping the perpetrator accept what they'd done. A kind of therapy. Some would go all the way to prison denying the truth. But many actually broke down and cried with relief. And yes, grief too.

Mirin was in no shape right now to admit anything. A slow drive to the station and then a little time by herself before bringing her to an interview room would help give her time.

Normally when Connie got to a crime scene it had already been *declared* a crime scene. Forensics were there or on their way. Uniform coppers had started taking statements from witnesses. Connie wasn't normally the one with the handcuffs, reading them their rights. As such, she would usually enter the scene in a clinical fashion, already primed with information. She'd cold-read the room, assessing the evidence as she found it. But this scene was still hot. The body was still warm. And there was too much about it that didn't make sense. The shattered glass from the display cases, the type and extent of the victim's injuries, the lack of a murder weapon. Mirin must have stowed it somewhere in the building.

But weirdest of all: where was the archaeological find they were working on? Why would Mirin take it and how could she have done it? When they had bumped into her, quite literally, outside the university building, she had been fleeing the scene still covered in blood. Not the actions of someone who had taken the time to steal and hide a priceless artefact. *Another body to locate.*

It was time to go. The scene needed preserving and they had the perpetrator bang to rights. It was an open and shut case, but what was the motive? Connie had some thoughts on that: ambition, a love tryst, and a little mental breakdown added into the mix. There was no hurry. They had time.

33

Ever since touching it at the crime scene, the black knife had stayed in Douglas Wallace's mind. It loomed in the recesses of his imagination. Slowly, it had grown, becoming clearer. He often thought back to holding it in his gloved hand, placing it into an evidence bag. He could still feel the weight of the knife. He was surprised at how light it was. Even caked in peat, he could tell the blade was deadly sharp.

Crows perched on the top of streetlamps, parked cars, windowsills and rooftops, as Douglas parked his ageing Vauxhall Astra in at the police station near Cowcaddens underground station. The crows cawed and hopped agitatedly from foot to foot, stretching their wings the same way boxers roll their shoulders before the opening bell. The autumn nights had drawn in significantly, but the broiling black clouds overhead had turned the city into the pitch of midnight. The streetlights struggled against the dark.

Douglas locked the car. He noticed a fog beginning to snake its way through the city. It wasn't a fog he was used to in Glasgow: usually a thin, wet haze. This was thick. He could see it oozing, low to the ground, opaque and yet emanating its own low, insipid green light. However, it did not strike Douglas as odd. Not after all that had happened. It was a confirmation of things coming to a head. The feeling had grown stronger along with the image of the knife, and with them an ever-strengthening sense of certainty about his true purpose in life. He had begun with setting his family on the right path. A few others since, who had crossed his path, he had helped see the light. These had all been a prelude for *tonight*. The end was nigh. All the brimstone he'd been taught in Sunday school, spat from the pulpit by a pious priest soon replaced by a liberal fairy, was going to come to fruition. He just knew it. It was a deep faith. A fervent belief.

Police cars and vans left and returned to the police station like busy little bees. He clicked a button on his keys, unlocking the boot. A mechanical clunk followed, and like a coffin lid at sundown, the boot cracked ajar.

There was a scuffle near the entrance. The back of a police van opened, and police hurried from the station steps to assist with the melee. It was a comical sight: handcuffed prisoners still trying to set about each other with kicks and headbutts. The police piled in, pulling them apart. The handcuffed prisoners immediately turned their attention to the police. One sank his teeth into the forearm of an officer and was pepper- sprayed as a result. When the perpetrator cried out and stumbled back, the officer flicked out his baton...

Suppressing a grin, Douglas turned back to the boot of his car and lifted out the heavy black duffle bag, bracing against the weight.

Threading his way through the now subdued bodies, Douglas mounted the pavement and, at the bottom of a small flight of stairs, gave a nod of acknowledgement to DCI Connie Shepherd and DI Stuart Blair, who were bringing in a suspect between them. The suspect was a slight, middle-class-looking brunette with tears in her eyes. 'Ah, there is no condemnation for those in union.' Douglas recalled Romans 8:1, ascending the stairs and entering the police station. When he reached the security door to go down to the evidence room, Douglas swiped his forensics identification card and was permitted entry. He'd never known the station to be so noisy and chaotic. Although he was normally based off-site, it wasn't unusual for Douglas to be in and out of all the various stations to collect evidence or to sign it back in.

Police officers strained to control the good citizens of the city. Those not requiring restraint sat sobbing, with looks of shock accompanying their bleeding noses, fat lips, and black eyes. A paramedic team attended to a person on the floor, the arresting officers hovering close by. The doors closed behind Douglas, and he descended another flight of stairs into the basement, where the sounds of the scene above grew faint and distant, like a party in full swing he was having to walk away from.

Douglas smiled at Charlie Davies, who sat on duty at the evidence room. He'd known Charlie quite a few years now. Having blown out his knee on duty a couple of years ago, Charlie often manned the evidence room, and then piled on the weight of a desk jockey. Charlie pulled out the earphones connected to his phone as Douglas placed the duffle bag in front of the desk, out of sight, unzipping the top before straightening up.

"Watching the game tonight?" Charlie asked, nodding towards his phone. He must have turned the volume up full, because the pre-match chat between the pundits was clearly audible from little earbuds discarded on the desk.

"Aye, if I can get this piece of work stowed away."

"I can't believe they're actually going ahead with the game, what with everything kicking off tonight."

"You would say that," Douglas said wryly. "There's no way Rangers are ready for the *Bhoys* right now."

"Aye, you reckon?" Charlie returned the banter as good as he got, pulling forward the keyboard of the computer terminal. "What can I do you for?" He tapped the return key with his index finger to wake up the computer. Then he frowned at the screen, hitting the return key hard with his index finger repeatedly. "Bastard thing!"

As if on cue, the lights overhead flickered, then stalled completely. There was a moment of darkness before they came back to life stutteringly. Charlie looked up. When he looked back, Douglas was nowhere to be seen. Puzzled, he looked around his desk, as though expecting to find Douglas in miniature-figurine form amidst his paraphernalia and jumped when Douglas stood upright again from in front of the desk.

"Bugger me, Dougie. You nearly gave me a heart attack!"

Douglas stood with his arms folded behind his back, as if standing at easy on a parade ground.

"Sorry. I'm here for the flint knife in the Stirlingshire peatland killings case."

Charlie sucked his teeth and looked at the computer screen with a pained and doubtful expression, which developed into a shake of the head. "Doesn't look like you are in any luck tonight. The system's gone down, and you've no chance – just like in the football. Unless the system comes back online soon. It's been playing up a little today."

"Seeing as you think you're gonna get lucky tonight in the football, maybe you could help a poor old Celtic *bhoy* out?" Douglas said, feeling the weight of the lump hammer he held behind his back.

Another pained expression came across Charlie's face. "No can do, Dougie. You know how it is now, especially with this computer system. Every I has to be dotted, every T crossed. It would be my neck if any evidence went missing."

"That it would," Douglas agreed, smiling gently, before using the hammer to add a full stop to the end of Charlie's life.

34

MIRIN OFFERED no resistance to Connie and Stuart as they led her from the police car, holding her at the elbow. She was a somnambulist with her eyes wide but her mind in some other place.

Neither Connie nor Stuart had ever seen the station like this. The whole city seemed to be going mad. Things often got out of hand on game days. It wasn't unusual for fights to break out in bars, or for the occasional small-scale riot on some city centre street once disappointed supporters were sufficiently filled with alcohol. It was a sad joke that whenever an Old Firm game happened, domestic violence rates increased along with the random assaults and even murders. But this was different. The game hadn't even started yet and people were losing their minds. They, the police, were still in control, but only just.

Connie and Stuart approached the desk sergeant, an old-timer by the name of Jackie Conway. He raised his overgrown eyebrows, looking over his spectacles like a tawny owl. "It's not like you to be getting your hands dirty, DCI Shepherd."

"It's not like you to be working the desk on a Friday night, Sarge," Connie quipped back.

"All hands on deck tonight. People are being called in left and right. Leave has been cancelled."

They began the tedious procedure of signing in their suspect, details of address, prompting Mirin when they didn't know the information themselves. They made sure Mirin understood what was happening. Her agitation grew, although she didn't try to pull away from them. Things weren't helped by the fact that they had to repeat themselves many times because Mirin spoke too quietly, and Jackie's hearing was past its best. The noise of the station seemed to be rising all the time as officers struggled with a high volume of uncooperative arrestees. Then suddenly, Mirin stiffened, tearing her elbow free of Stuart's grip, who quickly caught her by the collar.

"No, you don't," Stuart said flatly.

Panic had spread across Mirin's face. "I have to go. I need to get my son. Oran! He needs me."

Connie looked at Mirin, still covered in blood, and shook her head. "You can't go anywhere, Mirin. We can send someone to check in on your boy. We have to talk to you about David. You understand."

Mirin shook her head, still pulling away, but outnumbered, hands cuffed behind her back, she was unable to go anywhere.

"I need to go. We all need to go. Can't you see? All this..." She jerked her head, indicating the chaos that was around them. "This is all because of the boy."

Connie nodded, as if agreeing, and kept her voice calm and level. "It's okay, Mirin. We will send an officer around to check on your boy. Just give us the details of the sitter. I will personally make sure your son is looked after. It'll be fine. Your boy will be safe. You are here now, and we need to talk to you."

Part of the job was getting a suspect to relax, to get them to trust you and calm down. It wasn't unusual for the suspect to be in a heightened state of agitation after arrest, especially if they knew they were guilty. They didn't want to accept what they'd done. A good interviewing officer tried to get them to see the officer as an ally and calm them down. With some perpetrators, an adversarial approach wouldn't work, and Connie was sure it wouldn't work with Mirin. She was in shock and was worried about her son. She would need some time to quieten down before they interviewed her.

Connie looked around at the police station, straining at the seams, and hoped she could actually get an interview room tonight.

The lights flickered overhead. When the lights re-established themselves, the weak control the police had fought to maintain was broken. Another handcuffed suspect ran away from the clutches of two uniformed officers. One officer looked around frantically. The other was already in pursuit, but too late. The detainee hit Connie in the small of the back, knocking her ribs into Jackie's high desk. She went down, losing her grip on Mirin.

Fights erupted everywhere.

35

Dɪᴘ sᴛᴏᴘᴘᴇᴅ, bent over, hands on knees, swallowing back saliva, gasping for breath. He'd run up and down University Avenue, then around the main building, and found nothing. There was no sign of Mirin anywhere. A stitch burned in his side.

He straightened up, trying to think. The panic of losing Mirin had him in its grip. He was spinning, lost at sea with a storm gathering both figuratively and literally. What to do? Where to go? All his questions and indecisions spun around each other, whirling into a vortex of problems, until from that chaos formed something solid, like a hardened pearl: a feeling. It was like the stitch stabbing Dip in the gut, only instead of a stab it was a *pull*, like an ache in his chest pointing the way.

Home, he thought. He needed to get off the street and head back. On the way, he could try one of the police stations: they needed to know about David and what Dip had seen. What *had* he seen? No one would believe him. But the pull told him he needed Mirin. She was the key. He didn't understand why yet, or why Mirin wasn't affected by the boy, even though she worked closely with him.

The thought hadn't occurred to him until recently. She never looked ill and her personality seemed unaffected. In the midst of the hurricane, she was the storm's eye. That only convinced Dip further that she was important in all this. Everything he had seen and experienced, his visions of death incarnate, convinced Dip of the truth that possessed him: whatever was happening needed to be stopped, however impossible that might be. And he thought he knew what had to be done. The pieces were falling into place. At least, he hoped.

A taxi roared by. The window rolled down and the shout that left it drew him back to the present.

"Fucking Paki!" Following the words was a half-eaten kebab in its greasy wrapping. It tumbled through the air, shedding lettuce and hot sauce, landing with a wet slap at Dip's feet. The car didn't stop, gliding away until it turned, brakes whining around the corner. Twice in as many weeks Dip had been called that slur. Before that the last time was as a probationary officer on the beat in Glasgow, and then it was from a drunk. Normally he would have taken the licence plate, but the car was too far away now, and Dip had other things on his mind.

Dip needed to get his bearings. The university at his back, Kelvingrove Park to his right, and his parents' only a few minutes away down the hill, which his stitch would be thankful for. Overhead, clouds simmered blackly, churning in slow, restless eddies. Night had come even earlier than usual to the short autumnal day. Like beams bowing against the heat of a fire ranging unseen in the attic, the streetlights seemed barely up to the task of holding back the night.

Dip started to walk. He didn't let the racial slur get to him. It wasn't the first, though it could be the last if he couldn't find Mirin. That thought turned his walk into a jog as he rounded the corner of University Avenue; the stitch complained sharply. To Dip's surprise, there were students heading into the stone building of the union from the otherwise abandoned campus.

He looked back with a feeling of being pushed from behind, and a cold blade ran up his spine when he saw it. A viscous fog moved slowly up the road towards the park. It slunk forward, only a few feet high, glowing faintly green. It seeped through the iron railing, like syrup through a sieve, and into the park. Dip didn't have the time to investigate it, nor did he want to. The sight filled Dip with nothing but dread. He quickened his pace, the stitch now biting. There wasn't any time left. The fog told him that. He needed to find Mirin and something else, something black and marked with death.

Another glance back and the fog was moving quickly now, spreading out across the park and up towards the union building. He ran flat-out, weaving between students. He had to get to his parents before the fog got through the park. Death wasn't a cloaked figure on horseback any more. It was a silent cloud.

36

EVERY EVENING, without fail, Judy Maclean walked her dog, Timmy, through the park. The thunderstorm of earlier seemed to have petered out, and Judy thought they'd nip out during the calm.

Timmy was a mongrel Judy rescued from the pound when he was barely a pup at a year old, a cross between an Alsatian and maybe a collie. Now seven, he was still a bright and energetic boy, but very obedient, except when he gave her puppy eyes, often when Judy was dunking Rich Tea biscuits into a mug of tea. As such, Timmy was a tad overweight. Not by much, because they walked often, but those Rich Teas over the years did add up, and he had a little tooth decay, which meant he'd had a couple of teeth removed. Judy had been admonished by her vet about it on several occasions. Judy still thought of Timmy as having a hard life. She needed to smother him in love, her own children having flown the nest a few years before she got him. Even Judy acknowledged Timmy was filling the void that they had left.

The children had moved further afield, one over in Edinburgh, another down in London. Fingers crossed, they might start having children soon. One was engaged. The other was married. They had good job prospects. So, when Judy's husband, Roger, died three years ago, it was just her and Timmy left rattling around their large Edwardian apartment in Park Circus, which looked across Kelvingrove Park.

It was Judy and Timmy's early evening ritual to make a couple of circuits around the park before dinner. In reality, it was a couple of circuits for Judy. Timmy, however, when off the leash, would bound here and there, meeting other dogs, playing with them, stealing a ball from a grumpy terrier named Billy and bringing it back to Judy, for her to apologise and hand it back to its rightful, yappy owner.

Judy had thought twice about going out tonight. With all the peculiar weather and trouble on the news, Judy was definitely starting to feel a little on edge living by herself. But then, she reasoned, why should she let any of that ruin her walks with Timmy? She really looked forward to them, and so did he: one in the morning and one in the evening. She wouldn't let a little silliness on the news get in the way of them having their fun. You weren't a Glaswegian if you weren't prepared for all kinds of weather in one day. Admittedly, green lightning and a rain of frogs was a *wee* bit out of the ordinary. But the scientists did say climate change would bring more extreme weather conditions. Chickens coming home to roost, thought Judy, who always recycled, even carefully washing out all her plastic packaging. What did people expect if they were going to burn all those fossil fuels and throw away all those plastic bags?

Timmy had sat by the front door, wagging his tail, his ears pricked up expectantly. Judy picked up the keys and popped them in the pocket of her white raincoat, which she pulled over a woolly jumper to guard against the autumn chill. It was their usual pre-walk ritual, and Timmy would bounce excitedly on his front paws as Judy put on a red woollen hat she'd knitted herself, and then unlatched the front door. Timmy gave an excited little bark.

As soon as they stepped outside, Judy felt it wasn't as cold as it should have been for this time of year. In fact, it was quite muggy. She looked up warily at the clouds overhead. It wasn't raining yet, but those looked like the worst storm clouds she'd seen in a while. A gentle rumble of thunder would be the soundtrack of their walk. Perhaps they'd walk a little quicker tonight. They wouldn't want to get caught in a tropical downpour. It might actually rain cats and dogs, Judy thought.

As they got to the park entrance, Timmy was already pulling at the lead to be set free into the glorious fun of crispy leaves. Judy unclipped him and he was off, feet skittering on the concrete until they found grass. He kicked up clouds of leaves left and right, barking with joy, turning around to see whether Judy was coming, and then continued on his way, running in a large loop.

Thunder growled as Judy picked her way as quickly as she dared, following a path that led down the steep hill from Park Circus to the flatter levels of the lower park. But still no rain. She reached the small pond, not far from the bridge over the small, meandering River Kelvin, with the university beyond perched on the hill opposite Park Circus. That was when Judy noticed just how many other animals there were in the park tonight. Kelvingrove Park was a favourite for dog walkers. A typical evening would see dozens of people with their dogs. It was one of the reasons why Judy loved coming here with Timmy so much. She could socialise, and so could he. However, tonight there didn't seem to be any owners *with* the dogs. Judy and Timmy tended to meet the same dogs on the same days, dog walkers being sticklers for routine. However, tonight Judy didn't recognise any of the dogs wandering the park.

At first, the dogs paid no attention to Judy. She walked a little more of her route around the pond until she realised she had lost Timmy. She called his name. It wasn't unusual for him not to come straight away. He might be involved in some amazing game with another dog, and it would take Judy several attempts to get his attention, but he always came bounding back, ears pricked up, tail wagging, that bright-eyed canine grin on his face. Her husband, Roger, had said dogs couldn't smile, but Judy knew different. Timmy definitely smiled, a big, massive ear-to-ear toothsome beam, reflecting in his sparkling brown eyes.

"Timmy!" Judy shouted. The shout didn't seem to travel as it normally would, as if she were shouting in a padded room. More dogs she didn't recognise trotted past her. Turning full circle, Judy shouted for Timmy, her voice dying in the thick, oppressive air that smothered the park.

He'll come back, Judy told herself, her heart fluttering with nerves she hadn't felt since Roger died.

Judy turned again, squinting into the distance. Thunder rumbled in a slow, boiling growl. She took one further step forward, craning her neck, her eyes straining in the gloom of orange lamplight. Fog?

It oozed into the park from beyond the football pitches. Turning in a slow circle, Judy checked to see if the fog was anywhere else. And sure enough, it was descending the hill from Park Circus, where her home was, and from the other side of the park, slithering through the empty children's play park.

Suddenly, Judy felt terribly sick and afraid. She couldn't put her finger on why. There was something unnatural about the fog. It wasn't a normal Glaswegian fog, the wet, misty cloud that lay over the city very occasionally. Judy was hemmed in on all sides. She had nowhere else to go except towards that unearthly fog.

"Timmy," Judy cried again. Trying to muster the confidence in herself, telling herself that she was just being a silly old lady, Judy tried again. "Timmy," she shouted.

She started to walk away from the fog snaking towards her, heading to the fountain beyond the pond. That looked to be an island, free from the encircling spectral mass. She quickened, still calling Timmy's name.

The fountain stood where it always had been, a landmark to orientate herself by. Behind it was the huge bronze statue of a sabretooth cat, proudly roaring over the park from a prehistoric age, when all was claws and blood. It had always seemed odd to Judy that the statue was here. All the other statues were of dead scientists, generals, and lords of an equally dead empire. Judy could understand those, but what was the point of a giant, menacing cat? Yet now, the sabretooth looked at home, its paw coveting a bloody kill. In this fog, it could hunt the blind with the smell of fear alone.

"Timmy! Come on, boy. Please!" She came to the edge of the fountain, its stone lip giving back something solid and real. Fog had swallowed up the orange-brown football pitches, just as it had smothered the streets of the city.

The circle closed around Judy as she edged around the splendour of the Victorian fountain, calling for her once-faithful hound. Judy's heart swelled as she saw him at last. Timmy!

There was a congregation; that was the word that came to Judy's mind. A congregation of all the dogs that had been streaming into the park, including her Timmy. Unlike his usual self, he sat stock still. The congregation was not only made up of dogs, but cats too. Hundreds of them, perhaps more, sitting in the fog. They were all sat obediently, looking towards a small figure at their centre. It was a boy, with his back to Judy. The fog was all around her now, so she had no choice but to go in. She edged forward, terrible nausea rippling through her.

A burning fire raced up her throat and out of her mouth. Judy vomited into the empty pool. She wiped her mouth, a cold shiver washing over her, knowing that her stomach would convulse again soon.

"Timmy," Judy called weakly. The word hung in the air with no effect on her dog.

The small figure began to turn. Judy realised he could only be nine or ten years old and entirely naked.

No sooner did she look at him than a thought surfaced in Judy's mind. A cold memory she had worked to forget. Roger, wasting away in front of her, in so much pain, shitting the bed, vomiting up the meagre amounts of food she made for him, in agony, dying a slow, painful death. Judy remembered standing in the kitchen, harrowed by his cries of pain, her hands shaking, holding boxes of his medication. She could end it. Give him too many pills. End it. It would be a mercy. But mercy wasn't the reason. Selfish fear, a desire for her to be rid of him and his pain and his cancer.

Judy stumbled back, half pitching into the fountain. She fell heavily into the empty pool. The flash of Roger's emaciated face, globs of dried spittle in the corners of his mouth, stared back at her through eyes that were glaucous pools of morphine. Judy saw the face of the boy reflected in the memory of her dead husband's eyes.

So in heaven as in hell, a growl of thunder overhead was mirrored by a growl from the earth. As lightning followed, so did the keening screech of feral cats. All the animals were looking at Judy, who stumbled to her feet. Her white coat was stained with green algae and smears of dirt.

Judy climbed from the fountain, sobbing, looking for somewhere to run. The fog was everywhere. She did not want to go farther into that fog, just as she did not want to go back into Roger's room to listen to the death rattle of his necrotic lungs.

Dogs began to bark. They weren't like Timmy's playful bark. They were the barks of hellhounds guarding their master's crypt. Growling snarls filled the air. Saliva foamed around their maws. The cats hissed, aping their long-dead sabre-toothed cousin. The cacophony grew.

The fog was *at* the fountain now. Caught between it, and the boy and his denizens, Judy hesitated. The barks and hisses grew louder. Her hesitation was like a signal. They started to run toward her.

She gave a strangled scream and tried to get her old legs moving. Her heart burned in her chest as she ran into the fog that whirled around her thighs like an eddying current.

There was a steep hill running directly up towards Park Circus. It was the shortest route, but the ground was wet and sodden underfoot. She had to take the risk. She skidded on the mud, but Judy somehow stayed on her feet. The steep incline quickly made Judy's legs feel heavy and they burnt with effort.

She was already slowing, growing weaker. She fell to one knee and one hand. Looking behind, the cats and the dogs were at full clip, their eyes wild, their teeth bared. The rabid sounds the animals made did not echo. They stopped dead, sucked back in on themselves like a demonic recording played in reverse.

Judy cried. Every second step she stumbled, wheezing with the effort. Her white coat was drenched in mud. The fog, alive and predatory, rippled around her.

Judy screamed when jaws clamped around her ankle beneath the fog. Her scream was strangled by the night as she tried to pull her leg free, but it would not come. She knew that once a dog's jaws bit, they could lock, making it near impossible for them to be prised open. She kicked out and a second set of jaws fastened on her other leg.

Fumbling, Judy tried to punch the nose of the dog worrying at the flesh of her calf. As she did so, another pair of sharp feline jaws sunk their teeth into the skin of Judy's hand. More jaws and claws snapped. She screamed, trying to get back to her feet. If she stayed down, she was dead. She knew that, even through the pain.

Whatever was attached to her feet was snarling, thrashing its head from side to side. More teeth fastened onto Judy's upper arms, and claws dug into her back. Needle-like teeth sunk into her neck. Something with a soft, furry belly struck Judy on the head, latching on with piercing claws, mewling hungrily as it bit her ear. Judy screamed, feeling the blood running hotly from her wounds. A huge pair of jaws clamped on to her arm and the pain reached new levels as the bones began to crack.

"Timmy," Judy shouted. Yes, Timmy was there. He had come at her call. Just as he had been with her when Roger died, he would be with her now. Lovingly, he opened his mouth, as though to kiss her, and bit down sharply upon her face.

37

IT WAS Alex's first football match. He was nine years old and had been pestering his dad to go to a Rangers match since he was five. His dad, everyone called him "Big Alex", had always been reluctant to take his son, for some reason that *wee* Alex couldn't fathom, and his father wouldn't explain.

Alex was fascinated by the Saturday ritual his father performed every other weekend. Dad would always disappear shortly after lunch. Alex knew he would meet up with his friends in a pub, because he wouldn't take the car, walking out of the house with a red, white, and blue scarf wrapped around his neck. Then sometime later, his father returned, the sweet smell of beer on his breath, either elated or solemn, depending on the result. The closest Alex had ever got to these mysteries was watching a game on the telly with his father. They munched on crisps. He'd enjoy a can of Irn Bru while Big Alex drank his beer, and they'd both shout at the screen and jump off the sofa when Rangers scored. It was like becoming something else, something bigger than himself. When they watched football, Alex and his dad were parts of the same entity.

But as they approached the stadium, *wee* Alex started to get a true sense of the magic which television could only portray a pale reflection of. He could feel the palpable energy as they walked along the street. Everyone headed in the same direction, flowing towards Ibrox Stadium.

Slightly to Alex's annoyance, his dad had also capitulated to his younger sister's protestations that she wasn't allowed to go. So Karen was tagging along as well. She was two years younger than Alex, which meant she'd got to go to her first match two years before he did.

Like all younger sisters, Karen was full of annoying questions. Not just about football, which she knew nothing about, but other point- less stuff. Furthering Alex's annoyance, his mum had told him to "look after" his sister. He'd thought: *What's a dad for then*? but he didn't really mean it. Of course he would look after her. That didn't mean he had to like it.

Despite the presence of his questioning sister, Alex revelled in the excitement, nerves dancing and making his tummy flip. Not only was it his first game, but it was an Old Firm game between Rangers' greatest rival, Celtic. They could see the stadium now and hear the noise of the fans already chanting inside. The noise had a physical presence, humming in the air, rising from the stadium, calling them in.

Karen tugged at Alex's sleeve. Big Alex had got annoyed at all the questions and so she deferred to Alex.

"Alex, why are there so many crows here? Do they all live in Ibrox?"

"Shut up, you *wee dafty*. There aren't any..." Then Alex noticed the crows lining the stadium's upper scaffolding and banners, perched on top of cars, on window ledges, from the guttering of the tenement buildings and shopfronts. Their cries mixed with the calls from the stadium, as though they too had a team to support. He'd never seen this many crows before. Their shiny marble-like eyes watched the people pass underneath them. Alex squeezed Karen's hand just a little bit and pulled her a little closer.

"But there are crows, Alex. Look. Hundreds of them!" Karen said.

"I... I know," Alex said, trying to sound grown-up and confident. "This is just the time they go to bed. You're right. They must live round here or something." The last bit didn't come out quite as confidently as he hoped, but Karen seemed to accept it. Crows must have to live somewhere. Why not near the football stadium? Pigeons seemed to live absolutely everywhere, especially in the city centre.

A burst of noise behind them. As they passed a pub, its doors burst open. A man bundled out onto the pavement, shouting and swearing, holding a bottle in his hand. Everyone on the street turned to stare at him. Big Alex took both his children in his arms, pulling them away.

"Don't pay any attention to him. It's all right," Dad said.

"None of yous fuckers care," the man slurred. And then without further warning he smashed the beer bottle over his head.

Karen screamed, unable to take her eyes away.

"Don't look, love. He's just drunk," Big Alex said, trying to turn Karen's head away.

The man wasn't finished. He looked at the broken bottle in his hand. Blood and beer dripped from his head as he considered the hungry shards of glass in his hand. Then he looked to the broiling sky, exposing his neck.

"NO!" Big Alex almost shouted, covering his children's eyes.

The slamming of police car doors preceded the sounds of running feet and the cries of a struggle followed.

"Come on," Alex's dad said urgently, acting as though what they had just seen was nothing. The stadium wasn't far away now.

Alex's tummy did another flip in excitement. He'd seen playground fights before, plenty of violence on TV, and he'd blown off the heads of a few people in computer games. But he'd never seen *real violence*. All he could think of was: what if that was his dad? What if that man had tried to attack his dad instead of himself? What would happen then? Dad would probably handle it, he tried to reassure himself. He was a big guy, or at least he was in Alex's eyes.

The situation outside the pub well behind them, they finally reached the stadium, anticipation building with every step. Alex had been in the car as they passed it before, and walked by the stadium a few times as well, but this was different. It had become charged with the energy of those coming to watch the game.

Four huge stands stood sentinel around the pitch, rising to meet the sky. It was like a temple in everything but name. Even the smells of match day were like a Catholic priest's mysterious incense: cigarette smoke mixing with wafts of frying onions and beefburgers, the faint smell of beer, colognes, and body odour. It made Alex light-headed.

"Stay close," Big Alex said, letting go of their hands, fishing in his pocket for their tickets.

He handed one to Alex.

"I want *mine!*" Karen said.

"You're too little," Alex said.

"No, I'm not," Karen protested. "Daddy, please can I have my ticket too?"

"You'll lose it," Alex growled.

Big Alex was already handing her the ticket.

"She'll be all right, *wee* man. You're a big girl now, aren't you, hen?"

Alex couldn't hide the sourness from his face. Karen scrunched up her nose and stuck out her tongue at him. She snatched the ticket with glee away from their father.

"Tell you what. I'll go first and show you how it's done," Big Alex told them. "Then, Karen, you go next. Give the man the ticket. Alex, you run security and take up the rear. Keep your sister safe. Okay?"

Karen beamed and nodded. Alex shrugged in affirmation. They joined the queue, mostly men, but women and children lined up as well; the *beautiful game* drew all-comers. They were all being funnelled into a tight spot, pressing together, the smiles and the noises intensifying.

Big Alex disappeared through the turnstile with a click-clacking noise as he went. Karen bounced into the space left by their father, and Alex looked back one last time to the street. He saw something strange. Stranger even than the crows. Stranger than the man with the beer bottle. He squinted, trying to make out exactly what it was. He'd seen fog before, but not like this. It was glowing green. His stomach flipped a third time, though now it wasn't due to excitement. He didn't know why, but he wanted to run away from it. It seemed to be heading down the street *towards* them, moving with agency, floating low to the ground.

"Come on, Alex. What are you waiting for? You're holding up the queue!" Big Alex roared.

Alex snapped back to attention and gladly headed through the turnstile. The man taking the tickets saw the nerves on his face and probably interpreted them as excitement for the game, which was partly true.

"All right, *wee* man? That's it, you give me the ticket." The old man took the piece of paper and ripped it along its perforated edge, handing the stub with a seat number back to Alex. He took it and headed through the turnstile. It occurred to him — in the way ideas did naturally to a child — that turnstiles couldn't stop fog.

38

Douglas Wallace didn't have access to the whole police station. His forensics card only got him into the places relevant to his position. However, Charlie Davies, from the evidence room, had kindly given Douglas his card, and therefore access to any part of the station his heart desired.

Douglas had done the best he could, wiping the remains of Charlie off his hands and face. There'd been a spray of sticky red plasma after caving in the back of Charlie's head with the lump hammer. It got all over his face and coat. He'd hopped over the desk and purloined the obsidian knife, still in its plastic evidence bag. It felt comforting to have it, even though he could barely feel its weight in the pocket of his old tweed blazer.

He swiped the key card and a tiny green LED lit up. The lock clicked, and Douglas went through the door. The weight of the duffle bag bit into his shoulder; he had to shift it from hand to hand every so often. He'd never met any of the turnkeys before, so this was new territory. But Douglas felt even more confident than before (if that were even possible), even firmer in his commitment to his belief and his purpose. Tonight, he was going to help people set themselves free, to see the light, to be reborn in blood, as he himself had been.

Luck, or perhaps it was fate on Douglas' side, meant there were only two turnkeys. They were sitting at the end of the corridor in the small room leading to the cells beyond. They had just finished a conversation, and one was leaving, throwing Douglas a cheerful look as he passed, barely paying any attention to him. Douglas approached the desk. The remaining turnkey was a young man in his late twenties, at least six feet tall and athletic-looking. He had broad shoulders and a fat neck coupled to a big chest. He carried a little bit of fat around the middle, but not too much. He looked like the type of guy that lifted a lot of weights but didn't like to run much.

"Hello. How can I help you?" the turnkey asked affably.

"I was wondering if you could tell me if I'm in the right place." Douglas said.

"That depends," said the turnkey. "What are you looking for?"

"The evidence room."

The turnkey gave a small laugh and shook his head. "No, you're in the wrong place, pal. How did you get down here?"

As natural as could be, Douglas gave a shrug. "I think maybe one of the officers played a joke on me. I'm from forensics and they sent me down here. So easy to get lost, but I think they pointed me in the wrong direction on purpose. It was a red-headed guy, about this big."

The turnkey laughed again, getting up from his chair behind the desk. It was a nice laugh, deep and hearty. "That must have been Tony. He's always playing practical jokes on people."

It was a good guess on Douglas' part. Choosing someone with red hair in a Scottish police station meant there was bound to be somebody of that vague description.

The turnkey came around the other side of the desk, giving Douglas the quick once-over, looking down on him from his significant height, and clocking the black duffle bag. He took the reddish stains on Douglas' neck as merely dirt on a slightly dotty old man. Satisfied, he pointed the direction Douglas needed to go.

"You want to go out of these doors," he said, making brief eye contact with Douglas and then indicating the doors at the end of the corridor from where he'd come. "And then you take a left, and then a right." Douglas nodded affably in agreement, making it look as though he was paying attention to what the turnkey was telling him.

The man turned his head away, indicating the direction his next instructions referred to. "And then you get to another set of double doors. You might need a pass to get through, but you probably got a swipe card if you got in here. And then..."

After that only a wet gargling came out of the turnkey's mouth. A hot jet erupted from his jugular, spraying across Douglas' face and the wall behind him, as Douglas drew the obsidian knife from the neck of the turnkey.

He buried it to the hilt and twisted before pulling it out in one clean movement. The flint blade had cut through the big man's flesh as easily as a stone sinks in water. His eyes looked uncomprehendingly at Douglas as he choked up blood, like a child might let half-chewed pasta fall from their mouth to gross out their parents. The big man fell to his knees. Douglas took a step back, evading the turnkey's groping hand. All colour had drained from the turnkey's face. He pitched forward face first, dead before he hit the blood-splattered linoleum floor.

Douglas returned the knife to his pocket. He stepped around the crimson pool, squatting on his haunches. He unhooked the keyring and the key card from the turnkey's belt. Then he retrieved the duffle bag and unzipped it. He paused, taking a deep breath, savouring the moment. The lights blinked overhead, as though to applaud his work so far.

The name on the key card read *Dennis White*. Douglas swiped it while its previous owner twitched on the floor. The door to the cell block clicked heavily and opened. Douglas stepped through. Standing at the entrance to the cells, the lights still blinking on and off, he set down his heavy duffle bag. Slowly, Douglas undid the heavy-duty zip, with the precise and deliberate movement of a craftsman taking pride in his work. There was a selection of hammers, screwdrivers, two tyre irons, a blunt ornamental African hunting knife, and a pair of garden shears Douglas had inherited from his father.

These would be his gifts to those he was about to set free.

39

MIRIN STARED AT THE TABLE. Her two arresting officers sat across from her. A lawyer completed the quartet in the interview room, sitting closely at Mirin's side. Mirin had only ever needed a lawyer twice in her entire life: once to purchase their flat, and the second time was to sort the particulars of Omar's will after he died. Now she was in a police station, arrested for murder, picking at the skin around the nail of her thumb, avoiding eye contact, trying to think about how she was going to get out of this place as quickly as possible, get home to Oran and flee. Maybe they could outrun this, whatever it was. She just had to straighten this all out, make them see what was going on, that they were all in great danger and needed to leave. Mirin played the facts out in her head over and over, the whole story from the beginning, starting at the dig and ending with David's brutal death.

"Let's start back at the museum, okay, Mirin?" Connie kept her voice calm and conversational. There was a sympathetic edge to it. Mirin made a small movement, which was taken as an affirmation to the officer's question. "I want to talk about what happened to Professor Hamill, David. I know it'll probably be difficult, but I'd like for you to tell me in your own words what happened tonight."

Mirin bit her lip, eyes still on the table, staring into the negative space as though hoping it would yield a tool to get her out of here. "I went to see David back in the museum. I knew he'd be there working on the boy, our archaeological find. I was with Dip... Hardeep Bhaskar, Constable Bhaskar..." She wanted to be clear. "He's staying in Glasgow and I didn't know where else to go."

"Constable Bhaskar was there?" DI Blair asked. "Why were you with him?"

"I had been suspended. I needed somebody to talk to."

"Suspended?" DI Blair said. "Why did you get suspended, Professor?"

"David said that I was unstable, and he was worried about the things I was saying. He seemed concerned for my mental health. And I think deep down he thought I wanted his job." Mirin let out a bitter laugh. "Blind until the end."

"And did you?" Connie asked.

Mirin shook her head.

"So why didn't David believe you?" Connie pressed.

"David couldn't understand what I was trying to tell him. He couldn't believe it. It sounded incredible. Even I couldn't take it in at first. There's still a piece of me that doesn't. But I wanted David to see. He needed to understand. We needed to link together the pieces of information and step back. That's what good researchers do." Mirin looked up beseechingly into Connie's face. She saw someone sympathetic opposite. She wondered whether Connie had ever been disbelieved, whether she had gone to her superiors about a case and been told to drop it. She seemed to understand. She seemed to be listening.

"What was it that David couldn't see, Mirin? Why couldn't he believe you?" Connie asked.

Mirin shrank into her chair. "We're wasting time."

"Why are we wasting time?" Connie pressed, gentle in her tone but unrelenting in her focus.

Mirin chewed her lip again, her eyes returning to scanning the tabletop side to side as if she was reading something in her mind.

Mirin wrestled with herself. What could she say? There was a lawyer beside her. What would she do if she heard Mirin's *actual* explanation of what had taken place at the museum? Drop her case? Plead insanity? Mirin wished she could speak with Connie alone.

"What couldn't David believe?" Connie asked again. "Why was he so angry?"

"He couldn't believe the truth about the boy. Our find."

"What truth?" Stuart Blair asked. His voice was not so soft. He was direct, matter of fact.

Mirin shook her head. "He couldn't believe it. I really wouldn't have either, not completely, unless I'd seen it. I... I thought something strange was going on, but... but not that... not this."

"What, Mirin? What did you see? It's okay. You can tell us," Connie said.

Mirin rubbed her temples, scrunching her eyes closed. When she opened them, she took a deep breath. "The boy's alive," Mirin said. There, it was out in the world. *Truth.*

Stuart Blair cast a glance to his senior officer, who hadn't taken her eyes off Mirin.

"He rose up tonight," Mirin went on. "I saw it. David thought I was delusional, but we are all being *delusional.*" Mirin's fist slammed on the table. "All these things that have been happening, all these terrible things, the weather, the violence, everything, and we're still turning a blind eye. It's all connected to the boy." Mirin met Connie's eye, refusing to break contact. She had to believe her. She *had* to.

"You're telling us that a thousand-odd-year-old corpse rose from the dead and killed Professor Hamill?" Stuart said.

Slowly, Mirin bowed her head. "Yes," she whispered.

"For the benefit of the record," Connie said, "the suspect said *yes.*"

The word 'suspect' was the trigger. Mirin had to wake up to the true danger she, her son, that everyone was in.

"Look, you obviously think I killed David. Let's not beat around the bush here. How can I prove to you it wasn't me?"

Connie's face was totally unreadable.

"Tell us how the boy killed Professor Hamill," Connie said.

Mirin closed her eyes, trying to order the images playing in her mind. Replaying the terror and unbelievability of it. When she opened her eyes again, she said, "David saw the boy coming out of the storage unit. The boy grabbed him. He... he lifted David off the ground. Then he threw David across the hall, and when David hit the ground, we saw..." Mirin swallowed back the vomit wanting to surge up. "There was a wound in his abdomen. I think... I think it was the boy's hand that made it." Mirin's hand touched her own stomach.

"For clarification, and for the record, you're saying that the dead body of the boy you discovered in the peat bog, which you and Professor Hamill were studying, rose from the dead, and that that boy attacked Professor Hamill, somehow injuring him, lifting him from the ground and throwing him thirty feet across the hall of the Hunterian Museum. And when Professor Hamill landed, he was dead?" Connie summarised.

All Mirin could do was move her head in silent agreement.

"For the record, the suspect nodded in agreement," DC Blair added.

"I know this all sounds completely ridiculous, but you've got to get hold of Dip. He can confirm everything I've said..." Mirin was interrupted by a knock at the door.

Stuart Blair went and opened the door to another police officer, who handed him a note. He glanced at it briefly and then returned to his chair, passing the note to his commanding officer.

Mirin looked between the two officers opposite, searching them for some possibility they actually believed her.

"We are looking for Constable Bhaskar," Connie said, answering Mirin's question. "But we've another problem to deal with first." Connie folded the piece of paper. "We can't get hold of your babysitter."

"Did you copy the number down wrong?" Mirin said, panic rising.

"We didn't. The number doesn't exist. We checked with the mobile phone provider as well, and that number has *never* existed. The officer chased down the name that you gave us as well. He spoke to the woman and she said that she used to babysit for you, but that she hasn't done that job for you for over a year now."

Mirin looked between DCI Shepherd and DC Blair, searching to see if this was some sick joke. She felt cold, her skin prickled with goosebumps. Salty saliva started to fill her mouth. Then the room began to close in, the walls constricting, the ceiling pressed down, and the floor rushed up. The room became a swirling blur. A pounding roared up in her ears. Somewhere, some part of her mind screamed, *NO, NO, NO*. The words of the police officers echoed, and the sounds stretched out back through time, as if Mirin were trapped inside a glass bubble within which the outside world couldn't break in, and inside she was trapped in a personal hell. All of it, from now and the past, tumbled together in a cacophony of images, sounds and memories churning and tumbling, like white water flipping over a kayak and tossing its passengers into a frigid tumult to be buffeted mercilessly and relentlessly until a life was torn apart.

Mirin felt herself sway as something terrible flooded back to destroy her again, as it had twelve months ago. And she remembered.

40

INSIDE THE STANDS felt like being in the guts of a huge animal.

The assimilation had begun, and they were becoming part of the entity, the beast. The noises of the crowd reverberated in pulses, like the beast's enormous heartbeat. Supporters flowed between the stands and down the stairs, life blood coursing through the beast's veins, bunching in stairwell turns or at food kiosks, like blood backed up at a closed ventricle. Alex and his family sat in the stomach, the growling belly of the animal, ready to devour the beautiful game.

Alex held tight to his father's hand, as did his sister Karen. People pressed in at their sides, back, and front. Alex could feel how tightly his father held on to them. It wasn't like the gentle grip of holding hands in the park, although Alex was too grown up to hold hands with his dad in the park now. His friends would rip the hell out of him if they saw that. In the stand, he didn't care. It was all he could do not to be swept away.

The entrances to the stands outside stretched out in regular intervals along the concrete landing. Numbers above the entrances indicated the different sections and seats. Big Alex pulled them slowly through the ambling crowd to the seat numbers marked on their tickets. Suddenly a space opened in front of them, where there should be sardine-packed people, causing Alex to trip. A second later something barged into him, almost knocking him down.

"Fecksake!" Big Alex shouted. His voice was nearly lost in the pre-match hubbub.

Alex's father jerked him upright. Once Alex could feel his feet back under him, his father let go.

"Sorry, mate," said a man in a yellow high-visibility jacket. He had a shaved head, and his eyes looked dark and sunken. Karen wrinkled her nose, bringing the crook of her elbow up to protect her from the smell. Alex caught the staleness too. Days-old body odour and cigarettes. The man was younger than their father. Alex didn't like the look of him.

Another man passed behind them and started to chant *King Billy's on the Wall*, punctuating his words with jabbing points of his arm in the air. Other men joined in, including the steward with whom they'd collided. He began to shout the chant with a leer on his stubbly face, gesturing for the children to join in.

Hearing a roar from the crowd as the players took to the pitch, Alex's dad pulled them away.

"Best take our seats," Big Alex said, by way of excusing them. The steward continued shouting *King Billy's on the Wall*, waving at them as they went. Alex looked back. The man was watching them go through the crowd. He came and went from view as people jostled, until he was obscured completely by a wall of bodies. Alex was glad to see him go and hoped he never saw him again.

A FAT MAN with a moustache cast Eddie Burns a look as he finished off his rendition of *King Billy's on the Wall*, waving at the children with mirth in his eyes. The mirth vanished instantly.

"Wha' the fuck yous lookin' at?" he spat at the fat man, who averted his gaze and hurried on his way, carried in the tide of people out into the stand.

The landing underneath the seats had begun to thin as everyone took their place, leaving the figure of Eddie Burns in his bright yellow jacket alone. He put a hand in his pocket and brought out an almost obsolete flip phone he'd bought second-hand down at the Barrowlands Market. It still worked with a pay-as-you-go SIM card.

There were only four numbers programmed into it now. Eddie flipped open the phone and the screen came to life. He thumbed open the contacts folder, each of the four entries only marked with a number, one to four, corresponding to the other four flip phones he'd bought at Barrowlands. There wasn't much left of those phones, just the internal circuits, antennae, and the small, oblong grey-scale screens, each connected by wires to a simple trigger system, which in turn connected to the homemade explosives. Two were on top of kiosks. The others were out in the open.

Eddie had hidden bombs in backpacks placed under seats. He'd waited for the stands to start filling up, and then pretended to take a seat among them, carrying a backpack with him. After a few minutes, he'd got up, as if to take a leak, leaving the rucksack under the seat next to him. The difficult bit had been getting out of that stand and into the adjacent one without it looking odd or drawing attention, but he'd managed it. It was amazing how much suspicion a hi-vis deflected.

It had all gone to plan, as he believed in his soul it would. He had no doubt he was being called to fulfil his true destiny.

Eddie let his thumb scroll up and down the numbers.

"Which little piggy went to market?" he said to himself. A whistle sounded and a huge roar went up from the crowd.

"Not just yet, little piggies," he said, flipping the phone shut and slipping it back into his pocket. "We've one other bag of tricks to deliver."

41

"Please, Mum, go visit Auntie Mina in Leicester. You haven't seen her for ages." Dip was finding it difficult to disguise the rising panic in his voice. Jackie Chan barked around their feet, jumping up, pushing into Dip's shins, trying to get his attention while he talked to his parents.

"We can't leave now," his mother protested. "What about the restaurant? It's opening time. Things are ready for service."

"Mum, do it for me. Hardly anyone has come into the restaurant for the last few days."

Dip's father pried Jackie Chan away from Dip by the collar, lifting him up into his arms. The little pug licked his ear.

"But we had some bumper days recently," his father reasoned.

Dip had already made up his mind not to repeat past mistakes and tell them about *the boy*. His parents were old-fashioned. They believed in a world of order and orderly-functioning society. How could he tell them that was all about to end? Dip didn't even know whether getting his parents out of the city would be enough. In his heart of hearts, he doubted it. All these efforts, perhaps, were just delaying the inevitable; it was a weight he carried in his chest. There had to be another way.

"Look, I shouldn't be telling you this, but I have information from work."

Dip's mother's interest was piqued. The pride she had for her policeman son's position visibly swelled in her bosom.

"I got some intelligence from a friend on the force. "I really shouldn't be telling you this, but you have to get out of the city. It's not safe here tonight."

"What kind of trouble?"

"Mum, you know I can't tell you that," Dip continued to lie. "But it's serious. Please pack a bag, get on the road as soon as you can, and get out of the city and down to Auntie Mina tonight. I'll phone you later to let you know I'm okay."

His mother frowned. "You're not coming with us?"

"I have a duty."

"You're on sick leave," Dip's father interjected, putting Jackie Chan down, who scampered off into the kitchen to look for food.

"It doesn't matter. This is too big. It's all hands on deck. This isn't even really my beat, but I can't go if what they say is true. They are going to need everybody, even if it's just having someone to answer the phones." Dip held up his broken arm.

His mother and father exchanged looks.

"All right then, if it will make you happy. But only for a night or two. Phone as soon as you know everything is okay and we'll come straight back and open the restaurant." His mother pulled him into a hug.

"Don't go trying to be a hero in your condition. You did enough already this month," his father said.

"He's a brave boy!" his mother purred into his chest. "But your father is right," she said, becoming stern. "You have a broken arm, and you shouldn't be at work anyway." Her face softened again. She kissed him on the cheek, having to stand on her tiptoes.

Dip tried to help them pack, throwing clothes into a bag, which his mother would then take out and re-fold properly. Jackie Chan grew more excited with all the activity, skittering around the apartment above the restaurant, sliding on the wooden floors, and barking excitedly whenever they opened another drawer. Jackie Chan's watery-brown eyes grew reproachful at Dip when his mother picked the small dog up and carried him and her overnight bag out of the flat.

"Don't stop to do *anything*. Nothing. Do you understand? Get on the motorway and keep driving. Don't stop for anything until you get out of the city, as far away from here as you can possibly get."

That was the last thing Dip told them.

After he'd watched them go, he waited, intending to give them a thirty-minute head-start. He tried to get through to a police station, phoning both the local station and 999, but all lines were engaged. Unable to wait any longer, he grabbed his car keys, wishing he had his police gear with him. He consoled himself with the thought that pepper spray and a baton would probably be about as useful as an inflatable armband in a tsunami. They weren't the weapons he needed.

If what he thought he knew was right, and he could get it and find Mirin, maybe, just maybe, they had a chance. If he was wrong, it would be all over for them at least, and he wouldn't have to live with his mistake.

Jumping into his car, Dip took a moment to take a deep breath. "Maybe you're just traumatised and delusional, and this is all in your head," he said, looking at his eyes in the rear-view. "Now there's a happy thought."

The car revved maniacally as he punched it into gear. The thick low-lying fog had wormed out of the park, infecting every street. He was driving blind. Nerves twisted in Dip's stomach. He knew something big was about to happen. He could feel it, crackling in the air with the intensity of a storm.

He drove too fast for the visibility granted by the fog, heading towards the city centre and the police station, feeling a magnetic pull since he realised what they needed, since he'd put together the meaning contained in his visions. He was sure Mirin was there too. It was all falling into place.

Three dogs shot across the road in front of Dip, running towards Kelvingrove Park. He slammed the brakes.

"You told Mum and Dad not to stop for anything, you bloody

idiot," he told himself ruefully, hitting the accelerator again. He sped up Woodlands Road, past the bars and antique shops on the left-hand side. The greenish fog billowed in his wake.

Soon he encountered other cars trying to get to the city, all converging at the choke point at the top of the intersection with the motorway. He came to a halt.

Two cars had a fender-bender. The drivers were out, shouting and pushing each other. Children cried in the back seats of the cars, unsure what was going on, wedged between piles of hastily packed belongings. Dip fought his policeman's urge to get out and break up the fight. Instead, he threw the car into first gear and pulled around RTA, narrowly missing an oncoming car that blared its horn. In his rear-view mirror the two drivers lashed out at each other before falling in a grapple beneath the blanket of fog.

The wrong side of the road was clearer but only until the end of the road; everything came to a standstill at George's Cross junction. Countless car horns hooted in a tuneless cacophony. More people had alighted from their vehicles and were fighting. Passengers and other drivers got out to help, only to be dragged into fights of their own. All the while the green fog encircled, and the escalation continued.

Dip looked left and right and then over his shoulder, thinking about backing up, but three more cars had followed him up the wrong side of the road, trying to find their way out.

On the other side of the road, Dip could see a way through, and he floored the accelerator, screeching out into the space. Through the diffused light of the fog, Dip was met by the vision of a large four-by-four hurtling around the corner from an intersecting road. He pulled hard left on the steering wheel and the four-by-four clipped his back headlight, the red plastic shattering. Dip had turned off onto a road that ran parallel to the motorway; the way ahead was clearer, on the wrong side of the road. His heart pounded wildly in his chest. He daren't stop to reflect on how crazy everything was.

The magnetic pull in his chest told him he was heading away from his destination, but Dip knew what he was doing. The most direct route wouldn't work tonight. The old city was full of choke points where Victorian city streets met twentieth century motorways and traffic control systems. Dip weaved perpendicular to his goal, the small engine of his car protesting in a high whine. All the advanced driver training he received in the police force was brought to bear. He read the road ahead, seeing drivers making mistakes. He capitalised on their errors and accelerated into the spaces, downshifting, braking hard and making even harder turns, weaving through the traffic and fog, using people's hesitations against them, and their accidents too. He would never have done this as an officer of the law, but this went beyond training and rules and order.

Dip knew he needed to get onto West Graham Street, the road that ran over the many-lane junction of the motorway, cutting through into the heart of the city, but when he reached it a four-car crash completely blocked the road. Looking back over his shoulder, putting his broken arm against the passenger seat, Dip threw the car into reverse and swung around, mounting the pavement and accelerating around the crashed cars. Horns blared at him, people shouted, but he didn't care.

Once back on the road, he braked hard and performed a hand-brake turn, his wheels screaming, bringing the car around in a drifting U-turn. The car hit the side of a stationary vehicle and the back window cracked. Finding the gear, Dip slammed his foot into the floor, and the car went screeching up over the ramp to West Graham Street, which was surprisingly clear, probably due to the pileup he'd just avoided.

The road rose above the fog, granting visibility for a few brief moments before it sloped back down into the cloudy green haze. Dip had the feeling of descending into the maw of some malevolent leviathan as the fog rushed toward him.

The police station was only a couple of minutes away, at worst, as long as he could avoid meeting anything else.

Then the back end of his small car spun out. The world was a blurring whirl. The sound of twisting metal and breaking plastic filled his ears, along with the scream of tyres. He fought to regain control of the car but he couldn't. He was out of control.

Like the rest of the world, it seemed.

42

REMI HERNANDEZ KICKED at the crow strutting around the pitch. The bird looked like it owned it. As his boot came toward it, the crow made a protesting squawk and flew a couple of feet into the air before landing back on the pitch and rolling its shoulders like a thug. Remi hocked in the back of his throat and then spat at the bird. The glob of phlegm flew past it and landed on the grass.

Remi shook his head. "Fucking birds." His accent was Colombian, which made all the vowels richer, and hence his curse, more vitriolic.

Ibrox Stadium was nearly full. The public announcement system sent incomprehensible words echoing across the pitch, while the Rangers fans chanted one set of songs from three sides of the stadium. A smaller pocket of Celtic supporters battled against the overwhelming numbers of home fans to support their team in the green and white hoops. Remi appreciated their efforts, even if they were sorely outnumbered.

Remi walked up to the referee, adjusting his captain's armband. "We playing, ref?" Remi knew the guy. He was a good ref by the name of John Stuart, a wiry man with thinning brown hair and greying patches over the ears.

John surveyed the pitch. Ball boys and ground stewards had been marshalled to help clear the crows, hundreds of which had landed on the pitch. They hadn't got rid of them all, but it was probably clear enough to start playing.

"*Aye*, Remi, I think we can give it a go," John said and gave a quick toot on his whistle, calling for Colin McDermott, the stocky midfielder who captained Rangers, whose favourite move was a dirty tackle.

Colin seemed to pound the earth, even when jogging slowly. Remi hated the man. He had been on the end of a couple of his tackles over the last couple of seasons. Despite his animosity, Remi had come to appreciate Colin's skills in the close quarters of the Scottish game. There might be more flair in the Colombian style of football, but the Scots could pass the ball, play well as a team, and there was skill in their physicality. Remi had grown to understand the technical differences between the two games over two years playing in the Scottish league. The Scots played like boxers who could fight dirty without the ref seeing, unlike his hot-blooded Colombian brothers, who threw wild hay-making flying tackles.

The two captains shook hands. John gave them their instructions, repeating what he told them in the changing rooms, and then tossed the coin in the air. McDermott gave the only quarter Remi expected from him the whole night and let the Colombian call the toss. Remi won the coin-flip and chose to kick off. Colin McDermott didn't care. Whatever end they played to, it was all on home territory tonight and so he stuck with the end they already had.

The midfielder took a swipe at a crow as he jogged back to his position, catching the bird full in the chest, launching it eight feet. It landed like a deflated football. Both sets of fans cheered. Remi couldn't help but smile. A serendipitous moment in this shitstorm.

The bird shook its beaked head, tumble-turning back to its feet. It staggered a couple of steps and then took flight to another cheer of the crowd.

John was about to blow his whistle when he saw something in his periphery. Initially, he thought it was smoke from some kind of fire. Like any football-mad Scotsman, he knew about the stadium tragedies of the past, and it rang instant alarm bells. But then he noticed how it moved. Not like smoke, rising. Instead, it oozed low to the ground, seeping in from the corners between stands. Crows hopped excitedly on their myriad perches around the stadium: on advertisement boards, the crossbar of the goal posts, and the flood-lights. John hesitated, the breath to blow the whistle still held in his chest.

"C'mon, ref!" Colin shouted.

John took another look at the fog, deciding that was exactly what it was, and blew his whistle.

There were only a few touches of the ball. It pinged between Celtic players, first back, then laterally. Remi ran deep into Rangers' half, as his team passed the ball between opposition players. Remi felt the move coming, something they practised countless times on the training pitch. He drew the centre-half slightly out of position, and then checked sideways, shuffle-stepping into space. Or so he thought.

Shaun O'Neill, Celtic's young, but very skilful, central midfielder, laced a beautiful through pass deep into the final third of the pitch, right to Remi's feet, two yards shy of the eighteen-yard box. This was Remi's domain: deft control, turn on a sixpence, shrug off the defender, sidestep another then either pass laterally or find a space and hammer the ball at the goal. Remi prepared to trap the ball, soft-ening his knees, as the ball zipped to his feet. It never reached them. Remi heard the crack before he felt the pain. The studded soles of Colin McDermott's two feet connected with the side of Remi's shin just above the ankle. Both bones snapped under the full weight of the stocky midfielder multiplied by the velocity of his jump. Remi's body tilted sideways as his knee ligaments exploded, and his tibia and fibula bones punctured the skin on the inside of his shin.

A roar of complaint went up from the Celtic fans, only to be drowned out by the celebrant cheers for the Rangers supporters. And then the melee began. White-and- green-hooped players ran at Colin McDermott. Punches were thrown. Colin kicked one of the players in the balls. When the player doubled over, Colin grabbed him by the ears, and taking a punch in the mouth, he brought his knee up between his hands, smashing the nose to oblivion on his knee. He was tackled around the waist and felt studs all over his body, puncturing holes.

John Stewart blew his whistle ineffectually. Every player was involved in the fight. Even those who initially tried to keep the peace were being punched, kicked, and even bitten, drawing them into the fray. Fans from both sides vaulted the balustrades, barrelling through stewards and police in high-visibility jackets.

Giving up on his whistle, John spun around, trying to make sense of the madness. He had seen more than a few disasters on the pitch: tempers rising, fights, but never anything that got out of hand so quickly. Every member of the police was engaged in hand-to-hand combat now, literally fighting for their lives.

The fog spread out, reaching the grass and beginning to join up, enveloping those fighting on the pitch.

In the stands, thousands fought an all-out war. Those that did fight were tenderised, reduced to balls of flesh, kicked and trampled on, until in one corner of a stand there was a flash of yellow and white, accompanied by a bang that shook the recent thunder from its throne. Rubble flew into the air, reverse meteors. A segment of stadium collapsed in on itself, sending grey dust spraying like a rival fog across the field.

John Stewart found himself cowering on the grass. He opened his eyes as the moment of silence gave way to fresh screams of panic. Terror billowed up again like the smoke that followed the explosion in the stand. John looked up into the mangled face of Colin McDermott. His ear was hanging on by a thread. He sneered at John with bloodied gums and shards of teeth. It was a look that would make John join in with the screams of everyone else.

43

MIRIN HAD other things on her mind. She had three papers that needed finishing. She had a new graduate student, Portia, who seemed very bright indeed, but required a little direction at the start of the project. She had several faculty meetings and minutes to write up, and there was a big research council grant that needed finishing as well, including reconciling all the edits from collaborators. Her mind was on a million other things, like it usually was. She sat on a rock with her life jacket hanging open, and her boots still barely tied up.

Omar was knelt in front of Oran, making sure all his kit was correctly attached, and when they smiled at each other it was like a mirror through time. It was uncanny how similar they were. The same beautiful lips and gorgeous deep-brown eyes. Their hair was black and curly, and almost looked like it was dancing. The father's face always had a shadow of stubble.

"Mirin, my love, put your phone away. Let's get the show on the road," Omar said, his smile faltering.

"Will you just give me a minute?" Mirin said sternly. "Stop pestering me. I've one more email to send."

"We're on holiday. Let's go and have fun." Omar lifted Oran into the middle of the boat.

"What kind of message do you think that's sending? That work's not fun?"

"You know that isn't what I meant," Omar said. He picked up the two oars and held out one to Mirin. "Let's not argue, my love. Remember we used to do this nearly every weekend."

Yes, Mirin did remember, but this also felt like the start of an argument. She took the oar and laid it down next to her, while she stuffed her phone into the waterproof pouch. Then she stiffly zipped up the life jacket and fastened the buckles, before slipping the phone into the pocket of her cargo trousers. Standing up she said, "Happy now?"

Omar looked defeated. There was a sadness in his face, and worse than that, she thought he looked disappointed in her. That made her simultaneously sad and angry. The urge grew in her to go back to the car and open the laptop and start work again. But then that smile spread, became as big and bright as the sun, like a welcoming dawn after a cold, unforgiving night.

"Come," he said. "Let's be young again and tame the river like we did when we were students. Show Oran how it's done."

With anyone else it would have sounded clichéd, but from Omar it came out as passion falling from his Persian lips, like sherbet over-flowing from goblets at a banquet for the soul. And all the wonder of the world was contained within him, and by extension their child, ready to be feasted upon.

The anger abated enough for Mirin to muster a smile and grip her oar. Omar gave her a theatrical bow, like a lovestruck courtier allowing his queen to pass. She clambered into the boat, her body only half remembering how this was done, but the memory kindled a fire and a smile grew.

Omar pushed the boat away from the shale bank of the river and out far enough for them to be buoyed by the water flowing crystalline underneath the bow. He held it steady and clambered on himself, the boat rocking from side to side as he took his seat. Oran giggled at the instability and adventure that lay ahead. They plunged their oars into the water, initially hitting the stony bed of the river until they were out deep enough to catch full, satisfying pulls in the flow of the river. The boat quickly found the current and they were off.

This was a favourite place they used to come to years ago in graduate school, when they had first become a couple. Omar became enchanted by the Scottish Highlands and its rugged beauty. They had walked Munros, skied at Aviemore, then walked the glens, and climbed the Bens, but they had always loved kayaking. Omar had been an undergraduate in Colorado and acquired a taste for paddling up the Colorado River. He brought that love to Scotland with him. They had spent many weekends escaping from the grind of graduate school into the Scottish wilderness and had fallen deeply in love there. But it had been a long time since they had been back. The love was still there between them, but it had become a humdrum and everyday thing. Other things had taken the place of its passion. The passion for work and career advancement. Mirin had become the youngest professor in the Department of Archaeology's history. Even Oran's arrival seemed unable to stop Mirin's star rising in the academic firmament. So, the adventures into the Scottish wilderness had become fewer and fewer, until they ceased to be anything but a memory, something they did when they were practically children.

Their paddles cut through the surface, gliding them swiftly along. They moved into deeper water, the bottom of the boat bumping against an occasional unseen rock jutting from the riverbed. Hitting a larger rock, the boat misaligned, throwing Oran to the side. Mirin heard Oran giggle over the rush of the water. His father righted him, briefly breaking the strokes of his paddle into the water. "Hold on tightly, my little star," he told him.

Mirin's shoulders began to burn. She was sweating and didn't care. The rushing river kept her mind there with her family: laughing, living. They had fallen back into their old roles. Mirin watched the river, looking for obstacles; Omar powered the boat from the back and steered. They found their rhythm, keeping the boat straight, both working in unison, the oars chopping either side of the boat as necessary. Omar would point out the birds and animals with a gesture of his head, leaning forward over his son's shoulder. Then even the sun broke through the sky, bathing them in a glorious golden light. Mirin often thought Scottish sun was like a fabulous jewel or precious metal. Its beauty was appreciated all the more because of its rarity.

There had been a lot of rainfall recently in the late summer, and the river had swelled. This was their last chance for an expedition before Oran would have to start back at school in August. Omar had promised the boy adventures, told to him at bedtime, before singing Oran the lullabies in Omar's mother tongue. They had navigated this part of the river before, but many years ago. Mirin couldn't remember if the waters had been this high, or if it was merely time and the presence of Oran that made her feel a twinge of unease. Still, she silently consoled herself, it was only a short stretch with one difficult point. Omar had chosen it because he thought the small section of rapids would be sufficiently exciting enough for Oran, but not too dangerous. Mirin had agreed, only half paying attention, while she pored over her laptop in their Glasgow apartment. Omar had been trying to plan a lot of these small trips recently. Mirin had said no so many times, she finally capitulated if only to shut up the two boys. Now, she felt glad she had. With the river churning and undulating beneath them, she felt alive with every pore of her being, and with that happiness, Mirin nearly began to cry. For the first time she could see him, her little boy. She could see what a bundle of pure joy her Oran was, laughing as waves slapped against the side of the boat, spraying them with cold, refreshing water. "It's like ice," he screamed with delight when a particularly large wave drenched them.

"We are adventurers sailing in the Arctic north," Omar shouted from the back of the boat.

"We are Iroquois escaping the cavalry across Lake Michigan," Mirin shouted back over her shoulder.

"No, we are pirates on the seven seas. Argh, me hearties!" Oran shouted. Both Mirin and Omar gave a hearty, swashbuckling 'Ah-argh!' as well.

Then the front of the boat bumped against a rock and Mirin nearly lost her paddle. Oran slipped against the side of the boat, hitting his ribs, and cried out.

"It's okay," Omar said. "It's just the start of the rapids. We need to concentrate. Oran, hold on tight. It's going to get bumpy, but not too bad. We are the pirates sailing through dangerous waters. Okay, me hearty?"

"Aye, aye, Captain," shouted Oran.

Mirin concentrated on the river. It had become choppier. Waves hit them roughly from all sides. The kayak pitched up and down into the peaks and troughs. Ahead she saw where the river bent in a kink. There was the epicentre of the rapids, where the river narrowed suddenly and turned, frothing rabidly with the high waters. The rapids were far bigger than Mirin remembered. In fact, they were bigger than any rapids she had ever had to negotiate. With the worst section still a little way off, Mirin thought about saying they'd had enough fun, and they should pull the boat over to the side of the river and get out here. But then they would have to drag the boat across land, and they were surrounded by trees. The river was the quickest route to their pickup point, and it would be hard to get to the bank anyway. Still, Mirin thought, with her shoulders burning with the effort, this was the place to get out. She'd made up her mind when Omar shouted from behind her, "Argh, Jim lad, hold onto the rigging tight. Here comes the kraken."

"Aye, aye, Captain," Oran shouted back with glee. "I can see him, Captain. Let's give 'em all our cannons."

Omar had just finished reading *Robinson Crusoe* at bedtime and clearly the boys had decided to play out a pirate dream. Mirin didn't want to be the party-pooper, not again.

When the rapids began, all play stopped. Mirin could barely hear her own breath over the thrashing of the water. The river was like some great industrial engine pounding away relentlessly. They ground against the rocks below. Waves didn't slap the boat any more, they barged and swiped haymakers at their flanks. Foam splashed into the boat, filling the hull with water. Whichever way they tried to go the river pulled and pushed them in the opposite direction.

Now every thrust of her paddle was an effort as Mirin strained against the water, her muscles searing and chest heaving. She called out when she saw a large rock ahead and turned briefly to make sure Omar had seen it. He had and was paddling for all he was worth to turn the boat against the torrent. Oran wore an unsure smile, which

Mirin forced herself to return, hiding her fear. With their combined efforts, they shot past the side of the jagged boulder only to be sling-shot into a deep gully in the rapids. The boat pitched forward. Oran let out a scream. It wasn't one of joy but growing terror.

"It's okay, Jim lad," shouted Omar, his voice strained.

The boat plunged under the water, sending a bow wave over the prow of the kayak that engulfed Mirin up to the waist. She was still paddling hard. It was the only thing to be done. The boat righted only to be taken by another whipping current. Six inches of water now weighed down the hull, making steering the boat true even harder on them.

Another rock lay in their path, but there was also an eddy that could carry them around it. Mirin told them to *pull right*. They thrashed at the water with their paddles for all they were worth, as the churning engine of the river began to chew them up. They hit the eddy, and the boat cut away, grazing the rock, which gouged a scar into the fibreglass of their boat. The current flung them in an arc around the deadly obstacle as if they were on a rollercoaster. They rode its power, utilising this force of nature, paddling with it as one. The adrenaline surged in Mirin. She knew that Omar and Oran felt the same elation, the sense of control and oneness, terrifying and exhilarating at the same time.

They rode their fear around the arc, but by the time they reached its end, the current was too fast to react.

Two great jagged boulders hunkered down behind a bank of frothing white water, a tumbling chimera at the confluence of two powerful channels, brought together and then halted.

Mirin screamed a warning, but it was drowned out by the roaring of the river. The boat pitched forward once more in a trough, where the currents swept down and then back on themselves. The tip of the kayak was driven down, sucked under until its point hit a nock between the two rocks. The boat came to an abrupt stop, water engulfing Mirin as she fell back into Oran. Under the weight of the water and the force of the current pushing under the hull, the kayak flicked upright. Mirin fell forward into the churning white foam, unable to hear the scream of her little boy as he flew over her head and beyond the rocks. Omar was heavier and had seen the danger. Mirin thought she saw Omar reach out for her son, his other hand gripping the side of the boat, but she could not be sure. A second later she had disappeared under the icy flow and they were lost from view.

Her helmet cracked against the rocks. She took in water, too much. The current pinned her between the rock and the upright boat. A heavy weight fell on top of her. There was a flash of orange she assumed to be Omar's life vest. Mirin made a grab for it, but she could not lift her arms through the surging water. The flash of orange disappeared into the tumult of white foam, as the impact dislodged her from the current.

Spluttering and gasping for air, Mirin breached the surface. Kicking as hard as she could amid the roiling white water, she could see the boat standing preposterously upright, its pointed stern aimed to the heavens. Then it began to fall to the side on top of Mirin. No matter how hard she tried, the current held her in place. The boat fell like a tree: slowly at first before picking up speed. Its full weight loomed over her head, when at the last moment the boat turned on its axis. Mirin put her hands up to protect herself and was momentarily sucked under the water once more. Kicking and pulling with everything she had while the water pounded her from all sides, Mirin surfaced again.

The roar of the white water had changed, becoming a thunderous storm on a caravan roof. The capsized kayak cocooned her. The boat began to move with the chaotic flow of the current again. The plank in the middle of the kayak, on which Oran had been sat, came rushing towards Mirin's face. She grunted with the effort of catching hold of the plank, and she was propelled free of the rock they'd struck, but her grip on the wet slat slipped with fatigue. She managed a half-breath and pushed under the water before the boat could hit her. It clipped the top of her helmet, knocking her head back, and lifting her feet up, like taking a comic book uppercut from a heavyweight boxer. The swirling current caught her feet and flipped her into a tumbling spin. Disorientated and turning, with no sense of which way was up, the urge to breathe became desperation. She could be kicking herself deeper, but she had no choice but to kick. Two, three, four kicks and her hands touched something soft and Mirin knew who it was.

Oran's orange life jacket was the first thing she saw, and then his black curls. Mirin caught hold of his jacket, and in pulling herself to him realised three things: he was alive, she knew which way was up, and he was trapped.

Oran had begun to thrash, desperately needing air. His small hands clawed at his mother's jacket. Mirin's feet had found the bed of the river, or at least a boulder, and with her muscles burning she heaved with all her strength. Oran did not move.

Fighting the reflex to breathe, Mirin's chest began to hitch. She pulled her way down his body, exploring with her hands. Some water rushed into her mouth when her lungs attempted to expand. It burnt in her windpipe and choked in her chest but still she held on, feeling.

Oran's foot was caught between two boulders. Mirin shoved her hands into the gap between them and heaved, but the stone would not shift. The urge to breathe was almost unbearable but she fought the instinct hardwired into every cell of her body. She yanked at her son's leg, not caring if she hurt him. She needed to free him. His trainer, she thought, might come loose. A fingernail tore off down to the root as she clawed at the shoe. Nothing would move.

She needed air. If she could get a breath, she could swim back down and try again. Mirin felt her way to Oran's face. His eyes were wild with fear, experiencing the same feeling Mirin was: the body demanding air.

She took his face in her hands, his soft, beautiful face. He calmed for a moment and she kissed him on his delicate lips. Mirin pushed off to leave, but Oran caught her hand. It gripped her with desperation. She could feel every little bone in his fingers. She could stay, lie with him at the murky bottom of this place, but the current ripped her away.

Mirin surfaced choking. Even as she gasped for air, she realised her mistake. The current was whipping her away downstream, and no matter how hard she swam there was no way back. The place

Mirin thought her son was lost in the churning movement of the white water was rapidly growing farther and farther away.

She kicked and pulled at the water, shouting and screaming, until the rapids spat her out exhausted and battered into the calmer waters beyond. Still Mirin did not accept her fate and continued to try to swim back upstream until she choked on the river water and, unable to keep herself above the surface any longer, she slipped beneath. She was glad of it. The water could take her along with her family. They would go together. But as she gave up and her tired body relaxed, her feet found a stony bank submerged beneath her feet. Her body weight dragged along the bottom, flipping her onto her back, and her life jacket did its job, keeping her afloat. In the delirium of exhaustion, the current carried Mirin to the shallows until finally she came to rest at the shore.

PART III

"Live to the point of tears."

Albert Camus

"Those who have a 'why' to live can bear almost any 'how'."

Viktor Frankl

"Music gives soul to the universe, wings to the mind, flight to the imagination and life to everything."

Plato

1

"I think this is outrageous," Dorothy said. She was barely audible over the foot stomping that rattled through the student union's debating chamber, causing the small oak- panelled anteroom to vibrate as a result. They were using the debating chamber as a green room for the famous, or rather infamous, Professor Peter Jorgensen. He sat calmly in one of the worn green-leather chairs, his legs neatly crossed, his hands in his lap, wearing one of his trademark three-piece suits. His agent, Dorothy, was not happy with the delay, and was currently remonstrating with the vice principal of the university, who was supposed to be introducing Professor Jorgenson.

Strathclyde's chief constable had assigned extra security weeks ago when the visit, connected with Professor Jorgensen's controversial book tour, was announced. However, it had failed to turn up on the night.

The professor's last tour in the UK had seen him de-platformed at the Cambridge Union and Ellen Nesbit had asked him the same question thirty-four times on Channel Four News as he ran rings around her aggressive interview style, designed to put him into a box he couldn't accept. The resulting media backlash and viral exposure on the internet from both incidents had done wonders for book sales and advertising revenue on his YouTube channel.

This time they had received a number of anonymous threats when Professor Jorgensen's visit was announced. That was nothing new either. He'd become something of a controversial figure in the last two years when he quite innocuously refused to bow down to his Canadian university and his state legislature's edict for him to publicise potential trigger warnings in his undergraduate and master's classes. Being a trained clinical psychologist and having practised therapy for the past thirty-five years of his life, Professor Jorgensen felt it unethical to actually coddle the children or young adults with the so-called trigger warnings, when there was no clinical evidence that they would actually benefit them. Far from it. In his opinion it would go against the clinical teaching and exacerbate whatever emotionally fragile condition they believed they had. For this position he got suspended.

And then, to his complete surprise, he'd become an international celebrity after starting his own YouTube channel merely to scratch an itch to teach, presenting his lectures online. The university wasn't going to let him teach any more. After twelve months they paid out, but the money was inconsequential. Professor Jorgensen had quadrupled his salary from advertising through his YouTube channel. Then he wrote a book about how to take responsibility in an irresponsible world, which became a New York Times bestseller. Most peculiar of all, he now found himself one of the world's most famous public intellectuals, able to fill out five and even ten thousand-seater theatres with people who'd come to listen to him speak.

The promotion of his new book, *Return of the Individual*, with the subtitle *and the Death of Identity Politics*, was already causing controversy, mostly, the professor thought, with people who hadn't read it. This, among other of his 'apparent' opinions, most of which people ascribed to him but which he didn't actually hold, tended to excite certain groups on campuses around the world. And so, he was here tonight as an invited speaker to kick off his book tour. They paid his fee, and he was more than happy to talk to students and faculty. Peter still loved universities and the opportunity to engage with people who had come to the institution for, he hoped, the pure love of knowledge. He loved the free exchange of ideas, the rough and tumble of intellectual badinage he hoped wasn't dying, but deep down, knew it was.

To say the atmosphere was febrile tonight would have been something of an understatement. The university had some security and usually the students created a bit of a scene, more theatrics than anything. Occasionally, there was a scuffle outside, but nothing major. Professor Jorgensen knew, like all primates, the students needed to go through the motions, beat their chests and show their teeth. If they stopped him from speaking, he was still getting paid. Dorothy had made the contract quite clear on those matters. And the publicity would be even better for book sales.

Peter took a sip of black tea. He could no longer drink milk, having found that he had an allergy to dairy and wheat. He thought this was rather funny, as most of the evidence showed that the majority of people who believe they had wheat and dairy allergies had no such thing. In fact, to say he had an allergy was not quite accurate. He had an intolerance. And so, his tea was now black. He hadn't liked it at first, but he eventually got used to it. In fact, it had become part of his image: three-piece suit, neatly cropped salt and pepper hair, the old-fashioned Windsor knotted tie, and taking tea from an elegant China teacup. In fact, to Professor Jorgensen, tea was a perfect allegory for an ordered life. Most people, especially in Canada and North America, drank harsh and bitter coffee by the pint, laced with sickly syrups. Tea could be made badly, with or without milk. But even the English argument about whether to put the milk in first or last hinted at the ceremony that really underlay tea-drinking. It was a drink that required patience, waiting for it to brew, allowing mindfulness and reflection. The Japanese had elevated the tea ceremony to an act of spiritual transcendence, something referred to in his book *The Return of the Individual*. No one ever really asked him about tea. He would love it if they did.

"If he's going to go," the policeman said, speaking in a broad Glaswegian accent, "he needs to go now. Or we send that lot out there home. Waiting any longer is going to excite the crowd even more."

Professor Jorgensen had a number of pleasant conversations with the officer, from which he had understood absolutely nothing. The man had the warmest smile, but it was like being growled at by a friendly bear. Dorothy seemed to fare somewhat better.

Dorothy relayed the message to Peter. He put down his teacup, straightened his tie, and stood.

The vice principal looked ashen, clammy sweat sheening her forehead. "I guess this is it?" she said shakily.

Professor Jorgensen got the impression she wasn't used to such hostile crowds.

"Don't let them see the whites of your eyes," he said, offering for her to lead the way.

The reverberating roar battled with a cacophony of boos as they took to the stage.

2

THE CRYING WOULD NOT STOP. It racked Mirin's body. Burying her face into her arms on the interview desk, she let it out, she let it all go. The full truth of the memory and all the other unthinkable things that followed the accident.

The recovery of their lifeless bodies.

Mirin wished she could forget. To see the cold pallor of their faces, their blank staring eyes, never to come to life again. The unreality of it as the paramedics checked her over, and the police tried to ask questions. All their faces riddled with sympathy and pity. Mirin thought it was the only thing she would ever see in people's faces ever again.

Then followed the acquisition of new knowledge, knowledge she did not want. Organising funerals. The compassion with which an undertaker handles everyone, but particularly children. The sensitivity with which they help the bereaved choose a coffin.

After that came rituals of burying the bodies. The service, the music, eulogies. So many decisions to be made. Mirin couldn't remember specifics, only the general numb feeling of people coming in and out of her flat as she fell deeper and deeper into grief. She spent nights on Oran's bed crying with his sheets bunched in her fists, soaking up her tears, while she breathed his smell.

Mirin sat and stood through services and ceremonies and the parade of sympathisers, a mannequin finding itself somehow dressed in different clothes on different occasions, placed in different positions. She remembered being there. She remembered observing it, but she never felt part of it.

After that, they left her alone in an empty home with only silence for company. And everything was a reminder which reduced her to tears. Until it didn't any more, because only half the reminders came, and it started to become bearable, incrementally, imperceptible at first. There was a little light in her life. Some joy which grew and became more substantial. Maybe just a playful fantasy a few minutes a day. Such a nice place: to be thinking of her son so intensely it was like he was there. Gradually he stayed longer, becoming more vivid, more real, their interactions so needed in her life. Mirin was a mother again, a better mother than she'd ever been. And she loved her little boy and he loved her. Yes, they'd lost a husband and a father, but they still had each other and together they could get through this.

But it was all a lie.

In the interview room, Mirin's solicitor had laid an awkward arm around her shoulders, and Mirin heaved beneath it in great juddering sobs. She allowed this stranger to comfort her. But then something distracted the lawyer. The arm had drawn away. Mirin didn't care why. She was barely aware of the chair moving beside her, and the solicitor said something like, "I'll just go and see what the matter is." A knock at the door. A conversation, some curt words and eventually the door opened. The solicitor left, and Mirin was able to return to her misery. She didn't care what happened now. They could take her to prison. It didn't matter where she was. The solitude of a cell, without the complications of the world, sounded like the best of all options.

There was a loud bang, and the heavy door of the interview room rattled in its frame. It was a menacing noise. The door banged again, holding fast against the onslaught. But Mirin was somewhere else. The noise was to do with something else and Mirin did not care.

The toughened-glass pane cracked when something hard hit it. A second impact smashed it. Glass tinkled to the ground like doleful windchimes, broken with age. The gap let in the noise. Beyond, shouts from people who believed they were in authority, using institutionally commanding voices; voices that were being ignored. Then the scuffles of a violent struggle, of a strangled cry, followed by snapping and wet slapping noises, over and over. The voice of authority became weak, pleading like a child, before finally falling silent.

A lock turned and the door burst wide open. At that moment, an alarm began to sound in the police station, part of some centralised system. The noise was so loud it hurt Mirin's ears, but she did not look up. It was nothing to do with her

Sirens wailed. Footsteps crossed the room. Guttural swearing. A shadow cast over Mirin in her despair. A freeing angel?

Something metallic and heavy was being hoisted from the ground with a grunt of physical exertion. And then the squeak of rubber soles. A shout covering quickly moving feet, followed by a short grunt on impact, and the clattering of something metallic and heavy on to the floor near her.

"Mirin, we've got to go."

Mirin did not move. The voice was distant and irrelevant. She wanted to stay and curl up here forever.

She flinched when his hand touched her arm, waking her from her reverie. Mirin looked up to see through the fractal blur of tears Dip standing over her, a fire extinguisher in his good hand.

She could see the concern and questions written in his eyes. However, he didn't ask any questions. Instead, he bent down and threaded the potted arm of his fractured limb under her armpit and hoisted Mirin bodily to her feet, hefting the fire extinguisher with his other arm.

"You have to help me, Mirin. I can't carry you and fight at the same time. The city is falling apart, and that includes here. We have to try and end this."

Mirin's knees buckled. She fell to her knees. She didn't want to help. Whatever was going to happen, let it happen. She would lie on the floor of the interview room next to the body of this unconscious man with a bleeding head and wait for it to be over.

3

MARY CURSED HER ARTHRITIC KNEES. It had taken ages to shuffle from the city centre down Sauchiehall Street and into Finnieston. The town wasn't a place to be tonight. She had a few spots she might be able to hunker down in, nearer to the West End of the city. There was a back alley behind one of the Indian restaurants with a large recycling bin. She could just about clamber into it, and there was enough paper and plastic to provide insulation and a little comfort. And if it rained, those things were as watertight as Noah's Ark. The only problem was she had to wake up early to avoid being tipped into the back of a bin lorry. In all her years on the streets, she knew a couple of people that had happened to. Not a nice way to go, crushed up with all the dirty rubbish.

It was dark now, and those funny clouds Mary didn't like hung overhead. She'd never seen green lightning before. She hurried as much as she could.

Those bloody crows were everywhere, mocking her. "What are you doing, you silly bitch?" one of them squawked as Mary shuffled by.

"Shut up, *ya wee dafty*," she muttered, keeping on the move.

"Who you calling a *wee da*fty?" the crow retorted, and then went on, "You're going the wrong direction, Mary. All the fun is back the other way. Although you'll find a treat if you keep going."

"You shut your face, stupid bird."

"Stupid bird, me? You're the queen of the loony castle." The crow squawked and took flight, aiming some droppings as it flew over Mary's head. She skipped as quickly as she could into a doorway and the bird's excrement splattered on the pavement.

The thunder and lightning started again. Mary had never liked thunder. It made her wet herself when she lived in Lennox Castle. Not that she did that kind of thing any more, not often anyway, but thunder and lightning still frightened her. It was so loud and bright tonight, it hurt Mary's ears. She tried to comfort herself that at least it would drown out the birds.

The bin wasn't far. If she could just get inside it, no one would know she was there, and she could wait it out. Hopefully, it would rain. There was something quite nice about being inside the big plastic recycling bin when the rain started to fall. The drops would drum on the roof of the bin and always send Mary off to sleep. It reminded her of when the rain would hit the big glass windows of their dormitory at Lennox Castle, drowning out the noises of the other people she lived with, the sounds of people being naughty at night, touching them-selves where they were not supposed to, and the moans and groans would keep her up. Mary never did anything like that. She knew that was dirty and wrong. But when the rain came, she could drift off, listening, and imagine she lived somewhere else, in a real castle, some-where with a mum and dad who hadn't forgotten to come and get her. She would drift off in peaceful dreams. Mary never remembered what she dreamt about, only that she woke a little happier. If it could rain tonight. That would be beautiful. *Please let it rain*, she thought. *Please.*

Her eyes weren't as good as they used to be and so she saw the fog a little too late. Mary knew instinctively the fog was something to do with those naughty crows. It was all around her, snaking between her ankles, coming up to her knees. She couldn't see her feet. The fog was thick and distorted the glow from the streetlights, blurring the light in all directions. She didn't like standing in it. It reminded her of being a child walking over an old railway bridge, those rusting skeletons of iron, where if she looked down it made her dizzy. It was like that. There could have been a troll under the railway bridge. Or something worse. What was in this fog, she couldn't tell. It made things quiet, sucking the noise out of the street. There were no sounds of traffic or the gentle sounds of people inside their homes. No distant dogs barking, or cats padding along walls, all the little noises that go unnoticed until they are gone. Mary looked around furtively.

Just around the corner and down the first side alley she'd find the bin. Mary turned the corner and stopped still. Her old legs started to shake. The fog was everywhere, covering the street from building to building, and as far as she could see in front and behind her.

In the heart of the fog stood a little boy. He was naked. His skin was very dark, his hair too.

He wasn't a good little boy; even silly Mary knew that. He was what the stupid crows had been croaking about when they had said she would find a *treat*. Her feet were stuck to the pavement. Closing her eyes tight, she tried very hard not to wet herself like a scared little girl abandoned in the loony bin. When Mary opened her eyes again, she saw dogs and cats flanking the boy, as though summoned out of the green, pulsating mist. Overhead, a great murder of crows soared. Some came to roost, lining the streets and rooftops, cackling amongst themselves, so many Mary couldn't count them. She could hear the crows' dirty jokes and the horrible comments.

The little boy met Mary's eyes, and seemed to look right through her, as though she wasn't there at all. The boy moved forward. The sky roared and lightning struck the ground, shaking it. Mary cowered, huddling close to the red sandstone wall of the tenement. Lightning hit the top of the buildings, causing green showers of sparks to rain down. Green flashed in the sky like hungry eyes caught in the lamplight. The sky above was a swirl of towering black clouds, like a dirty pool that wanted to wash Mary and everyone else down the plug hole. The boy had blocked the alleyway entrance Mary wanted to get to. There was nowhere for her to go except back. Not that she could get far on her gammy leg.

As the boy came toward her, the windows of the building parallel with him shattered and blew out into the street. Car alarms triggered, blaring and flashing their lights. The boy trailed his fingers through the fog, as though across the spine of a rugged animal.

His eyes were black like coal, black as his smile, but he did not look like a happy little boy; it was not a nice smile. Mary had seen smiles like that on people crazier than her, a smile only bad people had when they were going to do bad things. Mary couldn't help it. She made water in her knickers, like a naughty girl, a dirty girl. She wasn't supposed to do that, but she couldn't help it. She wanted her mummy and daddy to come and get her, but she knew they were long dead. She was an old lady who'd never had a mummy or daddy, not ever. There was no one to clean her up, no one to help her.

The boy and his minions passed right by Mary as if she wasn't there. She felt the unmistakable scurry of rats' paws over her feet beneath the fog and let out a whimper. Dogs with wild eyes and cats with feral, hungry looks swept by Mary, parting around her like river water around a rock. The boy was the head of that river, and they followed in his wake.

People emerged from their homes in throes of anger. Some jumped from the floors high up, crashing out of windows, falling feet first right onto the street, screaming. She heard the shrill screams of children up in the flats. She looked up to see a woman crash through a window on the second floor, a man pinning her to the thin windowsill with one hand, raising what looked like a toaster above his head, its cord dangling. Mary flinched as the toaster came down.

"Silly Mary," squawked a crow. "He's not interested in you. Why would he be interested in you? Our master is heading for his witch. She is much better than you, Mary, much prettier she is. Silly, mad Mary." The other crows laughed, swearing and jabbering.

Mary put her hands over her ears and closed her eyes tightly. Lightning flashed and thunder rumbled. The dogs barked and the crows cawed as Mary sank to her knees and rocked until the procession had gone, leaving only the wail of car horns and people fighting in the street.

Mary knew she could see things most ordinary people could not because most ordinary people could not see Mary either. Sometimes, she wasn't sure if she was really there at all or if any of this was real. Reaching the edge of the alleyway, Mary looked left to right, half expecting this to be another trick played by the crows. The large brown recycling bin hid in the shadows. With difficulty, she opened the heavy lid and found just enough strength to pull herself inside. As the lid closed, the first drops of rain fell on her resting place. Safe inside, making a bed of cardboard and plastic, Mary could not see the colour of the rain, and for that, she would have been thankful.

4

WITH THE SECOND EXPLOSION, screams shredded the air. Alex's little sister, Karen, was one of those screaming, her wailing drowned by the thunder of explosions. The stand was chaos, a surge of bodies and sound.

Big Alex held them close, steadying himself between the rows of seats, shielding the children as other supporters climbed over the seats all around them. He was like a spear of rock in the sea, around which the waves crashed. He would not move.

From under his father's arms, Alex held his sister's coat in bunched fists. He could see the players down on the pitch fighting, bright colours amongst the confusion of green fog, and hundreds of people across the stands brawling. Figures fell from their seats into the fog, submerged, vanishing as though they had never existed.

The sky rumbled and the green lightning returned, forking down from the black, churning clouds, striking one of the floodlights. Sparks flew and the stadium fell into darkness. A fresh chorus of screams erupted. But Big Alex was being buffeted less and less now, as though the waters of the violent sea were calming. The crowd had moved past them into the upper tier of the stand, surging towards the bottleneck entrances. Emergency lighting kicked in, providing meagre light.

Gripping his children by the shoulder, Big Alex started to steer them. "This way. Come on now." He was stern but not harsh. They clung to him. Instead of upward, where most people had headed for the nearest exit, he took them down and along. There was an exit there the majority of panicking fans hadn't spotted, but Big Alex knew the stadium like the back of his hand. As they approached, Alex realised why it was clear. It was closer to where the explosion had taken place. An uneasy feeling came over Alex, but he couldn't bring himself to say no to his dad, who moved with such certainty.

Karen wept, her screams having quieted into sobs. Alex held her hand, holding the delicate fingers like he might have a little bird, fragile and quivering. She squeezed his hand in return. They edged their way between the narrow rows of seats and onto the steps down, with a handful of other fans who'd had the same idea. Big Alex broke Karen and Alex's grip on each other, pushing between them and taking their hands in his.

They didn't run, but hurried down the steps, the sounds of panic and fighting still burning in their ears. At the bottom of the stairs there was a steward in a bright yellow coat. She was a short, tubby, red-headed woman with black-rimmed spectacles. Her voice was high-pitched. "Not this way," she said, her face ashen white.

"There's no other way," Big Alex said, as they broke into a jog through the tunnel. The steward made no further attempt to stop them.

In the belly of the stand, the sounds of terror echoed, but there was less fighting. They joined the flow of people fleeing the stadium. The fans surged over each other, piling towards the stairs, but there were too many through such a narrow passage. One or two people fell and were run over, crying out, then silenced by the stampede.

Big Alex battled with the current of people, using his shoulders to barge people out of his way. They broke free and headed away from the direction everyone else had opted for. Big Alex had a better route in mind, away from the exit, near the burger and match-programme kiosks.

They could move more quickly now, still holding tight to their father's hands. The other exit, less used, was in sight when Alex saw a man standing in the middle of the thoroughfare ahead of them.

It was the man in the yellow steward's uniform with the shaved head, the one who'd smelled so badly of sweat and stale cigarettes. There was something about the way he stood: legs apart, arms by his sides, head tilted down. Why wasn't he panicking like everyone else? He had a phone in one hand, an old one by the look of it, and something long and straight and lethal in the other. The man lifted his right hand as if checking he had a new text message and pushed a button on the handset.

The explosion behind them shook the landing beneath their feet, knocking them off balance. There was a roar that drowned Karen and Alex's cries. Even their father cried out, a sound of pure terror swallowed by the roar of flame.

Big Alex tried to get his feet. Alex looked into his father's face and followed his gaze back to the explosion site. Sprawled bodies lay everywhere, torn to bloody tatters.

Through the clouds of dust they came. A stampede rushing towards them. Big Alex pulled them roughly to their feet. There was no more time for gentleness. Karen cried uncontrollably. Alex began to sob too. The man in the yellow jacket was coming towards them, the fire-axe swinging backwards and forwards as he walked, whistling a merry tune.

5

THE PRODUCERS of the show babbled in her earpiece. The countdown had begun, and they were giving Lucy regular time checks, as well as going over the usual pre-programme procedure. She hadn't felt this energised since getting her first big story, and even that paled into insignificance to how she was feeling right now. What she and David were going to achieve would be something stupendous. It felt preordained. And tonight, Lucy felt, would be a knockout show. They had Professor Jorgensen slated to come on at the end of the programme. The car was picking him up right now at the end of his speech at the university and rushing him over here. She was looking forward to creating a bit of controversy with him.

Hair and makeup buzzed around her, touching her up. They'd wittered on about her looking too skinny and pale these days and how hard it was to hide the bags under her eyes. One of them asked what her secret was for losing weight. Was she on some special new diet? She looked the makeup artists in the eye and said, very deadpan, "A good fuck, of course," and then threw her head back laughing. The makeup artist had joined in uncomfortably. Sandra, who always did her hair, asked if Lucy wanted to dye out the grey streak which had appeared very suddenly over the last few days. Lucy ignored her and took off the cape attached around her neck, protecting her clothes from dustings of makeup, and turned back to the camera.

"Sixty seconds," Lucy heard in her ear.

Cathy was doing the weather report. Lucy could see it on the monitor in front of her: the pictures of the horrible black clouds swirling over Glasgow, with yet another unexplained meteorological phenomenon of green lightning. Lucy watched with amusement, her heart quickening with every flash of green. She could feel the studio vibrating with energy; it pulsed through everything and through her.

"Thirty seconds, Lucy. We're kicking off with the piece on people trafficking tonight, something nice and light for a Friday, and then into that heart-warming piece about the homeless guy who got on Britain's Got Talent."

"I shall perform a fucking literal miracle linking those two together for you," Lucy said.

"It's all about light and dark, darling," her producer, Tim, said. "Twenty seconds."

Lucy checked her notes on the desk for the interview pieces. The rest was on the teleprompter. Her eyes scanned the words. Some part of her brain took notice of what they said, but some other part of her, which was growing stronger by the moment, felt those concerns beneath her. It basked in the energy she could feel running through everything. That part of her, lurking behind the journalistic profes-sionalism, sensed fate was in the driving seat tonight. Lucy thought that if she left the studio right now and went down to the newsagent's and bought a lottery ticket she would win. If she walked out into the middle of the motorway and didn't look, not a single car would hit her. She felt untouchable.

"And in five, four, three, two, and..." Tim went silent in her ear as the programme's intro music faded out and the red light above the camera came on.

"Good evening, and this is *Big Issues* with Lucy Walker."

Lucy could hear herself following the autocue, doing her thirty-second introductory piece on people trafficking. Her tone was sombre, inflecting the serious points with a staccato rhythm. Then the VT was introduced, and she was off the air, with Tim calling instructions from the booth. It all felt irrelevant, as though they were all reading a script for children and simpletons. But she had the *real* one. The message was in everything, encoded in the world, pulsing through this city and vibrating in every cell of her body. It would wipe away the old, tired script.

Above the BBC building, looming over the River Clyde, a vortex of clouds gathered. They spun, opening a covetous eye to gaze down at them. From the centre of the eye came a series of forked green lightning bolts, one after the other, stabbing like tridents into the antennae of the building.

Every piece of electrical equipment was suddenly over-charged. The energy surged through the building. Tim was about to fade out the VT, his hand on a slider, when his entire body became rigid, along with the rest of his team in the booth. They sat in front of the control desk, juddering on the spot, tendrils of green electricity crawling all over their bodies, making their hair stand on end, and their eyes bulge. Could lightning do that? Lucy wondered. It was mere curiosity. The room was filled with the smell of burning hair and charring flesh and then went black. Every light in the BBC blew; every light but for the red light on the camera focused on Lucy Walker.

When the lights came back up, they pulsed with a spectral green, casting dark shadows across Lucy Walker's sunken, pale face.

Now the silly, childish script was done away with. Its authors killed. Something had to come in its place, to fill the void. The true narrative.

The vibration was a low hum coming from the back of Lucy's mind. It grew like a gathering wave, tremendous and inevitable, until it roared with utter clarity. It would break over the city in a glorious flood of destruction and hate, and Lucy would be there riding its crest. She would bring them what they wanted. She would let them see the way, the way of darkness, the way of blood.

Lucy raised her head and looked into the red eye staring at her, waiting for her to talk. "For too long you have been lied to. For too long you have lied to yourselves. We all have. We have all been guilty. And guilt is such a terrible thing to carry around. We've all been told to be good, to stay in line, to know our places. Work hard, they say, follow the rules, do the right thing, then you get what you deserve. And did you? Did you all get what you deserved?" Lucy was smiling and shaking her head. "Of course you didn't. Because they were all lying to you. Taking what was really yours. Making you work your fingers to the bone, and you all work so hard, don't you? And why? So that they can get the things that you really deserve, that you really desire. But can you sense it? Can you feel that tonight is the night that all your dreams will come true? All you have to do is take it. Take whatever you want. Don't lie to yourself anymore. Don't believe the lies that you've been told. Whatever, whomever you think has been standing in your way, all this time, talking behind your back, stopping you from getting what you wanted, coming along and taking it. They have. Believe that little inner voice you always had. Tonight is the night that voice doesn't just get to speak; it gets to shout. It gets to be heard. You get to be heard. Get up. Get up off your lazy backsides. Stop sitting there being told what to do. Stop hoping for it and go and get it. Don't ask for it, take it. And if they won't give it, make them. Make them feel sorry for not giving it to you before, because tonight is the night, we all get what we deserve."

Lucy Walker felt like a priestess talking to her flock. And even though her cameramen lay unmoving on the floor, wisps of smoke rising from his still body, she knew that everyone with a television, radio, computer, even a mobile phone could hear every word she was saying. Tonight, there were so many of her flock tuned into her exact frequency.

6

"Thank you... Please... That's enough..." The Vice Principal stood at the lectern, her arms raised above her shoulders, palms down, trying to call for order for the third time that evening. "Yes, thank you... Thank you... Please... Order... That's it, yes. I would like to remind the floor, Professor Jorgensen is an invited guest of the University. And it is our tradition to let guests speak, in the spirit of openness of ideas and debate. I would ask you once again to allow Professor Jorgensen to finish, and if we can continue with no further interruptions, there may still be an opportunity for a question and answer afterwards."

A murmur spread quickly among the crowd. Some of the protesters immediately raised their murmur to a shout of protestation. This triggered those who wanted to hear the controversial professor, and they shouted back. But the Vice Principal cut in before the ruckus could amount to anything.

"Thank you. That will be quite enough... Thank you..." She cast a stony eye over the crowd. Her earlier nervousness had abated, and she had found her lecture hall feet firmly beneath her. "Professor Jorgensen, you have the floor." The Vice took a seat, keeping her firm stare wandering across the crowd, working to maintain the precarious grip of control that she had.

Professor Jorgensen quirked his mouth, stood, and walked up to the microphone again, nodding deferentially to the vice principal. He spoke without notes and took a moment, partly for dramatic effect, partly to establish control in the room, a trick he would use in therapy and undergraduate seminars. The control of silence had an uncanny effect of making *Homo sapiens* feel uncomfortable and he knew it could be used to establish dominance within the group. The pause was also to give him a moment as he picked up his previous train of thought.

"I think twenty years ago," he began, "the things that I'm saying now would not have been particularly controversial. Of course, in many ways, back then we lived in a society less tolerant than the one we live in today. However, then, the popularity of the idea of the sovereignty of the individual was paramount in Western thought. Of course, there have always been different interpretations of this idea, depending on time and place. The European notion of the individual and social democracy has always been different to that of your American cousins, but far more like my own homeland of Canada, no doubt because of our shared colonial history. Today, it is important to explore the various social changes which may have led to this idea going out of fashion. However, I contend that the idea of individuality remains as important today, if not more important, than it ever was. Not only because the forces of identity politics, which are on the rise in our society today, have the potential to be more pernicious than those we saw during the Cold War and up to the end of the 1980s. Rather than driven from the older, static geopolitics of liberal democracies and authoritarian regimes, or capitalism and communism respectively, the threat to the individual and the freedom that comes with it are due to technological changes. These changes have in turn driven huge social changes, namely, the diffusion of power, and the diffusion of complex systems of distribution such as the Internet."

The professor looked out over the crowd. Unsurprisingly, many of the students stared at shiny little screens they held in their hands. He noted, however, all of them were glowing green. He thought it must be some local trend in cell phone technology and filed it away with other irrelevant pieces of information in the back of his mind, and he went on.

"Essentially, my thesis is this: it is the individual who is paramount. It is the individual that lies at the heart of all of our problems and all of our solutions. It's a very old Enlightenment idea, but it is at the level of the individual through which you will do it. It doesn't matter whether you are a woman..." An uncomfortable murmur rose up through the hall and the Vice Principal cast her glare, feeling its grip weakening. "...or a man," Professor Jorgensen went on. "It doesn't matter what colour skin you have. It does not make you better or worse than anyone else." That murmur was then trampled by short shouts of protest.

"Order... Thank you..." the Vice Principal demanded.

The professor didn't feel like backing down from this point. "It doesn't matter what sexual orientation you have, what gender you identify with, or what country you were arbitrarily born in because your parents happened to have sex or were living there at the time of your birth. No one group..."

Individual shouts of outrage blended into one another, feeding and growing. Professor Jorgensen thought briefly about stopping but decided instead to finish his point.

"In sum, it is identity politics, the belief that one group is inherently bad, and other groups are somehow inherently better and more just, purely through the arbitrary denomination that they have assigned themselves, or which society has placed upon them, that will ultimately wreak more havoc than any benefit."

Even amplified by a microphone, his voice struggled to rise over the shouts decrying the professor and those who argued back and wished to hear him speak.

The Vice Principal was on her feet, arms raised, again calling for order, when Professor Jorgensen spotted something out of the corner of his eye. Even though the room wasn't in total darkness, the spotlights were on him, and he saw it far too late. It cut across the light like an eclipsing moon's shadow, drawing the professor's attention. He tilted his head up to see what it was. Initially, he had the preposterous notion that it was a bird or perhaps a bat that had got into the auditorium and fluttered across a light. He realised too late that the object was not coming from the ceiling of the high auditorium, but rather travelling in a fast arc. The glass beer bottle crystallised in his field of vision a split second before its thick glass bottom impacted on the bridge of his eyebrow, sending a spray of beer in an almost perfect circular arc eight feet in the air above his head. He didn't even have time to duck. The impact made him stagger back one step, catching the lectern with a hand.

A great cheer went up. Like a boxer caught behind the ear, he felt his legs wobble under him. He felt separated from the room. It swayed and reverberated before him.

The auditorium erupted. More bottles were thrown in all directions, showering the students below. Then they were throwing larger objects: chairs and even people.

A hot trickle of liquid had run into Professor Jorgensen's eyes. He inspected it with the tips of his fingers, noting they were covered in a thick, red mud. I'm bleeding, he dumbly thought, and slid down behind the lectern, one hand still holding on ineffectually until his backside hit the worn wooden floorboards of the stage. The professor held his bloodied hand in front of him, like Lady Macbeth inspecting the damned spot. He looked across the stage, befuddled, and saw the Vice Principal cowering, her hands over her head, crouched behind a chair, bottles and glasses smashing everywhere, some hitting her. The bottles lay like disused ordnance.

His thoughts felt slow and cumbersome and full of uncertainty. Some part of himself could observe them and how odd they were. He was used to being so certain. Having a clarity. He enjoyed questions and finding the answers to them. He enjoyed good questions, intellectually probing questions. However, the questions he was asking himself now were those of the simpleton, unsure if there were any answers. Should I go and help her? I think I should. I'm tired. Perhaps I will stay here. Am I bleeding? How did that happen? Someone threw something at me. Why did they throw something at me?

The Vice Principal was crying now. The blood from his forehead was running freely down his face and dripping copiously onto his immaculate Egyptian cotton herringbone shirt, staining its starched whiteness red.

The professor could see a security guard shepherding the Vice Principal off stage, enduring the slings and arrows thrown his way. The brave guard placed the middle-aged woman in the wings, shouting something to her before poking his head around the curtain and darting for the chair which the Vice Principal had previously taken cover behind. He is coming for me, Professor Jorgensen thought, detached, and then every light in the auditorium hummed.

The professor felt the very room vibrate as each light in the ceiling exploded in a shower of green sparks, plunging the room into darkness in a hail of screams. Some of the sparks landed on the old worn curtains of the debating chamber, and small fires began to kindle around the hall. They are quite pretty, the professor thought. The flames caught slowly for a moment, then swiftly became hungry to consume whatever they touched. As they grew even higher, they cast shadows through the gloom of the hall.

It vaguely reminded Professor Jorgensen of how he always imagined the mead hall would look in an epic poem of old. He had studied the archetypal myth structure of mediaeval stories as part of his PhD dissertation; after his clinical doctorate, of course. It had interested him how humans, psychologically speaking, were a conflict of angels and demons, and how those metaphors served as allegories for our mental conflict between emotion and reason. Stories, he agreed with Jung, were a culture's way of passing on information, encoded in archetypal narratives of self-development. And therein was the rub: a society and an individual's journey within it. The hero's journey. The idea had been everything he'd ever wanted to explore intellectually. He'd never wanted the fame that had been thrust upon him. He'd merely capitalised on it, using it as an opportunity to speak to more people. He'd seen his difficulties back in Canada, with his own run-ins with university authorities and the legislature as his own hero's journey. His own slings and arrows through which to grow, to learn and to bring back the knowledge gained as an elixir to his society. This was all that he was doing. It was for his but also their benefit. He had returned to the mead hall to show them how to vanquish their monsters. There should have been a feast as the fire licked and crackled ever brighter. And would a monster appear? Grendel? The Jabberwocky? The Minotaur? A serpent at the Tree of Knowledge?

Someone new had entered the stage. They climbed onto it, dragging themselves from the fray below and standing upright. They searched, and then found what they were looking for.

Professor Jorgensen's eyes locked with the young man. He was holding a cricket bat. Not something one expected to see in a debating hall, and certainly not a Scottish one.

The young man strode forward with his cricket bat, which could just as easily have been an Anglo-Saxon sword forged in the ironmaker's furnace, a priest casting spells upon the blade.

Was this boy the hero? Professor Jorgensen mused as the cricket bat rose above the young man's head. The professor looked up as the bat came down. He felt the spike of pain run from his face to the back of his skull. He fell to the ground, blood filling his eyes. The security guard had seen what was happening and made a dash for it, running at full clip to tackle the young assailant. He would not make it in time. As the bat swung for a second time, the last thing Professor Jorgensen ever thought would be his last and most profound revelation.

"I am not the hero," he murmured as the bat came down, an executioner's blow.

There was peace in that.

7

THE BLARING alarm reverberated in an endless cycle, while the strip lights struggled to stay on, blinking as if aghast at the horror of their reality.

Dip had dragged Mirin through the hell of the police station with his one good arm. He was tired, and Mirin slumped from his grip onto the floor.

"Get up," he shouted, but he had no time to wait for her to respond. A blur of movement headed towards them. Dip made a split-second decision, swinging the fire extinguisher in an upwards arc. The heavy metal cylinder rang like a broken bell. The man's jaw cracked as his head whipped back. His feet left the floor as momentum carried him forward, until he lay parallel to the ground in mid-air. Then he fell flat on his back, unconscious.

The cast on his arm prevented Dip from getting a good grip on Mirin. She was a limp dead weight, eyes full of tears, staring dumbly into the middle distance.

"Please, Mirin. Get up. We can't stay here."

Mirin could see Dip. His face was panicked. He was saying something, trying to lift her. What he was trying to tell her, she could not hear. Down the corridor and over Dip's shoulder, two men burst from a room, tumbling into the wall. One was a police officer, dressed in a dark uniform. The other man fell astride the policeman like a school-yard bully.

The bully was a stocky, bald man with tattoos on his thick arms. In one hand he held a hammer. The hammer began to rain down. The police officer brought up his hands to try and intercept the blows, letting out screams. The screams turned into a choked gargle, each rise and fall of the hammer bringing with it a spray of blood. He became a painted man. With each hammer blow, the now silent policeman's body twitched, legs kicking spasmodically.

Mirin watched it all through the blank eyes of a doll, until she saw something. In that madhouse of screams, she caught a flash of something, something impossible. At the end of the corridor, a small boy with black curly hair disappeared around the corner with a childish giggle. Her inert body came to life. Her back straightened. Mirin's eyes refocused. In the awfulness of everything around her coming into clarity, there was also a glimmer of something else.

"That's it, Mirin. That's it. You can do it." Dip heaved with all his might, getting Mirin to her feet.

CONNIE SHEPARD'S hands were covered in blood. She had only just met this woman and couldn't remember her name. Now Connie had a hand on her abdomen, trying to stop the bleeding from the multiple stab wounds inflicted by a screwdriver. The woman was a solicitor, and they had been discussing the case on which they had been on opposite sides. They had decided to call in a psychologist before proceeding. That was when the alarms began, and before they knew it, they were overrun with madmen armed with weapons, smashing everything and everyone in their way. They had been running for the interview suite, with Connie leading the way, when the lawyer had fallen into Connie, sending them both tumbling to the ground. Connie had been pinned between the wall and a vending machine, with the lawyer on top of her. The attacker had dark hair. That was all Connie could remember as he punched the screwdriver repeatedly into the lawyer's stomach. As suddenly and violently as the attack had started, it ended. The man looked up, as though he were a dog hearing the voice of his master. Screwdriver dripping with blood, he scanned for his next target, seemingly missing Connie. A moment later he was gone.

Easing herself out from underneath the lawyer, Connie had tried to make her comfortable, but she was slumped awkwardly against the edge of the vending machine. The lawyer had been wearing a waist-length navy blazer, matching her slacks, and a fitted white blouse, pink buttons matching the pinstripe of the suit. The shirt was now crimson with the blood leaking out of her belly. When Connie moved her hands under the shirt, she could feel the puncture holes. One of the holes was larger than the others and the blood pumped from it vigorously. Connie applied pressure and the lawyer let out an anguished cry, grabbing weakly at Connie's wrist as if to try and remove her hands.

"It's okay," Connie said softly. "I've got to push hard to stem the bleeding." But even as she said it, she thought it was too late. All the colour had drained from the lawyer's face, leaving her with a deathly white pallor.

Keeping her voice gentle and low, Connie repeated over and over that she would be okay, and that help was coming. They were words as much for herself as the lawyer. With noises of violence around them, Connie kept her eyes on the woman until her eyes went blank and her head lolled, bringing her chin to rest on her chest.

The blood on Connie's hands was already growing cold as she removed them from the dead woman. Another lost to the madness, then.

A shadow fell over her. Connie turned, squinting in the bad light. As her eyes adjusted, she recognised Douglas Wallace from forensics. He was a competent man. His reports were always impeccable. *But he shouldn't be here*, she thought. Not at the station.

The initial rush of gladness ebbed as Connie noticed what he was holding. The elegant black blade pointed down to the ground, Douglas's hand curled firmly around the bone handle.

"Douglas? Douglas, what are you doing with that?"

Douglas did not reply. He seemed incapable of response. Instead, he rushed her. Connie brought up her hands. The black blade slashed laterally through the air, cutting through the flesh of her forearm. The pain blossomed into a bright sting when Douglas cut again with a backhanded action, flaying Connie's wrists to the white bone. She fell back and started to crawl away. Douglas followed slowly. Red dripped from the blade to the tiled floor. Connie slipped in her own blood and that of the lawyer's. Douglas loomed over her, ready to make his final strike, when he was slammed against the tiled wall.

DI Stuart Blair gripped Douglas around the chest, trying to pin his arms. They hit the floor in a writhing knot of limbs, snarling, straining with every muscle. Their momentum rolled them again. They lost a grip on each other and came to their knees separated. With only a second's pause they sprang at each other. They collided with the wall of the corridor. There was a sharp intake of breath when they came to a juddering halt, Stuart on top, slumped forward.

Stuart turned and looked at her. There was only pain in his eyes.

"Connie," he whispered, and then he was dead.

Douglas pushed Stuart off him, the policeman's body falling limply. Kneeling up, Douglas reached forward and slid the obsidian knife from between the dead officer's ribs. His face was calm and considered, just as it was when Connie had seen him work a crime scene. His chest rose and fell in deep breaths, but his face remained sanguine in his task. Thick drops of blood fell from the blade, like the sands of time, tick-tocking on the tiled floor. Douglas moved silently towards Connie.

Connie held her injured arm to her chest, blood pulsing down her front. She felt woozy. She knew she had to move. She must try to run or stand and fight, or even cry out and hope that someone heard her. But it was all she could do to keep her eyelids open and stop herself swooning. She had lost a lot of blood.

Douglas was silhouetted in front of the light once more. It formed a halo, eclipsing his face, and like the angel of death he descended upon her. His weight was heavy as he sat astride her. She made to grab his knife hand, but her fingers would not move. The tendons in her wrist had been severed. Instead, her hand flapped pathetically, and Douglas batted it away. Placing the tip of the knife on her belly, holding it almost ceremonially in both hands, he pressed the blade into her stomach.

Blood flowed over the black stone as a celestial song rose in pitch. Connie had heard of hallucinating at the point of death, of people floating above their bodies, or seeing impossible things. Initially, she assumed this was one of those experiences. The song was not the choir of archangels harmonising with seraphim and cherubim that she had learned about in Sunday school as a child. No, the song was a rough, rhythmic chant. Her lips began to move in time with it, to words she didn't know. But the song pulsed like the beating of a heart. The rhythm was so natural it was impossible for her to get it wrong.

The blade did not hurt now as it slid millimetre by millimetre through the muscles of her abdomen. Soon it would break through muscle and plunge smoothly into her internal organs. But for now, blood fed the blade in ceremonial preparation. She had given herself to the song. It had become everything: sight, sound, smell, feeling, turning over and over until it coursed through her entire body, turning light into a dance of fractal colours. She could see the song in its entirety, reaching from the past to the future in an endless line of song.

And then the song ended.

Pain replaced the divinity of the song. Constable Hardeep Bhaskar eclipsed the light, Mirin Hassan stood by his side. The constable put down a fire extinguisher and hurriedly inspected Connie's injuries. Douglas lay in a heap. One more lifeless body among many. Dip looked around and, not finding what he wanted, hurried away.

Connie looked up into Mirin's eyes. "The knife," she whispered. "That black knife."

Mirin saw the obsidian knife lying on the floor. She was surprised to see it, and she felt a pang of terror in seeing the blade that had hurt Portia. No, *killed* Portia.

"You want the knife?" Mirin asked.

"It sang to me."

Connie knew by the look on Mirin's face that she didn't understand. She laughed. Now the doubting police inspector understood, now she believed the impossible. She had seen beyond the veil, if only for a moment. The laugh turned into a wince of pain.

Dip returned in a hurry, kneeling at Connie's side. He produced a necktie, salvaged from some poor dead soul, and applied it as a tourniquet to Connie's forearm, stemming the flow of blood. He pulled the fire extinguisher near and scouted the hall for any further threats. Connie could read in Dip's face the conclusion he'd already come to.

"Go!" Connie said.

"We can't leave you here," he said.

"You have to go. Take the knife."

Dip bent and picked it up, looking at it with solemnity. "She's right. This is what we need. It's the only weapon I've seen used against the boy in my dreams."

"It sings," Connie said. "Can you hear it?"

Dip nodded. "It's the song of my vision, it's the chant of the young woman waiting in the bog for the boy to come."

Mirin searched Dip's face to understand.

He offered the blade to Mirin. "Here, take it."

Mirin's fingers closed around the knife's handle with a feeling of trepidation. She gripped the antler heft and felt... nothing.

"I don't understand. It's just a knife, an old knife we dug up."

Connie's eyes filled with tears. "I'm sorry. You were right, Mirin. You were right about the boy. You must go to him and end this."

"I can't. I'm... insane." The last word came out as a hollow note. "I've been living a fantasy. I can't trust anything I see."

"You were the one who tried to make me see," Connie said. "Constable Bhaskar sees it too. We believe. If you can't see it then trust us. You're not mad, Mirin, no more than the rest of us on a night like this." She laughed and winced with pain. "Please, can't you see that it has to be you?"

"But why?" Mirin pleaded.

Dip's hand rested on Mirin's shoulder as Connie told her. "Because, for whatever reason, the boy doesn't affect you."

8

THE RED EYE maintained its unblinking stare. The more that Lucy Walker spoke to it, the more she could feel its power spread. A spectral green illumination, which crept through every electrical wire and material making up the room, spread like blood through veins and capillaries, connecting the surging energy to all the fractals of life beyond the conduit of the studio.

The more Lucy spoke the more she felt a presence grow, there but not there. Becoming more substantial by the moment. She felt it, black and scaly, breaking in between the atoms that made up everything. It entwined her limbs, its reptilian tail sliding with exquisite pain across the soft smoothness of her legs, coiling serpentine over her inner thighs and venturing further still. She felt the great weight of its belly, and the rumble of its hunger. Its breasts were full, and its grey nipples swollen, lactating a pus of insipid milk. On seeing a drop of the poisonous liquid in her mind, it fell upon her full lips. She savoured it on her tongue, licking her lips, whetting her own hunger.

Lucy spoke into the camera. The tinny voice in her ear, Tim the producer, had been replaced by another voice. The grey in her hair was growing more pronounced, as was the feral look in her eyes. Her mouth never stopped moving.

"I can feel you all. My brothers and sisters!" Lucy said. "Take what is yours. Sacrifice and you shall have all that you desire! I can feel many of you have already begun and the more we sacrifice the more we can take. Follow the example of these good works..."

There was no one alive to flip the switch to cue the VT to Lucy's introduction, but still the live feed began to play. All censorship had died with Tim the producer.

The footage showed the pitch from the Old Firm game at Ibrox, practically next door to the BBC. There was no ball to be seen. Instead, a battlefield covered with a blanket of fog. The camera cut together a montage of violence and death. The final cut switched to the image of two figures in the centre circle. Colin McDermott sat astride the referee whose face had become a bloody pulp. Colin's own three front teeth were missing, and his left ear hung on by only a thin thread of tissue. His left eye was closed completely. And while his right eye was technically open, the gelatinous orb dangled unnaturally from its socket. What had been his nose had been so broken it was pushed across his face in a destroyed smear of flesh that bled profusely. Colin placed his hands around the man's neck and squeezed. Blood from his nose dripped into the referee's mouth.

Once he had finished, Colin climbed off the dead referee. The television screen showed him wipe a hand over his shaven head, feeling the first drops of something. More drops of red splashed on his pallid skin. He looked up into the roiling black clouds overhead, and his face began to be bathed in the falling blood.

"And in the centre of the city tonight," Lucy purred, "the good people of this city, your brothers and sisters, are taking what they want. Join them. Join them now. The only price is a little blood." She winked.

Screens across the city changed to closed-circuit television footage. On the broad shopping parade of Buchanan Street, a man and woman had picked up a dazed and helpless beggar. They ran with the homeless man, using him like a battering ram, throwing him head-first through a shop window. The glass shattered and the victim was impaled on a resilient shard at the bottom of the frame. The man and woman kicked away extraneous pieces of glass and clambered into the shop. Others followed suit.

The CCTV camera panned out to take a wide angle on the scenes of chaos on George Square, the broad plaza in front of the city hall. There was nothing but violence. Rioting had taken over the whole city.

The camera passed over a troop of police officers, but they were being backed into a corner by a larger mob. They brandished batons and pepper spray as the overwhelming numbers hemmed them in. A few mob-members were put down by swift batons, but then the mob closed and the police were overrun by the crazed frenzy.

The camera switched two more times, accompanied with Lucy's words of encouragement to join in. One news feed came from a discarded camera on the ground, lying on its side, showing a short cobbled street. Feet went to and fro. Sirens sounded among the screams. The last showed footage from a mobile phone in a building nearby: vehicles were crashing on a dual carriageway, some in flames. Drivers and passengers ran from the fires, and more cars crashed, mowing down pedestrians, skidding and crashing into the barriers.

With each image Lucy could feel the boy's presence. He was coming closer, making his way through the city. Beneath the broadcast desk, Lucy felt the black scaly tail move beneath her skirt, sandpaper grating exquisitely over her inner thighs. The tip of its tail played at the thin elastic hem of her panties. Acrid milk dripped from its grey nipple onto her lips. A second streak of grey hair had spread from her temple.

The camera cut a final time.

The boy walked through the fog down a wide street. His entire chest and every inch of his arms were covered in black symbols. His eyes were the colour of flint, reflecting the diffuse light emanating from the fog. Building and car windows exploded as he passed. Dogs followed in his wake. Crows flew across the camera, breaking the image with a strobe of shadows. Car tyres burst, shaking their steel skeletons as their alarms wailed and their lights flashed in a carnival display.

"He is coming. Can you see him? The boy. He has come to collect the blood price. Give it and you will be rewarded your heart's desire. Give and you shall receive. He comes to me now, and through me to everyone, to all of you. Pay the price and through us he will spread his message to the ends of the earth."

9

"You drive," Dip shouted to Mirin. He flung open the back door of the police Range Rover and bundled in Connie. Getting out of the station had seemed an impossible stroke of luck. The three of them now working together, with the knife, they had somehow moved unseen through the violence.

Dip thought Mirin was going to protest about driving and handed her the keys to force the issue. If they didn't get out of here soon, they might never get out alive. Mirin nodded, placing a hand briefly on the glass of the passenger-side window, and then pulling away, as if the glass were hot. She ran quickly to the driver's side.

She fastened her seatbelt, throwing a glance at Dip.

"There's no Green Cross Code tonight. Don't stop for anything," Dip told her, tending to Connie in the back, who flitted in and out of consciousness.

Mirin had never driven a large Range Rover before. She looked at the numerous screens. Dip leant forward and pointed to where the key slotted in the console. Something hit the four-by-four, bouncing off the roof.

"Hold the brake and hit the start button," Dip shouted, spotting three men who had noticed them and were heading their way, weapons in hand.

Mirin pressed the start button and the engine revved into the red. She cast a nervous glance to the passenger seat before turning to look out the back window and putting the car into reverse. A scaffolding pole came swinging at the side windscreen. The Range Rover lurched back, and the pole missed by a hair's breadth. They were jolted forward as the vehicle braked sharply, and Connie moaned. Putting it into drive, Mirin floored it, and the three men tumbled out of their way as the four-by-four sped off.

In the corner of her eye, Mirin could see Oran sitting in the front seat next to her. In the back, Dip was loosening Connie's tourniquet. Then he was checking the wound on her belly.

"It's still bleeding," he said. "But I don't think it was as deep as it looked. You must have iron stomach muscles!" The humour faded when he looked at her arms again. "I'm more worried about these."

"The tourniquet is working," Connie said, trying to control the pain. But neither of them sounded sure.

"Which way?" Mirin shouted.

Before anyone could suggest anything, the radio turned itself on. At the same moment, the mobile phones in Dip and Connie's pockets sang with notifications. Connie was too weak to fetch hers, but Dip fished his out to find the screen glowing green. He looked at it as if it were an infected piece of flesh. The words leaving his phone's tiny speaker matched the radio exactly, but his phone screen also had an accompanying video feed of Lucy Walker's deranged face making proclamations.

He showed the screen to Connie. She nodded in agreement. "The BBC," Dip said.

Mirin tried to keep her eyes on the road but found them drawn again and again to the little boy sitting next to her.

"Which way?" she asked, swerving in and out of abandoned cars. "We'll never get through to the motorway."

"The motorways are properly out of the question," Dip said. "Too many people were trying to get out of the city when I was coming to get you. I think our best bet is the waterfront. The Arc Bridge is the closest road bridge to the BBC."

Lucy Walker's voice floated out of the glowing radio on the central console. "Pay the blood price and receive all that you deserve. The higher the sacrifice, the greater the reward. Friends, brothers, sisters, mothers, fathers, husbands, wives..." And then she paused for effect. "Children. Oh yes, children. They give us so much, but they are worth so much more."

"Faster!" called Dip.

"What are we going to do?" Mirin said. She swerved around two cars abandoned in the middle of the road. They hit the kerb heavily as they mounted it. She drove along the pavement, the engine revving. Someone ran out from a residential building carrying a flat-screen TV. Mirin hit the brakes and hauled on the wheel, narrowly missing the person, who dropped the television screen. Instinctively, she checked if Oran was okay in the passenger seat, but the little boy smiled happily at his mother, unaffected by the world around him.

"The knife," croaked Connie, answering Mirin's question. She swallowed hard with the discomfort she felt in her abdomen, wincing at the pain. "It's something to do with the knife. I felt it when it cut me. It sang to me."

A hand still on Connie's belly, Dip stared intently at her. He scanned the memories of his visions and nightmares which followed him into his fitful sleeps, piecing things together. "That's it," he said half to himself. "The songs. They were lost without the songs. The songs protected them. They connected them." Dip reached with his mind, trying to make connections, trying to make sense of it all.

Still confused, Mirin asked, "Who was singing?"

Looking inside himself again, Dip consulted his memories for an explanation. "Right from when we uncovered him, the boy affects people. He magnifies things, people's feelings, their emotions and desires. He did it to me. I felt sick as soon as I drove onto the building site."

"But you didn't become a killer," Mirin said, clipping a parked van and turning a corner as the tyres screeched.

"You're right. I felt violently ill when I first saw him. But I think he affects different people in different ways."

"Portia was ill before..." Mirin's voice trailed off and she bit her lip, wanting to hold her little boy, but knowing she could only clutch at the wheel of the four-by-four.

"Sometimes he changes their thoughts, sometimes he just makes them ill, but why? What's the difference?" Connie said, a cold sweat on her brow.

Dip's mind was racing. "I don't know. Maybe some people have something inside already, something to turn or grow. The ones that don't, his presence makes them ill instead. Maybe it's like a natural warning. I don't know."

"There's a third group," Mirin said. "What about me? I didn't get ill and I haven't become violent."

For a moment there was only the noise of the Range Rover racing through the streets, before Connie broke the silence between them.

"Your little boy. You've been living with him for a long time, haven't you?"

Mirin fought not to look at the passenger seat. "But he's not real."

"And I think that is what makes you immune to the boy," Connie said, and Dip nodded in agreement.

"Because I'm crazy?" Mirin said hollowly.

"We're living in a world of killer crows and raining frogs. There's green lightning in the sky, and a boy thousands of years old has risen from the dead. I think crazy doesn't matter any more," Dip said. "But I've not finished telling you everything yet. My first vision of the boy was on that night we dug him up, in my shower at home. I saw his *death* on the bog. My dreams were filled with fragments of images after that. Nothing made sense or gave me a complete picture. I had only seen the end. But then I took a bath yesterday."

"Does your mum often tell you to wash?" Connie said wryly.

"Funny. I hadn't washed since the vision in the shower, the day we found the boy."

"Christ, you need your mum to tell you to wash more often," Connie said, her humour becoming a painful cough.

"Very good, DCI Shephard. Now rest up," Dip said, helping her relax back. "I knew I needed to get in the water, but I was still scared from the first vision."

"So, what happened?" Connie asked. Mirin weaved down side streets, turning whenever she saw trouble ahead.

"When I submerged myself, I wasn't *me* any more, and I wasn't here, not in this time. I went back, way back through time. I was a hunter-gatherer walking the landscape with his brothers, going to exchange food and trinkets with farmers. We sang through the forest until the trees stopped where our tribal lands ended. The farmers had cleared the land of all the trees, to turn the land over to their crops and animals. But their crops had failed, and their animals lay dying. We should have been singing songs, but the farmers, in clearing the land, had cleared away all the songs. We finally found them at a great circle of stones, like Stonehenge, only larger and built on a hill. And they had carved animals into the stones: lizards and jaguars. There were hundreds if not thousands of people there, gathered at the stones, and they were making great sacrifices of blood."

"What were they sacrificing?" Mirin asked. "What kind of animals?"

"There weren't sacrificing animals," Dip continued. "They sacrificed every one of their children to a black lizard god. They had slit their throats on a sacrificial stone and bled them of so much blood that the centre of the circle had become a pool. Black clouds, just like these, swirled overhead." Dip cast a worried eye to the sky. "The boy was the last of their children. God, he cried out. He was so terrified. Once they had bled him dry, they discarded him face down in the pool of blood. And do you know what they slit his throat with?"

"A black stone knife, by any chance?" Connie said.

"Ten points for the newly impaled DCI," Dip said, trying to smile.

"Then what happened?" Mirin asked, pulling her eyes from Oran.

"The green lightning struck and nearly killed everyone, everyone but me and my hunting brothers. We saw the boy come back to life in the pool of blood, and when he stood, the thousands of crows began to eat the dead. We ran back to our lands, and as we ran, we sang the songs of our homeland, our dreaming songs of life and creation. The other glimpses I've had are of the destruction that followed the boy as he walked through the land. I don't have the full story, only pieces here and there, until he came here and reached people who finally put him in the bog. They were singing too. There was a woman. She held the black stone knife."

"That's it," Connie said. "The song and the knife."

Mirin shook her head. It was all too much. "But how are we going to stop this?"

"It's you, Mirin," Connie said. "The knife in the song. *You* must take the knife, and go to him."

They raced along a clear stretch of road. The engine screamed. Mirin drove on the edge of control, close to crashing at any moment.

"But I can't. Why me?" Mirin said, close to tears. "You just arrested me and told me that my son is dead, and that I have imagined him for the last twelve months. And if you are right, and he is dead, then I'm just some..." She hit the steering wheel with the pad of her fist. "A fucking madwoman."

"Hey, hey, you're not crazy, okay? Doesn't all this prove it?" he said.

"He's right," said Connie. "Maybe that's why he doesn't affect you. Clearly, the boy has some miraculous powers. The weather is pretty incredible. And obviously he affects people in a bad way. Portia, she was very ill, and the doctors couldn't explain her getting weaker and thinner. Now, Lucy Walker is clearly in league with him, and his power is growing. But the question is why hasn't he affected you, Mirin? That's what we're all wondering. I've got a hunch. That's all it is, but it's all we've got."

"What is it?" Mirin was desperate for an explanation.

"I think your trauma protects you. I don't know how else to explain it."

Tick, tick, tick. Heavy raindrops began to drum on the car.

Mirin fumbled for the wipers, hitting the indicators first, but then the wipers came on automatically. The thin arms waved across the windscreen, spreading out the thick, dark globules landing on the glass. Soon, the windshield was covered in red smears.

"What the...?" whispered Dip.

Mirin sprayed the windscreen with water, clearing their view. A flash of green lightning came and a second later the clouds rumbled overhead. The rain grew heavier still, pounding out a loud tattoo on the roof. The wipers waved ineffectually against the torrent of blood, and Mirin could see nothing but the blur of shapes behind a liquid red curtain.

"You have to stop, Mummy," Oran said. Only Mirin heard him. She threw him a glance. Both Connie and Dip saw her do it. "Stop now, Mummy, please."

Mirin hit the brakes and they screeched to a halt.

10

THE CONCRETE LANDING of the football stadium was a churning roil of people running from the second explosion. When a person fell – man or woman, adult or child – they were consumed by the rolling surge of bodies. The flames from the bomb flickered orange and red, their light refracted through the smoke and dust, which appeared to follow the wave of people like the spray from tumbling breakers crashing towards the shore. Karen screamed. She and Alex held hands with their father, clinging to him as they would a lifebuoy. They were stranded in the open waters between two dangers. From one way, the rush of people was almost upon them, and in the other direction the sneering man in the high-visibility jacket with his long, heavy axe. Time had run out.

What happened next would stay in Alex's dreams forever.

"Hang on to the railings," Big Alex shouted.

"But Dad..." Alex cried.

"Son!" Alex had never seen his father look at him that way, had never seen him shaking with emotion. Not the wild euphoria of watching a game. A different emotion, one that had run so deep in his father, Alex hadn't been sure, until now, it was ever there.

"Do as you're told! Climb!"

He flung his children to the outer wall of the stadium, where a blue steel balustrade lined the concrete. Alex collided with the steel railing, the force of the blow bruising his ribs. He could see the stampede of fans was nearly upon them. He climbed up on top of the balustrade, pulling Karen up onto the metal runner with him. He pressed his sister's arms around a concrete pillar and threw his arms around it and her. He closed his eyes and waited for whatever came next. But *through* his eyelids, he could still see the high-visibility jacket man, raising a fire axe above his head.

The man's eyes glared above a mouth that was a snarling smile. The axe came down towards Big Alex, but Big Alex bravely met it halfway, catching the haft. The weight and momentum of the axe's head was too great. Four inches of sharpened metal buried in the muscle of Big Alex's shoulder. He screamed, falling to one knee, as the man in the high-visibility jacket pulled his axe free with a gory spray of blood.

"Climb!" Big Alex screamed again. "Climb! Alex! Karen! Climb!"

The stampede of terrified fans was moments away. But Alex didn't care. He screamed with rage, leaping from his point of safety as the shaven-headed man raised the axe once more to perform the death-blow. Alex charged the short distance across the landing, dropping his shoulder low, and barrelled into the man's stomach, flailing his fists. The man regarded him with amusement. He gripped Alex roughly by the ear, the boy's screams of pain mixed with his cries of fury. The man peeled Alex away, like one might a used plaster, tossing him aside. Alex tumbled, spinning as if caught in an undertow, and only saw what happened next in a gyrating blur.

The crowd was about rush over Big Alex and the axe-man. Blood poured through the fingers holding Big Alex's shoulder together. His son had bought him the moment he needed, and he plunged his free hand into his coat pocket.

The axe-man raised his weapon to finish the job. The crowd would take them both, but he didn't care. One last kill for the road. Big Alex rose suddenly, finding the speed and strength he needed and slammed a fist full of keys into the man's throat. The axe fell. Big

Alex screamed. Another gout of blood pumped into the air, as the axe-man and Alex's father were enveloped by the panicked stampede.

Alex clung to the balustrade, buffeted by the surge. His sister stood atop the thin metal railing, a screaming siren rising above the tide of terror. But their father had saved them, and Alex would never forget that.

11

THEY CAME to a stop with a jolt, sprays of blood kicking up from their tyres.

"What's wrong?" Dip asked.

"I-" Mirin began.

A car horn blared from their left, followed by the scream of braking tyres. It was a BMW cutting between fountains of red. Suddenly, thirty yards in front of them, where their road intersected with the braking car, a supermarket delivery truck hurtled from the opposite direction. It didn't stop, colliding with the BMW at full speed. The noise of the crash was like an explosion. The front end of the BMW disappeared, folding in on itself, as its back end continued forward and up, plastering it upright to the front of the truck. The truck now hit the brakes, but its larger size and momentum carried the BMW back the way it came and out of sight, metal grinding on asphalt.

With the engine idling, they sat in silence for a moment, the metronome of the wipers ticking side to side, a timer running out.

"We need to go," Connie said with difficulty.

"I can hardly see," Mirin said, looking through the smeared windscreen.

"Take it steady," Dip said. "Just keep us moving."

Mirin moved off again, hesitating at the junction and hoping her phantom son beside her would let her know if anything else was coming their way.

The city was a cobweb of dangers. Every road presented an obstacle of rioters and crashed vehicles, but Oran anticipated them all, telling Mirin to slow, or turn left, sometimes directing them back on themselves before taking them forward.

They progressed laterally as much as forward until reaching the motorway, which cut through the city north to south at George's Cross, and turned into the Kingston Bridge, which swept high over the Clyde. The power was out. Only car lights and the numerous outbreaks of fire inadequately illuminated the city.

Seeming almost black in the near dark, the rain fell heavily: fat droplets of blood. As they made for a gap between crashed cars, which would enable them to follow the road down by the many hotels flanking the motorway bridge, a crowd of rioters emerged from the dark. They wore the rain as macabre shrouds. The group stood hunched, their chests rising and falling as one rabid animal in the car headlights.

Dip looked around for somewhere to go. More of the blood-soaked figures appeared behind them from beneath the Kingston Bridge overpass, brandishing makeshift cudgels and missiles.

"Shit!" Dip rasped. "Shit! We've got to go. Drive!" Panic coloured his words.

All the while the blood rain fell, bathing the city in red.

"Where to?" Mirin shouted.

"Drive through them, Mirin," Connie said. "It's the only option."

"I can't do that. They're *people*."

"Wait, Mummy," only Mirin heard Oran say.

Tick, tick, tick, the rain counted down.

"Feck's sake, Mirin. It's them or..." Dip didn't finish the sentence.

They all jumped at the bang of the brick on the passenger-side window next to Oran. It cracked into a web, which immediately began to channel the rain into a fractured kaleidoscope of red.

Together Connie and Dip shouted for Mirin to go. They screamed while the blood-soaked figures moved closer. More projectiles hit the four-by-four, bouncing from its metal body. Dip leant forward between the two front seats, shouting at Mirin to go.

"Wait, Mummy. Not yet."

The main group of the mob came into the full beam of their headlights. Their eyes glared out of their red masks, like angry white pustules ready to burst poisonously. Between them they had a sledge-hammer, two baseball bats, a spade, and two crowbars; enough to get the job done. One of the red figures from the side of their vehicle swung at the window next to Connie. It cracked but held.

Connie and Dip shouted in desperation. Dip was preparing to climb into the front seat and drag Mirin out of the way.

The boiling black sky flashed green and thunder rolled, as though the heavens were about to split open. The thunder disguised the sound of an engine revving in freefall.

From the motorway above, a transit van plunged headlong into the road in front of them. Its engine housing crumbled into the body of the van, along with five of the mob. A concertina of metal, the vehicle burst into flames, scattering the rest of the mob.

"Now, Mummy. Drive."

Mirin floored the accelerator and Dip was flung into the backseat. They skirted the burning van. A man with a crowbar dived out of the way. The road was now a river of blood and they skidded on the slick surface. The back wheels began to kick out but then they clipped a kerb, correcting their spin into the other direction. Mirin's control over the vehicle was slipping. She wanted to slow down when Dip shouted from the back.

"Go, go, go. There's more."

"Left, Mummy," Oran said.

Mirin turned the wheel just in time, narrowly avoiding another vehicle falling from the motorway above. It collapsed into a twisted mass of metal barely recognisable as a car. Dip, looking out of the back window, saw more cars falling like the blood rain from a broken gutter, smashing over the concourse sixty feet below.

The Range Rover began to aquaplane on the flow of blood covering the tarmac. For each correction Mirin made in one direc-tion, the car swung back in the other. The four-by-four had a mind of its own and its desire was to waltz in a danse macabre. Mirin finally gave in to the fact that she was not the one leading this dance. The four-by-four spun around and around, throwing them around inside the vehicle. Mirin held tightly to the wheel, white-knuckled, seatbelt pinning her back into her seat. They spun and spun, until they hit the kerb again. Something beneath the car crunched. Connie winced as they mounted the pavement, performing one more half-turn and stopping when the front quarter of the Range Rover collided with a low brick wall of the Marriott Hotel's carpark.

The airbags deployed, protecting Mirin and Connie, but buffeting Dip, unsecured by a seatbelt, between the two front seats.

The car alarm kicked in. The engine stalled and died.

The sidelights flashed orange through the heavily thrumming red rain.

Mirin pressed the start button; the engine gave out a wheezing electrical whine, which came to nothing. She tried again. The engine still refused to come to life. A third attempt convinced them they weren't going anywhere else in this vehicle.

Groaning, Dip pulled himself up from between the seats.

"How far?" said Connie, her face taut with pain, a hand holding her stomach while the other still clung to the door frame. She looked ashen and weak.

Mirin squinted out through the torrent of red. "Not far. The river is a few hundred yards straight down. Then right along the riverfront."

"We should get moving," Connie gasped, trying to pull herself up.

"Wait! I'll come around to help." Dip opened the door and jumped out into the blood rain and immediately felt a compulsion to get back in the car. The rain was thick and oily on his skin. When he wiped it from his face, red smears remained on his palm. Dip's hand began to shake at the unnatural warmth of the rain on his skin, as hot as fresh blood. Before it had time to grow, Dip clenched his fist on that idea, and skirted around the edge of the car. As he did, every memory of guilt, or anger, and every petty injustice he'd had to suffer blistered under the surface of his mind, ready to weep bile into his conscious-ness. He fought them down, searching for something to control them.

Before he was even aware of it, a song appeared on his lips: *Blackbird* by the Beatles. He'd never been a huge Beatles fan but his first serious girlfriend in high school loved them, and *Blackbird* was her favourite. She had played it over and over in her bedroom when he'd come over (under the pretence of studying). She was the first girl he'd loved, and the first one to break his heart too. The song had evoked a pang in him ever since, whenever it would come on the radio or start playing in a department store. He was already humming it when he opened Connie's door, the pang of emotion surfacing above all the others fighting for his attention.

Slinging her arm around his shoulders, Connie leant heavily on Dip. "You're singing," she said softly, blood soaking her hair and dripping down her face.

Mirin was out of the vehicle too, the car headlights shining through the crimson downpour. "Ready?" she said, as much asking herself as her companions. She felt nothing but the same empty sorrow that had consumed her in the police station. She stood, an insignificant person, blood raining on her city, cars falling from the bridge overhead and burning on the ground below, black storm clouds gathering once more, and lightning blazing across the sky. The green flash of light showed Oran, standing a little way off from them. *The world is ending*, she thought. *It ended the day he died.*

What was the point in going on? She had already lived through her own personal apocalypse, and she now doubted whether it had been worth surviving. Her hand curled around the knife in her pocket, looking for something, anything, to hold on to.

Dip and Connie had lurched around the four-by-four, joining her in the headlights.

"Are you singing?" Mirin said. Connie was singing. *Take Me Home, Country Roads.*

"Yes." Connie broke in, between lines about West Virginia being mighty. "My mum loved John Denver. It always reminds me of her." She went back to humming about going home on country roads.

Mirin tightened her grip on the knife, looking at their vehicle with a wordless prayer. She turned to her companions, who looked at her with white eyes blinking from their scarlet masks.

"Sing, Mirin," said Connie. "You've got to."

But Mirin had no song in her heart.

Thunder cracked so loud it rang in their ears. A jagged emerald fork speared from the black belly of the sky, hitting the river. The usually brown water of the Clyde had run red. Ghostly rubicund steam rose from the strike point with sparks of green, only glimpsed before the night swallowed the spectre back into the shadows of imagination.

"I... " But Mirin had no words to answer Connie.

Oran stood, untouched by the crimson rain. He beckoned to his mother happily, like he might have for her to join a game he and his father were playing while she worked. And love, longing, craving, they all moved her feet to follow her heart.

12

MIRIN FOLLOWED Oran to the river. The two police officers followed her, Connie leaning heavily on Dip, struggling to keep up. It was like wading through a bog of emotion. Their feet squelched in their shoes. Each step had become an act of will. Blood ran into their eyes and into their mouths. Dip spat it out onto the pavement, where it was absorbed into the stream flowing downhill, like them, toward the river.

They tracked the motorway running overhead. Blood fell over its edge, like overflowing buckets in a slaughterhouse.

Oran reached the road running parallel to the Clyde River, stuttering in and out of sight between flashes of lightning. Despite the abandoned and wrecked cars, vehicles still careered in either direction, trying to escape the city, or riding like madmen around Hell looking for destruction. Still untouched by the rain, the little boy did not look before he crossed the road in the dark. A lorry tore down the dual carriageway between two bloody crests surging from its wheels, and narrowly missed the boy. It did not sound its horn because it could not see him.

Dip and Connie came up behind Mirin, singing louder now. They paused and looked into the dark, seeing only the outline of shapes which lurked there. They began to cross the road, itself now a small river running alongside the Clyde.

They crossed the wide road, led by Mirin, Mirin in turn led by something they couldn't see. Dip and Connie were almost shouting their songs, fighting back the violence in their own skulls. Dip sang of broken wings and learning to fly; Connie of the mighty mama of country roads. Mirin still heard no song in her heart, but she clung to the knife in her pocket, gripping the bone shaft as if holding onto a buoy in a storm.

In time with the flashes of lightning, Oran would turn and wave them on, smiling as if there was some great game that they should come and join.

Finally, through the gloom, the bridge came into view. The bridge's cables looked like a great white ribcage, laid open, as though upon an altar.

Another fork of lightning, fizzing across the river's surface, confirmed what before they had thought to be their imagination.

The boy, the Wee Man, stood at the foot of the bridge.

While Oran was untouched by the rain, the boy was bathed in blood. His beautiful silk and black locks hung sodden around his face and his naked body dripped red. He was not alone. The murder of crows, a thousand strong, had settled on the banks of the Clyde, covering lampposts, railings, and discarded vehicles. Thousands more of his familiars, cats, dogs, and a numberless horde of rats, formed a trail of insidious living ermine. A coronation procession for their lord.

The black belly of the sky gave a low, hungry rumble and a fork of lightning spasmed from the heavens, striking the BBC building, showering it in viridescent sparks. Several more strikes came in quick succession, then the fifth struck *unbroken*, connecting the heavens and the earth with a pulsing, opaline tether. Shadows bowed penitently. It was done.

Mirin watched as Oran began to walk towards the boy.

"No!" The word choked in her throat. "Stop!" she shouted. She took the knife from her pocket and followed her son towards death.

13

At the cusp of the bridge, the boy turned to face them. Oran was running, beckoning for his mother to follow him, as though into the haunted house at a travelling carnival. Oran could have been looking at himself in the hall mirrors; a dark inversion of his innocence looking back at him.

The boy looked straight through Oran at the three adults behind. He inclined his head, inspecting them through his impassive flint-black eyes. He raised a hand towards them, and then turned, returning to his path.

As one, the familiars launched at Mirin and her companions. The crows took flight with a thousand discordant cries. The mass of four-legged animals ran in unison, every pair of eyes reflecting the spectral green lightning.

Connie and Dip stopped singing as they came to a halt seeing the oncoming horde.

"Mirin, this way, quickly," Dip shouted, veering to the right, splashing through the blood running down the road. They reached the other side, where a wall about seven feet high ran along the pavement in front of a waterfront block of modern apartments. Connie rested against the wall. Backing up, Dip sized up the jump. He could make it and pull himself out of danger from the pack of dogs, cats, and rats. But then he looked at Connie, barely able to stand. Could he pull her up with only one good arm? Could she even stand and reach up to him? Time was up. The rabid mass of animals was closing fast.

Mirin had not moved. The crows were almost on her. Hurrying to collect Connie from the ground, Dip screamed Mirin's name, but she was standing steadfast, knife in hand. A large Alsatian led the pack, a delirious anger in its eyes, its gums and teeth bared. Over the susurration of the rain, Dip and Connie could hear the snarls and shrieks of the horde.

Dip was preparing to run and get Mirin, knowing it would be the end of all of them, when Connie pointed and croaked, "The SUV."

He hesitated, caught between a slim chance and no chance. "Mirin," he screamed, having made up his mind.

Dip pulled Connie, hefting her roughly so she cried out in pain, and finding new depths of strength he didn't think his tired and battered body had, he carried her the short distance to the SUV.

The crows were a churning phantom ready to envelope Mirin from the sky, but as they reached her, their flock was flayed in two by an invisible blade seen only by the cleft it cleaved six feet above Mirin's head. They became two surging channels in the air, like the powerful flow of a river parted by a great boulder midstream. The phantom mass of wings screeched in anger and swerved around Mirin. They veered, changing direction and fixing on the SUV, as moments later the ground attack reached Mirin.

Theirs would be the same fate. Every snapping jaw and writhing head was deflected as Mirin ploughed a path through them. Now, unable to devour Mirin, and with one mind with their brothers of the air, every rat, dog, and cat changed direction.

It already seemed too late and if the door was locked, they were done for. They would be eaten alive, ripped apart by teeth, beaks, and claws.

Dip tried the handle. Their luck had finally washed away, along with the sanity of the city. Desperately Dip yanked at the door. He let go of Connie to use both hands. She fell awkwardly and cried out again but did not complain.

"Come on. Please," Dip pleaded.

The thunder cracked and the sky blazed green, burning his words from the air. Mirin was still on the path by the river. As Dip screamed, she had begun to walk, advancing on the pack, both hands clutching the dagger and raising it above her head.

Dip threw his shoulder against the SUV's window, shooting pain through his broken arm.

"Dip," Connie shouted, seeing the rabid pack, knowing it was too late for them all.

Dip didn't listen. He raised the heavy cast of his broken arm and smashed it into the window. The pain was electric, but he did it again. A small crack appeared on the glass. Dip hit it again, every nerve in his arm on fire.

The pack was only a few yards away, drowning out almost everything else.

Connie started to sing again.

Dip halted. It was over. He held his arm in agony, defeated. He dropped to his knees next to Connie. They would die together. When he heard her song faintly, moments before the horde would rip them apart, he could think of no better way to die. He began to sing *Blackbird* again, as the surging animals still cleft apart from Mirin's blade set upon them.

They were covered by a writhing mass, scratching and clawing. Snarls and maniacal snuffles from the dogs. Fevered mewling from the cats. Frenzied squeaks of the rodents. But none could touch them as they sang in each other's arms, sang the songs from their souls.

Forcing each leg forward, Mirin walked on, the blade raised before her. She would not lose her little boy again. She forged on into the calamity which seemed inevitable. Now on the foot of the bridge, Oran turned back and waved to his mummy.

"Wait, Oran!"

The little boy did not listen.

The thrumming rain sounded like a torrent of white water in Mirin's ears. All Mirin could think about was how she wished they had steered the kayak over to the side of the river and got out before the rapids. This all had the feeling of a recurring nightmare. Mirin recognised the sadistic logic of the dream, a logic that would not let her wake up, and which must be followed to the end, even though she knew how this ended.

Mirin stepped onto the foot of the bridge. The boy was halfway across, heading to his witch at the BBC, to that centre of power connected to the black sky with the massive unbroken pulse of lightning. Only a few steps behind, Oran would catch the boy any second. She would not lose him a second time. And with that thought, her past and present merged. The muscles in her legs burnt as her shoulders had pulling frantically against the danger on the river.

Suddenly, the boy stopped, as though he sensed her, or perhaps, even more strangely, sensed the knife. He turned and his black eyes met Mirin's. Oran had caught up with the boy. They stood like twins: one boy soaked in blood, the other untouched. Oran spoke to his mother. His voice sounded in her head more clearly than if he was standing in front of her alive.

"Sing, Mummy. You *have* to sing."

As the crashing rapids of fear swirled all around her, finally a song came. It was the song that Omar used to sing to Oran. The old Persian lullaby. She only knew the Arabic, but every word was committed to memory. As the first words issued from Mirin's mouth, the black stone blade in her hands began to harmonise with the song.

"Sleep well
Your sleep is flawless
The flowers of moonlight are a thousand colours
Don't awaken from your fairy tale dreams
Don't step into the world of despair"

The blade came to life, resonating with power. The fear did not evaporate and neither did Mirin's struggle, but somehow each step was possible. She advanced on her son and his dark twin.

The boy's face darkened. His mirthful smile fell away. Mirin felt the vibrating blade drawn to the water some twenty feet below her feet. The boy turned his face skyward and raised his arms above his head. There was a heavy rumbling but not from the thunderous sky but from below. It shook the earth. The bridge swayed and oscillated, its rib-like cables groaning as they twisted. Mirin stumbled as one of the support cables broke with a terrible snap. Like a striking serpent, the cable fell and whipped across the bridge. The vibration under her feet grew, rumbling louder. Mirin walked on, coming closer to her son and the boy, singing her lullaby.

"That's it, Mummy, sing. You must sing louder."

So she did. The blade's power grew in her hands.

"Sleep well
Mother's eyes are wide awake
Like every night there is a monster behind the walls
And there is no longer a string attached to your kite
It will no longer reach the clouds broken
Sleep well, sleep well
Mother won't leave your side
She loves you
She loves you
She'll be by your crib"

The noise of the rain was sucked from the air. Still the earth shook, and stumbling again, Mirin steadied herself on the railing. It was then she saw that the level of the bloody river had fallen drastically, so that the flotsam of supermarket trolleys, car tyres, glass, and plastic bottles jutted from the surface like bones from a rotting carcass. She squinted downstream, and the electric green light impaling the BBC headquarters showed her a new horror.

A tidal wave of blood, thirty feet high, was charging down the Clyde towards them, swallowing abandoned vehicles and the small silhouettes of humans. It moved impossibly fast.

For the first time, Mirin knew she was alone, and remembering her companions, she looked for them and saw the mass of animals writhing over one another next to an SUV. Wiping blood ineffectually from her eyes with her sodden sleeve, she looked through the gloom but could not see them. Still she sang, but the wave was upon them. It sucked up the SUV and the rabid familiars of the boy, and seconds later it would consume her and the bridge as well.

14

Pushing a fetid wind before it, the wall of blood towered above Mirin, blocking out the sullied sky. The wave made a deafening roar, consuming all the sounds of the besieged city.

A smile grew on the boy's face once more, a dark mirroring of Oran. Chaos and death were the boy's playthings.

Mirin sang as loud as she could, but her words were barely audible to her ears, nothing but a vibration in harmony with the knife clenched in her fists.

The wave crested, the detritus of the city turning in its body.

Then the wave stopped, halted by an invisible barrier. It was emanating from Mirin and surrounding her son and the dark boy. Her lullaby was now a scream, but it could not be stopped.

"If you throw a stone into the sea
The devil will come to fight me
The clouds will take you from me
As our garden will die without you"

The wave fell, splitting around the invisible field, washing upstream, flooding the banks on either side of the Clyde. The red wave was broken. It flowed on, up the Clyde, sloshing along the roads and walkways, depositing its cargo.

Still Mirin sang, holding onto the knife as though it were a paddle, an oar. She knew that all was lost, and that any moment they would pitch into a gully and be thrown into the mouth of the churning monster. Trapped in the infernal logic of the recurring nightmare she had once worked so hard to forget, she could do little more than paddle against the inevitable forces raging around her. Her little boy was so close, within arm's reach.

The blade hummed.

The mirth disappeared from the boy's face to be replaced with a grimace of rage. His dark eyes became terrible black holes at the centre of a rotting universe, swallowing everything, sucking all life from Mirin. He was her punishment, her just deserts. He was the end to her dream, surfacing from beyond the rapids, alone, husbandless, childless. Not a wife. A widow. Not a mother, but something for which there was no word.

She sang and the knife sang with her.

There was her little Oran. If only she could touch him, she could hold him and never let go.

The boy opened his mouth and as he screamed, the sky erupted in sheets of phosphorus green so bright they might set light to the heavens and burn down the world. Thunder roared, and forks of lightning stabbed the city. Through the flashing light shone green, invidious eyes, the eyes of something beyond even the boy, glaring from some other place, some other time, at what transpired upon the bridge.

The boy flew at Mirin. Each footstep on the bridge cracked the tarmac. He leapt, rising in the air, his knees pulled up to his chest, his hands stretched out as talons. He descended, a dark wraith against a blinding green sky. Mirin still sang, taking one last step to meet the boy as he fell upon her.

She was in the waves now, spat forth from the rock that flipped their kayak, searching for her son.

The obsidian knife impaled the boy's chest. Blood as black as oil flowed from the wound, cold as the river rapids over Mirin's fingers, and his child's screams spat in her face.

And in that deathly embrace she found Oran, trapped between

the rocks. She drew him close. He writhed in panic, struggling to breathe.

Mirin and the boy began to rise above the bridge, turning in the phosphorus light. He clawed and raged at Mirin, while she sang him her lullaby, holding him in a deathly embrace, the stone knife vibrating in the boy's chest. Their song was coming to an end.

"Sleep well, sleep well
Mother won't leave your side
She loves you, she loves you
She'll be by your crib
Sleep well, sleep well
Mother won't leave your side
She loves you, she loves you"

With the lullaby finished, Mirin planted a kiss upon her son's lips.

The sky exploded, a shockwave rushing from the pair floating above the bridge. The shockwave rippled as it spread, speeding through the city, severing the lightning connection between the black sky and the chaos it had wrought on the city below.

Mirin and the boy hurtled down into the river of blood below.

The water enveloped them, separating them from the world, plunging them into cold silence. Still the boy struggled, and Mirin held on, her loving kiss fixed to his dead mouth.

They descended to the bottom of the river. Every fibre of Mirin wanted to breathe. She had reached the point of the dream where she would have to leave and rise to the surface and then realise her mistake, as the current pulled her away from her precious boy. But if she could do one thing, if she could live that moment over, she would not stay her kiss. She would not leave her beautiful boy again.

They drifted to the silty bottom, the boy pinned under Mirin, struggling against her embrace. Her weight plunged the knife deeper into his black heart. They came to rest. His body pressed into the sludge, swallowing him slowly, covering him in neither water nor earth, trapping him in the hinterland between.

Refusing to accept his fate, the boy wrestled with Mirin.

The eddies of the rapids pounded Mirin's body. She must leave now to breathe and seek the surface. Breathing was as inevitable as the sunrise. However, this time Mirin would not leave her son to die alone.

The inevitable breath came. The blood-water burnt her throat, clogging her lungs with dirty gore. The kiss remained, loving, unbreakable.

The boy's struggles became laboured. His limbs followed his torso into the heavy sludge. Then even his head sunk beneath the mud, ensnaring the last of his silken black locks. Icy liquid filled Mirin's lungs as the boy's limbs went slack in her embrace, and he lived no more.

Their fond kiss broke.

All Mirin's pain and guilt and suffering were washed away, and Mirin died with her son beneath the rapids.

15

SHE SAT AT THE WINDOW, idly looking out of the coffee shop. Around her buzzed the life of the city, students and office workers, pensioners on shopping trips, tourists come to investigate the city where it had all happened. Dip saw Connie sitting calmly among the frenetic flow of life around her. He waved and indicated he would get a coffee.

"You're out of the plaster," Connie said when Dip sat down.

He flexed his hand. "Three weeks now. When do you start back?"

"Two weeks before the doctor sees me again, but that's why I wanted to meet. I'm thinking of travelling."

"Where will you go?"

"West Virginia," she said with a wry smile.

They chatted, making small talk about small things. Since that fateful night they'd remained in touch on and off, friends through circumstance. Now things were returning to normal Dip could feel they were drifting apart. It felt natural. It was the way of normality, he supposed.

Everyone was trying to do the same. The events of two months ago had already been rationalised into something people could understand: freak weather, something in the water, old tribal rivalries, Catholics and Protestants, Celtic and Rangers, a combination. Something. Anything. But not the truth. The truth of it, the horror of it, what people had done, that was too much for them to live with. Dip and Connie both knew someone who'd tried to live with such horror, and she wasn't here any more, but she was the reason *they* were. So Dip understood, and he was prepared to let Connie go. They didn't need to hang on to each other. They knew the truth, even if other people couldn't accept it. It was time to move on, and he would have if the dreams, the visions, hadn't begun again.

He was working up the courage to tell Connie, letting her talk.

She shrugged understandingly when they spoke about the trials that had started to clean up the violent mess of that bloody night. Both she and Dip would be called as witnesses in several cases and tribunals to get to the (rational) bottom of things. They had gone back and forth over email about what they'd say about that night and the events leading up to it.

Douglas Wallace had become a convenient scapegoat. It had been Connie's idea. He linked most of the players together. It was entirely plausible that he had become obsessed with the Wee Man from the peat bog when he was discovered after that initial terrible event, and Douglas had worked the crime scene. He could be made responsible for Portia and David's deaths, among many others, including his family. Clearly the man had lost his mind.

Dip and Connie were trying to protect a witness in the case, Professor Mirin Hassan, and unfortunately in the nightmare that played out that night, Professor Hassan had fallen into the Clyde and drowned as they escaped a mob. It kind of made sense, certainly enough for people to happily buy it.

They'd buried Mirin on a rainy day four weeks later, laying her to rest along with her beloved son and husband in a family plot. Through the entire graveside liturgy, Dip felt the urge to hum the tune to *Blackbird,* but he didn't.

Dip looked out of the window over to George Square, where so much violence had taken place at the heart of the city, while Connie had moved on to telling Dip about Stuart Blair's funeral. Dip was about to tell her of his returning dreams, about the darkness which fought with a song he could never quite remember. It was trauma, he'd been telling himself, just his brain's way of coming to terms with it all. He'd let Connie talk it through with him in just a minute.

Outside Dip saw an old bag lady standing in the middle of George Square. She had her arms outstretched and all around her and perched on her arms and woolly hat were dozens of pigeons. They fed from her hands. She looked happy, and Dip could see she was talking to them like old friends.

Suddenly, the pigeons took flight. Standing in front of the old woman was a single large crow. Dip flushed cold with memories of the squawking birds that haunted his dreams.

"What? What is it, Dip?" Connie said.

"Shoo! Go away!" Mary said. "I'm not talking to you."

"Mary, Mary, quite contrary," the crow laughed.

"You go away, crow. I'm off to get tea and a bun." Mary kicked at the crow, but it merely took flight and floated back down out of reach.

"Well, you better be quick, Mary. It might be the last tea and cake you ever enjoy." The crow laughed heartily at this, although Mary didn't see the joke.

"Stupid bird, you go 'way. Everything is okay now." Mary was annoyed and started to shuffle away as quickly as she could.

"Silly Mary. Stupid Mary, what would you know? Can't you feel it, Mary? You know you can." And the crow gave a cawing laugh and took flight.

EPILOGUE

Tk'lo's soul was carried in the great tumult of the heavenly waters singing all the songs of the Dreaming Time. As he sang, he felt the voices of his ancestors in the firmament, where all memory was never lost in the harmony of existence.

He left the pain of the world far below, where he could see the last of his tribe walk into strange lands and begin to forget themselves, having already forgotten an old man, whose body lay savaged in a snow-covered clearing, his fire snuffed out.

The crows pecked at Tk'lo's eyes, pulling the gelatinous globules from the sockets of his skull. Wolves filled their bellies with the meat torn from the old man's bones. It was a meagre meal that would not satiate them.

The little boy covered in markings looked to the lands beyond. As long as they would forget themselves, he would be there forever to help them do so. They had made him, and wherever they ran, whatever fantasies they tried to fill their lives with, he would find them and give them what they desired. He would never stop. They had made him, and it was not within their power to destroy him. Smiling to himself, the little boy walked into the blackness of the lands beyond.

The last embers of the dead man's fire danced before the boy's face. Its fading glow reflected in his black eyes, throwing in through time along infinite, unseen connections until it found its way to the opioid stare of Lucy Walker. Drool fell from her slack mouth. The spark ignited her imagination and a fool's grin bloomed on her face. A nurse was preparing a syringe to keep Lucy sedated, restrained as she was by all four limbs in her padded room. Concentrated on the task at hand, the nurse did not see the maniacal grin grow, nor that Lucy had dislocated her thumb while her back was turned.

"There you are," said the nurse, tapping Lucy's forearm until a vein emerged. Carefully, lining up the needle, she would never know how ironic her final words would be. "This won't hurt a bit."

Lucy seized the syringe from the nurse with her free hand, thumb hanging loose, and with preternatural strength stabbed it into the nurse's ear. A look of shock flashed across the woman's face before death washed it away. The final electrical signals sent from her brain sparked her body into twitching spasms as she hit the floor and her light went out like the dying embers of a fire. And with gleeful mutterings, Lucy Walker freed herself from her restraints.

NEOLITHICA READER BONUS

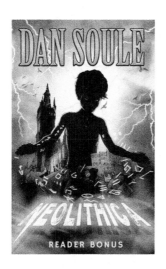

If you loved this novel, here is a link to a bonus behind the scenes ebook, exclusive only for NEOLITHICA readers. It includes an alternative ending and an in-depth interview with the author, Dan Soule, about the writing of this epic story. Go to the following link.

Reviews greatly help readers and authors alike. If you could leave a review on Amazon, Goodreads, and Bookbub, or on your own blog and social media pages it would be a big help in spreading the word.

You can follow Dan on:
Bookbub https://www.bookbub.com/profile/dan-soule
Facebook https://www.facebook.com/WriterDanielSoule/
Instagram https://www.instagram.com/writerdansoule/

MORE BOOKS BY THE AUTHOR

WITCHOPPER

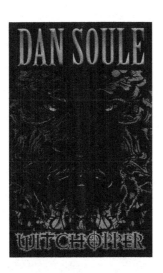

If you see her, then you're dead...

In the vein of *The Wickerman* and *Midsommar, Witchopper* is an epic ordeal of a father and son relationship, where past sins echo in the present. Dan Soule delivers another terrifying Fright Night book, a story of love, lies and truth that will leave you sleeping with the light on. Available from Amazon.

THE ASH

You know the drill: mushroom clouds, end of the world, only the clichés survive. This isn't that...

A blend of *The Mist* meets *Alien* in the English countryside, *The Ash* is a breakneck horror ride. Another of Dan Soule's *Fright Night* tales, where even if one man can face his demons, it still might not be enough. So turn the page and get pulled screaming into... The Ash.

SAVAGE

Jack is back, but he isn't even the worst thing on the streets of Whitechapel...

Dan Soule delivers another of his *Fright Night* novels, reviving the vampire mythos with aplomb. If you can't get enough of dark and gripping suspense with compelling characters set in a gritty world, then you'll love *Savage*.

5 FREE BOOKS

SWEET DREAMS AREN'T MADE OF THESE. If you love spine chilling horror, full of monsters and great characters, then Dan Soule's two anthologies of short fiction are the perfect introduction to one of the new talents in horror. Not only that but you also get three of the all time classics to keep you up at night.

Join the growing horde of insomniacs who've said goodbye to sleep and hello to NIGHT TERRORS. Free from www.dansoule.com.

ACKNOWLEDGMENTS

There are a number of people who make any book possible. Neolithica was no exception. I'm indebted to my editor Joe Sale for his comments and surgeon's knife. He made some deep cuts into the initial draft, but ultimately he helped craft a beautiful monster, at least in my biased eyes. I had an alternative ending, which Joe cut. You can read this in the Reader Bonus download, if you are interested in how I originally ended things for Mirin. Everything is the same up until that fateful meeting on the bridge.

My wife, Jenny, was the first to read the complete story, with the alternative ending. Her encouragement and tolerance for my sometimes obsessiveness to writing time remains so central to making my stories happen. My brother in arms, Ross Jeffery, did a great beta-read for me, as did Sandra Hould and Kate Anderson. Their keen eyes helped clean up the draft and spot small inconsistencies which often get away from the author in such a large writing project. Kate and Niall Anderson, my one-time Shorinji Kempo comrades from our undergraduate days at the University of Glasgow. Kate was also my archaeological consultant for Neolithica. On that front any inaccuracies are mine and not hers. I tried to be faithful to reality but sometimes the conveniences of the story took priority, mainly in the time at the dig site and omission of certain procedures. And a big thanks to Sherie O'Neil for her tremendous final proofread. As a dyslexic writer, I am greatly indebted to all these wonderful folk.

The cover design, which I love, was done by Stuart Millan, another former martial arts friend, from when we used to train in Brazilian Jiujitsu together in Coatbridge, Scotland. Stuart has illustrated a number of my stories over the years. You can see those illustrations in my collection of short fiction IN TOOTH AND CLAW, which is available for free on Amazon.

Lastly, I have to give a special mention to Glasgow. It is a city in which I lived from the ages of 19 to 34. My daughters were born in the Royal Infirmary there. I went to the University of Glasgow from undergraduate to PhD degree, and then went on to work at Glasgow Caledonian University for over seven years as an academic. It was the city in which I met my wife, made many friends, started a family, and became an adult. I mean this book to be an homage to that great city, because it is a great city, bustling with life and a unique culture, and to which I owe so much. I'm fortunate enough to return there often, and it still feels like coming home every time I'm there. And to the University of Glasgow, my *alma mater*, and the department of English Language, where I learnt to think, I have nothing but thanks.

Dan Soule, Islandmagee, 18th December 2019

Printed in Great Britain
by Amazon